BECKY RYAN

BECKY RYAN

Sheila Jansen

severn
House

This first world edition published in Great Britain 2002 by
SEVERN HOUSE PUBLISHERS LTD of
9–15 High Street, Sutton, Surrey SM1 1DF.
This first world edition published in the USA 2003 by
SEVERN HOUSE PUBLISHERS INC of
595 Madison Avenue, New York, N.Y. 10022.

British Library Cataloguing in Publication Data

Jansen,   Sheila
    Becky Ryan
    1.   Sisters - Fiction
    2.   Newcastle (England) - Social life and customs - 20th century
    I.   Title
    823.9'14 [F]

    ISBN 0-7278-5897-1

Typeset by Palimpsest Book Production Ltd.,
Polmont, Stirlingshire, Scotland.
Printed and bound in Great Britain by
MPG Books Ltd., Bodmin, Cornwall.

Man for the field, woman for the hearth,
Man for the sword and for the needle she,
Man with the head and woman with the heart,
Man to command and woman to obey.
                              Tennyson, 'The Princess'

As always, to my husband, Henricus,
and my sister, Shirley

One

'Shhh, Becky, try to go to sleep.' Liz patted her sister's back to stop her whimpering but Becky, now almost fourteen, couldn't be so easily consoled as in the old days. She sat up in the double bed they shared and pressed her palms against her ears. The raucous strains of their mother and older sister singing 'I'm Forever Blowing Bubbles' blustered up the stairs.

'I can't, Liz. I'm scared when they're drunk. And I can't sleep when they're making such a racket. Thank heavens that bloody boyfriend's coming for his machine tomorrow. Pray Dora doesn't bribe him into lending it to her again. Their singing's bad enough without the background screeching. Please, sneak down and close the kitchen door?'

Although only two years older, Liz had always been Becky's guardian angel in times of trouble, which were almost constant in the Ryan household. She sat up and pulled the blankets round her sister's bony shoulders. 'They're too far gone, Becky. I'll just get the back of one of their hands.'

'Aye, likely our Dora's. The witch isn't right in the head when she's sober, but she's dead dangerous when she's drunk.'

'Well, luv, we just have to learn to live with Dora without upsetting her.'

'Aye, live with both of them.' Becky's voice trailed away and she began to cry. She hugged her knees and pressed her forehead against the rough wool blankets. After a few moments she raised her head and wiped her eyes with her knuckles. 'I hate Dora, *and* Ma. Especially when they get this drunk. I'm scared.'

'I'm scared an' all, luv. But we can't do nothing about it, and you know you don't really hate Ma.'

Their father's voice rose from the front parlour. He'd slept downstairs for the past six years – since that terrible night when their mother had thrown him out of the bedroom, shouting that he was useless and spineless and some other words they hadn't understood. The only blessing was that, since then, Dora had slept with their mother. This left Becky and Liz the bed to themselves – the only place where they felt safe.

Their father was still shouting to the two in the kitchen: 'How many times do I have to tell you to cut it out? Can't you let a poor bugger get some sleep? It's nearly two o'clock and some of us has to get up for work in the morning.' Rarely did Jim Ryan dare to raise his voice against his wife and stepdaughter and, when he did, it was always futile.

The singing stopped, while Dora, just turned eighteen, screeched at him: 'Shut ya yap, y'ould fart. You can't shtand nobody having a good time.'

'Aye, get losht, you miserable shpoil-shport,' her mother echoed.

Liz reached out to find Becky's hand. 'Don't cry, luv. They'll conk out soon. And please lie down. You're letting the cold in the bed.'

Becky wriggled under the meagre covers, gripping her sister's hand like a lifeline. Liz was the only person in the world who loved her; not even her da loved her, though he didn't hit her like Dora and Ma did – mostly Dora. Ma wasn't so bad when she was sober. 'I *hate* our Dora.' Becky thumped her fist into the bare, lumpy, bolster that served as a pillow. Ma and Dora had soft pillows on top of their bolster, with white pillowcases.

'You know Miss Donlan says you shouldn't say you *hate* anyone, or even think it.' Liz squeezed Becky's hand tighter.

'Oh, you're so good, It's all right for you. It's me our Dora hates, and Da. She never gets on at you.'

'Only because I let her boss me around. If you didn't answer her back . . . if you just did as she tells you—'

2

'I won't! I won't, I won't!' Becky cut in with fervour. 'Why should I do what she tells me when she hates me? I'll *never* let her boss me around. And when we run away she can't boss *you* around neither.' The singing had resumed and she turned on her side and put her hands over her ears.

Liz snuggled in to Becky's back. 'Aye, poor Da'll get the brunt of it then. Come on, go to sleep.'

The two blonde heads drew closer on the grey and white striped bolster and the two pairs of blue eyes screwed shut.

When Becky followed Liz downstairs the next morning the dingy kitchen was a mess. Empty gin bottles and two tumblers stood on the table, records littered the floor, cigarette butts overflowed on saucers, and the room stank of gin.

They threw on their coats and crossed the twenty-foot wide road at the rear of the row of colliery houses to the privy middens, coalhouses, and gardens.

The coal company, which owned all the properties, was progressive in some ways, but overlooked the substandard living conditions of its workers. The town's medical officers complained about the poor water supply, lack of surfaced roads and pavements, and the need for public baths, water closets, and proper sewage disposal. Sewage was dumped untreated into the nearby River Wansbeck and the Hayden Letch. Still, nothing was done.

After an icy wash at the sink in the pantry, Becky and Liz set to work. Liz attacked the empty fire grate while Becky cleared away the mess and set the oilcloth-covered table with bowls for porridge. Liz always insisted that Becky did the lighter jobs, and for this Becky was grateful. She hated getting her hands dirty.

The kettle snorted steam and Becky filled the teapot and their father's enamelled tea canteen for his midday bait. She set it on the table beside his bait tin, which contained his usual sugar sandwich.

Like all miner's families, they feared their men going on shift, though the fear wasn't discussed. Becky supposed it was because mothers didn't want to worry their children. But an unexpected blow from the dreaded pit buzzer set terror in every heart in every house. Anyway, she cheered herself, Da had always come back, *and* in one piece.

'Your breakfast's nearly ready, Da,' Liz said as Jim Ryan shuffled in like a man going to the gallows. He wore the traditional miner's clothing – over his shirt, the woollen waistcoat that helped to ward off the cold rush of air from the ventilation system, the knee britches and rough jacket, and the cloth cap that was his sole head protection. Only officials wore the more protective leather caps.

When he returned from the privy Liz set a bowl of porridge before him and Becky poured his tea.

'Ta,' he said. His grey, hopeless eyes didn't look at them – he rarely looked at them – and he bent his haggard face over his bowl. The downward lines of his cheeks and about his eyes and mouth were deep and dark, as if the coal dust he inhaled every day had lodged in the cracks.

Becky sat next to him. 'Ma and Dora's still abed,' she said unnecessarily. She never knew what to say to her father. He didn't seem interested in anything she said.

'Aye, what's new?' He slurped his tea, sucking in his hollow cheeks until they seemed to disappear into the back of his skull.

She persevered. 'How're things at work, Da?'

He shook his head. 'Aw, what's the point? So long as the government rejects nationalization there's no use fighting for better conditions and wages. As long as the owners have control, the government'll put them first. We haven't the power to get action.'

Becky was encouraged that he'd responded in such detail. 'I've got cookery at school today,' she went on. 'I'm making bread pudding. You can have some for your tea.'

He put down his mug. 'Where'd you get the money?'

Liz joined them at the table, eyes lowered. 'Ma was drunk when I gave her me wage packet so I sneaked sixpence out. I didn't want Becky to miss cookery again.'

4

'But we'll *all* have the pudding for tea.' Becky felt guilty that Liz did bad things only to help *her*, never for herself.

'Aye, well next time tell me when you've got cookery and I'll give you the money afore them two get their hands on it. At least it's food on the table.' He scraped back his chair and trailed to the door, where he pulled on his tattered overcoat. His clothes hung on his skinny, stooped figure, as if he'd been a bigger and more upright man when he'd first acquired them.

'Ta-ra, Da,' they chorused, both praying silently he would come home safely.

The girls washed the dishes and set the table for their mother and Dora, then Liz banked up the fire with small coals. Ma and Dora complained if the fire went out before they got up.

Liz grabbed her shabby wool coat from the mound that hung on the nails behind the door. As always, the coat was a hand-me-down of Dora's. 'You coming then?'

In a second Becky dived into her own coat, again a hand-me-down of Dora's, via Liz. Twice she had taken in the seams, first to fit Liz, then herself. She enjoyed sewing and couldn't bear to wear oversized, obviously second-hand clothes. She longed for the day when she would earn her own money and buy new material to make beautiful clothes for herself and Liz.

They wound about their heads and necks the striped wool scarves Becky had knitted from old jumpers, then strode arm-in-arm down Long Row.

The winding wheel and chimney stacks towered over the colliery rows. The sulphurous fumes from the cokeworks, and ashes and coal dust, merged with the stink from the middens and pervaded the town.

Becky always walked with Liz to the Co-operative Store at the end of Station Road, where she worked in the tailoring department. During the war she'd made underwear for the troops, but now she made shirts to be sold in the store, and laying-out shirts for the dead. Somebody was always being killed down the pits, or dying, especially since the influenza epidemic had reached the Northumberland pit town of Ashington.

The mining town had grown fast as the Great War increased the nation's already greedy demand for coal. Becky considered Ashington well named, for that's what it thrived on – coal ash.

Her basket of ingredients for the bread pudding hooked over one arm, she stepped carefully lest she trip. The cracked, badly surfaced lane of Long Row was deep in dust, which turned to dark mud when it rained. Yet the rain didn't wash the smell of coal from the air, but made it smell like a wet ashtray.

'It's freezing.' Becky's voice came muffled through her scarf. 'I'm glad it's cookery today. It's nice and warm in the Domestic Science room.'

'Better not burn the pudding like the pasties last time. There's only leek soup for tea.'

'Aye, I know.' Becky kept her eyes on the ground. She always felt gloomy walking down the familiar lane of back-to-back, two-up two-down pit houses. Yet they were fortunate to have gardens in which to grow vegetables, and the Ashington Coal Company provided the house and supplied concessionary coal. But even with the four pounds a week Da earned and the eleven shillings Liz earned at the Ashington Industrial Co-operative Society, after they'd bought food there wasn't much left for clothing.

Of course, the gin ran away with most of the money, and Dora had never worked in her life. Sometimes she helped behind the bar at the miners' clubs when somebody was ill and they needed an extra hand, but she did this for free drinks and the opportunity to flirt with the men.

In their almost identical coats and headscarves, from a distance Becky and Liz could have passed for twins. But Liz was two inches taller than Becky and her blonde hair was pinned in a knot behind her head according to work regulations. Becky hated the blonde schoolgirl plaits that stuck out from under her scarf. Her blue eyes looked at the ground, her mouth set in a permanently taut line – too old for her child's face. Liz's identical blue eyes looked up and out on the world, but not without a hint of fear. Her face

6

was rounder, without her sister's haunted air, though already heavy with responsibility.

They had some qualities in common, such as the sparkle that lurked behind their frightened expressions, and the love that lit up their faces whenever they shared some simple pleasure – a practical joke, singing a silly song, playing 'I spy' or word games in bed. Their love for each other was the only light that guided them through the shadows of their lives.

As they neared the end of Long Row, Becky nudged Liz in the ribs. 'There's Will Bennett giving you the eye, as usual.' Her voice was vehement. She was jealous of Liz's affections and hated anyone who paid her attention.

Liz blushed as they neared the youth leaning against the outside wall of the built-on pantry. He lived in the last house on the row and, at seventeen, was a seasoned miner.

He lifted his cap and smiled at both of them, but mainly at Liz. 'Hello, Liz . . . Becky.'

Becky glared at his dark, nice-looking face. But Liz smiled at him, her eyes shining. 'Hello, Will. Why aren't you at work?'

'Night shift.' He twisted the cap in his hands and swallowed, making his Adam's apple ride up and down his neck.

'Er, could I have a word with you, Liz?'

Becky stiffened and hung on to Liz's hand. But Liz shook her off gently. 'I'll only be a second.' She walked the few steps to where Will now posed awkwardly in the centre of the path, still twirling his cap.

They spoke in hushed whispers, and though Becky strained her ears she couldn't hear what they said. Liz came back looking pink and pleased. Becky took her hand in a proprietary manner and pulled her past Will. But she knew he'd be staring after Liz. 'What did *he* want?' Though her voice was petulant, there was fear in it.

'He just asked if I'd go for a walk on Sunday.'

'But you said you wouldn't, didn't you?'

'I said I would.'

'You didn't!' Becky dropped Liz's hand as if it burned her.

Liz gave her sister a pleading look. 'Oh, what's the harm?'
'He's rough, and he's a miner, and you don't want nothing
to do with him.'
'It's not a crime to be a miner. What's the matter with you?'
Becky pouted. 'You know you *can't* get stuck with a pit
lad! Then we couldn't run away and meet two rich men with
clean jobs, and we couldn't live next door to each other in
nice houses. You promised you'd come with me. You can't
marry that Will Thingamabob.'

Laughing, Liz tucked Becky's arm in hers and they left the
colliery rows behind and reached the outskirts of the town,
turning down Station Road.

The townspeople were a strange mixture. Ragged, barefoot
children walked the same pavements as children in fancy
school uniforms. Women, huddled in moth-eaten shawls, and
men in inadequate jackets and cloth caps, mingled with pros-
perous businessmen and their well-dressed womenfolk.

Becky, obsessed with her fear of Will Bennett, clung to Liz
like a blind person. 'Promise me you would never in a million
years marry that lout.'

This time Liz didn't laugh, but gave Becky's hand a reassur-
ing squeeze. 'Don't get yourself in a stew. Going out for a walk
with a lad doesn't mean I'm going to marry him.'

'It could.' Becky stuck out her lower lip as far as it would
go. 'He's got a crush on you and you have on him, I know it.
You look all funny when he talks to you.'

'Don't be a ninny.'

'I'm not a ninny, and anyway, what about *me*? I'm not
staying in that house without you on Sunday. Saturdays are
bad enough.'

'I'll only be out for an hour or so in the afternoon. I'll be
back to make the tea with you.'

Becky turned on the sad, pleading look that always won over
her sister. 'Can I come, then?'

'You know you can't. You'd be a gooseberry.'

'I'd be your bodyguard. I'd make sure he doesn't try to kiss
you or nothing.'

Outside the Co-op, Liz gently disengaged Becky's clinging arm. 'I've got to go. I'm late. See you at the food kitchen at dinner time.'

Becky pulled a face. The food kitchen was charity, but better than school dinners, and it was nice to get out and meet Liz. Best of all, she didn't have to go home.

She crossed the road to the station. At the bottom of her basket she'd hidden the book she'd found under Dora's side of the bed when she'd made it yesterday. It was called *Love's Passion Lost* and the cover showed a man and a woman holding each other. You could see almost all the woman's chest.

Becky sat on her usual bench in the waiting room. When there were enough people it could get quite warm. Sometimes, if her hands weren't too cold, she would knit or sew to pass the time, but whenever she could, she would sneak one of Ma's or Dora's books or penny dreadful women's magazines out of the house.

Failing this, she would do what little homework the teachers gave. Girls weren't expected to know much beyond basic reading, writing and arithmetic. Cookery and sewing were vital to their futures as housewives and mothers. When Becky had nothing else to do she even borrowed English grammar books from school, which she studied to improve her speech for when she went to Newcastle. Sometimes she practised on Liz and tried to teach her to use proper words, but they didn't dare put their learning into practice yet. People would laugh at them, especially Ma and Dora. Nevertheless, Becky stored her knowledge for the future and read anything she could, even Da's newspapers. She spent an hour at the station every morning after leaving Liz, and another hour and a half waiting for her to finish at half past five. It kept her out of the way when Da got home from the pit, so Ma and Dora didn't mind. While he had his bath they took a nap upstairs.

For Becky the cold waiting room was better than being at the house without Liz. She had nightmares about Liz dying. If Liz died, Becky wouldn't want to live.

Two

L iz was stamping her feet to keep warm outside the Co-op entrance when Becky ran to her with a contrite face. Even in the dim gaslight Liz looked tired. She was always tired after bending over the sewing machine all day.

'Sorry I'm late, Liz. I got carried away with that book of our Dora's.'

Liz smiled. 'It must be dirty to keep you sitting in the cold all this time.'

Arm in arm they turned for home and Becky giggled. 'It's the usual – about a man and a woman and, *you know*, soppy stuff and passion and all that. It's got lots of juicy bits.'

'Aye, our Dora wouldn't bother with it if it hadn't. Did you learn anything?'

Becky wrinkled her nose. 'A bit. They always tell you a lot about what they do, but I wish they'd say more about how it *feels*. I get that funny tingling down below just reading it. I can't imagine what it's like to *do* all those weird things.'

'I bags it after you. But put it straight back under Dora's bed when we get home. There'll be hell to pay if she misses it.'

'Aw, I wanted to read bits to you in bed tonight.'

'We can't till we know she's finished it and forgotten about it.'

Becky pouted and they walked on in silence. The dark street was filled with huddled figures scurrying home from work. 'Liz,' she said at length. 'I've been thinking. The heroine in the book's an artist's model. It doesn't pay much but she meets interesting men, and some people in the arty set are rich – you know, patrons of the arts, and famous artists, or just artists who can afford to play around because they come from rich families. When we go to Newcastle we could be artists' models.'

Liz's laughter rang down the street. 'Take our clothes off? To earn a living? What would Ma say?'

'Ma wouldn't know. If you're daft enough to come back to see them after we leave, you can. But don't expect me to.'

The thought that had gnawed at Becky's mind all day began to nibble once more. She dropped Liz's arm. 'Of course, if you go out with that Will Bennett, we might never get away.'

'Now don't start that again.' Liz sounded unusually impatient. 'Besides, one of us has to get *some* experience. City lads are worse than here, and we'd better know what to expect.'

Becky was mollified. Will Bennett might serve a purpose after all.

As always when they entered the kitchen door, Becky found herself stiffening in readiness for an onslaught.

'Where d'you think *you two*'s been? Gallivanting around the town and worrying me into me grave! You should've been home twenty minutes ago,' their mother said. Florrie Ryan sat by the fire opposite Dora, her podgy hand nursing her forehead.

Becky noticed that her mother *did* look paler than usual and the bluish shadows under her eyes seemed almost black. The sharp brown eyes above the shadows pierced her two younger daughters.

'Sorry, Ma. I had to work late to finish a laying-out shirt for tomorrow.' Liz lowered her head, as she always did when lying.

But Florrie's round face was still clamped in a disapproving scowl, her mouth set in a lipless line. Her mousy hair was turning grey and she'd grown fat almost overnight. But it wasn't the kind of fat rich people got. She was saggy and droopy and sometimes her ankles hung over her shoes like rising dough over loaf tins. Becky was sad that her mother looked so bad, but she was afraid of that disapproving scowl on her face. She should have known they would get it for being late. Ma and Dora didn't like to wait for their meals. She was also sad that Liz had had to lie to cover up for her again.

Dora rose and minced towards the table, her high heels clicking on the linoleum and her large buttocks rolling like the swell of the sea. She wore the white blouse and green cardigan and skirt her mother had bought her from the Co-op for Christmas. Dora was proud of her bosom and always left her blouse unbuttoned at the top, even in winter.

Becky had to admit that Dora was pretty, in an overblown way. She looked like her mother must have when she was young, except that Dora's eyes were lighter – almost the colour of marmalade. She dyed her hair bright red with henna and put metal curlers in it every night. The resulting tight curls she piled on top of her head. She glanced at the basket on the table and lifted the old newspaper that covered Becky's creation. 'What you got here?'

'It's bread pudding, for tonight.' Becky braced herself. Dora took pleasure in ridiculing everything Becky did.

'Looks more like dried-up boily.' Dora lifted the pudding from the basket to scrutinize it, revealing the book hidden underneath. 'What in hell's name? Me book! You stole me book! I've been looking high and low for it.' Red flashes blazed in her marmalade eyes, but Becky was grateful the eyes weren't popping. When Dora was really mad, her eyes exploded almost out of her head.

'I just borrowed it.' Trembling, Becky hung up her coat.

Dora turned to her mother, her great bosom heaving with indignation under her tight blouse. 'She's a thieving little bugger, Ma. And she's too young to read that stuff anyway.'

Florrie Ryan nodded and gave Becky a stern look, but her eyes were never so frightening as Dora's. 'Don't you ever touch our Dora's things again, Becky. Not unless you want the back of me hand.'

'Yes, Ma.'

'And now go and get me some Aspro. Me head's bad and I don't want no shouting in here the night.'

Becky didn't want to go back out in the cold but she was

relieved that that seemed to be the end of the book business. Obviously Dora had finished it and hadn't been looking for it or she would have made a bigger scene.

'And while you're at it, fill up the gin bottle at Mr Brown's,' Florrie said.

Dora returned to her chair by the fire. 'Aye, I'm ready for a wet an' all. It's dead boring now that Bill's taken his bloody gramophone back.'

Florrie pulled half a crown from her pinafore pocket and handed it to Becky. 'And make sure he gets the change right this time.'

Becky shrugged into her coat, leaving Liz washing the leeks in the pantry. 'I'll help you when I get back,' she said. She hated going for gin. Mr Brown lived on Third Row. He made his living as a booky, taking illegal bets on horse races, and doing the local rabbit coursing, also illegal. But he made most of his illicit earnings distilling gin and whisky in his garden shed. Everybody knew how he made his living yet nobody told on him. Even policemen greeted him in the street and were among his customers.

The men usually drank in the clubs. It was mostly the women who bought drink from Mr Brown, leaving little to be spent at the Co-op on food. Approaching Mr Brown's shed, Becky wrinkled her nose. The place was filthy and it stank something awful. Not just of gin and whisky, but also another strange smell, like paraffin. Becky was glad at least that Mr Brown charged little more than half the off-licence price, or they'd never have any food except the garden vegetables.

When Becky returned, her father was seated at the table. The two armchairs by the fire were invisibly marked *Florrie* and *Dora*. Becky could smell beer on his breath. Occasionally he popped out for a couple of pints at the Miners' Club, one of seventeen in Ashington. The beer was to wash the dust out of his craw, he said. Unlike Ma and Dora, he didn't drink to get stinking drunk. He said it was bad enough working eight hours down the pit without doing it with a hangover.

13

Becky worried about his going to the club in case he caught the enteric fever. The poor water supply and infection caused by the proximity of the ash-pits brought annual epidemics. But the risk of getting it was worst at the clubs because of the dirty conveniences. Yet Da had to have some relaxation away from the house.

Becky gave her mother the Aspros and gin.

'Ta, hen,' Florrie said. 'And a couple of glasses.'

Becky handed two glasses from the dresser to Dora.

'It took you long enough,' she said.

'Your teas are ready,' Liz said before Dora grumbled further. She placed the black pot of soup from the fire on the trivet, and Becky filled the bowls and set them on the table.

Florrie threw Liz something like a smile. 'Eey, it's grand to sit down to me tea all made. I just don't feel well enough to cook these days.'

Becky took her place at the table and lowered her eyes. Aye, she thought, Ma hadn't felt well enough to cook since Liz and she had been old enough to do it. But she remembered the days when sometimes she would come home from school to an appetizing smell.

'There's hopeful news in the *Chronicle*,' Jim Ryan said.

Becky looked at him in surprise. He rarely spoke at meals. 'What, Da?'

'It says the government's commission agreed to change the Eight Hour Act. By July sixteenth we should be working seven hours underground and maybe only six by the end of 1920. But the bloody coal owners want no less than seven hours.'

Florrie finished her soup and clattered her spoon on the plate. 'That'll mean you'll have more time to get in folks way around the house and spend more money at the club. What about a rise? Didn't they say anything about that?'

'Aye, the union want two bob a day and a shilling for lads under sixteen, but the owners say one-and-six, ninepence for under sixteens.'

Dora spoke without looking up from her plate. 'The stingy

buggers! But it's better than nothing. Now we might get some decent food on the table instead of bloody leek soup.'

'Any more news about nationalization, Da?' Becky was glad her father's life would become a bit easier.

He finished his soup, wiped his mouth with his hand and lit a Woodbine cigarette with nicotine-stained fingers. 'Nah, the owners said nowt about it, but if we *do* strike, they'll use all the resources of the state to stop us.'

'But you won't need to strike now, will you?' Liz's voice held a plea.

Her father shrugged. 'Who can say, lass? We're a long way from getting what we want. They still haven't agreed to more machinery and safer working conditions, or compensation payments for death and accidents. That could take years.'

'Well, let's just be happy that for the moment they've agreed to a bit more money and shorter hours.' Becky smiled at her father but he didn't smile back. She wished she could get through to him. It was as if he'd grown a shell around himself as protection from the women of the house. It was sad that it also kept out Liz and her. Ma and Dora had each other, Liz and she had each other, but he had no one.

Liz served the pudding and Dora stuck her spoon in hers. 'Bloody hell! It's as tough as old boots. When are you going to learn to do anything right, our Becky?'

Liz gave Becky a pleading glance to keep silent, but the outrage inside Becky swelled, stretching tight the skin on her face, expanding her scalp, even her skull. The blood pounded in her veins and she longed to reach across the table and squeeze Dora's plump throat until those mocking eyes really *did* pop out of her face.

She compromised. 'I can cook better than you, our Dora,' she dared to say, and got carried away. 'You never do nothing but sit on your backside and drink gin and read women's magazines and dirty books – that is, when you're not tarting yourself up to catch a man.' She rolled her eyes. 'Eey, that'll be the day! What man in his right mind would want to take you on?'

Dora's face turned maroon and the red flashes started in her eyes. 'That's enough of your lip! Don't you dare speak to me like that!'

'It's the truth.' Becky knew she'd gone too far but couldn't stop now.

Dora leaned across the table and with the flat of her hand walloped the side of Becky's face. 'Next time I'll pull your stinking knickers down and you won't be able to sit for a week.'

'Ow! Ma!' Becky's hand flew to her stinging cheek. But it was to Liz, not to her mother, that she turned with a silent plea for help. Liz did what she could by patting Becky's knee under the table.

Her father plodded on eating his pudding, eyes down, pretending nothing was happening. Florrie's hand was on the table, balled into a fist, ready to let fly. Instead, she glowered at Becky. 'You brazen hussy!' she said. 'Apologize to Dora or you'll get the back of *my* hand an' all.'

Becky, still nursing her cheek, began to cry, deep, dark tears of frustration. Her insides were screaming at the injustice of always having to apologize to Dora, the injustice of Dora's criticizing everything Becky did. But she knew she had to give in. Dora wouldn't stop until she'd reduced her to a whimpering, snivelling heap. Then, when she'd finally humiliated her to the limit, she'd get that triumphant, gloating look on her face. Becky hated to see that expression. She jumped up and ran from the room, shouting a blatantly insincere 'I'm sorry!' apology only when she'd reached the door.

She flew up the stairs, flung herself into bed and pulled the blankets over her head.

'Beck, are you all right?' Liz peered at the bed in the strip of light from the landing and groped to find the bump under the blankets that was Becky. Becky's head emerged.

'That bitch! I want to strangle her.' She dried her eyes on her jumper sleeve and sniffed.

'I couldn't come up before I'd cleared away and done the

dishes. Dora's getting ready to go out on the hunt. The football club's having a dance at the Princess. She's had more gin and she's in a better mood. You can come down if you like.' Liz stroked Becky's hair in encouragement.

'So that's why our Dora's all dolled up!'

'Aye, she'll be leaving soon. Come down.'

'Not on your nellie! I'm staying here till she's off. I pray to God she finds some idiot like Da, who won't see through her, to marry her and get her out of here.'

Liz shivered in the frigid room and climbed under the blankets. 'Da's not an idiot, Beck.'

'But he was daft to marry Ma in the first place! I wish he'd stand up to them. They've knocked all the stuffing out of him.'

'He's a gentle soul. All he wants is peace and quiet.'

'And he's never going to get it with those two lunatics in the house.'

'Please, Beck, stop it. Dora is Dora and we have to live with her. Try not to let her get to you. Da copes with them both by cutting himself off, and it works.'

'Aye, even with *us*, and we've never done him any harm.'

'I'm sure he doesn't ignore us deliberately. He's sort of like a caterpillar that curls into a ball to protect itself from people poking it with sticks,' Liz said.

Becky ballooned her cheeks and let out the air in a burst of frustration. 'I'll never understand why he married Ma. Why would any man take on a grouchy woman and another man's bastard brat?'

'Don't dig up that old muck, Beck, and don't *ever* say anything about it to them, no matter how upset you are. Promise?'

'Phweeow! Think I'm mad? I'd get me face bashed in.'

Liz pulled the blankets tighter round her neck. 'I'll stay with you till Dora's gone.'

'What are Ma and Da doing?'

'Da's reading the paper and Ma's just sitting.'

'Just sitting drinking, you mean.' Becky sat up, her voice

suddenly eager. 'Liz, why don't we leave home sooner? I'll be finished school this term and getting a job anyway. Why wait till I'm fifteen. If fourteen's old enough to earn me own living, it's old enough to leave home. And you'll be almost seventeen.'

Liz was silent for a moment. 'Let's not talk about it just now, luv. I get scared when I think about it. And I start to worry about leaving them, especially Ma and Da.'

'You're too soft, Liz.' Becky's voice was small and sad. 'Ma doesn't care about you. She only cares about what you do for her. You know Dora's the only one she gives tuppence about. We committed the mortal sin of being Da's bairns and we can't do nothing about that. The only thing we can do is get away from here.'

Liz let out a long sigh. 'I suppose you're right. It won't make that much difference whether we do it sooner or later.'

Becky bounced on the ancient bedsprings in excitement. 'I'll start looking in the papers for jobs. We could take a single room for the both of us at first and sleep in a single bed till we're earning decent wages.'

Liz climbed out of bed. 'Aye, we'll talk more later. Let's go down now. I'm freezing.'

Three

After the midday meal on Sunday Liz washed up and Becky dried. 'Are you really going?' Becky whispered.

Liz threw an anxious glance into the kitchen and whispered back, 'Yes. And keep your lip buttoned, do you hear?'

Filled with self-pity, Becky nodded. 'How long will you be?' She forgot to keep her voice low and they both peeked into the kitchen and emitted a joint sigh of relief. Their father was reading the paper at the table, their mother nodding off by the fire, and Dora sitting opposite immersed in the *Sunday Pictorial*.

'I'll only be a couple of hours, you ninny.' Liz squeezed Becky's hand before going to the mirror over the mantelpiece to tidy her hair. By the time she'd reached the door, Becky was into her coat and winding her scarf about her head.

'Where do you think you're off to?' Dora looked up from her newspaper.

'Out for a walk,' Becky said.

Liz's mouth fell open, but she said nothing until the door was closed behind them. 'Beck!' she cried. 'You can't come. I'd feel stupid taking you along.'

'Don't worry. I'm going the other way. Enjoy your silly walk with your stupid pit lad.' She tossed her head and flounced off in the opposite direction.

When Liz returned some two hours later, Becky was leaning against the back gate, her eyelids swollen like puff pastries in her pinched face. Liz gasped. 'Beck! You've been waiting all this time? You should've gone in. I hope you're not crying because I went out with a lad.'

Becky wiped her wet eyes on her scarf. 'Are you seeing him again?'

'Oh, luv.' Liz hugged her, but Becky remained rigid.

'Are you?'

'Well, just for a walk next Sunday.' Liz's voice was apologetic.

'I knew it!' Becky burst into fresh tears.

Liz sighed and hugged her tighter. 'All right. I promise I won't see him again if it makes you that unhappy. I'm sorry.'

Becky sniffed and took a long breath. 'No, *I'm* sorry. I'm being selfish. If you want to see him, go. Just promise me you'll never marry him and we're still going away at the end of term.'

'Of course we are, you daft thing.' Liz's face brightened and she gave Becky another hug.

'I'll be your alibi again next Sunday.' Becky sniffed one last time. Now that her anxiety had abated, curiosity took over. 'What was it like, then? Did he do anything? Did you learn anything? Was it like they say in the books?'

Liz giggled. 'He didn't even hold my hand. He's very nice, and polite.'

Becky's face cracked into a grin. 'Well, you'd better learn something next week. It'll be a waste of time otherwise.'

It poured the following Sunday. Becky dashed across the cold linoleum in her bare feet to open the faded green curtains. 'Liz, it's bucketing. You can't go for a walk.'

Liz yawned and rubbed her eyes. 'He said if it rains we could go for a cup of tea somewhere.'

Becky climbed back into bed and snuggled up to Liz to keep warm. 'But what excuse could you make for going out in the rain?'

'You're good at that. Think of something.'

Now Becky truly felt a part of the conspiracy. 'We'll say

Mary asked us over, but I'll pretend to have a bad head and go to bed.'

Liz chuckled. 'Aye, bad heads run in the family. They'll believe that. And I haven't seen Mary for ages anyway. You're the best little liar in the world, Beck.'

'You know what Ma says – *Needs must when the devil drives*.'

They burst out laughing and Becky pulled the blankets over her head to smother the noise, but Liz pushed her out of bed with her feet and followed her. 'We'd better get the fire on and the place cleared up before they get down.'

They crept downstairs and tiptoed into the kitchen. Florrie was asleep in her chair, head lolling sideways on her shoulder, arms dangling limp over the armrests.

They began their chores, making no more noise than dust settling in a deserted church. They were used to being invisible and silent while their mother slept the dead sleep of the drunk. Even after the fire was blazing, the table set and the tea made, Florrie hadn't stirred.

'Shall I give her a cup now?' Becky looked uncertain. It was impossible to know when their mother would want a cup of tea before going upstairs to sleep off her hangover, or when she would yell at them for waking her.

'I'll ask her.' Liz tapped her mother's shoulder. 'Ma, do you want a cup of tea?' No response. She tried again, shaking the shoulder gently. Florrie's head dropped to her chest. 'Ma? Ma?' Liz raised the yellowish-white face. 'Ma!' Her voice was anxious. 'She won't wake up, Beck.'

'Better leave her alone. She must've had a right skinful.'

But suddenly their mother made a small choking sound, and her eyes opened and rolled back in her head before closing again. They stared in horror.

'She's bad,' Liz said. 'Quick, go for the doctor. I'll get Da and Dora.'

Becky was into her coat and out of the door almost before Liz had got out the words. Though the main emotion she now felt for her mother was fear, tears stung her eyes at the thought of her dying. As she ran, memories flashed through her head like scenes from a moving picture – a younger Ma picking her up after she'd fallen and rocking her to stop her tears, dabbing iodine on her finger when she'd cut it with the bread knife, and soothing her with words. Maybe one day she would stop drinking, and that same Ma would come back. Although Becky found it hard to imagine, she felt a sort of love for her now. She desperately didn't want her to die.

A weeping Becky held open the door while Dr Maynard's large frame pushed through it. Dora was kneeling in her dressing gown, holding her mother's limp hand and wailing, 'Don't die, Ma. Don't die!' Her mascara from the previous night ran in rivers down her cheeks. Jim Ryan sat at the table staring at his wife and biting his lower lip.

Dr Maynard's long legs crossed the small room in a couple of strides. He gently moved Dora aside and bent over Florrie. After rolling her eyelids upwards, he took a stethoscope from his bag.

Liz stood beside Becky and took her hand. Liz wasn't crying, but she trembled as much as Becky and her face was almost the colour of her mother's. Becky knew that Liz had never really stopped loving Ma, in spite of being treated like a servant.

Dr Maynard grunted and put away his stethoscope, then he poked Florrie all over. She moaned a few times. 'Help me to get her upstairs,' he said to Jim Ryan. The doctor's strong arms raised Florrie's heavy figure by the shoulders while their father supported her legs.

Dora, still wailing, followed them. 'You two stay here,' she said, turning her red eyes on them.

'How is she, Da?' Liz dropped Becky's hand and ran to her father when he returned.

'Her heart's not beating properly. The doctor's got to examine her.' He ran his hands through his wiry hair and sat heavily at the table again.

Ten minutes later Dr Maynard came down, his handsome face grim.

'She'll be all right if she takes care of herself. I've been warning her for years to stay off the gin. Her heart's not strong, that's why she fainted. And her liver's enlarged. If she doesn't stop drinking, it *will* be serious.' He took a bottle of pills from his bag. 'I've already given her one of these. See that she takes them according to the directions. She needs to lose weight. Keep her diet light, cut down on fat and salt. Dropsy's common with heart problems.'

Liz took the bottle of pills. 'Thank you, Doctor. I can try to make her eat better and keep the salt out of her food, but I can't do anything about the gin.'

He turned to Jim Ryan, who gave a helpless shrug. 'She won't take no notice of me.'

'She doesn't drink that much.' Dora was indignant in her mother's defence, but for once her father turned on her.

'She bloody well does. And you an' all. You'll be the next one that takes bad.'

'And what about you? Nobody knows how much you put away at the club.' Dora's eyes flashed as she gave him a look of pure malice. Becky closed her own eyes. She couldn't bear to see that look, even when directed at someone else.

Dr Maynard cleared his throat. 'I'll be off now. Let me know should there be any change for the worse. Otherwise, I'll pop in again in the morning.'

Liz saw him to the door and Dora turned on Becky. 'Little bitch! A spot of gin does Ma good. It's the only pleasure she gets in this dump.' She stalked to the dresser and poured herself a large gin. 'Me an' all.'

Becky thanked God that her mother wasn't going to die, and that they paid fourpence a week panel money to the doctor. Otherwise, his bills could land them in the workhouse.

Dora sat back in her chair, lit a Woodbine and exhaled through her nostrils, piercing Becky with her steely-eyed stare. 'You'll have to stay off school till she's better.'

Becky's pent-up fear for her mother and her rage at Dora

exploded. 'You sit at home on your backside all day. Why should I have to stay off school?'

'Because I say so. It's about bloody time you made yourself useful. You could've sat the leaving exam last year and been bringing in some money instead of wasting your time making bread puddings. Anyway, I've got some interviews next week and I'm helping out at the club. You're the only one who's not earning.'

Becky knew what helping out at the club meant. Dora tarted herself up, pulled a few pints, hung her bosom over the bar, flirted with the men, and came home drunk in the afternoons.

As for interviews, Becky knew they were an invention of the moment. Although, mysteriously, Dora always had money to spend, she'd never even tried to get a job. She lay in bed till eleven or so each morning, then sat on her bottom and read rubbish and drank gin until it was time to tart herself up to go out on the tiles. Becky's anger bubbled over like boiling toffee. 'Since when have you ever been to an interview? You've never earned a penny to help in this house.' Her voice went on without her consent. 'All you do is sit on your fat arse all day. You're—'

A whack across the side of Becky's head checked her runaway tongue. Dora stood over her, her face purple with fury. 'Don't you dare speak to me like that. I'm in charge when Ma's ill and you'll do as I say – or else!'

'Da?' Becky made a futile appeal to her father, but he only grunted and went to the door for his coat.

'Keep me out of it. I'm off to the club. I'm sick of bickering women.' He slammed the door, still muttering.

Liz rose from the table to go to Becky's aid. 'Couldn't you help out at home half days, Dora, and let Becky go to school the other half?' She was rewarded with one of Dora's looks.

'And *you* watch your mouth an' all or you'll get your ears boxed. You're always sticking up for the little bitch.'

'I'd rather be a bitch than a bastard!' Becky had said the forbidden word. Tears stung behind her eyes but she wouldn't let them out. She was determined not to give Dora the satisfaction of reducing her to a snivelling schoolgirl.

'What did you call me?' Dora loomed towards her and shook her by the shoulders. Becky felt as if her teeth were rattling loose in her head like dried peas in a jar. 'Ooww! Stop it! You're hurting me!'

'Stop it, the both of you!' Liz begged. 'You'll wake Ma. Doesn't anybody care about Ma?'

'Care about Ma?' Dora's eyes popped. 'I'm the only one in this bloody house who does. This selfish little monkey bloody well doesn't.' She gave Becky a push that sent her flying across the room.

Becky landed against the wall, head first, and slid to the floor weeping. Dora had won again. One of these days she would— But before she could think of what she would do, Liz was kneeling beside her gripping her shoulder, and there was a dull pain in her head.

'Are you all right, Beck?' She ran her hand over Becky's head. 'You've got a bump.'

'I hate her! I hate her!'

'Shh. I'll get a wet cloth to reduce the swelling.'

Dora sat back in her chair and gave Becky her cool, superior look. 'If Ma wasn't up there poorly, I'd give you more than a bump on the head. I'll bash the living daylights out of you if you ever dare use that word to me again. You don't care a bugger about anybody – not even Liz. You only pretend to because she's as soft as clarts, and you know you can wiggle your way round her like a little worm. She's the only one who doesn't see through you.'

Liz placed a damp cloth on Becky's forehead. Becky held it in place as she got up from the floor and, between sobs, attempted a final fling at Dora. 'You're just jealous because Liz loves *me* and not *you*. Nobody but a mother could love a piece of snot like you anyway!'

Dora's voice came slow and measured, as always when she was taking particular pleasure in flattening Becky's self-esteem. 'You know damn well our Liz's just sorry for you because you're an ugly, skinny, stupid little brat. You should have half her brains – and looks.'

'Please, stop! Both of you!' Liz moved next to Becky, squeezing her hand to calm her.

Dora lit another cigarette, her victory smile on her face. 'Aye, it's time you got on with the dinner. And try to make something we can eat this time.'

Liz led Becky to the pantry and whispered, 'Stay here with me and keep quiet. I'll see to the dinner.' Becky propped herself against the wall, her stomach still going round like a butter churn. She pressed the wet rag hard against her head and moaned.

Her glass in one hand, Dora took her coat from the door peg. 'I'm going up to sit with Ma to make sure she's all right.'

'That wicked witch!' Becky said when she'd gone. 'How could we be sisters – even half-sisters?'

Liz began peeling potatoes. 'But she *does* love Ma in her strange way.'

Becky shuddered. 'Aye, that's the only good thing you could say about her. But it spooks me that she has no conscience or guilt.'

'Harping on Dora's faults won't change her. We just have to put up with her.'

'Only till the summer though. Then we're off.' Becky tied the wet cloth round her head and moved to the sink to help Liz to peel the potatoes.

Liz handed her a knife. 'Would you mind if I sneaked out after dinner to tell Will I can't see him because Ma's poorly?'

'You *are* going to see him. Dora'll be keeping Ma company anyway. Just say your friend, Mary, is bad in bed and you promised to visit her. I'll cover for you. It's not fair that our Dora's the only one in this house who has a life of her own.' She rinsed the potatoes under the tap and gave Liz a wary look. 'But remember you promised not to fall for him! You'll just find out about things.'

Liz nodded.

* * *

Florrie slept most of the day. It was an eerie Sunday. Becky was glad when ten o'clock came and she and Liz could slip up to bed.

'If Ma needs anything during the night I'll give you a shout,' Dora said, twirling her hair round her metal curlers at the mantelpiece mirror.

Becky paused on the stairs and bit her tongue to keep it still. Dora slept with Ma. She could at least see to her during the night.

Liz gave her a push from behind. 'Get a move on, Beck. I'm tired.'

Becky pulled her flannel nightgown over her liberty bodice and knickers, though she removed her long black wool stockings and pulled on an old pair of ankle socks with holes in them. The stockings went baggy at the knees if she slept in them. She burrowed under the blankets and, after visualizing Dora with a metal stake protruding four feet from the centre of her chest, her massive tits flopping to each side, she felt satisfied enough to put her out of her mind.

This was the first chance she'd had to talk to Liz about her outing with Will Bennett. Exploding with curiosity, she whispered, 'Go on, what happened, Liz?'

'Nothing really. We just had a cup of tea at the tea shop in Laburnum Terrace and talked about things. I told him Ma was took bad and he said he was sorry, he knows what it's like. His ma's poorly a lot and he helps his da to look after her. His married brother and sister live in Durham, so they're not much help. We had a walk in the park on the way back and he held me hand. It was nice, but I couldn't feel much through me gloves.'

'He didn't try nothing? Not even a kiss?'

'Becky!' Liz's teeth chattered as she undressed. 'Do you think he's going to grab me in a passionate embrace in broad daylight?' She pulled her nightgown over her brassiere and vest.

Ma had bought Liz the brassiere when she'd started work. Becky stared at it with her usual envy but knew she didn't have enough up there to put into one. She prayed every night to wake up with a pair like Liz's – not like Dora's, they were disgusting. She put tits out of her mind. She was more interested in Will Bennett. 'He could have found a secluded place in the park and kissed you,' she said.

'Aw, come on, Beck. I've told you. He's a nice, polite lad and, when he said he was sorry Ma was took bad, I felt he really meant it.'

'Aye, *I'm* sorry Ma's bad an' all,' Becky said. 'Can you believe our Dora making me stay off school and get up in the night to look after her, when she sits on her bum in the house all day? I mean, even for Dora, that's the flaming limit.'

'Aye, she's got the nerve of the devil. I'm sorry about you missing school, but let's pray Ma gets better soon.'

'Aye, please God she does.' Becky closed her eyes, but suddenly a tight fist of panic clutched at her chest. What if Ma stayed an invalid and always needed looking after? No! She wouldn't even think about that. Ma *would* get well, and at the end of term she and Liz would be off to Newcastle.

Four

To Becky the next week passed like a month. Her mother, never in a good humour, became even more querulous and demanding on her sickbed. Becky ran up and down the stairs constantly, attending to her needs and complaints. Relief refreshed her spirits like spring rain when, on Friday, Dr Maynard said her mother could get up for a while the following day.

On Saturday afternoon, Becky supported Florrie as she shuffled downstairs in her ancient slippers and dressing gown. She seemed to have shrunk, but her voice was as loud and irritable as ever. 'Not so fast! You're knocking the breath out of me.'

'Sorry, Ma.' Becky inched her down the last few stairs.

Dora sat by the fire with a book, another one showing an almost bare-breasted woman and a man with a shirt open to his waist. She flicked half an inch of ash from her cigarette on to the hearth and glanced up. 'Eey, Ma! It's grand to see you downstairs.'

'Aye, I'm sick of lying up there staring at the ceiling.'

Becky lowered her mother into her chair. Her face was still tinged with yellow, but it was less bloated, and her ankles didn't overflow her slippers so much.

Florrie puffed and fanned herself from the effort of lowering herself into her chair, then looked around the kitchen. She ran her fingers down the wooden armrest and held them up to Becky. 'Call that clean? The place is a pigsty.'

'I dusted this morning, Ma. It's the coal, it's all slack, not a roundy in it. It belches back when you throw it on.' Becky hated it when her mother pursed her lips like that.

29

'Aye, always ready with excuses. One of these days you'll learn how to keep a house.' She peered at the pan on the stove, a plate on top with a lid over it. 'I'm starving. Is that me tea, or have you got an excuse for that an' all?'

Dora yawned. 'Aye, that's your tea, Ma. It smells like sweaty socks.'

Becky ignored Dora. She'd ignored her a lot this week and was pleased with her self-control. 'It's poached plaice, Ma. I got it special for you.'

Florrie screwed up her nose. 'Fish again! Haven't you got no imagination, lass?'

Becky bit her lip before confessing, 'It was all we could afford. The housekeeping money's finished. There's only tuppence left and I've kept it for the gas meter.'

'Begod! You've gone through the lot?' Florrie shook her head. 'You'd better start learning how to make ends meet, lass. You'll make a lousy wife.'

Dora snickered over the top of her book. 'What man would ever want our Becky?'

Becky took a breath that caused her thin shoulders to rise and fall two inches. 'I did the fish in milk for you, Ma, and mashed potatoes.' She set the meal on a tray and placed it on her mother's lap. Her hands shook.

Florrie began to eat, then screwed up her face. 'For God's sake, give me the salt. I can't take another bite of this invalid rubbish.'

'But the doctor said—'

'Never you mind what the doctor said,' Dora cut in. 'You heard Ma.'

Resigned, Becky handed her mother the salt. Florrie tipped it over the food. 'Eey, that's a bit more like it,' she said after tasting it. 'But I'd slit me granny's throat for a noggin to wash it down.'

Dora jumped up with a grin. 'Why not, Ma? No harm in celebrating your first day up. I could do with a drop meself.' She bounced to the dresser and returned with two large gins. 'Here's to your health, Ma.'

Yes, Becky thought, that's the only time you'll get off your backside and serve yourself. Dora didn't trust her to pour the gin.

Florrie stared at the glass in her hand. 'Eey, by God! I could do with it. But the doctor said no.'

'Aw, now you're getting better you can have the odd nip. Here's to being on your feet again.' Dora raised her glass to her mother in encouragement.

'Aye, if you put it like that.' Florrie sipped cautiously, then the urge seemed to overcome her and she emptied the glass with a sigh. 'Eey by! I'm starting to feel like me old self again.'

'Hello, Ma.' Liz arrived and stood by the fire. 'How are you feeling?'

Florrie nodded. 'Better now I've had a sup. But I'm sick of this filthy invalid food.' She contorted her face and thrust the tray with the unfinished meal at Liz.

Becky straightened from checking the panhacklety in the oven. 'Nice to see you home early, Liz.'

'Aye, for once I didn't have to stay late.'

'You finally getting the hang of the job then?' Dora lit another Woodbine from the one she'd just finished. 'About time an' all. Be an angel and go to the fishy later on for some chips and batter. Ma needs some real food.' She cast a sarcastic smile at Becky. 'Don't we all?'

Liz glanced at Becky, who fumed quietly. All week she'd managed to keep her mother to her diet, and on Ma's first day up Dora was ruining it. Besides, she only had tuppence left. At closing time you could get a big newspaper-wrapped parcel of chips and batter for tuppence. But not the *last* tuppence! And certainly not for greasy food for Ma.

She fingered the coins in her pinafore pocket and sneaked out to the hall. The gas was still on but it wouldn't last the night and they'd be sitting in the dark. Da and Liz got paid fortnightly. It was pay day tomorrow but, in the meantime, she needed light to do the mending. She opened the cupboard under the stairs quietly and slipped the coin into the meter slot. When she turned the handle the penny dropped with a clatter. Her breath came heavily as she turned the handle on the second penny. She would get hell for this.

'Our Becky!' Dora's voice rang out. 'What the blazes do you think you're doing? We've *got* gas.'

Becky braced herself and returned to the kitchen. 'Aye, but it'll be going out any minute and I've got to sew tonight.'

'Sewing! You selfish cow! All you ever think about is tarting up your clothes. Now Ma can't have her treat.'

'I'm not tarting up me clothes,' Becky said with relish. Now was her chance to get one over on Dora. 'I'm doing Da's mending and *your* stockings.' Becky used a tiny embroidery hook to pick up the ladders in Dora's imitation silk stockings, a task she found relaxing, despite her resentment at having to do anything for Dora. Watching Dora's anticipated reaction, satisfaction swelled inside her.

Dora's pursed lips crept into the sugary smile she used when forced to eat her words, which she always managed to do without admitting she'd been wrong. Her voice, as sugary as her smile, floated towards Becky, 'Oh, ta, Beck. Do you mind, Ma?' She turned her smile on Florrie.

'Nah, hinny. I shouldn't have chips and batter anyway.'

Becky gave Liz a sly smile, which she returned with a nod. That evening passed peacefully, despite the fact that Dora spent it at home.

The following Monday when Liz came home, Becky said, 'I can't stay off school any longer. The kiddy-catcher came when Ma and Dora were snoozing in their chairs.'

Liz clapped her hand to her mouth. 'Oh! He *would* come when they were both up. Dr Maynard might give me a note if I tell him Dora drinks too much to be trusted to look after Ma. Where is she now?'

'Upstairs.'

'Good! I'll go while the surgery's still open.' She disappeared in a flash.

Becky prayed that Liz would be back before Dora came

down. Her prayers were answered. The door opened and Liz waved an envelope. 'I got a note. I know you'd rather go back to school, but it won't be for long.'

'Did you tell him about Dora?' Becky's eyes were wide.

'Aye.'

Though Becky didn't relish continuing to nurse Ma, a smile puckered her face. At least Dr Maynard knew the truth about Dora.

Five

B ecky couldn't keep her mother on her diet. 'I'll just have one little tipple to keep you company, pet,' she would say to Dora, but it never stopped at one. And when she was drunk she refused her diet food and demanded a 'real meal'. There was nothing anyone could do against the combined forces of Ma and Dora. Dr Maynard became a regular visitor.

The strain exhausted Becky, but she clung to her dream of escape at the end of the term. Just a few more weeks!

Liz went out with Will Bennett more often now, but she insisted they were just friends and she simply enjoyed his company. He hadn't progressed beyond a goodnight peck on the mouth.

Becky was mollified. If they hadn't done anything yet, there couldn't be anything in it. But that Will Bennett was probably retarded or something, she thought

Though reconciled to Liz's outings, Becky was miserable at home without her. On the rare occasions when she was allowed out, she would go to the pictures or for a walk with her old school friend, Carol Billings, but it wasn't the same as being with Liz.

One morning she was scrubbing the kitchen floor when she heard the milk lad shouting in the lane. On her way to the door she picked up the tin jug from the dresser. She didn't realize it was raining until she stepped outside, and couldn't be bothered to go back for her coat. She held out her jug to the milk lad, Bob Baker, without a greeting.

'Good day, Becky,' he said.

'Aye, maybes for some,' Becky retorted, anxious to get back inside.

He smiled at her as he filled her jug. 'What's wrong, then? Got out of the wrong side of the bed this morning?'

'Less of your cheek, Bob Baker.' Becky's face flamed with anger.

He smiled again and filled her jug but didn't hand it to her. Instead he set it on the cart, pushed back his cap and scratched his forehead. 'You look right pretty when you're angry, Becky.'

Her hand flew to her hot face. She felt embarrassed. Her hair was tied back with a rag, and she wore her mother's sacking apron over an old work dress of Liz's. 'Very funny,' she said and stretched out a work-reddened hand. 'Now can I have me milk? You'll get your money at the end of the week.'

His fresh, boyish face turned serious. 'I wasn't being funny, Becky. You're the prettiest lass on me rounds. I've been wanting to ask you out, but you're always so . . .'

'Always so what?' In her astonishment Becky's voice was curious, even courteous. Was he really asking her out? Bob Baker wasn't a bad-looking lad, though he was shortish, blond and fair-skinned, and she preferred tall, dark boys.

'Well, you're sort of off-putting, you know, distant like.' He scratched his forehead again and pulled his cap back down. 'I don't mean snooty,' he added quickly, 'but there's something about you that, well . . . It's taken me a long time to get round to asking you.'

Becky's head spun in amazement and delight – that a lad, any lad, could fancy her, even in her old work clothes, but Bob Baker was almost seventeen and she'd seen him in the town with quite a few pretty girls, older than she was. 'Now, if I was to say yes, where would you take me?' She tried to sound teasing.

'Well, we could go to the pictures. Charlie Chaplin's on at the Hippodrome in *Shoulder Arms*. It's a rotten night to do anything else.'

'You mean tonight?' She was amazed.

'Aye, if you're not doing anything, like.'

'No . . . I *could*,' she said, slowly, as if deliberating, but she was reasoning quickly – while Dora was still at the club she would wash her hair and press her best blue serge dress.

'I'll come for you at about half past six, then.'

Her stomach jumped into her throat, then plummeted to her feet. 'No, don't come.' She tried to still her rocketing insides. 'Me ma doesn't like people coming when she's poorly. I'll meet you at the end of the row.' Phweew! It would be more than her life was worth to have him come to the house.

He handed her the milk jug and grinned. 'See you later, then.'

She stood for a moment, transfixed, as he pushed his cart down the lane. Then she carried her head high as she walked back to the house.

Inside, she looked at her reflection in the mirror and her shoulders slumped. Her face looked as if the pieces didn't belong together. Her eyes were too round, her nose too short. Her mouth, that was all right. But it looked as if it should belong to a prettier face. Lord, her hair! What a mess! But she preened herself and felt a warm glow all over. Bob Baker had asked her out, so she couldn't be as ugly as Dora always said.

She did a little dance over the now dry floor. She was going out with a lad! Not that she intended to get serious over Bob Baker, a milk lad, but there was no harm in getting some experience before Newcastle. After all, she'd had her fourteenth birthday last month. She was old enough, but Dora and Ma wouldn't think so.

Though Liz had turned seventeen two weeks ago, she still had to lie that she was going out with her friend, Mary, when she saw Will Bennett. Becky would say she was going out with Carol Billings.

Bob Baker was a different story from Will Bennett. He was a lot more experienced, judging by all the lasses he took out. Not that she would let him get away with too much, mind you. Just enough to get an idea of what it felt

36

like to be kissed by a lad and all that, to see what all the fuss was about.

She wished she could tell Dora, just to get it into her big thick skull that she, Becky, could get a lad. Eey! Dora would be dead mad, and dead jealous.

At the thought of Dora, Becky glanced at the clock. Half past twelve. She would just have time to wash her hair and iron her dress before Dora got home from the club.

A plaintive cry drifted down the stairs. 'Our Becky, that you? Where the hell've you been? I've been shouting me lungs out for ten minutes.'

Ma! In her excitement, Becky had forgotten the irons she'd put on the fire for her mother's feet, and it was time for her dinner. The liver she'd bought for tea that night was still in its wrapping paper on the table, blood seeping out of one corner. She would braise some of it for her mother now and give her a boiled egg for tea tonight. She still couldn't eat fried foods and if she smelled everybody else's dinner frying she wouldn't eat her own.

'I had to wait at the milk cart, Ma,' she shouted up the stairs. 'I'm bringing your irons up and your dinner's in the pan.'

With a thick cloth, she picked up one of the irons and spat on it. It sizzled furiously. Phew! Too hot! She wrapped both irons in extra layers of rags and ran up the stairs and tucked them at her mother's feet. 'Your dinner's nearly ready, Ma,' she lied.

'An' about time an' all. Me belly's eating itself.'

While the liver simmered, Becky rummaged in the cupboard under the stairs, where the family hung the overflow of clothes from Ma's wardrobe. There were so many of Dora's clothes in the cupboard that the few items the others owned got pushed to the back or fell to the floor. The hooks near the front were invisibly marked *Dora*, just like her favourite chair by the fire.

At last Becky retrieved her dress and threw it on the kitchen table. She would iron it after she'd washed her hair. Dora mustn't see her with wet hair on a Tuesday. It wasn't due to be washed until bath night on Friday.

When she'd made the tea and refilled the kettle to wash her hair, the liver and onions were ready. She hid the greyish, soggy slice of liver under the onions and put a piece of bread and dripping at the side. She braced herself as she carried up the tray.

Florrie sat up and peered at the plate. 'What's this then?'

'Liver and onions, Ma, your favourite.'

'Aye, them were the days, when I could have a nice fry-up. I suppose you've boiled it again.' She scraped the onions off the liver with the knife and peered at it in disgust.

'It's not boiled, it's *braised*, Ma, and I've put dripping on your bread.'

'Braised! A fancy name for boiling if ever I heard one, and you've scraped the dripping on and off again as usual.'

'The doctor says you have to lose weight.'

'Aye, I know. Thank God at least I can still have me cup of tea the way I like it.' Becky backed to the door, sighing with relief. Ma hadn't thrown the food at her. That meant she would eat it.

The kettle was steaming again and she filled two jugs and topped them up with cold from the pantry before setting them on the draining board. She would have to rinse her hair in cold under the tap. She strained to reach the high shelf in the pantry where Dora hid her Amami shampoo and Lux soap flakes for her bath.

A thrill ran through Becky at her crime. She couldn't sit next to Bob Baker in the pictures with her hair smelling of carbolic soap. She'd used the last of the Fairy soap yesterday when she'd washed Dora's smalls by hand. Dora's underwear was too delicate to go in the big tub with the posser.

Her hair washed and smelling dreamy, Becky combed it out in front of the mirror and tried to twist it into little curls. But it dropped, straight as ever. She toyed with the idea of Dora's metal curlers but dismissed it. Too notice-able! Never mind, after real shampoo her hair would prob-ably shine when it dried. She'd have to keep her distance from Dora in case she smelled the Amami or noticed the shine.

She glanced at the clock again. Quarter to two. She'd better iron the dress before Dora got home. Then horror stuck in her throat like a fish hook. The irons were in Ma's bed. With sudden determination, she marched upstairs.

'I'll take your tray, Ma, and could I borrow the irons for a while? I washed our Dora's smalls yesterday and I haven't had a chance to iron them yet. She needs them tonight. She's going out.'

Florrie grunted. 'Aye, but bring them back hot, mind you.'

Downstairs, Becky reheated the irons. She hoped Ma wouldn't let anything slip to Dora about the smalls, because she'd ironed them and given them to her last night.

She spread the flannelette sheet used for ironing over one end of the table and washed Ma's dishes while she waited for the irons. A century later, they were hot enough, but the rough wool serge barely responded to the heat.

In desperation Becky soaked a rag and pressed the dress damp. Half an hour later it looked crease free, though plain and ugly. In fact it looked more like a school gym slip than a dress. She had a sudden urge to help herself to one of Dora's dresses from the hall cupboard. She could wear it underneath her own and slip off hers in the washhouse.

She returned the irons to the fire before Ma started wailing for them again and hung her dress over the top of the hall cupboard door, then, with shaking fingers, rummaged among Dora's dresses. She was due any minute and Becky knew that she'd be a dead duck if Dora caught her going through her clothes. Somehow the danger excited her. But as she held up each frock in turn, her excitement drained away like Monday's murky washing water. Of course, all Dora's dresses were too big. Except! She spied a bright pink clinging wool one with a tie belt. Dora hadn't worn that for ages. It had been too tight when she'd bought it anyway, and now she'd put on more weight.

Becky fingered the smooth wool with longing. If she tied the belt tightly, the skirt might look as if it were meant to be gathered. She put the dress back in the cupboard underneath her own. She would sneak them up and hang them behind her bedroom door when she took up Ma's irons.

Barely had she returned from her mission when the back door opened. Dora threw her coat over the heap on the door, teetered across the floor and flopped into her chair, kicking off her shoes. 'Phweeew, standing behind the bar gives me feet jip. Tell Ma I'll be up later. I'm knackered and frozen.'

Dora was wobbly on her feet. A good sign! She would lie down with Ma when she was warmed up and it would be tea time before she surfaced. Becky felt guilty and elated at the approaching adventure, as if she were about to pour Dora's gin bottle down the sink.

Six

Becky was in the back yard scrubbing out the scum in the zinc tub after Da's bath when Liz came home. She grabbed Liz's arm and pulled her into the lean-to that served as the washhouse.

In the dim interior she said, 'Guess what? Bob Baker's asked me to go out with him – *tonight*. He must be keen.' She flicked her hands under her shining hair and let it fall to her shoulders, but it seemed the gesture was lost on Liz in the gloom. 'Now, there's a lad who can get any girl he wants,' Becky continued, 'so I must be pretty, no matter what our Dora says.'

'Of course you're pretty. But you're just fourteen. *Bob Baker* must be at least seventeen, *and* he's got a reputation. I hope you said no.'

Becky's spirits sagged like a soggy Yorkshire pudding. 'Are you daft? Say *no* to a nice-looking lad asking me out? He's taking me to the Hippodrome to see Charlie Chaplin.' She added mutinously, 'As you're not learning anything from Will Bennett, I'll have to find out for the both of us, won't I?'

'Beck! You're not serious. He could get you into trouble.'

At the anxiety in Liz's voice, Becky softened. 'Oh, Liz, don't be crazy. You know I wouldn't let him go too far. He was right polite and nice today. He can't be as bad with the lasses as you say.'

'Even if he turns out to be a gentleman, if Dora or Ma find out, they'll skin the hide off you.'

'They haven't caught on about you and Will Bennett yet, and it's been months now.'

Liz leaned against the mangle, her face tired and worried.

41

'You know you'll catch it much worse than me if they do find out. I'm older, and Will Bennett hasn't got a reputation like Bob Baker.' She let out a hopeless sigh. 'I can't stop you, but stay where there are people. Promise?'

Becky grinned. 'I promise. And I've got another surprise. Come up with me when I get changed and you'll find out. We'd better go in now.'

'How's Ma?' Liz asked as they hurried to the house.

'Grumpy, but she's eaten everything I've given her so far, and Dora's going out.'

'Thank the Lord for that,' Liz said, opening the door.

'For what?' Dora yawned and stretched in her chair.

'The rain's letting up,' Becky said, turning into the pantry to smother a giggle.

Becky was too excited to eat. She lied that she'd had hers earlier and sat at the table sipping a cup of tea. She was relieved that Dora hadn't noticed her clean hair. She must be in a good mood because she was going out, she thought. Then, her breath stopped and she choked on the tea. What if Dora was going to see Charlie Chaplin? Or what if they bumped into each other in the street?

Liz thumped her back. 'Don't drink so fast.'

Becky swallowed hard and gasped until air once more trickled into her lungs. 'I'm all right,' she said. Ashington was a big enough place. Liz had never met Dora when she was with Will, so why worry? She rose. 'Do you mind clearing away, Liz? I'm going to see Carol the night.'

Dora put down her knife and fork and wiped her mouth with her fingers. 'Oh, aye? What for?'

'Just to play cards or something.'

'You'd better.' Dora pushed away her plate and lit a cigarette. 'If you spend the housekeeping money on the pictures again you'll be in even bigger trouble than last time.'

Becky fumed as she darted into the pantry to wash. She'd only once used ninepence of the housekeeping when she'd gone to the pictures with Carol and bought some Maltesers.

What the blazes could she do on sixpence a week pocket money? And Dora was smoking a Gold Flake, not even a Woodbine. Where *did* she get the money? Ma couldn't possibly keep her in all her fancy clothes, booze and cigarettes, and she got mainly drinks for tips from the men at the clubs. Perhaps she pilfered from the tills? Dora didn't have a conscience about anything, why should she about stealing? Funny, Becky had never thought of that. She must tell Liz. That *must* be the answer.

As instructed, Liz followed Becky when she went upstairs to change. Becky closed the bedroom door softly and lifted the heavy blue dress from the top of the clothes on the door hook, revealing Dora's pink wool beneath.

Liz gaped. 'Beck! Are you mad? If she finds out, she'll kill you.'

'She won't find out.' Becky waved the blue serge dress in front of Liz. 'I'm wearing this over it and I'll take it off in the washhouse. Dora'll still be out gallivanting when I get home and I can sneak it back in the cupboard.'

Liz ran a hand over her forehead. 'Becky, it's not worth the risk. You'll be in the dark in the pictures anyway, and the rest of the time you'll have your coat on.'

'I'll take it off as soon as we get there and the lights'll be on – and they'll be on in the interval and at the end. He'll see plenty.' She twisted her face as if in pain. 'I just couldn't wear that schoolgirl thing.'

'All right, I'll keep me fingers crossed for you.' Liz's voice was resigned. 'And I didn't dare ask in front of Da and Dora, but what have you done to your hair?'

Becky removed her liberty bodice and flung the soft pink wool over her head. When her face emerged she beamed at Liz. 'I washed it in our Dora's Amami.' She swung her head to show off the silky blonde mane. 'Not bad, eh?'

'Eey, our Beck, you're going to catch it one of these days.'

'Aw, Dora's so wrapped up in herself she didn't even

43

notice.' Becky smoothed the dress over her slim body and looked down at herself, disappointed. 'I wish I had tits like yours, Liz. Mine look like two cherries without stalks.'

Liz's tight face relaxed and they giggled. Then Liz held her at arms' length and considered her chest for a moment. 'Nah, not cherries, they're more like crab apples now.'

They giggled again, and Liz said, 'They're coming on grand. Don't worry about them, or you'll stunt their growth.' They burst out laughing, but Liz clapped her hand over her mouth. 'Shush, or Ma'll want to know what's going on.' Still shaking with stifled laughter, she picked up the dress belt. 'Let me help.'

She tied the sash round Becky's hips and pulled the dress bodice over it, blouson style. 'There now! You could have tits the size of Dora's under there and nobody would notice the difference.'

'Ugh, I wouldn't want her revolting floppy things anyway.'

Next Liz arranged the skirt in a couple of pleats at the sides to take up the excess material. 'Wow! That looks fashionable – and slinky, Beck. You can see the shape of your bum.'

'Eey, does it look tarty?'

Liz smiled. 'It would if it had our Dora's bum in it, but not your little cheeks.'

'Oh, I wish I could look in the mirror in Ma's room.'

'Well you can't, just take my word for it. In fact, you look too nice for that Bob lad. I hope he doesn't get any ideas.'

Becky sat on the bed and put on her school shoes. 'If he does get any ideas, they'll be squashed when he sees these.'

'Never mind, pet. You're due for a new pair soon. I'll see if we can wangle a teensy heel and a strap instead of laces. We can say they're for when Ma's better and you get a job.'

'Aye, but we won't say that the job'll be in Newcastle.' The shoes tied, Becky lifted a radiant face.

Liz glanced away. 'I'd better go down and clear up. You look lovely, pet. Promise you'll be careful.'

'Don't worry! You know I wouldn't get serious about any old Ashington milk lad and ruin our plans.'

* * *

Bob Baker was leaning against the wall at the end of the row, huddled in his overcoat, his cap pulled low against the rain.

'So, you came, then.'

'Did you think I wouldn't?' It gave her confidence that he believed she could treat lads that carelessly.

He took her arm and they walked, huddled against the rain, towards the town. 'It's a good night for the pictures,' he said.

'Aye, the end of May and still like winter.'

Becky made a mental note. She'd said *aye* instead of *yes*. She must remember not to use Geordie words. It was time she started practising for Newcastle. And she would nag Liz to practise with her. When the time came, they would be able to talk like Miss Dulwich, the headmistress, and some of the other teachers. They pronounced all their words precisely and never used slang.

Bob broke into her thoughts. 'I take it you don't work, seeing as you've been getting the milk the past few months.'

'Not at the minute. I'm looking after my mother while she's poorly.' *My mother.* She thought how much better that sounded than *me ma*, and was glad that she was good at acting.

'What's wrong with your ma?' Bob interrupted her thoughts.

'It's her liver, and things. Not serious, but she's taking a while to get better.' She wished he wouldn't ask so many questions. 'How long have you been doing your milk round?' Her cleverness pleased her.

'Couple of years, but I don't think I'll do it all me life.'

They'd reached the outskirts of the town and the street was cluttered with sodden figures hurrying home from work or, like them, striding out to find temporary escape from their hard lives.

But not all people led hard lives, Becky thought, as they passed the Grand Hotel. A well-dressed man in a fancy overcoat and Trilby hat held an umbrella over a fur-coated woman as he helped her out of the largest motor Becky had ever seen. She peered in the gaslight. It said *Sunbeam* something. One of these days she would ride in a car like that.

'I never see you at dances,' Bob said.

Hot embarrassment drenched her as if he'd poured boiling water over her face and neck. 'My mother doesn't approve of dancing, at least not until I'm eighteen.' She could admit that, because it was obvious she wasn't eighteen.

'How old are you, then?'

'Old enough.'

'I don't see why she won't let you go to dances if she lets you go out with lads anyway.'

'She just has a bee in her bonnet about dancing – she thinks it's sinful.'

'She doesn't know you're out with a lad the night, does she?' His chuckle was so deep it made her arm quiver in his.

'Aye, I told her.' Damn! She'd said *aye* again.

He was still chuckling. 'That's why you had to meet me at the end of the lane, isn't it?'

'So what if it was!' She felt like a boxer in a corner losing a fight. But she wouldn't let him know everything. 'She has a bee in her bonnet about lads as well, so I just tell her I'm going out with a girlfriend. Me older sister does an' all. Me ma—' (Oops! She'd slipped into Geordie again.) She continued, 'Ma only lets me oldest sister go out with lads because she's twenty.' She lied because, if she said her oldest sister was only eighteen, and there was another sister between, he would guess she was younger than she looked.

They were early for the first house and there was no queue at the cinema. They ducked into the foyer and he helped her off with her coat and scarf, then he stared at her in the pink dress. 'By, you look grand, Becky.' He grinned as he removed his wet cap and overcoat. She drank in her first compliment. Slinging the wet coats over his arm, he went to the box office. When he joined her she noticed that the tickets were pink – the front stalls. But as they were early they found seats in the last row, only one row in front of the back stalls, which cost ninepence. That was almost as good.

The cigarette girls wandered the aisles with their trays of cigarettes and sweets slung from leather straps round their necks.

'Would you like some sweets?' Bob said.

She hesitated. He was only a milk lad, but he delivered for his father, who had a small dairy on the outskirts of town. It was all that was left of what had been a big farm before Ashington had grown out into the countryside and swallowed up many farms. Still, it was his father's business. He couldn't be that badly off.

'Yes, please. I'd love some Liquorice Allsorts.' She'd remembered to say *yes*, not *aye*. Soon it would come naturally.

Her eyes followed him down the aisle and she noticed he was wearing a navy-blue serge suit. It was tight across the shoulders and the pants were shiny where he sat. It must be old but it still looked nice and showed off his broad build. She felt proud to be out with him.

'Here you are, then.' He handed her the box of Liquorice Allsorts before opening the packet of Park Lane cigarettes he'd bought for himself.

Just then the lights dimmed and the curtains opened to reveal the screen. The prospect of entering the fantasy world of moving pictures always thrilled Becky, but tonight it was especially nice to be taken by a lad and bought sweets. She chewed contentedly and settled into her seat.

His hand fumbled in the dark for hers, but she was clutching the box of sweets. He slid it on to her lap and took her hand. She waited for her breath to stop, but it didn't. Never mind, it was a pleasant sensation to feel his skin against hers. Then she felt a strange excitement as he began to fondle her fingers, one by one. She wished they weren't so rough from housework and that her nails were manicured.

He worked on her fingers through the trailers showing the coming attractions, and the news, which was bad. Lots more people were dying from influenza and there was talk about more food rationing because the economy couldn't get back on its feet after the war.

She was glad when the big picture started, but it was hard to concentrate with him playing with her hand like that. He'd moved it to his lap and now had both his hands around it. He ran his fingers up and down her palms and her wrist. It felt funny but nice. Then he put her hand on his thigh, and she felt his hard muscles and sinews under the rough serge.

By the time the lights went on at the end of the picture, she felt hot all over and kept her head down until they were outside in the cool air. It had stopped raining. He took her hand again but now she wore her gloves. 'I enjoyed the picture,' she said.

'Aye, Charlie Chaplin's dead funny.'

They were talking normally and yet this unspoken *thing* hung between them. She still had that funny feeling, and knew he must as well, from doing those things with her hand.

'Let's take a turn round the park. It's still early and the rain's stopped.'

Becky opened her mouth to say she'd better get straight home, then closed it. It was dark, but a walk in the park would be romantic. He would try to kiss her and she would let him, but no more. 'All right,' she said, as if she regularly walked in the park with lads at night.

They exchanged small talk as they strolled along the deserted paths, drops from the wet elm and sycamore trees falling like sparse drizzle, until the drizzle increased and Becky realized it was raining again. 'Oh, drat!' she said.

'We could sit in the shelter. The benches'll be dry.' His arm went round her waist and he pulled her closer. Even through their thick coats she felt the movement of his leg against hers and a pleasant, prickly sensation ran through her. In silence, they reached the shelter, and a man's voice, barely a whisper, was followed by a woman's low giggle.

'Too late,' Bob said, and led Becky to the back of the structure. He pulled her underneath the overhang. It jutted out about a foot, giving some shelter from the rain, which now pelted them like heavy glass beads.

He leaned her against the wall and put his arms round her, his bulk protecting her. Becky waited, silent, trembling inside, and he bent his head and pressed his mouth against hers, still, at first; then he moved his lips from side to side and increased the pressure. Becky's knees felt wobbly and a little flame of pleasure licked at her insides. She found herself returning his pressure. When the tip of his tongue forced her lips apart, it felt strange, not what she'd expected from reading Dora's books. Fancy, poking your tongue inside someone else's mouth! The thought was revolting. Yet she liked it.

From the other side of the wooden partition the noise increased, and the shelter shook with violent thumping. The woman cried out, 'Yes! Yes! Yes! Joe, oh, Joe!' over and over. Becky froze in horror. The thumping and shouting grew louder until the shelter shuddered and the woman yelled, 'Oh, God! Oh, God!'

Becky pulled away from Bob.

'Come on,' he said. 'It's only a couple having it off.' He pulled her back, breathing heavier now.

'No, stop a minute,' Becky said in a barely audible whisper. 'That's a girl I know. I don't want them to know we're here.'

He loosened his grip only slightly and they stood, silent.

The man's voice from the shelter, still breathless, was accompanied by the chink of coins. 'Half a crown! It was only two bob last time.'

Becky closed her eyes as if in pain. So that was how Dora got money – not from the club tills at all.

Bob, also listening to the couple's conversation, ran his hands up and down her back. 'So, she's a professional, eh?'

'Shush and hold still.'

'They'll be going soon, and we can go inside,' he said, then gave a low chuckle. 'Is it your friend?'

'Quiet,' Becky hissed, as Dora spoke.

'Aye, well, the cost of living's gone up, hasn't it, luv?

You've got to admit I'm still a bargain at that. And anyways, it's sixpence less for your wife to blow on gin.'

'Knock it off about Maggie, Dora. She's a good soul and there's nowt wrong with her having an odd nip, she doesn't get much else. She's not like you – at the bottle all the time.'

Dora tittered. 'Aye, you're dead right she doesn't get much else, or you wouldn't have to get your fun from me.'

'Less of your lip, now. Be glad I help to keep you in business. You must be making a packet.'

Dora laughed. 'Not enough to live on, but so long as you like your work, the money's not everything, is it?' High heels sounded on the wooden boards. 'I've got to see somebody else.'

'Aye, and I know who it is.' The man sounded disapproving. 'I saw you coming out of Ben Jackson's place last week – and his wife hardly underground a month.'

'Why, the poor sod needs comforting, and it's nice for me to be in a warm house and a real bed for a change.'

'You don't give a bugger, do you? What'll them poor bairns think? And the neighbours?'

'Aw man, the brats are too young to think, and anyway it's none of the neighbours' business if I help a poor widower to look after his bairns now and then.'

'You get away with murder, Dora. I don't know how you do it. Come on, let's go.'

Becky didn't realize she'd been holding her breath until it suddenly spurted from her lips, but she couldn't move.

'Was it your friend?'

'It . . . it sounded like her.' She let out more air through her mouth, but she felt as if screws were being driven into both sides of her head. Tears welled inside her, but they couldn't get any higher than her throat.

His arm round her waist, Bob tried to steer her towards the front of the shelter, but her body was as unrelenting as if it were nailed to the woodwork. She forced her voice to say no, but the pain in her head was unbearable. Then everything went black. She couldn't see. Her stomach whizzed round like a Ferris wheel. She was going to be sick. 'I . . . I,' she began, but choked on the last words. She bent over in the blackness and felt the entire packet of Liquorice Allsorts leave her stomach.

'What the—! Jesus Christ!'

She heard Bob's voice loud, yet as if from a distance, then he backed away.

She'd never felt so wretched or so embarrassed. 'I'm sorry,' she said. 'I don't feel well.'

'You're not bloody kidding. You could at least have puked the other way.'

Though still dizzy, she looked down. She could see again, fuzzily. He was scrubbing his trouser legs ferociously with a white handkerchief.

Dear God! She'd been sick down his trousers. Tears of humiliation welled but she forced herself not to cry and make an even bigger fool of herself. 'Here, let me help.' She made her shaking legs kneel on the wet grass while she rubbed his trousers with her handkerchief.

He stepped aside, as if her touch might contaminate him. 'Don't bother. I'll go back to the Hippodrome and clean it off in the Gents. Can you see yourself home?'

'Aye.' She wasn't sure if she could, but she turned in the direction of the path, slowly putting one foot in front of the other. She was glad it was dark.

Hazily, she thought she hadn't thanked Bob for taking her out. But he'd never want to see her again anyway.

Seven

'Are you all right, Beck?' Liz threw down the stocking she was darning and stared at Becky's chalky face as she stood in the doorway.

'Shut the door for the draught, lass,' her father said from behind the *Evening Chronicle*.

Becky closed the door and warned Liz with a look. 'I'm just tired. I'm going to bed.' She removed her coat, revealing the pink dress.

Liz's eyes darted like an astonished fish.

Becky looked down at herself. In her misery she'd forgotten to change in the washhouse. She climbed the stairs as fast as she could, out of sight of her father. Liz followed, whispering, 'Quiet, Ma's asleep.' They tiptoed to their bedroom and shut the door.

'Did that Bob Baker *do* anything to you?' Liz's face was tight, as if she had a stomach cramp.

'No, I'm all right.' Becky pulled off the dress as she spoke. 'Before I tell you, put this damn thing back in the cupboard.'

Liz obeyed and, when she returned, Becky was in bed with the blankets up to her chin, her tears falling freely now that she was safe with her sister. Liz climbed into bed and put her arm over her in the protective gesture she'd used since they were toddlers. 'You poor lamb. Just let it all come out when you're ready.'

Becky drew in a long shuddering breath and related her tale. 'I don't know why I'm crying over our Dora when I hate her. It was just that it was so . . . so horrible.'

Liz felt Becky's forehead. 'Forget about blasted Dora. How's the head now? And your stomach?'

'Me head's just fuzzy, and I don't feel sick now. Of all the times I've said our Dora makes me sick, and tonight she really did. And, what a laugh! When she was smoking her fancy cigarettes at tea time it dawned on me that she must pilfer from the tills at the clubs. I thought I'd solved her money mystery. What daft buggers we are not to have guessed.'

'Aye, I wouldn't have thought even Dora would stoop that low.'

'Can you imagine? That poor sod paying Dora his hard-earned money just to get into her knickers.' Becky turned down the corners of her mouth in revulsion.

'Poor lamb! How awful to find out like that.'

'Serves me right for breaking me promise to you.'

'Never mind about that. You still look like a ghost. I could make you some bicarb soda to settle your stomach.'

'No, I don't feel sick, just sick to death of our Dora.'

'Me an' all.'

'And I feel such a fool about Bob Baker. I wanted him to ask me out again.'

'*I*'d like to bash his face in. He shouldn't have taken you to the park in the first place – and then he just left you, when you were poorly. You're an idiot if you want to see him again.'

'But I *let* him take me to the park, and he probably thought I puked because I'd eaten too many sweets. I admit he *was* a bit fast, but he stopped when I said to. And I quite liked it – at least going that far. I wouldn't go an inch farther, mind you, after hearing our Dora's performance.'

'It must be different when you love somebody.' Liz's voice sounded dreamy.

As if she hadn't heard, Becky moaned, 'Oh, Liz, how on earth am I going to face Bob Baker in the morning when I get the milk?'

'Just act normal. Pretend it never happened.'

'Aye, you're right. Thank God he didn't know it was me sister.' She pulled the blankets back up to her neck, rested one elbow on the bolster and looked at Liz, puzzled. 'Do you think Ma knows?'

Liz also propped herself up, her brow furrowed in thought. 'I hate to say it,' she said at last, 'but she must know that Dora's money doesn't fall from heaven. Everybody knows she's the town tart – the way she dresses and flirts with men. But the town prostitute! That's horrible. Anyway, even if Ma knows, she couldn't stop her.'

'Aye, Ma couldn't stop Dora committing murder. And what about the neighbours and people? You can't hide a thing like that in a little place like Ashington. Look how I found out. It could have been somebody else we know.'

Liz bit her lip. 'And she must do it with Da's mates. Men brag about that sort of thing. I bet he knows an' all. But he wouldn't dare say anything.'

With unexpected determination Becky sat upright. 'We don't have to put up with it any longer, Liz. I'll start looking in the paper tomorrow for jobs and a room in Newcastle.'

Liz took some time to answer and, when she did, she stared past Becky at the faded green curtains. 'We can't go until Ma's on her feet again.'

'If we're not here, our Dora'll just *have* to look after her, the lazy bitch. You've admitted that Dora loves Ma in her funny way. She couldn't let her starve. And she wouldn't need to give up her work,' she added vehemently. 'Da's at home at nights when she's *working*. Ma wouldn't be alone. We can't sacrifice *our* lives for *theirs* any longer.'

'Beck, you know Dora would have Ma up and drinking gin and eating fish and chips the whole time. And we should wait till we know if Da has to strike. The hearings'll be going on for a while, Will says.' Liz still gazed at the curtains. 'Will's always up to date with what's going on and he says they're almost certain to strike. If so, they couldn't manage without my wages.'

Will! Something in the tone of Liz's voice as she said his name jolted Becky to some other place. *Will Bennett.* She stared across the few inches separating her from Liz, as if from a great distance. 'It's Will Bennett, isn't it? You've fallen for him and you don't want to leave him. It's not only Ma, is it?' Her face puckered and she let out a yowl like a tortured animal. 'How *could* you? You *promised* you wouldn't! You're as big a liar as our Dora.'

'Sshh,' Liz said urgently. But too late.

'What the devil's going on in there?' Florrie shouted from the next room.

'Nothing, Ma. Our Beck just stubbed her toe in the dark.'

'One of you bring me a cup of tea and a sandwich. I'm famished. And while you're downstairs, try to find a magazine I haven't read. I can't sleep and I'm bored out of me bloody skull.'

Liz darted out of bed. 'I'll get you something, Ma.' At the door she turned and whispered to Becky, 'I'll be back in a few minutes.'

'I brought tea and bread and dripping.' Liz set the tin tray on the bed between them and climbed in.

Becky's head was under the blankets. 'I don't *want* anything.' After a moment, her head poked out and, in a voice more anguished because she was forced to keep it hushed, said, 'You *are* in love with him, *aren't* you? She thumped her forehead with her palm. 'How could I be so bloody blind all this time?'

Tears started down Liz's face. 'I want to be with both of you. I've been torn in two since I got fond of Will. I've tried to tell you a million times, but I knew you'd be so upset, I couldn't. I thought it would be a long time before the Newcastle business got serious, so I put it off, hoping things would sort themselves out by then.'

'You've been lying to me all this time. You said you were just fond of him. Lies! Lies! Lies!' Becky shook her head in pain and disbelief. 'It must run in the family – you and our Dora – both lying bitches.'

Liz looked as if she'd been slapped in the face. 'I was trying to break it gently to spare your feelings. It seems I did the wrong thing. I'm sorry.'

'Sorry, my foot!' Becky rammed her fist into her mouth to muffle her sobs. But even screaming from the rooftop would have given no relief from the racking misery of her loss. Will Bennett had taken Liz away from her, and that made her feel even emptier than if someone had cut out her insides. At length she found her voice. 'You've been talking to him about me behind me back, and about our plans, haven't you?'

Liz put a trembling arm over Becky's shoulders again, and her voice shook. 'Oh, luv, I had to tell him about us when he asked me to go steady with him. I just said I'd sort of made plans to go with you to Newcastle.'

'*Sort of made plans*,' Becky mimicked, forgetting to whisper, but no sound came from the other room. She went on, controlling her voice with difficulty. 'I suppose our *sort of plans* were just something you thought you might do if you didn't find a lad first. I knew it would happen, but not this fast. You've only been seeing him on Sundays . . . or have you?' She stared at her sister, realization slowly penetrating the turmoil in her mind. 'You've been seeing him on the quiet!' Her voice rose in accusation.

With shaking fingers, Liz picked at the fluff on the blanket. 'Sometimes he'd walk me home from work, or if I was finished early, we'd have a cup of tea somewhere. I'm sorry, Beck. I kept trying to pluck up the courage to tell you. And I swear Will didn't persuade me to break me plans with you. He said I could only make up me own mind. I realized that, if I went with you, I couldn't make you happy because I'd miss Will something terrible.' Her face crumpled and she mewled like a kitten in pain. 'If only I didn't have to choose between you.'

'You love him more than me.' Becky's voice was dead. Her misery had swallowed up her earlier shock and anger.

Liz tried to put her arm round Becky's shoulder, but the tray between them tilted perilously. She held it steady. 'You ninny, you know loving Will's different from loving you. I still love you and I always will, but when you love a man, your life changes.'

Becky nodded. 'Apart from the fact that you're not coming

away with me, you're settling to marry a miner and go on living like Ma and Da in this pit dump. I can't believe it.'

'I'd marry Will no matter what. Mining's an honest living and it takes a strong man to do it.' Liz's voice was defensive.

'Aye, they work like dogs underground and have to strike to get the slightest improvement in their rotten lives. You'll live in a dump like this and count the pennies he gives you every fortnight. And how will you manage when he's on strike? Oh, yes, if they don't strike for nationalization this time, it'll be for something else next time. Nothing comes easy to the miners. I thought you had more ambition than that.'

'Love's more important than ambition, Becky. You'll know one day.'

Weariness, like a crushing weight over the empty shell of her body, began to blur Becky's pain. She laid her head back against the bolster and her eyelids fluttered. 'Aye, I've still got a lot to learn, but I've learned enough today to last a lifetime. First our Dora, then you. I don't want to hear any more. Just leave me alone, get that damned tray off the bed, and put the light out.'

Eight

B ecky cleared away the breakfast dishes, her head still throbbing. She'd barely spoken to Liz, who looked as if she hadn't slept. Da had eaten no breakfast and he'd coughed more than usual. They'd gone to work, and Dora was still in bed, sleeping off her night on the town.

At the thought of Dora, Becky's stomach felt queasy again. *Why didn't Dora catch the pox and die*? She clapped her hands over her mouth as if she'd spoken the thought aloud. It was a terrible sin to wish death on anybody – even Dora.

Becky wished she hadn't ignored Liz. She dumped the dishes in the sink and sat by the fire. For the first time since she'd woken, she allowed herself to cry – long, shuddering sobs that left her feeling limp, like a rag that been through the mangle. But she felt calmer.

Without Liz to lean on, she must make her own life. Strangely, she felt stronger. From now on she was going to act like a grown-up. She must tell Liz she was sorry she'd been so selfish. Drawing in a renewing breath, she decided to say a prayer every night that Will would make Liz happy and that they wouldn't be too poor.

It would be more frightening and less fun going away without Liz, but she *could* do it, and when she made a good wage she would help them out and send Liz the bus fare to come to see her.

From the dresser she took a sheet of paper, an envelope, and a stub of a pencil. She sat at the table and began:

58

Dearest Liz,

I'm sorry I was so awful to you. You have a right to fall in love with anyone you want, and I know you didn't do it on purpose. I was just so hurt and frightened that we won't be together any more. That upset me a whole lot more even than the Dora business. But wanting to keep you with me always is selfish. You've got to lead your own life.

I still love you and I'll miss you when I go away at the end of the term, but you'll come to see me often, won't you?

Sealed with a kiss.

Love,

Beck

After writing Liz's name and PRIVATE AND CONFIDEN-TIAL on the envelope, she sealed it, grabbed her coat and slipped silently into the lane.

Another smell mingled with the sulphur today. Ugh, the middens! Sometimes when it rained heavily, like last night, they overflowed into the street.

She held her breath for long periods till she reached town. The rain had stopped and the sun was trying to penetrate the clouds. Avoiding the sooty puddles, she thought of the future without Liz to lean on.

At the Co-op outer office, Miss Miles sat typing at the reception desk. She glanced up, surprised. 'Hello, Becky. Is something wrong?'

Becky hesitated. She knew Miss Miles from meeting Liz at the Co-op every day, but she didn't want to tell her such private business. 'Well, there *was* something wrong but there isn't any more, and I want Liz to know so she won't worry all day.'

Miss Miles pulled the sheet of paper from the typewriter. 'Well, I have to take this report up to the boss. I'll pop in to the workshop on me way. It's nice of you to think about your sister.'

'Thank you!' As Becky handed her the envelope, her

shoulders dropped as though a concrete collar had been lifted from her neck. How childish of her to sulk with Liz! This time yesterday she'd still been a schoolgirl, but *now* she was a woman. She would write applications and have a job and a place to stay waiting for her by the end of term. She'd do it sooner, but the kiddy-catcher from the School Board would be after her if she didn't send the doctor's notes every week saying that Ma was poorly. She prayed Ma would be better by then but, if not, Dora would just have to do her duty. She smiled at the thought. Ha! Ha! One in the eye for Dora! Then she sobered, and prayed that Da and Will wouldn't have to strike.

When she turned down the back lane, Bob Baker was pushing his cart at the far end. She shouted to him, forcing a big smile on to her face and a gay note into her voice. 'Hey, you've passed me house. Wait till I get the jug.'

He stopped and turned but said nothing.

'Here you are.' Breathless, she ran from the house and handed him the jug.

'I see you're feeling better.' He filled the jug from one of the churns without looking at her.

'Aye, I'm grand now. Just a bit of a stomach upset. I'm sorry about your trousers. Did they come out all right?' She smiled again.

'Aye.' He handed her the jug, replaced the lid on the churn, and began up the lane again.

She grimaced at his back. Sourpuss! I didn't want to see you again anyway. I can do better than you in Newcastle.

Becky set Ma's breakfast tray and laid the table for Dora. She didn't dare take up Ma's breakfast while Dora was still asleep or all hell would be let loose. Ma had to lie quiet, waiting for her breakfast until Dora got up.

Becky was satisfied. The kettle was simmering for the tea and the bread was cut ready for the butties. She'd fry her own bacon now and have hers in peace, but as she popped a rasher into the pan, Jim Ryan came in, bent even more than usual.

Becky's heart lurched. 'What's wrong, Da?'

'I feel bad, lass. They sent me home.' He blew his nose into the sooty square of old sheet he used as a handkerchief, then coughed until Becky thought his insides would come up.

'Oh, Da! That's a nasty cold. Sit down and I'll sponge your hands and face. Then you're going to bed and I'll go to the chemist for a cough bottle.'

'Aye, lass, I'll have to lie down.' He sat like a child while Becky sponged his black face and hands, dipping a clean rag into a bowl of warm soapy water. She felt overcome by sadness and pity for this emaciated man and his emaciated life. She could do nothing about his life, but she could at least make him comfortable in his illness.

When she'd patted him dry with a towel, he held on to the furniture and made his way across the kitchen to the front room.

Becky helped him undress to his body shirt and linings. They were thick with coal dust but he was too ill to change them. He coughed something awful when he lay down on the bunk that served as his bed, but she propped him up with the cushion from Ma's chair. 'That'll help a bit, Da. Now you get some rest. I'm going to the chemist's.'

She grabbed some money from the dresser drawer and pulled on her coat in the lane.

The bacon rasher sizzled in the frying pan.

When she returned, smoke gushed out of the open door. She could barely see into the kitchen and the smell of burning was terrible.

'What the hell do you think you're doing, trying to burn the place down?'

Even through the smoke, Becky could see Dora's eyes blazing. 'I had to go to the chemist's for some medicine for Da. I forgot about the bacon.'

Dora was opening the window and flapping a towel to get the

smoke out. The tie of her chenille dressing gown was undone and her huge bosom bounced about under her cotton nighty like two cats in a sack. Becky thought of all the eager male hands that had grasped those revolting things the night before. Her stomach turned again. She closed her eyes and pressed her palms against her temple. Thank goodness, the headache didn't come.

Dora ranted on, 'I didn't dream even you could be that stupid. Poor Ma's coughing her lungs out. You could've bloody killed her. Get her a drink or something.'

'I've got to see to Da! Can't you *bloody* hear *him* coughing an' all?' She knew she'd get it for being cheeky but she didn't care. She darted into the front room and closed the door on Dora's outrage.

Jim Ryan was kneeling at the open window.

'Da, are you all right? I forgot the bacon on the fire.'

'Aye, stop your worrying, lass. Did you get me a bottle?' His voice was choked, as if he were holding back the cough.

'I got some cherry linctus and Vick's Vapour Rub for your chest.' She handed him the red bottle from her pocket and he took a long draught.

'Stay beside the window till the smoke goes,' she said, and took the bottle from him. 'I'll have to give Ma some an' all.'

'And what's *he* doing at home?' Dora was still flapping a towel about the kitchen.

Becky paused on the bottom step and said in a surprisingly calm voice, 'He's got a bad cold and they sent him home. That's why I had to run out for medicine in a hurry and forgot the bacon. If you got your lazy arse out of bed and lifted a finger to help around here, I wouldn't have to do everything at once, would I? I'm taking some medicine up to Ma.'

Dora's mouth fell open, making her look stupid as well as surprised, but before the usual torrent of abuse could tumble out, Becky darted up the stairs. Now that she was taking her life into her own hands, she didn't care tuppence about Dora.

'Jesus God Almighty!' Florrie Ryan sat up in bed when

Becky arrived. 'Are you trying to kill us all or just burn the house down? I'm choking to death.'

The smoke wasn't so bad upstairs and her mother had stopped coughing, though her eyes watered.

'I'm sorry, Ma. Here's some cough medicine. Da's in bed with a bad cold. I had to go out for the medicine and forgot the bacon was on the fire.'

Florrie pushed the bottle away. 'Do you mean to tell me you've burnt the bacon ration?'

'No, Ma, just one rasher. I'll bring your bacon butty as soon as the smoke goes.' In case her mother hadn't heard her, she repeated, 'They sent Da home with a bad cold.'

'Aye, I heard you the first time. That's all we need. Him off work and no money coming in. He'd better get his backside out of that bed quickstick, or that's the last bacon we'll be having.'

Becky searched her mother's face for any sign of concern for her father, but there was only anger in the eyes and the pursed mouth.

She curled up in disgust, like a withered leaf. Yet this was her mother. As a child, she'd loved and needed her. When had that child's love turned into . . . whatever it was now? She didn't hate her exactly, not the way she hated Dora. She didn't feel *anything* for her, and somehow that was worse.

She took the irons from the bed. 'I'll heat these up. Would you mind if I gave one to Da? The warmer I keep him, the sooner he'll get well enough to go back to work,' she said in a tight voice.

Florrie pulled a face. 'I suppose so, and hurry up with me breakfast, for God's sake.'

Dora was sitting by the fire smoking a Gold Flake, the door and window still open to let out the last of the smoke. 'It's bloody freezing in here, you gaumless lump, and look at that!' She pointed to the frying pan on the hearth. The twisted piece of sooty metal, minus its wooden handle, testified to

63

Becky's stupidity. 'You'd better get another one out of your pocket money.

'Don't be daft. It would take weeks.'

'Get it on tick! And don't you dare call me daft. It's time you learned to respect your elders.'

Becky thought of the thumping and the animal noises of the night before. Respect Dora? She wanted to laugh. She shrugged as if she didn't give a fig about the pocket money. That would get Dora's goat.

But she *was* worried about how to cook the bacon for Ma's and Dora's breakfasts. Her own rasher had gone up in smoke. Literally, she thought with warped amusement. The meat tin! She'd stand that on the trivet over the fire. She'd make Da a butty as well. He needed to eat. Longing for Liz's support, she gave herself a mental slap on the hand. Hadn't she decided it was time she took control of her own life?

She went to ask if Da wanted a butty. He was already in bed, asleep, but tossing and moaning. His face looked scarlet. She felt his forehead. It was burning and beaded with sweat. She would have to go back to the chemist.

Returning to the kitchen, she grabbed her coat again.

'Where the hell do you think you're off to now?' Dora said.

'To get some Aspros for Da. He's boiling hot and soaked in sweat. You'll have to wait for your breakfast.'

She turned in the doorway, unable to resist glimpsing Dora's face. It was tight. She'd put a cage round her fury but Becky could see it bursting to come out. Satisfied, she banged the door behind her.

Mashing potatoes in the pantry, a deep frown furrowed Becky's forehead. She was worried about her father, and felt a strange sadness. It was a revelation to realize now, by her deep concern for him, that she *did* love him. Though he'd taken no active part in her life – Ma wouldn't have allowed him to if he'd tried – he'd never said a harsh word to her or Liz. She prayed he would get better soon.

Liz came home and, without taking off her coat, ran straight to the pantry. 'Oh, Beck, you're an angel. Thank you for the note.' She flung her arms about her and squeezed her.

Becky returned the hug before easing her away. 'Da's bad in bed, Liz. I'm worried.'

'What's wrong?'

'They sent him home from work. He's got a temperature and everything. I think it's the flu.'

Liz's face paled. 'We'd better get the doctor.'

'Ma and Dora'll say he doesn't need the doctor. But they haven't seen him. They don't believe how bad he is. Dora's having a lie down. She's going out tonight – working, no doubt. Neither of them gives a bugger about Da. He only has us.'

Liz's mouth tightened. 'I'll go and see him, and if I think he's bad enough, I'll get Dr Maynard anyway.' Still wearing her coat, she went to the front room.

A few minutes later she returned and almost stomped through the kitchen to the back door. 'I'm going for the doctor, Beck. If it's the flu, the sooner we find out the better.'

'We won't tell them two upstairs. If it's only a cold, we'll get into trouble.'

Dr Maynard looked grave when he left Da's room. 'I'm afraid your father's got the flu. I'll arrange for an ambulance.'

'Oh, doctor, is it the epidemic flu? Is he going to die?' Becky's eyes brimmed. Automatically she grabbed Liz's hand for comfort.

Dr Maynard shook his head. 'I'm not sure. They'll take tests at the hospital. But wash everything he's eaten or drunk from with carbolic soap and disinfect his bedding and clothes. Boil whatever you can.'

'What's going on?' Dora was halfway down the stairs, still in her dressing gown. She stared at Dr Maynard. 'I thought you weren't seeing Ma till Friday.'

'I'm here about your father. He's got the flu.'

Dora had reached the bottom of the stairs and stopped dead.

65

'Dear God! Is it the epidemic flu? Are we all going to get it?' Her voice rose like a soprano reaching high C.

Dr Maynard stared coolly at her. 'Not if you take precautions. I'll get an ambulance.'

Dora's shoulders sagged visibly with relief. 'Oh, thank heaven! He can't stay here, especially with Ma poorly. We can't risk *her* getting it.'

Becky gave Dora a look of disgust, but it was wasted on her. Dora's full gaze was on Dr Maynard, her lips curved in an inviting smile. 'We're grateful that you came, doctor,' she said, mincing towards the fireplace.

After he'd washed his hands, Becky showed him out. 'Thank you, doctor,' she said, and wondered why she was thanking him for telling them their father was probably going to die.

Nine

Though visitors weren't allowed in the infectious wards, Liz called at the hospital reception desk on her way to work each morning, at lunchtimes, and on her way home. On the third day, she came home at lunchtime, her eyes red. Becky, chopping rhubarb for a tart, put her hand over her mouth. 'No, Liz, no!'

Liz nodded. 'The doctor says his lungs were so bad to start with they couldn't take the extra strain.'

Becky thought her legs would buckle under her as she moved from the pantry towards Liz. They locked themselves together and wept.

Dora stared at them, her hand poised halfway to her mouth, a Gold Flake between her fingers. 'Aw, for God's sake, stop snivelling. He's gone, and you can't do nowt about it. I don't know why you're whining. He never acted like a father to you anyway.'

'He *was* our father,' Becky said between her teeth. 'And we loved him and we'll miss him, even if nobody else around here does.' In her new loss she wanted to hurt somebody, anybody, but especially Dora. She moved away from Liz and deliberately provoked Dora. 'At least *we* know who our father was.'

'Beck, don't—' But Liz's plea was cut short as Dora jumped up and landed a resounding slap on Becky's cheek.

'That's right,' Becky said, feeling dangerously calm. 'The only thing you know how to do is lash out and hurt people, any way you can. And when you're not doing that you're selling your wares to any old man in the street who'll have you, even if

67

you've got to filch them from their wives. There's not a shred of decency or real feeling in you.'

'Stop it, Beck,' Liz pleaded, but a noise like a motor car backfiring exploded from Dora's open mouth before she threw herself at Becky and the pair landed on the floor.

'For God Almighty's sake, what's going on down there?' Florrie shrieked from upstairs.

'It's all right, Ma, I'll be up in a minute.' Liz's voice was laboured as she tried to push Dora's weight off Becky.

Dora gripped Becky's shoulders and banged her head against the floor. 'What did you say, you cow?'

Flattened underneath Dora's bulk, Becky felt as substantial as a paper doll pasted to the floor. 'I said—' But her head hit the floor a second time. She closed her eyes.

Liz tried to pull Dora back by her shoulders but was helpless against the strength of her fury. 'Stop it!' she begged. 'You'll kill her.'

Dora sat up and astride Becky's skinny body. 'Take back what you just said, or else.' She held Becky down with her left hand while she raised her right, ready to strike her in the face if she refused.

Liz crouched and leaned over Becky's face to protect it from Dora's waiting blow. 'Please, Becky, please – for Da's sake.'

'All right, I take it back.' Becky's voice was barely a whisper. She held both hands to her head.

'*And* say you're sorry and that it's not true.' Dora waved her fist again.

'I'm sorry and it's not true.'

Dora gave her a final shake and rose, panting. 'Next time I won't let you off so lightly.' She grabbed two glasses and the gin bottle. 'I'm going up to tell Ma about Da. She'll need this. You damn well know we'll be out on the street now that we haven't got a miner in the house. Start crying about that instead of feeling sorry for yourselves because your precious Da's dead.'

Liz helped Becky to stand, then sat her in Ma's chair at the fire.

Becky slumped back, still holding her head. 'I'm sorry, Liz, something snapped in me when she went on about Da. And after all me good resolutions to be grown-up and behave meself.'

Liz sat on the armrest and held Becky's shoulders. 'It's all right, luv, it's only human to break resolutions sometimes.'

'We could've done more for Da, even if we'd only made him laugh once in a while.'

Liz sighed. 'Feeling guilty now won't help him. Anyway, you often tried to talk to him. And you looked after him like an angel that last day. He'll remember that in heaven.'

Becky looked up at the ceiling. 'Listen to that din up there. Ma doesn't need Dora to encourage her to get blind drunk.' Tears trickled down her cheeks. 'And poor Da's not even cold yet.'

Liz went to get her coat. 'Just stay still and relax. I'll be back as soon as I can.'

'Where you going?'

'To the pit to tell the manager about Da. When a miner dies, they're supposed to pay a lump sum compensation or something.'

'I thought that was only if they died in a pit accident.'

'I don't know, but it's worth finding out. Then I'll go to the undertakers. We'll have to see to the funeral. If Dora comes down, give her some soup and rhubarb tart for both of them. And be civil to her, promise?'

'Aye, it's not worth letting her get to me. I'll help you with the funeral and things.' Suddenly the practicality of their situation hit Becky like a blow. 'How much notice do we get to leave the house?'

'I think four weeks.'

'Then what? The workhouse?'

Liz looked at the floor. 'No, luv. Things won't be that bad. Ma won't get a widow's pension, because Da was a hewer. Only the officials' wives get pensions. But I remember years ago she took out some sort of worker's insurance for him every week. We should get something from that.'

69

'Fat lot of good that'll do when we have to pay rent for another house.'

Her hand on the door latch, Liz went back and sat on Becky's armrest. 'We won't lose the house, luv. I didn't tell you before because I didn't want you to even think that Da might die, but when I told Will, he said if the worst happened, we'd get married straight away and he'd move in. We'll still have a miner in the family and we won't lose the house.'

Becky closed her eyes in pain. Not for herself, but for Liz. So that was the life that lay ahead of her. Being married to a miner was bad enough, but to live *here* with him, with Ma and Dora! That would be sheer hell. 'I'm glad you've got Will to take care of you,' was all she said. 'When are you going to tell those two upstairs?' The chatter from the bedroom had grown louder.

'Later. It doesn't sound as if they're doing much grieving. It seems that in their rosy glow they've forgotten they'll be homeless.' She rose. 'I have to go.'

Left alone, Becky closed her eyes and slid down in the chair. She felt herself crying inside, though the tears wouldn't come out. But this time they weren't for Da, they were for Liz.

When Liz returned, Becky sat up at the sight of her white face. 'Will the pit pay?'

'They gave me a cheque for five quid to help with expenses, as a goodwill gesture, they said. His death wasn't work-related, so he wasn't due anything.'

'Big of them! And Da hacked coal for them his whole rotten life. What about the insurance?'

Liz hung up her coat. 'I checked at the office. Ma stopped paying into it years ago and cashed in what there was.' She indicated upstairs. 'What's going on?'

'They're asleep – conked out.' Becky raised herself slowly, having trouble taking in the news. 'I'll give you some soup. You look terrible.' She served two bowls and set them on the table, then glanced at the clock. 'Quarter to seven already?'

'Aye, I went to see Will on the way back to tell him the news.'

'What did he say?'

Liz put down her spoon. 'He was wonderful. He says we'll announce our engagement in tomorrow's paper and have the banns called on Sunday. Then we can prove we're getting married in six weeks and surely they won't throw us out. He's telling them at the office tomorrow.'

'Will you tell Ma and Dora tonight?'

'Aye, if and when they wake up.'

'They'll be furious that you've been going out with Will behind their backs.'

'Don't worry, I'll break it gently. Have your soup while it's hot.'

Florrie shouted downstairs. 'Becky, for God's sake, I've got to go to the pot. Hurry up or I'll wet the flaming bed.'

Forgetting her still-aching head, Becky bounded up the stairs, grabbed the pot from under the bed and helped her mother on to it.

'Hell's bells! Just in time.' Florrie gasped with relief.

'For Christ's sake, Ma!' Dora twisted her face. 'Isn't it enough that you wake me up yelling, without stinking the place out an' all.'

'Would you like me to help you downstairs for a bit after I've emptied the pot, Ma?'

'Aye, a sit by the fire would be nice. And change the sheets while I'm up. I expect I'll be getting visitors when news of your da gets out.' Sober now, she crumpled her face and let out a noise like the hooter that signalled the change of the pit shifts. 'Eey by God! What are we going to do? No wages from your da and no place to live!'

'We can stay. Liz can arrange it. She'll tell you herself.'

'Oh, aye! What's she going to do? Get a job down the pit?'

Becky kept silent. She put the old towel she kept for the purpose over the pot and averted her face as she carried it downstairs. Liz picked up the coal bucket and opened the door.

'We need some coal an' all.' Both held their breath until they were outside.

They made the trek to the toilets and coal houses. As always, glad that the middens were a long way from the house.

Liz built up the fire while Becky helped Ma downstairs. Dora was slumped in her chair, the open Aspro bottle beside her.

'Now what's this news about the house, lass?' Florrie said as she reached the bottom stair.

Becky lowered Ma into her chair as Liz returned from the pantry with the tart. She cleared her throat. 'We won't have to leave, Ma. Will Bennett's asked me to marry him. If we do it in six weeks, they won't kick us out. We'll still have a miner in the family.'

'*You're getting married*! To Will Bennett?' Dora looked stupefied.

'I didn't know you even knew the lad.' Ma shook her head, unable to take in the news.

'I've known him for quite a while,' Liz said, her eyes lowered.

'You've been going out with him on the sly?' Dora's eyes began to pop, then slowly returned to their sockets and a sickly smile slid over her face. 'Eey, you're right, we wouldn't be thrown out if you married him.'

'What does he do down the pit? He can't earn much at his age,' Florrie said.

'He's a putter, but he's being promoted to hewer next. He can hew more coal than Da could and earn more. Does that not make you happy?'

'Eey, aye,' Florrie muttered. 'And *your* wages.' She thought for a bit. 'We could get by for a while, but not for ever. Will'll eat more than your da.'

'He's strong and clever, Ma. He'll get more promotions,' Liz said.

'Aye, and maybe you will, if you stick at it.' Dora leaned back in her chair with a satisfied look. 'Just make bloody sure you don't get in the family way. We couldn't manage without your wages, and we don't want any screaming bairns around the place.'

'And Becky can get a job at the end of term,' Florrie said. Dora glowered at her. 'Not while you're poorly, Ma. She has to look after you. But if you hurry up and get your lazy body out of bed, she *could* get a job.'

Becky counted to ten several times, and clomped upstairs to change her mother's bed. She must be alone to stay calm.

She pulled the sheets off the bed and flung them to the floor. An uninvited smile spread over her face. She wished she could be a fly on the wall to see Dora's and Ma's faces the day after Liz's wedding. They'd get up to an empty house. And what would dear Dora do then, poor thing? Becky's smile grew. Would dear Dora stay at home and do her duty by her ma? Or would she sacrifice Liz's wages and have her play nurse and housewife? Whatever happened, Liz at least had Will.

Ten

On the day of the funeral a few pale yellow rays squeezed through the clouds, though a strong breeze wafted coal dust and smoke in the air.

Becky and Liz stood by the graveside holding hands. Becky wore her blue serge dress and Liz an old black one of Dora's that Becky had altered. Dora stood apart, wearing a new black costume and a little black hat with a spotted veil. Florrie, though not well enough to sit through the mass and the funeral, had dressed in her best black dress, and waited at home for the funeral party to return.

The priest's vestments flapped like wings in the breeze as the mourners – Jim Ryan's mates from the pit who were not on shift, and neighbours – bowed their heads and repeated, 'Amen.' These people were not real friends. Da had never had any friends to the house, and he had no other family. There was a brother somewhere near Newcastle but they hadn't seen each other for years. Becky and Liz could barely remember him. The crowd shuffled back to Long Row, forming a crocodile of human bodies, like a class of children on a school outing. Becky and Liz, still holding hands, were the last to leave the grave. Becky felt sad, less for her father's death than for his life.

Back at the house, Becky glowered at the laden table. The funeral money, plus Da's wage packet for the half week he'd worked, had gone on ham and tongue sandwiches, assorted cakes and pastries, sherry, port and beer – and gin. There was only one shilling and sixpence left for the housekeeping.

They'd have to live on bread and dripping, and all this food for people who weren't really Da's friends! But Ma insisted it was custom, and only proper, to have a good wake for Da.

The truth was, Ma enjoyed a party. She sat in her black dress, waving a glass of sherry, nodding as people muttered their sympathies and doing a fine imitation of the grieving widow. Dora also held a glass of sherry. She'd turned back the veil of her hat and minced about in her high heels, dabbing a lace handkerchief to her eyes.

The food was disappearing at an alarming rate. Becky nudged Liz. 'Cover me at the pantry door.' Liz obeyed, and Becky picked up a plate of tongue sandwiches and a plate of angel cakes and stashed them in the pantry.

As the drink flowed faster and the conversation grew louder, a small man, dressed in pit clothes, knocked on the table and called for silence. 'I just want to say that me and me mates are that sorry to lose Jim. He was a right canny lad and no shirker when it came to work. Like us, he was praying that we'd get our rights and won't have to strike. Don't worry, Jim, we'll carry on the fight.' He drew from his trouser pocket a small black drawstring bag and held it up. 'We had a collection at work and it's my pleasure to give it to Florrie. It'll help out a bit at this bad time.'

Florrie dabbed her black-edged mourning handkerchief to her eyes before she grabbed the bag. 'Eey, that's right kind of you,' she said. 'Thank you all very much.' She set the bag on her lap, kneading it as if to guess how much was in it. She raised her glass. 'To Jim, as grand a husband as any woman could wish for.'

Becky looked at the bag on her mother's lap and wondered how much, if any, she'd get for the housekeeping. Now she felt guilty that she'd begrudged the guests the food.

Florrie continued her public address, her face flushed from the sherry, her voice slurred. 'I know it's not usual to announce such a thing at a funeral, but things being as they are, I'm happy to tell you that we'll not be put out of the house.' She pointed a pudgy finger at Liz, standing in the corner with Becky. 'I take this opportunity to announce, with pride, that my daughter, Liz, is to be wed to Will Bennett six weeks on Sunday. Sadly, Will couldn't be here today because he's on shift.'

A loud murmur came from the guests. Becky supposed they were giving congratulations, though she noted their surprised expressions.

Liz flushed as all eyes turned on her.

'Aye,' Florrie went on. 'I know it sounds quick like, but not what you're thinking. The happy couple were going to get wed soon anyway, but it's been brought forward so as we can keep the house.' She raised her glass, slopping sherry on the floor. 'To Liz and Will! I just wish her dear da could've been here to give his daughter away.'

While all glasses and eyes were raised to Liz, Becky saw the bag slip down her mother's lap, coming to rest halfway down the perilous slope of her stout thighs. Florrie seemed unaware, and no one else appeared to have noticed the black bag's journey down the black-clad lap. Becky couldn't take her eyes off it.

'And you're all invited to the wedding,' Florrie said, waving her now empty glass.

Becky made for the fireplace. The crowd made a good cover. She knelt, brushing her mother's knee in the process, and picked up the poker. Her right hand stirred the fire while her left grabbed the bag she'd dislodged from its precarious resting place. Hiding it in the folds of her skirt, she sidled into the pantry.

With shaking hands, she opened the cupboard door and poked her head inside as if looking for something. Thus shielded from view, she undid the string and stifled a gasp. There was a load of rolled-up notes as well as coins – all half-crowns. She pulled out as many notes as she could and grabbed a small handful of coins. The bag mustn't look noticeably lighter. As she stashed the money in her pocket, for the first time she was glad of the bulky serge dress.

It took a lifetime for the guests to leave. Ma was so drunk she could hardly keep her eyes open and Dora so far gone she'd had to take off her shoes to walk straight.

Florrie leaned back in her chair. 'Eey, that was a right good send-off we gave your da.'

'What did you do with the bag, Ma?' Dora said. 'Let's see how much is in it.' She flopped into her chair, her eyes expectant.

Florrie felt around on her lap, her mouth open and her baggy eyes suddenly wide.

'It's all right, Ma,' Becky said. 'You dropped it, so I put it in the pantry.'

Florrie clapped her hand to her chest. 'Eey! I thought somebody had nicked it.'

Becky retrieved the bag and handed it to Florrie, who fumbled in frustration with the string.

'I can't get it open. You do it,' she said, handing it to Dora.

Dora emptied the contents into her lap. 'Bugger me! Pound notes! Who can afford to give those away?'

'They get the coins changed at the bank,' Liz said. 'Mary's ma got one when her da was killed. The bag's probably got a message embroidered on it.' She picked it up and read the grey silk stitching. '*In loving memory of Jim Ryan, to his family, from his mates.*'

'Bloody nice of them. It's a lot of money,' Florrie said.

'Aye, well there's plenty of men at the pit to fork out a bit each.' Dora began counting the notes. Then she closed her eyes, shook her head and blinked at the pile in her lap. 'You two do it. I'm too tired.'

Too drunk, you mean, Becky thought as she scooped the money from Dora's lap. She and Liz counted it on the table. 'Nineteen pounds, twelve and six,' Liz announced.

'Eey, by!' Florrie said.

Dora yawned. 'I thought it might be more, with all those people who turned up.'

'It'll be a big help towards the housekeeping and Liz's wedding,' Becky dared to say.

Dora pushed herself out of the chair. 'We're not going to waste it on no flash wedding. I'm off for a nap. Try to clear up quietly.'

Downstairs again after helping her mother into bed, Becky poured two glasses of sherry and sat defiantly in Dora's chair. 'Come and relax, Liz. I've got something to show you.'

Liz was stacking plates. 'Are you crazy? Drink sherry? We've got to clean up.'

'Aw, they'll be unconscious for hours. Get off your legs and take this.' She pushed a glass towards Liz, who took it obediently and sat in Florrie's chair.

'Cheers!' Becky raised her glass.

'What's got into you?'

Becky put the glass on the hearth and emptied the contents of her pocket into her lap. 'That's what's got into me.' Her grin was gleeful.

Liz gaped. 'Beck, where? Oh my God! You took it from the bag?'

'Now where else would I have got it? And thank your lucky stars I had the presence of mind to do it. That money was for the family. It even said so on the bag. I just made sure that not all of it goes to fill the gin bottle and buy Dora new outfits.'

Liz ran her hand across her forehead. 'I can't believe it. And so many notes.'

'Aye, I grabbed mostly notes so Ma wouldn't notice the bag was lighter.' She counted first the notes, then the half-crowns. 'Twelve pounds, ten shillings. A nice round number. That's six pounds five shillings each.' She handed half to Liz. 'This is like my wedding present to you, luv, for you and Will.'

Tears hovered in Liz's eyes, then a smile overcame them. 'Oh, thank you! Even if you did pinch it. What are you going to do with yours?'

Becky hooded her eyes. 'You know I wouldn't miss your wedding for the world, but straight after it I'm going to Newcastle.'

'So soon?' Liz put her money on the floor and knelt beside

Becky. 'I'll miss you terribly, but I'll be dead happy when you've found yourself a nice job and a nice room – and a nice fellah,' she added, sniffing. 'I'm glad you've got some money to get started.'

'That was exactly what I had in mind for both of us, and I know Da would've wanted it.' Becky trembled at the thought of life in Newcastle without Liz. 'I'll write often, and you'll come and see me, won't you?' She felt ashamed of the plea in her voice.

Liz's arms went round her. 'You know wild horses couldn't keep me away.'

'And I'm not jealous any more. I'm dead happy you've got Will,' Becky said.

Eleven

The following evening Will was to be formally introduced to his future in-laws, though they had known him as one of the lads up the row for some years. Becky made the tea, serving the sandwiches and angel cakes she'd saved from the wake. She'd covered them with damp cloths to keep them fresh and, with her illicit money, had bought ingredients to make sausage rolls and jam tarts. It was a fine meal.

Liz's eyes were bright, her face flushed with excitement. Becky couldn't imagine this kind of love. It must be special for Liz to choose it, despite having to live with the family.

As she was still officially in mourning, Ma wore her black dress. She sat in her chair, her face grey and puffy from yesterday's excesses, her feet so swollen she had to wear her slippers. 'By God,' she said. 'It's a bugger when I can't even enjoy a little party without feeling like the black death the next day.'

Dora, painting her face at the mirror, said, 'You need some gin to perk you up. It was that sherry upset your stomach. It's too rich. I'll get you a nip. I fancy one meself.' She spat into her mascara box, rubbed the brush over the paste and applied it to her eyelashes. After appraising her image, she smoothed the tight black costume skirt over her hips, undid another blouse button, then poured two gins.

Liz, looking fresh in her floral-patterned dress, despite it's being three years old, raised her eyebrows at Becky as they set the table. 'You don't need gin, Ma,' Liz said, almost begging. 'Will's coming any minute. A nice cuppa will perk you up more than booze.'

Florrie dragged on her Woodbine and thought for a minute. 'Nah, I fancy a nip, then some tea.'

Dora handed Ma a half-full tumbler and Becky saw Liz's face lose its glow. Once Ma started on the gin with Dora, there would be no stopping her. Will would get a swift introduction to his new family. But like everyone in the row, he knew that Ma and Dora were Mr Brown's best customers.

There was a tentative tap on the door. Liz smoothed her hair, braced her shoulders and opened it. 'Hello, Will.' She smiled as shyly as if he were a stranger.

'Hello, Liz.' Will stood inside the doorway holding what looked like a new Sunday cap.

Becky stared at him. Had he changed that much in the few months since he'd stopped Liz in the street to ask her out? Of course, he'd been dirty and in his pit clothes then. Or had she in her jealousy not wanted to admit that he was handsome?

He stood with his legs apart, at least six feet tall and broad shouldered, wearing a dark-blue suit that also looked new. His brown hair was neatly cut and his face shaved and shining. He hadn't worked underground long enough to get the hunched back and grey, gaunt look of the men who spent their lives bent double in tunnels, hacking out coal to make the mine owners rich and barely to keep starvation from their own doors. Now Becky knew what Liz saw in Will and prayed that he would never look hunchbacked and gaunt, like Da.

Liz introduced him. 'Ma, you know Will.'

'Nice to meet you, Mrs Ryan.' He held out his hand.

Florrie seemed undecided whether to put down her cigarette or her glass. Finally, she put the cigarette in her mouth and it clung to her lip as she said, 'Aye, and you too, lad. We're right happy about you and our Liz.'

Dora rearranged her surly face and an unveiled interest lit up her marmalade eyes like signal lights. 'Aye, welcome to the family.' She extended a languid hand with scarlet-tipped nails. 'I wouldn't have known you, Will. It's a while since I saw you.'

A deep blush crawled up Will's neck to his forehead like a spreading stain. He turned to Becky as if for help.

'Hello, Will. Nice to see you,' she said

He nodded back and grinned with visible relief.

Liz ushered him to the table. 'Sit down and make yourself comfortable.'

Comfortable! Becky thought, with Dora ogling him like that. The bitch had a fancy for him! And she was brazen enough to make a pass at him. Becky took refuge in silent prayer again. *Dear God, don't let Dora cause trouble between Liz and Will.*

Working on the dresses, Becky wished she had a sewing machine. But it was a treat to work with new material and a pattern, though she'd always managed well making patterns from newspapers.

The bride's dress had a nipped-in waist and full skirt with a train. A couple of days later the bridesmaid's dresses were at the trying-on stage.

Dora held up her dress. 'Oh Lord! It's straight up and down. Where's the waistline?'

'On the hips, where the sash is.' Becky could barely keep her face straight.

They were in Ma's bedroom to use the full-length mirror. Liz and Becky sat on the bed.

'Go on,' Ma urged. 'Try it on, Dora. That blue suits you.'

Dora pulled the blue creation over her head.

'No, the other way, it buttons down the back.' Becky had to dig her fingernails into her palms till she winced or she would have burst out laughing. She'd deliberately buttoned it at the back so that Dora couldn't reveal her bosom.

'Bugger me! Why aren't they down the front?'

'That was the pattern,' Liz fibbed. 'I'll fasten you up.'

Becky could hear the control in Liz's voice.

Dora glowered into the mirror. 'Jesus Christ! I look like a bloody schoolgirl at a birthday party. I should carry balloons, not flowers.'

As she rejoined Becky on the bed, Liz nudged her foot. Becky pressed back, hard. Dora did look like a schoolgirl, and a plump one at that. The straight, elegant line of the dress concealed her curves but not her girth.

Carrying the dresses, Liz and Becky retreated to their bedroom and closed the door. As one, they threw themselves on to the bed and kicked their legs in the air like overturned beetles, smothering their laughter. Becky wiped her eyes with the back of her hand and croaked, 'I . . . I was determined she wouldn't flaunt her tits at your wedding. I knew the straight bodice wouldn't suit her, but I swear I didn't know she would look like a suet pudding.' She spluttered in her efforts not laugh.

On the wedding day a grey sheet of stratus cloud obliterated the sky. The resulting humidity hung over Ashington like a damp serge cloak and made the smoke particles more visible than usual.

The service was at eleven. Liz had hired two carriages – one to take the groom and best man to the church, then to collect the bride and bridesmaids, and Will's father, who was to give her away.

The second carriage was for the two families. Florrie, resplendent in a new lavender costume and hat, sat with Mrs Bennett. Will's married sister and her husband faced them.

Liz looked beautiful in her white gown, carrying a bouquet of pink roses. Secured to her head with a single rose above each ear, was her mother's lace veil, which Florrie had kept in a box all these years.

At the church, Will stood stiffly waiting with his best man.

Becky felt warm inside watching Liz and Will, hand in hand, shedding happiness as they mingled with the guests.

The wedding presents waited on the table in the front room. There wouldn't be time to open them until after the honeymoon. Becky had hidden her present under the bed.

As the drinking increased, some of the men forgot the

occasion and brought up the burning topic of the moment. One burly man thumped his fist on the wall. His voice boomed, 'I'm telling you! Them owners has deliberately kept us ignorant of the industry long enough. When we're nationalized we'll take our rightful place as men. We won't stop fighting till then, by God.'

His neighbour shook his head. 'Nah, Mick, the press and the whole bloody country's dead against us. All the blasted upper class is with the coal owners now. They're even handing out pamphlets saying what a catastrophe it'll be if the owners lose control.'

'Aye, he's right,' said an old man with a froth of beer on his upper lip. 'Things are going to stay the same, strikes and lock-outs and short time. We don't stand a chance.'

'Hey!' Will's falsely cheerful voice resounded across the room. 'This is a happy occasion; save your maudlin talk for over your beer at the club.'

One large matron with a voice like the pit's hooter hollered, 'Aye, do you have to spoil the poor lass's *one* day in her life when she can feel like royalty? After that she'll be down on her knees every day scrubbing floors and feeding bairns and trying to make ends meet. I should know!'

Will patted her jovially on the rump. 'Aye, you should, Lilly. Is it fourteen or fifteen you've got? Don't worry too much about Liz. I don't think I can compete with Harry.'

Will had broken the tension. Everyone laughed and toasted Lilly's embarrassed husband.

Becky helped Liz to change into her beige going-away costume and blue veiled hat. They'd bought both in the sales with some of Liz's money from Da's collection.

As soon as the door was closed they flung themselves at each other and sobbed. Tears as hot as the coke furnace at the gasworks seared Becky's eyes. 'Oh, Lord! I'm going to miss you, luv.'

Liz sniffed. 'Me an' all. Promise you'll be careful in Newcastle and write often. I want to know everything.'

Becky nodded. 'And promise *you'll* write. I'll let you know me address as soon as I'm settled.'

'Write to me at work,' Liz said. 'Miss Miles gets the post and she'll understand.'

'Aye, I can't have them two poking into me letters and finding out where I am.' Becky took a large breath. 'Come on, they're waiting for you.' She straightened Liz's hat and kissed her gently on the cheek. 'Have a heavenly honeymoon.'

'Of course I will, silly. And I'll see you on my first free Sunday.'

They returned downstairs, but when they reached the waiting guests, Becky sneaked back to her room, unable to watch Liz driving out of her life for ever. She hoped Liz wouldn't miss her in the crowd when she threw her bouquet.

Heedless of her immaculate dress, she climbed under the covers and curled up, pulled the blankets over her head and pressed her face into the bolster. She let the tears flow. It was a relief to let go after all the weeks of putting on a happy front for Liz's sake. Now the time had come to go to Newcastle and Becky had never felt so alone and miserable and frightened in her entire life.

Twelve

B ecky prized her swollen eyes open to peer at the alarm
clock. It was eight o'clock and quiet downstairs. The
wedding guests must have left.

She took off her bridesmaid's dress. It was creased like
a rag. She would shorten the hem and iron it before she
left. At least she would have one decent dress to go away
with. After throwing on her work dress, she trudged downstairs.

Ma and Dora were stretched out in their chairs, holding gin
glasses and cigarettes. The room smelt like a public bar and
looked like a pigsty.

'Weeeell! Look who's here!' Dora eyed Becky from under
half-closed lids.

Becky counted to ten and ignored Dora. 'Are you all right,
Ma? Shall I help you up to bed before I clean up?'

'Aye, I'm tired,' Florrie said.

Dora yawned. 'If you're going to start making an almighty
din down here, I'll pop upstairs for a nap an' all.'

Florrie attempted to push herself up and knocked the ashtray
off the armrest. Drunk as a louse! Becky groaned as her
mother's head lolled on her chest. 'Could you give me a
hand to get Ma up the stairs? She's passed out.' It was the
first time she'd asked Dora for help.

Dora's eyes narrowed like gunslits. 'Don't you dare say
that about your mother. She's just tired, and so am I. Get
her upstairs yourself. You should be rested after your sleep,
or whatever it was you were doing up there.'

Becky counted to ten again and put both arms under her

mother's armpits. She couldn't move her an inch. 'You'll *have* to help,' she said to Dora. 'I can't budge her.'

'Bugger! I swear the older she gets the less she can take it. She'll be all right there. You can still clean up around her.'

Becky put the cracket under Ma's feet for a footstool, then got Da's blankets from the hall cupboard and tucked them round her. She was secretly pleased that Ma was in such a state. Dr Maynard was coming in the morning. She wouldn't wake her till he came. He would be furious, and Ma would take more notice of him for a while.

Dora put a hand to her head as she straightened. 'Ooh, I feel a bit woozy. I'm off to bed. No banging dishes and clomping around.'

'I'll be quiet.' Becky surveyed the mess. Tonight she would have time only to wash and pack the rented dishes ready for the company to pick up. Tomorrow she would clean the house from top to bottom. She wanted it immaculate for Liz . . . and Will. She'd tried hard to shake off her jealousy and had succeeded about 99 per cent. Will was nice, quiet and gentle, and he obviously worshipped Liz. In time she would learn to love him like a brother.

Florrie opened her eyes as Becky shook her. 'Ma, the doctor's here.' Dr Maynard stood by Ma's chair, his face stern, like a book of rules.

'Eh?' Florrie rubbed her eyes, groaned and blinked. 'Hell's Bells! Where am I?'

'You've spent the night in your chair, Mrs Ryan, with your clothes on. It seems you were too drunk to go to bed,' Dr Maynard said.

Florrie turned a startled face up to him. 'Good God! Dr Maynard!' She glowered at Becky. 'Why did you get the doctor?'

'It's my regular morning, Mrs Ryan,' Dr Maynard said. 'And Becky doesn't need to tell me anything. This is my last warning. If you don't stop the drink and stick to your diet, I'm putting you in hospital. You'll have no choice.'

'No! Not hospital, please.' Florrie winced as if he'd slapped her in the face. Becky tried not to feel sorry for her.

He pressed his stethoscope against her chest. 'If you don't want to go to hospital, you'd better follow my instructions. If you'd done so from the start, you would have been on your feet weeks ago.' After listening to the stethoscope, he felt her pulse, prodded her bloated body and examined her ankles. He tutted. 'I have a mind to put you in hospital this moment.'

Florrie's face, as white as distemper, screwed up ready to cry. 'It was me lass's wedding and I celebrated a bit too much, that's all.'

'Mrs Ryan, I've been your doctor long enough to know that you don't need a cause to celebrate. You must see sense. Your body can't take any more punishment.' He scribbled on his prescription pad and gave the sheet to Becky. 'This should reduce the bloating.'

Becky decided to beg for Dr Maynard's help. Perhaps it would make Liz's life a bit easier. She followed him to the pantry while he washed his hands. 'Doctor,' she whispered. 'We could keep the drink out of Ma's way if it wasn't for Dora. If you really scared Ma that she's going to die if she doesn't stop drinking, it might help.'

Dr Maynard raised his eyebrows. He left the water running and took the towel Becky held out, giving her a caring look, as a father might. 'Where is Dora, Becky?'

'Upstairs, sleeping it off an' all.'

'I could drop in again on my way to surgery at five.' He put his hand on her shoulder and his voice was sad and gentle: 'I know you've been doing your best with your mother. I'll do whatever I can to help.'

'Thank you, doctor.' She led him back to the kitchen.

'You two's been talking behind me back in there. I'm not stupid.' Florrie's voice had regained some of its authority.

'I've been giving instructions to Becky about your medicine,' Dr Maynard said. 'Good day, Mrs Ryan.'

Becky closed the door behind him. *What had she done*? She felt as if she stood on the edge of a frozen lake. She had to go forward but didn't know how thick the ice was. Dora would know she'd told on her and would kill her. She ran outside and caught up with Dr Maynard. 'Doctor, there's one more thing. Could . . . could you please not tell our Dora I told you or she'll murder me.'

He put his hand on her shoulder again. 'I promise I'll find a way round it without incriminating you. Just say I'm calling back later to check on your mother.'

'Oh, thank you.' Becky felt like a prisoner reprieved from the gallows. She closed the door again.

'All right now, what you been saying about me behind me back?'

'Doctor was just asking what would be a good time to pop in again.'

'Jesus! He's coming back? The day?'

'He's worried about you.'

'And why the hell didn't you wake me and put me to bed before he came? It was a disgrace, him seeing me like this.'

'I'm sorry, Ma. I forgot he was coming, the same as you. All the excitement of Liz's wedding, I suppose.'

'Next time see that you remember when he's due.'

Florrie clicked her tongue against the roof of her mouth and pulled a face. 'Why did you let me sleep with me teeth in? Me mouth tastes like something the cat spewed up. Clean me up down here first. And I need the pot.'

'Yes, Ma.'

After attending to Ma and managing to get her into bed without waking Dora, Becky slumped into Ma's chair in the kitchen and poked the kettle over the hob to boil for tea. She'd better hurry up with the breakfasts and start cleaning if she was to have the place spotless before she left. And they'd better not muck it up before Liz and Will came home.

At ten minutes to five there was a tap on the door. Becky's stomach fluttered as she opened it.

'Good evening, Becky, Dora,' Dr Maynard said. 'How's your mother? That new medicine had any effect?'

'Aye, doctor, she's been yelling for the pot all day.'

He nodded. 'Good, that's what I hoped for. Is she upstairs now?'

'Yes.'

'Then I'll go up.'

Dora, sitting by the fire with her gin, watched him as he disappeared up the stairs. 'He's never come twice in one day before.'

'That's because he's never been as worried about Ma as he was this morning. I told you he was coming back to check up on her.' Becky was glad the gin bottle was out on the dresser.

'Aye, I forgot. He's dishy, isn't he? A bit toffee-nosed for me though.'

Becky smothered a smile. As if Dr Maynard would even look at someone as vulgar as Dora!

Dr Maynard came downstairs, shaking his head.

Trembling, Becky straightened from forking the potatoes on the fire. 'Is she all right, doctor?'

'A slight improvement, but not as much as I'd hoped for.' Instead of going to wash his hands, he took a chair from the table and sat, looking at them both.

Dora pulled down her shoulders and stuck out her bosom. The open neckline of her scarlet blouse revealed two inches of cleavage. 'Nice of you to pop in twice, Doctor.'

'I came because your mother is very ill. I know that she's been drinking alcohol and eating forbidden foods. If she continues, she'll soon be in hospital.' He looked at the gin bottle on the dresser, then at the glass in Dora's hand. 'In future, please don't leave gin or any alcohol in the house where she can get it, and *never* give it to her if she asks for it.' He raised his gaze from Dora's glass to her eyes. 'As the eldest in the family, can I leave you in charge to make sure that nobody gives your mother alcohol, or food that is not listed on her diet sheet?'

Becky was gratified to see that Dora actually turned pink,

but only for a second. Then she leaned forward to give him a better view of her cleavage. 'Of course, Doctor. I'll keep me eye on what everybody gives her.'

He waved towards the bottle on the dresser. 'Then would you keep your gin hidden in the washhouse or somewhere she can't get to it? And, *please*, never drink in front of her or allow anyone else to. It's too much temptation for her, and she might as well drink arsenic.' He aimed his words at Dora like darts.

Those red dots came into her eyes. She stood, tight-lipped, still clasping the give-away glass. 'Is that all? I have an appointment.'

'That's all for thc moment. Please call me if your mother gets any worse.'

Becky opened the back door for him and when he was in the yard and screened by the door he winked at her.

The wink told her that he *had* exaggerated Ma's condition for Dora's sake. 'Thank you, Doctor.' Relief made the tightness in her belly melt away like warmed wax. She closed the door and leaned against it to collect herself.

'Hell's bloody bells! He's not only toffee-nosed, he's a cheeky swine, an' all.' Dora refilled her glass. 'Who does he think he is to tell me what to do?'

'I'm sure it won't be so bad, Dora,' she said. 'I mean, he didn't say you couldn't drink, just to hide it from Ma and not to drink in front of her or give it to her.' Becky felt so pleased with herself that nothing Dora said tonight could upset her.

That evening, Becky washed her hair with Dora's Amami again, took up the hem of her bridesmaid's dress and ironed it. Then she pressed the blue serge. She would have to travel in that. It was a blessing she had the house to herself.

She rummaged at the back of the hall cupboard for the old brown cardboard suitcase that had lain there since she could remember. It was just the right size to hold her few summer clothes, her winter coat and the one wool skirt and jumper that were good enough to take with her. It was only

July. By winter she would have money to buy more warm clothes.

In her room she packed her few belongings. She trod carefully down the stairs with the heavy suitcase, avoiding the creaking step, and stashed the case back in the cupboard. Then she returned to her room and retrieved from under the bed the paper bag she'd managed to hide there for the past three days. Inside was a set of fine linen sheets with scalloped embroidered edges, a matching bolster case and two pillowcases. Next she pulled out a bulging parcel tied with string. Inside were two striped kapok-filled pillows. She held one to her cheek and sighed at the softness of it. She was determined that Liz would not have to sleep on that lumpy bolster all her married life. Even though she'd bought them in the sales, the presents had cost over two pounds. But she would still have enough money to last until she found work.

Sitting on the bed, she took from her bag the silver-edged card and envelope she'd bought. She crept downstairs, avoiding the creaking step again, and sat at the table in the immaculate kitchen, chewing her nails and thinking what to write. She dipped the pen and began:

> Dearest Liz and Will,
>
> I hope you enjoy your present. By the time you read this I will be gone. Don't worry about me, I can look after myself.
>
> Have a very happy life together.
> All my love,
> Becky

Adding a cross for a kiss, she placed it in the envelope and wrote their names on it. Her tongue against the envelope to seal it, she paused. She should tell Liz about her little subterfuge with Doctor Maynard. It would give her hope that Dora might take some notice of him. On a separate sheet of paper she wrote of the morning's events and placed it in the envelope with the card on top. She would slip the envelope between the sheets where they would find it when they got into bed.

What about Ma? Should she write her a note? She owed her mother nothing, but it wouldn't hurt to say goodbye. She took out a sheet of paper and an envelope and began:

> Dear Ma,
>
> I'm sorry I had to leave without letting you know, but if I had told you before, you would have got mad.
>
> I want to have a life of my own, and now that I'm old enough to work and look after myself, that's what I'm going to do.
>
> I pray you get well soon, Ma.
>
> Love,
> Becky

Feeling a fraud as she wrote the word *love*, she added no kiss. She'd felt no real love for her mother for a long time, and she'd received none from her for even longer. She licked the envelope and wrote, *Ma* on it. She would sneak it on to the chair that served as Ma's bedside table.

Barely had she closed her bedroom door when she heard Dora's footsteps in the yard. That was close! She pulled off her work dress for the last time and crept into bed. It was only eleven o'clock, early for Dora. *Please let her be stinking drunk and sleep late tomorrow*, she prayed.

Trembling with half excitement and half fear, she went over her plans. She would get up at half past three, before daylight. No one would see her carrying a suitcase. The first bus didn't leave till seven, but she could snooze in the bus shelter. It was unlikely that anyone they knew would be taking the bus that early on a weekday.

Hopefully, when Liz and Will came back later that day, the worst of Ma's and Dora's fury would be over.

Thirteen

Competing with other buses, motor cars, tramcars, and horses and carts for a piece of the road, the bus pulled into the Haymarket bus station. The driver seemed fearless. Becky was not. Shaking, she dismounted and steadied herself with one hand against the side of the bus to collect her luggage.

'There you are, hinny.' The driver set her suitcase beside her.

She couldn't move. Her muscles were tied in complicated knots, like the embroidery stitches she'd learned at school. Where to go? What to do? She longed for Liz's hand to hold.

The noise of the city swept over her like a tidal wave. Motors honked, trams clanged and screeched along their iron rails, wooden horse-drawn carts clattered over the cobbles, and amidst the cacophony, drivers shouted insults at one another.

She felt like an upside-down bag of sugar. If she let a single grain escape, all her insides would spill out. She mustn't panic. She would walk about and get her bearings. 'Is there somewhere I could leave my case?' she asked the driver.

'Aye, at the office.' He pointed to the far end of the parking area.

Becky thanked him and, squinting against the low rays of the morning sun, she jumped in and out of the traffic. It seemed finding a parking place was like playing on the dodgem cars. But she reached the office and emerged without her suitcase, clutching a map of Newcastle.

Every nerve in her body twittered like a tree of sparrows. What now? She stood on the pavement and, out of reach of the traffic for the first time, dared to look about her.

A square clock tower dominated what looked like several small steeples. Ten minutes to nine! No wonder she was hungry. The sign on the main thoroughfare said Northumberland Street. It was a wide, imposing, and busy shopping street. Everything was so big and moved so fast. People were hurrying to work, presumably shop and office workers. Surely there must be some cafés around here.

About halfway down the street she was impressed by a large department store, called Fenwick's. She dodged the traffic to get a closer look and gazed in Fenwick's windows. These were quality clothes – the latest fashions by Poiret. They were mainly classic style but cut with extra-narrow lines. Becky strained to take in every detail – shimmering satin evening dresses, and cotton or voile day dresses, most with low waistlines or none at all, some amazingly short, just reaching the models' knees, some even sleeveless. Her stomach growled and she pulled herself away. Styles were changing so fast and becoming so outrageous she could design almost anything she liked and call it the latest fashion. And she would.

She walked on, looking for a café to have breakfast. The morning rush hour was almost over and shoppers milled about her. She'd never seen so many well-dressed people, yet, just as in Ashington, they were outnumbered by the ill-clad poor, and barefoot children, many with the skinny, bent legs of rickets victims.

Her blue serge was too warm, even in the morning sun, and her feet hurt in the cheap beige high heels she'd been allowed for the wedding. But she was grateful that she was well enough clad and her legs weren't bent with rickets.

She walked on, staying on the main streets. Eventually she found herself on the corner of Westgate Road and Pink Lane.

She walked down Pink Lane, narrow and uninteresting, but was delighted to see a dingy sign saying *Johnson's Café*, with an *Open* notice in the window.

The smell of grease and smoke met her at the door, but mixed with it was the aroma of bacon and sausage frying. She went into the gloomy room, scattered with oilcloth-covered tables and wooden chairs. It was shabby but clean.

Flopping into the nearest chair, she kicked off her shoes with a sigh. A woman approached, most of her steel-grey hair gathered in a bun on her neck, the remainder falling about her face, despite the white frilled cap intended to anchor it. Her eyes and mouth crinkled upwards as if she'd spent her whole life laughing.

'Morning, hinny, what can I get you?' Her voice rang like a huge silver bell, and her green eyes, snug in their wrinkled nooks, smiled a welcome.

Becky felt less nervous. She'd never eaten in a café. 'I'd love a cup of tea and . . . a sandwich.'

'What kind, luv? It's all on the board.' She pointed to a blackboard on the wall, where the day's menu was scribbled, and took a stubby pencil and notepad from a pocket behind her white apron.

Becky scanned the board and wondered how restaurants could get butchers' meat when it was rationed. But she didn't care. 'I'll have a sausage sandwich please, with tomato sauce.' The tea was tuppence and the sandwich fivepence. She wasn't sure if that was reasonable or not.

'Right you are, luv.' The woman scribbled on her pad and disappeared.

Becky studied the other customers. She saw none of the elegant people from the streets, only workmen, perhaps coming off duty or going on, and shabby men with blank, beaten faces, playing cards. Not looking the type to have free time on a weekday, they must be some of the many unemployed since the war. She sighed. Why did she think she could find a job?

Her tea and sandwich arrived almost immediately. 'Here you are, hen.'

Becky stared at the sandwich. The two slices of bread were as thick as doorsteps, two fat, juicy sausages poked out of the sides, and tomato sauce oozed everywhere. It was a feast. She took a large bite and didn't stop eating until she was half way through, when she paused to sip the strong, milky tea. It was condensed milk, and sweet. She emptied half the cup before returning to the sandwich.

Afterwards she leaned back in her chair, savouring the comfort of warm food and drink filling the void in her belly and her being.

'Anything else, hinny? You polished that off quickstick for a little one.'

Becky flushed. 'It was lovely, thank you.'

'That doesn't tell me if you've had enough though.'

Thinking of the three pounds she had left after buying the wedding present and the bus ticket and map, Becky said, 'I'm fine, thank you.'

The woman looked at her closely. 'It's been a bit since you ate, eh?'

Becky flushed deeper.

'Bet you could do with another cup of tea at any rate, luv.'

She took the cup before Becky could speak and returned with it, refilled, and a plate with two digestive biscuits. 'On the house. Don't say nowt. The old goat only pops in at the end of the day to pick up the cash. I'm in charge the rest of the time.'

Embarrassing tears filled Becky's eyes.

'No need to cry, hinny.' The woman said. 'Are you in trouble?'

Becky shook her head. She'd felt so alone and lost since she'd left home, such kindness overwhelmed her. More tears came.

The woman pulled out the neighbouring chair and sat down. 'Look, hen, I've got a lass near your age meself. I know when something's up. You can tell me.'

Wiping her eyes with the backs of her hands, Becky forced a smile, but her face felt funny. It was her first smile since Liz had left her. 'There's nothing wrong, really. I'm doing what I want to do. It's just that it's me first day and I'm a bit scared. I've run away from home.'

'Aye, I had a feeling. Why, pet?'

'It was bad. I couldn't take it any more. I'm fourteen now and I've come to Newcastle to find work and a place to live. I'm tired of being the family skivvy. I want a life of me own.'

'And you just arrived this morning and you don't know nobody and you've got nowhere to stay and not much money. Right, eh?'

Becky nodded. 'I've got three pounds, but I don't know how long that'll last, or how long it'll take me to find a room and a job.'

The woman drummed her fingers on the table. 'I wish I could give you a job, luv. I've asked me boss till I'm blue in the face for help, even just in the busy hours, but he's too flaming mean. I do know somewhere you can stay though. It'll tide you over till you get work. It's not fancy but it's clean.'

'Oh, anything would be fine.' Becky suddenly felt brighter, as if someone had lit a candle in her head. 'Thank you . . .' She hesitated, unsure how to address the woman.

'Call me Annie. Everybody does.' She wrote on her pad. 'It's just across Westgate Road, that's the big street on the right, turn left then first right.' Pausing to lick the pencil, she continued, 'Go into Dunn's hardware shop and ask for Mrs Dunn. She'll show you the room. Her last lodger just left to get married. She only takes girls.' With a wide smile, she handed Becky the paper.

Gratitude enveloped Becky like a cloak. 'Thank you, you're very kind,' she said, though she wanted to fling her arms round the woman and kiss her.

'Aye, well, as I said, I've got one of me own like you. But, thank God, she's happy to stay at home with her ma, at least for now. Mrs Dunn's a bit poker-faced but don't let her get to you, she's all right at bottom.'

Becky handed her a pound note.

'Thanks hen.' She punched the keys of the ornate till on the counter and returned with the change.

98

Becky knew you were supposed to tip waitresses. Shyly she held out two pennies, but the woman pushed her hand away and shook her head. 'Nah, hen. You're going to need every ha'penny you've got.'

'Thank you, it was wonderful.' Becky put the money in her purse.

Annie smiled at her. 'I see you've got a good appetite, and Mrs Dunn's a bit stingy on the food. You come to me if you're hungry, hinny, or if you need anything at all.'

'Oh, I will, thank you.' Becky tried to keep a smile on her face as she ground her feet back into her shoes under the table.

Dunn's Hardware was a decaying building in a narrow street, but far enough from Westgate Road to be away from the main traffic noise. There were several small shops, some boarded up and, judging by the lace curtains at the upper windows, two storeys of living quarters above each.

She entered the shop, gritting her teeth against the screeching that met her, like fingernails on a blackboard magnified a thousand times. A thin, bald man was cutting a key in a machine that looked like a giant pencil sharpener bolted to the wooden counter. From the odd bobbing of his body, he must be operating the machine with a pedal. He nodded and went on grinding.

Becky continued gritting her teeth and looked around. The shop was crammed from floor to ceiling with boxes of ironware – various tools, nails, screws, files, and even some iron kitchen pots and utensils. A familiar smell, though she couldn't quite identify it, made her tongue feel unpleasant and dry.

The man stopped, and Becky unclenched her teeth.

'Aye?' He wiped the key on his dirty blue apron and placed blackened hands on the wooden counter.

'Annie sent me to see Mrs Dunn. I'm looking for a room.'

He pulled back a green curtain and yelled into the back of the shop, 'Edie, Annie's sent a lass about the room.'

Edie appeared, fastening a flower-patterned pinafore over a

black dress. She was tall and skinny, with greying brown hair plaited in tight coils round her head, not at all like Annie's untidy mop. Her flat grey eyes examined what she could see of Becky from behind the counter. 'You know Annie?'

'I went there for something to eat and she helped me.'

'Aye, that's Annie! She thinks God put her on this earth to save the human race.'

'She's very nice.'

The woman's gaunt face cracked into something like a smile. 'She's a soft touch, that one. It's a small room, top floor. Breakfast and high tea, and midday dinner on Sundays. Baths Friday and Saturday nights. You've got to book ahead as there's five of us. The washhouse is in the yard. But no washing on the Lord's day. And no eating in your room. It encourages mice. You clean the room yourself and I check it once a week. You want to see it?'

Becky was impatient to see it, but cautious. 'How much?' She held her breath.

'Nine and six a week all in. That's cheap for around here. It's not a fancy area but it's right in the town, no fares to work. I take it you work in the town?'

'I hope to. I still have to find a job.'

Mrs Dunn's face closed like a fist.

Becky knew why. 'But I can pay the rent.' She calculated as she spoke. Even if it took her a month to find a job, she could still pay the rent and have some left for emergencies. She would make do on the two meals a day.

Mrs Dunn beckoned her beyond the curtain that separated the shop from the rear. 'This is supposed to be the back shop but me man made it into a kitchen to give us an extra room upstairs to let. We all eat here together.'

Becky looked at Mr Dunn's handiwork. It was hard to believe the dirty shop was in the next room. The kitchen was large and immaculate – a white sink and draining board, a workbench and wall cupboards, a scrubbed wooden table and chairs. She noticed the white metal geyser above the sink. She'd seen them advertised in magazines – *Hot water at a touch*! There must be two other lodgers, she reasoned, counting five chairs. And Mr and Mrs Dunn obviously used this as their sitting room. A green patterned sofa stood under the window and two matching chairs by the fire.

Examining Becky for the first time from head to toe, Mrs Dunn asked, 'You got no luggage?'

'It's at the bus station.' Becky was pleased to say she had possessions.

The woman grunted and opened a door to a narrow hall and stairway. The green linoleum was patterned with worn spots, some bare to the wood below. 'You can get here from the front door at the side of the shop, and the privy's in the yard by the washhouse.'

Becky followed her to the first landing.

'This is the bathroom.' Mrs Dunn turned a switch outside the door, which opened on to a rectangular room with no window. 'The switch is outside the door. Remember to turn it off. Me man moved it outside so I could keep an eye on it. Electricity costs money. All the rooms has it, so you be minding to switch your light off when you go out, and don't have it on in the day.'

'Yes, of course.' Such luxury! A special room for a bathroom. Becky stared at the sink, the claw-footed bathtub, and a geyser like the one in the kitchen. The bath had hot and cold taps. How wonderful to turn on a tap and get hot water!

'Me man put in the partition and the bath. But he left the room next door big enough for a lodger. Aye, if you can't marry a rich man, marry a handyman,' Mrs Dunn said.

When she opened one of the two doors on the landing, Becky hid her disappointment. It was a boxroom, with a skylight. A single bunk with a candlewick bedspread was squeezed under the roof slope. There was no room for a proper bed. On the floor by the bunk was an alarm clock, on the opposite wall a chest of drawers, and some hooks for clothes. There was nowhere to sit except the bunk, and you'd have to watch you didn't bump your head on the ceiling even when sitting.

Mrs Dunn studied her. 'It's small, but that's why it's cheap. You want it, lass?'

'Yes,' Becky said quickly. She couldn't afford to refuse a cheap room and almost full board. She was pleased to see a tall, round paraffin stove in the corner.

Following her glance, Mrs Dunn said, 'Oh, aye, and you buy your own paraffin.'

Becky groaned inwardly. But the room wouldn't need much heating. 'I'll go for my luggage now, if that's all right?'

'I'll be needing the rent in advance, and your special foods card.' Mrs Dunn folded her arms over her skinny chest as if to say, *No entry without it.*

Becky grappled in her bag and handed her a ten-shilling note and her food card.

'Well now, everything's above board.' She tucked the money into her skirt pocket and withdrew a sixpence for Becky's change.

Becky made her way out, blinking in the daylight. She breathed in the fresh air and pushed the hair off her face with her hand. Grey metal filings clung to her fingers. She must have picked them up from the counter. Iron! That was the strange sensation on her tongue she'd noticed earlier. It was like licking a penny.

She hobbled back to the Haymarket, blisters biting her heels at each step. After retrieving her case, she sat on the step to change into her school shoes. When she removed her high heels she discovered that the blisters had burst and were glued to her lisle stockings. She foraged in the suitcase for a pair of socks, glanced around to make sure no one was looking, then pulled down her stockings and gritted her teeth as she peeled them off the blisters. She pulled on the socks, not caring that she looked childish. Ohhh, that was better. She could make it back to Mrs Dunn's now. On the way, she would pick up a newspaper for job advertisements, and a writing pad, envelopes and a pen and ink. It was amazing how small expenses mounted up. Tomorrow she would also go to the labour exchange.

Breathless after hauling her suitcase up the three flights, she dropped it in her room then fell on to the bunk.

She looked at the clock. It wasn't set. Her throat was dry, her face and body wet, and she needed to go to the privy. She dragged herself up and tiptoed down to the yard.

Although what Mrs Dunn had called the privy was outside, it was a proper lavatory with a porcelain bowl and a pull chain. Becky began to realize that Mrs Dunn was right. The sound of water flushing was like music. But *she* wouldn't need a handyman, because she was going to marry a *rich* man.

Back in her room, she sat on the bunk with the newspaper. The skylight didn't shed enough light to read by. She turned on the light switch and watched with awe as the naked bulb hanging from the ceiling lit itself without a match. She hoped Mrs Dunn wouldn't come in and see her with the light on during the day, but she had to see to read.

Opening the papers, she tried to focus, but her eyelids were heavy. The day had been exhausting. She yawned as she lay down and closed her eyes. Within minutes she was asleep.

The knocking on the door persisted after Becky opened her eyes. She wasn't dreaming. 'I'm coming.' *Please don't let it be Mrs Dunn.* She switched off the light and opened the door.

A thin, dark girl raised her heavily made-up eyelids and parted her scarlet lips in feigned surprise. 'Oh, you *are* there. I thought you were out – or deaf. I'm Janine.' She jerked her head towards the other door on the landing. 'I live there. I just came to warn you that Mrs Dunn'll make mincemeat out of you if she catches you with the light on in the daytime.'

Janine sauntered in and sat on the bed. 'Wedge your coat or a blanket along the bottom of the door. There's an inch of light shows through otherwise.'

'Thank you.' Becky closed the door and sat beside her uninvited but welcome guest. 'I'm Becky. Janine's a lovely name.'

'It's really Jane but I changed it to Janine when I left home. It's more chic.' She examined her long scarlet fingernails. 'Blast! A chip. And I only did them last night.'

'How long have you been here?' Becky hid her own bitten and unvarnished nails.

Janine was scraping off the damaged varnish with her thumbnail. 'Would you believe it? I've stuck it out with Mrs Dunn a year now, but I've been in Newcastle two years. The first year, I shuffled around from one bug or flea-ridden room to another. At least this place is clean, and old Dunners isn't so bad when you get used to her ways – and learn how to get around them. I'll show you a few tricks.' She stopped concentrating on her nail varnish and her luminous brown eyes inspected Becky for the first time.

Becky's face burned with embarrassment. She'd studied Janine's fashionably short hair, high-heeled pumps and imitation silk stockings, her clinging red crêpe dress with a daring neckline, as stylish as any in Fenwick's window. Becky felt excruciatingly aware of her crumpled serge dress, school shoes and ankle socks, and her schoolgirl shoulder-length hair.

'How old are you?' Janine's voice made her jump.

Becky hesitated, but she couldn't lie. 'Fourteen.'

Janine raised her pencilled eyebrows. 'I was fourteen when I came, an' all. Me family lives in Gateshead, but I had to get away. Me da's always drunk and me ma's always nagging. I only go home occasionally to see me little brother. Have you got a job?'

'I started looking in the paper but I fell asleep.'

'Poor thing! It's hell finding work. You'd better make yourself look older, luv.'

Becky bit her lip, then defended herself in a voice verging on tears. 'I've got smarter things to wear, but I didn't want to travel in them.'

'Oh, hen, I'm sorry.' Janine put an arm round her. 'Me and me big gob. I always open it first and think after.'

'That's all right.' Becky absorbed the feeling of Janine's arm round her shoulders and wished it were Liz's arm. But she enjoyed the affectionate gesture, and began to like Janine.

'I'll do your hair for you after tea if you like. I'm a hairdresser.'

'Ooh, that's a glamorous job.'

Janine kicked off her high heels and wiggled her liberated toes with a sigh. 'Aye, it sounds like it, but it's bloody hard work standing on your feet all day. Not many people can afford to have their hair done these days, and them that can skimp on the tips. What sort of work are *you* looking for?'

'Anything! The only thing I can do is sew, by hand. But me sister got a job sewing shirts on a machine and she can't sew a stitch. She says everything's cut out and marked, and all she has to do is keep the seams straight under the needle.'

Janine curled her feet beneath her. 'What do you sew?'

'Dresses and skirts and blouses and things.'

'Wow! Would you make something for me?'

'If you like, but I've got nothing with me. You'd have to get needles and thread and scissors as well as the material.'

'And a pattern?'

'It'll be cheaper if you just show me what you want in a magazine or a shop window and I can copy it.'

'Aren't you clever! I've got a half day on Saturday. We could go shopping.'

Becky felt herself relaxing. She'd found a room and made a friend in the process. She'd struck lucky. Please let it continue.

Janine stretched out her legs and stood, bumping her head on the sloping wall. 'Damn and blast! You'd think I'd be used to that bloody wall by now. This was *my* room when I first came. We'll go to mine to do your hair after tea. Dunners'll be ringing the bell any minute, and I've got to go to the lav first.'

'What time is it?'

'Nearly six. That's tea time, but if you're kept late at work or anything she serves it up on a tin plate and puts a pan lid on it. You heat it up yourself and you have to eat it with them in their armchairs, staring at you, waiting for you to finish. And she's dead stingy with the helpings.'

'So long as I eat, I don't care. Will the other lodger be there?'

Wincing, Janine squeezed her feet back into her high heels

and stood. 'Aye, Mildred – Milly Mouse, I call her. Never opens her mouth, just keeps her eyes down and eats. She's a funny lass, educated, posh like, works at the *Evening Chronicle*, copy editing or something. Goes to church almost every night and Sundays, and once a week she cleans the minister's house. Never goes home neither.'

'That makes three of us,' Becky said.

'Aye! Well, it's almost gruel time.' She crossed her legs and put her hands between her thighs like a little girl. 'If I don't go to the lav now, I'll wet me knickers.'

Mrs Dunn sat at the head of the table serving the shepherd's pie. Mr Dunn, stripped of his apron, sat opposite, and between them sat a pale brown-haired girl in a brown skirt and cardigan and a white cotton blouse. Now Becky knew why Janine called her Milly Mouse. The only bright thing about her was a pretty gold pin in her blouse collar. She didn't look up when they entered.

'Hello everyone,' Janine said. 'Mildred, this is Becky, our new lodger.'

Mildred raised her head and held out her hand. 'How do you do,' she said in a formal voice.

Becky returned the greeting.

Throughout the meal, not a word was spoken, other than an occasional *Pass the salt, please*, or *Anyone else want pepper?*

'Phweeoow, you'd think someone had died,' Becky said on the way upstairs. 'Are they always that talkative?'

Janine giggled. 'No, it was lively tonight. At least you got a *How do you do* from Milly Mouse.'

'Aye, what a shame! She'd be pretty if she didn't drag her hair back like Mrs Dunn, and dress like a spinster in that awful brown.'

'It matches her hair. Everything she owns is brown, except her white blouses, and I swear they're left over from her school uniform. But there's no harm in her.'

'She sounds educated,' Becky said. 'I wish I talked like that.'

'Nothing to stop you, hen. I put it on when I have to, especially at work and when I'm with a posh boyfriend. But when I'm with another Geordie, it's nice to let meself go.'

'I want to learn to talk properly. At home they would've laughed at me, so I used to practise in me head.'

'Practise on me all you like. I promise not to laugh.' She grinned. 'I need somebody to keep me on me toes. I'd like to have me own hairdressing business one of these days.' Outside her door, she said, in a formal voice, 'Come into my salon, Modom, and I'll style your hair.'

Becky imitated Janine's accent: 'How strange! I'm going to have my own business too – the best fashion house in town.'

Fourteen

B ecky turned back from the offices of Messrs Talbot and Maxwell in despair. The firm had given their address in the advertisement and she'd rushed there as soon as the paper had come out, only to be confronted by a queue of women ahead of her, all after one seamstress job.

She wandered home, eyes down, wondering when her luck would change. When she looked up she realized she was lost. She must have turned off Newbridge Street. She stopped abruptly to get her bearings and collided with a tall young man carrying an armful of books. As they scattered to the ground, he let out an exclamation that might have been an oath, though in her confusion Becky couldn't make it out.

'I'm sorry,' she said.

'It's policy to look where you're going.' The young man's voice was only mildly irritated.

'It was stupid of me. Let me help.' She picked up some of the volumes, mostly leather-covered and very old. 'I hope they're not damaged.'

'Me too. A fine would eat up my week's groceries.'

He was perhaps eighteen, dressed in shabby flannels and a blazer with frayed cuffs. He must be a student, and obviously a poor one. His brown curly hair looked as if he cut it himself.

Filled with guilt, Becky examined each book she picked up. 'If they're damaged, I'll pay the fine.' She said a silent prayer, *Please God, don't let them be damaged.*

He stacked them under his arm and glanced at her for the first time. 'It's nice of you to offer, but I don't think they're much the worse for wear. Partly my fault anyway. If *I'd* been looking where I was going, I would've seen you. Sorry for the outburst and thanks for helping.'

She smiled. 'I didn't hear the outburst. And let me help some more. They're too many to carry at once.'

He stepped backwards, his clear blue eyes looking at her through his rimmed spectacles. 'My digs are just across the road. But thanks anyway.'

Becky watched his tall frame and thatch of brown curls bobbing among the traffic and noticed that his blazer elbows were patched. There was something strangely attractive about him that disturbed her.

Becky hobbled up the stairs, verging on tears. Two weeks of trudging about looking for work had broken in her new shoes too well. The strap had snapped on the last leg of her journey home.

Janine yelled from her room. 'Hey, that you, Becky? You sound like an old woman. What's wrong with your feet?'

'My shoe strap's had it.' Becky leaned against the doorpost and Janine's lively face turned sympathetic.

'Come on in, you don't need to tell me. No luck again, eh?'

Becky flopped on to the bed. 'There were a hundred women waiting before me. But I did bump into a lad I fancied, a student, though he didn't ask to see me again.'

'Never mind, hen. I'll make you a nice cup of tea, accompanied by Cadbury's chocolate biscuits. And no questions about where they came from.'

Becky smiled. She was used to Janine's illicit tea parties and midnight feasts. She talked openly about some of her *friends* who were *in business for themselves, so to speak*, and Becky guessed it was the black market. She knew better than to ask where Janine's little luxuries came from, and had learned many tips from her on how to survive in the Dunn household.

'Abracadabra!' Janine pulled out her huge suitcase and unlocked it. They removed a rubber hot-water bottle, a small kettle, a tin of condensed milk, and an unopened packet of chocolate biscuits. Janine waved them under Becky's nose.

Becky inhaled the chocolate aroma. 'Mmmmm, heaven! I feel better already. I'll get the water.' She began to rise but Janine pushed her back.

'You rest, you're the one that's buggered. I've had a day off, if you can call it that. They sent me and Bella home because there was only half a dozen customers booked for the day. That means a day's pay docked and no tips. But who's worried about being on short time? I can spend me day going out on a wild shopping spree.' She made a clown's face.

'Oh, Janine, I'm sorry.' That was the third time she'd been sent home in two weeks. Becky knew that under Janine's brash exterior she was worried about her job.

'Don't be sorry, I'm still better off than you, pet.' Janine picked up the rubber hot-water bottle, stuffed it under her arm and threw a cardigan round her shoulders. The flat, soft bottle was easier to hide than the kettle, and if Mrs Dunn ever caught her filling it, Janine had her answer ready – it was a cold pack for her headache.

Becky's joy at the thought of instant hot water from the tap had been squashed when she discovered the pilot light was lit only on Fridays and Saturdays for baths. Janine had found out how to light it, but they only dared do so when Mrs Dunn was not at home, or late at night, when the Dunns weren't likely to use the water and find it still warm. They both revelled in an occasional late-night warm bath.

Becky lit the paraffin stove and set the top of the suitcase as a table. On it sat condensed milk, a tin teapot, two tin mugs and two plates that, with a couple of knives, spoons, and forks, completed Janine's kitchen equipment.

Suddenly Becky felt more cheerful. Because forbidden, these treats were all the more enjoyable. 'Janine to the rescue, as usual,' she said. 'I was wondering how I could last another two hours till tea.' She looked down, embarrassed. 'As soon as I get a job, I'll get me own kitchen things and treat you. You're always feeding me.'

'And who's just made me the most glamorous frock I've ever had in me life?'

'But I enjoyed doing it. Sewing, I mean making nice clothes, is the only thing that keeps me sane. It occupies me hands and me mind and I love to see the finished work, especially when I've made up the pattern meself. It would be heaven to design and make glamorous dresses for a living.'

Janine spooned tea into the pot and poured on the water. 'You *will* have your own business one day, I'm sure, but in the meantime, I bet that dress you made me would sell in Fenwick's for twenty times what you paid for the material and thread at the Quayside.'

Becky laughed, delighted. 'And have you any suggestions how I'm going to sell my creations, made from remnants at the market, to Fenwick's?'

Janine sat on the bed and poured the tea. 'Not straight away, but somewhere down the line you might. You'd have to start small. And *don't* tell them how you make them. Have a biscuit.'

Becky shook with more laughter as she took the biscuit. 'Aye, *small*'s the word. And can you imagine me starting a business from me little room? Having me clients traipsing up the stairs to me showroom?'

'Old Dunners as your receptionist leading them up.' Janine burst out laughing and choked on a mouthful of biscuit. Becky slapped her back.

'Thanks.' With tears in her eyes, Janine went on. 'But I'm serious. You make things incredibly fast for doing them by hand, all we have to do is think of an outlet to sell them. A stall on the Quayside would be a start.'

'Don't be daft. Those poor people are looking for second-hand rags the same as I am. They wear them as they are. They wouldn't want my fancy makeovers anyway – even if they could afford the extra money. First I need a steady job to pay the rent, then I'll find a way to tout my wares. In the meantime, what's one more wasted day?'

'Oops, I forgot! I brought your post up and stuck it under

your door. There's a letter from Liz, and another one – could be a job.'

Becky jumped up, almost spilling her tea. She kicked off the loose shoe, hobbled to her room and back. As predicted, one letter was a job refusal. She sat back on Janine's bed to read Liz's, the third she'd had so far:

Dear Becky,

At last I'm coming to you. Will's off on Sunday, and he's got a mate who's married and lives in Blyth. He wants to see him anyway and we can go to the bus station together and meet on the way back. As far as Ma and Dora will know, he's taking his wife to visit his friends, and he says nobody, not even *them*, can stop him doing that.

I'm catching the 7.30 bus. Even if I don't hear back in time, I know you'll be there to meet me. I can't wait to see you.

All my love,

Liz

Becky threw the letter into the air, bounced off the bed and hopped about in delight. 'She's coming on Sunday. I can't believe it.'

'Then you'd better stop doing the one-shoe tap dance on the floor or Mrs Dunn'll have you homeless by Sunday.' She poured two more cups of tea. 'I'm that glad for you. What other news?'

'She didn't say any more, but she's always protected me. I read about the miners' troubles meself in the papers, but she never mentions anything. Though she let it slip in her last letter that Dora and Ma are still drinking together. Even Dr Maynard's warning that the booze will kill Ma doesn't stop Dora.'

'It'll be grand to see your sister anyway. I'm sorry I'll miss her. I'm going home – only to see our Rick, of course, not Ma and Da. You know, them two bickering all the time's getting to him. I'm that worried about him, Beck. He's so miserable at home, and I suspect he's getting in with the wrong gang at school.'

'What'll you do with him?'

'Take him to the park to fish for tiddlers and whatever I can think of to entertain a ten-year-old. I feel as bad about leaving him at home as you feel about your sister.'

Admonishing her with a scowl, Becky said, 'And, as you're always telling me, there's nothing you can do about it.'

Janine sighed. 'Aye, I know. You can use my room, and eat whatever's in Mother Hubbard's suitcase.' She opened her eyes wide as if struck by a revelation. 'And I'll be away for Sunday dinner. I'll tell Mrs Dunn your sister can have mine.'

Becky's mouth fell open. 'You can't do that. I wouldn't dare.'

'Why not? Every time I go home on a Sunday old stingy mingy gets out of giving me my dinner. I pay for it. Your sister can have it.'

'Phew! If she sounds all right about it, but I'm not going to have Liz sitting eating your dinner with Mrs Dunn's evil eye on her, and Mildred and Mr Dunn's eyes glued to their plates. Without you to liven things up it'll be like taking communion for half an hour. Anyway, thanks for the tea.'

On Sunday morning Becky wore her blue bridesmaid's dress. She'd shortened the hem and the sleeves and it looked like a pretty summer dress. But she'd need a cardigan over it. No sun shone through the skylight.

Excited, she undid the newspapers Janine insisted she use every night to curl her hair and combed it out. She would surprise Liz. She hadn't told her that Janine had cut her hair short. Next, the lipstick, again courtesy of Janine. It was too bright for Becky's colouring but she smeared just a touch over her lips and cheeks. It made her look older.

Elated by the prospect of seeing Liz, she floated down the stairs and all the way to the bus station. A few drops of rain started, then stopped. She prayed it would stay dry for the sake of her dress, but nothing could dampen her spirits.

At last the bus pulled in. Becky's breath came so fast she almost choked. It seemed every passenger alighted before Liz. When she climbed down the stairs they clung together and cried and laughed.

'Oh, Beck, it's so wonderful to see you,' Liz said, when they separated for breath.

'You an' all. You've no idea how I've missed you.'

'Move along, please,' the driver said. 'Don't block the exit.'

Becky took Liz's hand and pulled her towards Northumberland Street. 'You look lovely in your going-away suit, luv, but you're going to get wet.'

'Aye, it wasn't raining when I left. But I don't care about anything. I'm here!' She searched Becky's face. 'And just look at you. Your hair! It looks very fashionable. And lipstick! You look thinner, though. Are you eating all right?'

'Oh, aye, plenty.' Becky laughed. 'It's all the walking, looking for jobs. Come on, we go down here. This is Northumberland Street, my favourite shopping street.'

Liz looked about her. 'Eey, isn't it grand! Such tall buildings.'

'Aye, I'll show you all the best shops. Of course, they're closed today, but we can only window-shop anyway. What you got in that carrier bag?'

'Don't be nosy.'

'Why don't we go home first and have a cup of tea and a natter? We can have a look round the town later. Maybe the weather'll clear up by then. I've loads to tell you.'

'Tea and a natter. Oh, we haven't had that for such a long time!'

Becky studied Liz's face. It was pink and glowing and her eyes shone. 'You look grand, Liz. It must be married life. Nobody could look that happy living with Ma and Dora.

'How's Dora been? You never say much in your letters.'

'Oh, just the same. What's the point of moaning about her?

Anyway, she's a much smaller part of me life now than she used to be – *and* Ma. I can put them out of me mind when I'm with Will.'

They walked on. 'How is he putting up with them?' Becky asked.

'He's wonderful. He just acts normal with them most of the time, but if one of them raises their voice to me, he tells them to shut their traps.'

Becky's eyes grew round. 'In those very words?'

'Well, not exactly, but he stands up for me.'

'How?'

Liz's eyes studied the pavement as she walked. 'You know, he tells them to leave me alone, or to knock it off. That sort of thing.'

'And do they?'

'Sometimes.'

'How's Dora with him?' Becky glanced sideways at Liz's face. She didn't want to lay any suspicion if Liz wasn't already aware that Dora had a fancy for Will.

Liz's voice didn't change. 'Oh, you know, she's just Dora being Dora. He doesn't take any notice of her.'

Becky couldn't tell if Liz meant that Dora flirted with him, or that she was rude to him. She let the subject rest. 'How's Ma doing?'

'The same. Dr Maynard's mad at her, but Dora's goaded her into talking back to him and telling him to stop nagging her. He just gives me the prescription every week. Says there's no more he can do if she won't help herself. I can only do me best and hope.' She stopped and stared in Fenwick's window.

Becky smiled proudly. 'Aye, this is me favourite shop. Isn't it lovely? Me friend Janine says I should make dresses and sell them here. She loved the one I made for *her*.'

Liz laughed. 'I like the sound of your friend. I'm so glad you found someone nice for company.'

'Aye, you'll like her, but she's gone home today. She insisted on telling the landlady to give you her Sunday dinner, and she says we can use her room, it's bigger than mine.'

'And what about your other friend?'

'Oh, Annie. She's really nice. I pop in for a cup of tea and a chat, and she always slips me something to eat. She's like a mother to me. We'll go to see her this afternoon. I want you to meself for a bit first.'

'It seems everything's going well, except the job. I'm sorry about that, but it'll take time, luv. I've got two pounds left of the money you gave me and I've brought it for you.'

'Oh, Liz, you shouldn't.'

'Just to tide you over until you find work.'

'Then I'll pay you back.'

'If you want.'

Settled in Janine's room enjoying a mid-morning cup of tea and one of the currant scones Liz had baked, the secret contents of the carrier bag, Becky thought she was in heaven.

Liz stared into her mug. 'Beck . . . there's something I want to tell you, but I'm almost afraid to say it in case I'm wrong.'

Becky's stomach skidded down to her feet. 'Go on,' she said.

'Well, I know it's ridiculously early to tell, but me usual's five days late.'

Becky closed her eyes and felt the room spin. No! It's not possible, not so soon. Please, God, let it not be that. She looked at Liz's excited face before she spoke. 'Would you be happy about it if it was?'

'Oh, Beck, I never knew it would be like this just to *think* you might be going to have a baby. I feel all mushy and motherly already.'

'But you were late once before and it was nothing.' Becky tried not to sound hopeful.

'But that was because I had pleurisy and a temperature of a hundred and three. You know I'm always regular to the day.'

In her mind Becky saw Liz carrying a baby over her shoulder and running up and down stairs looking after Ma, then laying the crying bundle in its cot while she scrubbed the floor and made the dinner and did the washing. Dora would go bonkers with a screaming bairn around. What sort of life would it be for Liz? Becky swallowed hard and tried not to sound too dismayed. 'How would you manage with a baby though?'

'The same as everybody else.' Liz's face split into a grin. 'You're the only one I've told. I'd feel that daft if I told Will and it came to nothing.'

'And what about money?' Becky felt hollow with despair for Liz and the narrowing road of freedom that loomed ahead of her.

'We'd just have to manage the same as everybody else. Nobody knows what's going to happen and I refuse to expect the worst.' She grinned. 'Perhaps if Dora's belly doesn't get as full as she likes, she'll fork out some of her earnings.'

'Hmph! That's a laugh! She'd go hungry before she'd contribute to her keep. How do you think she'd react to a baby in the house, Liz? I mean when it cries and stinks the place out and all that.'

'She'll just have to get used to it or move out, won't she? It's Will's house now, and mine.' The joy had left Liz's voice.

Becky felt like a murderess with a knife dripping blood. If she inflicted her worries on Liz, she would ruin her happiness. 'I forgot, of course the house is yours, and your Will could kick her out and she couldn't do a thing about it.' She laughed to lighten the mood. 'I wish I could be a fly on the wall if he did.'

Liz was smiling again. 'If it's true, I'll still come to see you whenever I can, Beck. Women travel on buses with babies.'

'And promise you'll write the moment you know for sure, one way or the other.'

'You'll be the first, you daft thing – after Will, of course. I mean, he had something to do with it.'

Yes, Becky thought, *after Will*. Already she came second place in Liz's life, and soon perhaps third. She felt like a kite with a broken string, detached and floating further and further from its owner. But it wasn't distance that was separating her from Liz, it was people taking what had been her place. First Will, and now a family. Don't be childish, she told herself. Be happy for Liz. It's what she wants.

'You're very quiet,' Liz said.

'Aye, I haven't got over me surprise. But now I think we should get on with our day and not talk about bairns any more until we know for sure – it might be bad luck.'

'You're right, and the sun's coming out.' Liz picked up the dishes.

'We can't wash them till everyone's in bed or we'd get chucked out for eating in our rooms. Let's go to the Quayside now, you'll love it. It's more like a fair than a Sunday morning market.'

'It sounds lovely. Maybe I can find a present for Will.'

After seeing Liz off on the nine o'clock bus, Becky climbed the stairs, kicked off her shoes, curled up on the bunk with the blanket over her head and wept. Liz was so simple and straightforward. She never saw problems looming until it was too late.

Yes, Becky admitted, part of her misery was selfish, but her fears were for Liz. What a hard life she would have bringing up a baby in that household. And if she fell so easily with this one, dear God, she might be one of those women who fell every year.

Fifteen

Near the end of August Becky plodded home, tired, elated, yet nervous. She'd found a job as a junior seamstress at a men's coat factory, Jacob & Sons, near the quayside. She could easily walk there. It paid sixteen and sixpence, working from seven thirty to five thirty. Quotas were assigned each day, according to which piece of the garment each person was allotted, and wages docked for unfilled quotas. She would be slow at first, but would soon catch up.

After the rent there wouldn't be much to live on, but she could manage. The firm provided an overall, and her old serge dress would do to wear under it. She wouldn't need to buy many winter clothes.

If only she hadn't lied about the sewing machine! She'd said she'd used one before. But she told herself she would learn so fast nobody would notice she was a beginner. The secretary who had interviewed her had shown her the downstairs sewing shop where the final touches were added to the garments, and the top floor shop where Becky would assemble the various parts. The machines looked just like the one Liz used and Becky had often watched her at work. Without the lie she wouldn't have got the job. Honesty so far had got her nowhere.

Something was happening up the street. Becky ran to see. Crowds shouted and jostled one another, others threw stones or any object that came to hand. A newspaper stand flew about twelve inches in front of her face. When it missed its target, a policeman on a horse, and landed face upwards, the words glowered up at her as if written in blood:

LLOYD GEORGE SAYS NO TO MINERS. SANKEY'S REPORT FOR NATIONALIZATION BASED SOLELY ON PRODUCING GREATER HARMONY BETWEEN EMPLOYER AND WORKER, NOT ON ECONOMIC GROUNDS. GOVERNMENT MUST PROTECT NATIONAL ECONOMY.

Dear God! What now? The miners would strike. Becky's happiness at finding work drained out of her like water through a leaky pail. She reached home, trembling, and leafed through the post on the hall shelf. Another letter from Liz! She'd written almost daily since her visit two weeks ago. She'd lost a tiny spot of blood, and in her last two letters had been worried. Ashamed, Becky prayed even harder now that the letter would say she wasn't in the family way after all. She tore it open.

Dearest Beck,

It's true! I can hardly believe it. Dr Maynard examined me this morning and says, even though it's early days, he would stake his life on it. He also said that one spot of blood was nothing to worry about.

I'm going to tell Will tonight, but I'll wait a bit before I tell Ma and Dora. Wish me luck.

Just think! You're going to be an auntie. Oh, Beck, I'm so excited I don't know where to put myself.

I pray that you find a job soon, and soon after that a wonderful husband like mine.

All my love,

Liz

If only it hadn't happened now. There was bound to be a major strike. There would be shortages, and Liz would be burdened with a new baby. She would have to send her something each week and would return the two pounds Liz had lent her immediately.

*　　*　　*

120

Half an hour later she was sitting on her bunk staring into space when Janine burst in. 'It's like a war going on in our own backyard.' She sat on the bunk and took Becky's hand. 'I'm that sorry they lost, luv. Try not to worry.'

'Aye.' Becky handed her Liz's letter.

'Phweew! So the bairn's definite. Rotten timing.'

'I got a job today.'

'Well, congratulations! The world's not all bad, then. What is it?'

Becky told her in a dull voice.

'Aw, come on, pet. It doesn't sound very glamorous but it's a start. On a normal day you'd have been over the moon about it. Do they know you can't use a machine?'

'I lied. I had to, Jan. I'm getting nowhere telling the truth. I've watched Liz at work and it looks easy.'

'Brave lass! I'm sure you can do it.'

'Thanks, I'll repeat those words over and over on Monday morning.'

The bell resounded up the stairs. Janine yawned. 'Tea's ready. Let's go down for a little spirited conversation accompanied by tripe and onions.'

As they left the room Janine yawned again. 'I'm bored. There was a dishy fellah at Annie's last night but I looked a mess. I'm going to tart meself up and if he's there tonight I swear I'll nab him. Coming?'

'I'm too tired.'

'All right. Wish me luck.'

A tap on Becky's door woke her and Janine bounded in, beaming. 'I did it! His name's Victor. He's gorgeous! And he's in with the arty crowd. Could open some doors.'

'I'm glad. Goodnight.'

'Aw, spoilsport! Goodnight.'

On Monday morning Becky embarked on her new life, wearing her winter coat over her serge dress, and her old school shoes. High heels weren't allowed while operating the foot treadles.

In any case, she'd mended the strap of her high heels so often it was too tight over her instep.

It would be interesting to work in the old area of the city, near the river and the castle, but there was nothing royal about King Street. Some buildings that had been shops were boarded up, but people still lived in the flats above. Other buildings were larger, some as many as four windows wide, though most had been bricked up before the window tax was repealed in the mid-nineteenth century. Becky remembered that from school. That made the remaining windows incredibly old and dilapidated. Such was the seat of Jacob & Sons.

Girls and women filed through the door. Becky climbed to the second-floor workshop, where Mr Jacob's secretary had told her she would be working. On the landing, she stood against the wall, people milling past her as if she were invisible. She prayed the secretary would appear.

The noise of the women chatting and scraping chairs across the bare wooden floor suddenly changed to the whirr and screech of what sounded like a hundred sewing-machine treadles in motion.

Heavy footsteps thudded up the stairs. Then a voice startled her. 'There you are! You're late. We start at half past seven and tardiness is not tolerated.' The serrated voice came from a tall woman, her face long and rigid, the mouth like a slipped thread in a sack. Her hair was hidden under a canvas cap, washed to the colour of stone, like her face. 'You were supposed to report at the secretary's office for a time card.'

Becky's heart sank. 'I . . . I've been waiting here.'

'Get your card before you leave.' She beckoned with her head. 'I'll set you up. I'm Miss Pratt.'

'How do you do, Miss Pratt.' Becky followed the woman. She wore what looked like army boots. They clattered on the floorboards, outdoing even the noise of the treadles.

'Leave your coat here and get into that cap and overall.' She pointed to rows of hooks holding coats. Only one held a cap and overall, the same as Miss Pratt wore.

Becky's hands shook as she changed into the uniform.

'Make sure you tuck every bit of hair in that cap,' Miss Pratt said. 'It can get caught in the machines, so can loose clothing. We have a good safety record and we mean to keep it that way.' She marched ahead and Becky followed her to an end machine, squeezed against the wall. Relief at being out of view warmed her like cocoa on a cold night.

'You'll be working here.' Miss Pratt pointed to a cardboard box on the floor filled with what looked like cut-out sleeves. 'You're on seams and cuffs. Your daily quota is sixty. The box is filled up regular. She'll get you started.' She nodded to the woman at the next machine. Becky couldn't tell if she was old or young. She had a pale, thin, worn-out look, yet she wasn't wrinkled. Like the building, she looked like a victim of overuse and neglect. She nodded and Becky nodded back.

'You'd better get started if you're going to make your quota,' Miss Pratt said. 'Remember, wages is docked if you don't.' She strode off and Becky pulled out her chair to get off her wobbly legs.

The pale woman said, 'I'm Eileen.' Her voice was small, as if it cost her effort to squeeze it out. It was soothing after Miss Pratt's metallic screech.

'I'm Becky.'

'Nice to meet you, Becky. I'll show you the ropes.' She stood and took a sleeve from Becky's box.

Becky stared in horror at the machine. It was threadless.

Eileen held up the rough brown wool sleeve, a cutting of the same material pinned to the bottom. 'It's quite easy but the material's hard on your hands.'

Becky stared at the threadless sewing machine, the brown sleeve Eileen held out. Panic rose in her throat as thick as dripping. Should she get up and run or try to brazen it out? She heard her voice say, 'There's no thread in the machine.'

'In the drawer, luv.' Eileen pointed to a flat drawer at the front of the machine.

Becky opened it, revealing a row of assorted coloured threads and matching shuttles. She picked out a brown bobbin and dropped it on to the metal post. That much she knew. What next? She sat, rigid.

'Here, luv.' Eileen's soft voice wafted to her. 'I'll do it. Just get up quietly and sit in my chair. If Pratt comes nosing about, there's something wrong with the machine, all right? I'll do the talking.'

Becky squeezed her eyes to keep in the tears and lifted her body from one chair to the other as if it didn't belong to her. Eileen had guessed. How kind of her to help!

'Watch carefully.' She slowly pushed the thread through one obstacle after another towards the needle. 'It's easy, luv. Just be careful you don't miss one. They're in a sort of order. And always thread the needle from left to right.'

Becky, teeth clenched in concentration, began to feel her jaw relax a second before the army boots approached again.

'What's going on here?'

'Just a little problem with the machine, Miss Pratt,' Eileen said. 'I've had the same trouble. I know what to do.'

'I'll get George. That's what he's paid for. You're both getting behind on your quotas.'

Eileen persevered. 'It's all right now. I'm just about to put the shuttle in and test it.'

'Let *her* do that and get on with your own work.'

'Yes, Miss Pratt.'

Again panic seized Becky. She felt like a rabbit in front of the dogs. She wanted to run, but Eileen rose and signalled with a barely perceptible twitch of her head for Becky to return to her own chair. She obeyed and Miss Pratt went off satisfied.

Eileen kept her head down and spoke through the side of her mouth. 'I'm going to take out my shuttle and put it back in, very slowly. Watch me.'

Becky forced herself to concentrate on Eileen's movements as she removed and replaced her shuttle twice.

'Now do yours and I'll watch.'

Despite her still-shaking hands, Becky followed Eileen's example and the shuttle clicked into place. 'Oh, thank you,

you're very kind.' Words weren't enough to express her gratitude.

Eileen's hand slid to her drawer and sidled across to Becky's machine and back, leaving behind another brown-threaded shuttle. 'Use that one when you run out. I'll have to show you another time how to thread it. Start sewing. I'll keep an eye on you.'

Becky inserted the material into the machine, eased it through the feeder and treadled, as she'd seen Liz do.

Perspiration ran down her face, her damp dress clung to her armpits, and already her fingers prickled from handling the rough wool. But she'd finished her first sleeve. She felt Eileen's glance again and gave her a triumphant smile. She could do it.

At midday, a high whistle punctured the din in the workshop. Instantly the machines stopped and the women charged towards the door.

Eileen touched Becky's shoulder. 'Come on, luv. We eat now.'

'I'm not hungry,' Becky said.

'But it's the only chance you get. We make our tea and eat our bait in the basement.'

Becky thought quickly and said, 'I didn't bring any bait. I'm going to eat at a friend's in Queen Street.' She rose, and together they walked to the exit.

'Eey, you're lucky to have a friend nearby. The canteen's a madhouse.' Eileen gave her her soft smile. 'You did well, pet. You've got spunk.'

Letting out a long breath of relief, Becky said, 'I couldn't have got away with it without you. You saved me bacon. Thank you.'

'It's nothing, luv. I'm glad to help. Whenever you're stuck just ask me, but keep your head down while you talk.'

'Aye, I will. Thanks again.'

Outside, Becky walked aimlessly, the events of the morning

jumbling about in her head like tumblers at a circus. It felt good to move. It seemed as if she'd been hunched over a sewing machine all her life.

Why had Liz never complained? But Liz never complained about anything. Becky walked on, head down. The smell of liver and onions wafted from a café. She tightened her stomach. But she could afford a cup of tea. No! She must get her belly used to going from breakfast to tea time.

The usual groups of unemployed men lounged on street corners, their hopeless, worn faces underneath the uniform cloth caps. They were silent and weren't playing marbles. Perhaps the riots had stripped them of the last of their spirit. Dear God! *Don't let Will lose his spirit.*

After five minutes walking, her tight shoulders relaxed somewhat and she turned back. She would sneak in early and do some more sleeves to give to Eileen. She didn't mind missing her own quota on her first day, but she couldn't let Eileen lose money by helping her.

Well, this was her first job, but it certainly wouldn't be her last. Why did those women stay, working killing hours at a boring and hard job? Once she had proved herself a good worker she would have skills, a job history, and a reference. Then she would find something better.

Sixteen

On Christmas Eve Becky sat on Janine's bed rubbing Vaseline into her rough, red hands. 'I can't believe Victor didn't invite you over Christmas, or even *ask* what you were doing.'

Janine stood and stretched. 'I'm not exactly the nice Jewish girl he'd want to take home to Momma. And that's that! We're going to have a lousy Christmas. Let's make the most of it. I'll put the kettle on for tea, and we've got two mince pies left.'

Becky put down the Vaseline and continued rubbing her sore hands. 'But I don't understand about Victor.'

Janine retrieved the hot-water bottle from the suitcase and hid it under her cardigan. 'You know he never tells anyone his business.' She removed her coat from the bottom of the door, where it served as a draft stopper, and went to the bathroom.

When she returned, Becky sat chewing what was left of her fingernails. 'What a flaming awful Christmas!' she said. 'The man *you* love deserts you and the only person *I've* ever loved is six months in the pudding club and tied for life to poverty. Happy Christmas to one and all!'

'Aw, it's not that bad. Liz is coming to see you after New Year and I'll see Victor after Christmas.'

'But it's Christmas *now*, and I've got two days off from that bloody sweatshop. I want to enjoy meself. Why don't we go to that pub where you and Victor go with his arty friends? You know everyone. We'll tart ourselves up. I bothered to make us new dresses for the holidays and all they're doing is hanging on the wall.'

Janine dropped the full water bottle back into the suitcase

127

and slammed the lid. 'You have a point. Why should I bury meself alive at Christmas because Victor doesn't believe in it? Let's go out and have a good time.'

Becky's eyes brightened. 'You mean it? I don't think I know what a good time is.'

Seeming embarrassed, Janine lowered her gaze. 'There's just one thing, Beck. You know Victor's friends are artists and poets and writers and actors and hangers-on and all that, but you might be shocked. I mean, they're not like that milk lad you went out with.'

'I promise, I won't be shocked. It'll be the start of me education. And it's only for one night anyway. I'll be too bloody tired to go out at night when I'm working again.' The plea in Becky's voice surprised her. She *would* go mad if she didn't go out and have some fun.

Janine looked serious. 'All right! You'll get a chance to put on your best voice around Victor's friends. And stick beside me or you could get into hot water.'

'Oooh, I'd love to practise my pronunciation, *and* to soak in hot water.'

'And why not do both? It's Christmas Eve.' Janine looked dangerously determined. 'I'll light the pilot and we can have a sneaky bath together. Then I'll see if my talents with make-up stretch to passing you off as eighteen.'

At the top of the staircase to the cellar at the Barley Inn, Becky peered down in amazement through the smoke haze at a carpet of people's heads.

As she followed Janine to the bar, a voice rang out, 'Hey, Janine. Out on the town without Victor? Come and give us a kiss, then.'

Janine dug her elbow into Becky's ribs. 'Come on.'

Becky felt embarrassed in her old school coat. She slipped it off and folded it over her arm. She'd never seen so many fashionably dressed people in one place, though some looked like typical starving artists. She was proud of the red wool dress she'd made from a second-hand one bought at Paddy's

Market on the Quayside, and prayed that her now dangerously frayed beige shoe strap would last the night.

A large red-headed man, the lower two-thirds of his face hidden by hair, engulfed Janine in his huge arms. Her face disappeared into his red undergrowth.

'Pheew, Ronny, your breath smells like a pig's trough,' she said when he finally let her go. 'How long have you been here?'

'Since opening time, my love. You should get started, and your little friend. What'll you have?'

Janine drew Becky to her. 'This is Becky. She's a dress designer, and we'll both have a gin and orange, please. All right, Becky?'

Becky squirmed.

When Ronny handed them the drinks, Janine swivelled her head towards Becky's ear, as if adjusting her hair, and whispered, 'Drink it slowly.'

For a moment the smell of gin in her glass made Becky feel sick. She'd always vowed she would never touch gin. What if she grew to like it as much as Ma and Dora?

A medley of people greeted Janine warmly. 'Hello, angel! Who's your lovely friend, and where's your lovely Victor?' A foppishly dressed young man scrutinized them through bleary eyes.

'My lovely friend is Becky,' Janine said, 'and my lovely Victor is spending Christmas with Mummy and Daddy, so I'm available tonight.'

'Whatcheor!' One of the men shouted in a broad Geordie accent. He put his arm round Becky's shoulders. 'Stick with me, my lovely, and I'll give you something to remember me by.'

An educated voice from behind said, 'Stay clear of Stan, sweetheart, or you'll be stuck with his souvenir for life.'

'Hello, Andrew,' Janine said. 'Don't worry. I wouldn't let any friend of mine near Stan.'

He flicked back the forelock of silky black hair that hung straight, almost covering one eye, and said to Becky, 'Don't let Janine's friends influence you. They're a rotten lot.'

Becky smiled, but her knees knocked. Tall, slim, and wearing an expensive-looking tweed suit, he was one of the few men who appeared neither flashy nor destitute. He surveyed her through amused blue eyes, his parted lips showing neat white teeth.

'Janine's already warned me about her friends,' she heard herself say.

'Then take heed. But that doesn't include me, of course.'

'Hey, Andrew,' a man's voice hailed from the rear of the crowd and Andrew bowed and disappeared.

Janine took Becky's hand. 'Come on, you look as if you'd just seen God the Almighty.'

'Who's Andrew?' she whispered.

'Oh, for heaven's sake, don't fall for him. He's not in our league. He's polite, but posh and uppity. He's an artist. That's how he knows this lot. But he keeps himself to himself.'

'He's *georgeous*.' Becky let Janine lead her across the room, though she kept her eyes on Andrew, talking and laughing with a group of young men, though now a stunning girl had joined them. Her long red hair was coiled on top of her head and secured with what looked like diamond clips, her shoulders swathed in a fur wrap, and her slim waist and hips wrapped in a clinging black-sequinned dress. She held a cigarette in a long silver holder.

Becky sighed in despair. Andrew was by far the most handsome man in the group. This must be his girlfriend.

'Another gin and orange, luv? I take it there's gin in there. I'm Jake. I saw you come in with Janine.' His round, pink face smiled a kind, wholesome, and completely uninteresting smile.

Becky tore her gaze from Andrew. 'No thank you, I'm still busy with this one.'

He squeezed his way towards her. 'How do you know our Janine then?'

'We're at the same lodgings.'

'I'll smack her hands and face for not bringing you before. We always welcome another pretty face.'

'I don't have much time for going out at night.'

'Is that when you do your dress designing?'

Becky remembered Janine's remark about her being a dress designer. He must have heard. Her face burned. 'Janine exaggerates. It'll be a long time before I get anywhere.' She sipped her drink. 'What do you do?'

He pushed the fair, pink-tinged lock off his forehead with a pink, freckled hand. His skin, his hair, his eyebrows and lashes were all tinged pink. 'I write poetry and stuff.'

'Really!' she said, amazed that this simple, peasant-faced, stocky lad was a poet.

He chuckled. 'You sound surprised.'

She looked at the floor before she could face him again. 'It's just that I think of poets as being thin and pale with deep shadows under their eyes from working in garrets by candlelight. You look too healthy.'

This time he threw back his head and laughed, revealing slightly crooked but startlingly white teeth. 'You've been reading too many romance novels. I write those an' all. And articles and short stories. Anything I can make a bob on. Poetry's me main love, but I couldn't live on it. I'm working on a novel now, hopefully to earn enough for rent and food for a year so I can concentrate on poetry.'

'Wouldn't it be nice if we didn't have to worry about rent and food,' Becky said with feeling.

His grey eyes studied her. 'Aye, I'm sure being a designer's pretty much like being a writer or painter.'

'I told you Janine exaggerates. I work at a garment factory and in my spare time I make clothes for Janine and meself. But, when I have enough money, I intend to start me own business.' She realized she'd slipped into Geordie. It was because she was speaking to another Geordie. But he didn't bother to hide his accent, so what did it matter?

His grey eyes appraised her. 'I take me hat off to you, Becky. Most people here try to blow up their achievements.'

'You're from Newcastle?'

'Oh aye, I was brought up in St Joseph's Orphanage till I was fourteen and then I was out on me own.'

131

Becky felt a sudden surge of empathy for Jake. He'd had no home or family at all. That must be even worse than having a family like hers. At least she'd had Liz. 'You must have worked hard to get where you are,' she said.

'Where I am?' He took a swig of his pint and gave her a rueful smile. 'It's not exactly where I want to be, but I'll get there.'

'Last call,' the barman yelled and everyone booed.

Becky couldn't believe the evening had gone so quickly. While involved in her conversation with Jake, she'd had to take her eyes off Andrew. Now she looked at the corner where he'd been. He'd gone. She searched the room. It was hopeless to find anyone in this crowd.

Janine put her arm through hers. 'Hello, luv. Let's go now before the stampede to the bar for last call.'

'Stan's having a party at his place after,' Jake said.

Janine laughed. 'It's one thing to have a drink at the pub, but Victor would have me guts for garters if I went to one of Stan's parties on me tod.'

Becky felt relieved, and disappointed. Andrew might be at the party. But she was exhausted, and didn't feel up to more social chit-chat tonight. She'd like to be on better form when she met him again.

'Jake's smitten with you,' Janine said as they walked home, huddled against the damp chill.

'Oh, he just talked to me because nobody else did.'

'Rubbish! It's written all over him.'

'He's nice, but he's like an overstuffed saveloy sausage. I *am* smitten with Andrew though. He's gorgeous.'

'And dangerous. Didn't you notice the huge *KEEP OFF* sign written all over him?'

They reached the house and tiptoed up the stairs, but Becky stopped and tugged at Janine's coat. 'Sshh.'

A stifled cry came from Mildred's room. There was no light under the door.

'There is something wrong with Mildred,' Becky whispered.

She tapped lightly on the door and was greeted by another sound like the first. She went in and switched on the light. 'Mildred, are you— Oh, my God!' Mildred lay on the bed in a white nightdress on a pile of blood-soaked newspapers. She'd thrown the top sheet and blankets to the floor, no doubt to avoid soiling them, and clutched the pillow to her bosom and over her face.

'God Almighty! Stay with her,' Janine ordered. 'I'm going to telephone for an ambulance. Raise her legs and keep them up.' She tiptoed out.

It was difficult to keep Mildred's legs raised as she tossed, wracked with pain. Becky had never seen anything so terrible, so much blood. Mildred must be dying.

By the time the ambulance arrived Becky was exhausted from the effort of supporting Mildred. Two men bearing a stretcher set it down by the bed, rolled her in a white sheet, then laid her on the stretcher and covered her with a red blanket. 'Another one fresh from the slaughter,' one of them said with disgust as they raised the stretcher and miraculously manoeuvred it round the landing and down the stairs with hardly a sound.

'I told them to be quick and quiet or the girl would be thrown out of her lodgings,' Janine said.

'What's wrong with her? One of them seemed angry.'

'Aye, but not necessarily at poor Mildred. They have too many cases like that.'

'Like what?' Becky put her hands to her face. 'Oh no! Mildred was having an abortion?'

'More like Mildred had *had* the abortion, luv, or rather a botch job. She's haemorrhaging badly.'

'Mildred?' Becky said in disbelief.

'Never mind that now. We'd better clean up this mess before Dunners sees it. We'll tell her tomorrow Mildred's in hospital with appendicitis. Take off your shoes and keep quiet.'

Afterwards, slumped on Janine's bed, they waited for the kettle to boil.

'I can't believe it,' Becky said. 'Anyone but Mildred!'

'Aye, it's often the quiet ones.' Janine let out a bitter laugh. 'It's the likes of me that people think do it all over the place, not little Miss Butter-Wouldn't-Melt-in-the-Mouth.'

'I wish we knew who she went to,' Becky said.

'Why?'

'Because he must have done something terribly wrong. Can't doctors be reported for – what's it called – bad practice?'

'Beck! You're nuts. Do you honestly think Mildred would let you report it? And even if she did, what good would it do? There's always plenty of dirty doctors and backstreet women, and plenty of business for them.' She paused and lit a cigarette with shaking hands, a treat she rarely allowed herself except when out socializing. 'Anyway, she might have done it herself.'

'Herself!' Becky's voice rose to a squeak. 'How?'

Janine exhaled loudly. 'It's easy, hen – a knitting needle or other long sharp object. Women do it all the time.'

'Oh, how terrible!' Becky was stunned. The kettle steamed and, in a daze, she made the tea.

'Aye, it's always the woman who gets it in the neck.' Janine made a face. 'Well, not exactly in the neck. The men, of course, get off scot free.'

Becky handed Janine her mug and sat again on the bed, curling her legs under her.

'Where did they take her?'

'The General Hospital, not far up the road.'

'I'll go to see her tomorrow.'

'Just one thing, luv. Don't let on that you're shocked or surprised. That's the last thing she needs.'

'Oh, I wouldn't. I'm really sorry for her. I can't believe we didn't wake the Dunns.'

'Nah, he sleeps like the dead and she's taking sedatives for her cold.'

'Eileen's expecting me at twelve o'clock for Christmas dinner. I'll go to see Mildred afterwards.'

'I have to go home or I'd come. Give her my love if you see her.'

They uncurled themselves and stood. Janine put her arms round Becky and squeezed her. 'Happy Christmas, luv.'

'Oh, aye, you an' all.' Becky grimaced and got as far as the door before she turned. 'Does that Andrew go to the pub all the time?'

Janine gave her a warning look. 'Nope! That's the first time I've seen him for ages. He diddles off here, there, and everywhere. He's a regular mystery man, *and* he acts superior. Forget about him.'

Becky shrugged. 'If you say so.'

Seventeen

At breakfast the next morning Janine said that Mildred was in hospital with appendicitis.

'Dear Lord! Poor Mildred!' Mrs Dunn, frying sausages, waved her fork in consternation, though she regained enough presence of mind to remove one sausage – presumably Mildred's – from the pan and return it to the larder. 'Fancy, and me not knowing a thing about it. I'll go to see her.'

Janine quickly put in, 'Mildred asked the hospital to let her family know, and visitors are limited to two. But we'll telephone every day.'

Becky sat open-mouthed at the table, as always amazed by Janine's ingenuity. Of course, Mildred would be in a gynaecological ward! Eating her sausage and baked beans, she mulled over her day. She must finish embroidering the baby's nightgown. The dress she'd made for Liz was already wrapped in Christmas paper. Her stomach fluttered like a cage full of canaries at the thought of seeing them tomorrow. She would telephone the hospital on her way to Eileen's.

In the telephone box she placed a precious penny in the slot and dialled the hospital. A brisk voice informed her that the patient was doing as well as could be expected, but was sedated and unable to see visitors.

Becky walked on, her coat pockets bulging with seven mesh bags of gold-wrapped chocolate coins for the children and a bar of Cadbury's chocolate each for Eileen and her mother.

Though they had become good friends, they didn't usually see each other outside of work. With seven children, Eileen had neither time nor energy for a social life. Her ageing mother helped during the day but Eileen took over when she got home. She and her husband were separated, Becky knew that much. Otherwise, Eileen didn't discuss her private life.

As she reached Blackfriars, originally a monastery, but now slum dwellings, a door opened and Eileen shouted, 'Becky! Merry Christmas!'

Becky started like a nervous horse. 'Oh, Merry Christmas, Eileen. You made me jump.'

'Come on in, luv.'

Becky entered the low doorway, followed Eileen down a stone-flagged passage and turned into the kitchen at the rear. Despite the pleasant cooking aromas, there was a strong smell of mould.

'Here we are then. Ma, this is me friend Becky.'

Ma munched on her gums and gaped a smile. 'Merry Christmas, lass.'

'Now you bairns,' Eileen said to the seven excited faces. 'This is Becky. Say Merry Christmas then go next door till the dinner's ready.' She explained to Becky. 'I put the fire on in the bedroom so they'd have more room to play today. It's a rare treat for Ma and me.'

The children, ranging from two to ten years, yelled Merry Christmas, and looked at Becky with increased excitement as she emptied her pockets.

When the children had filed out with their treasures, Becky presented Eileen and her mother with their bars of chocolate.

'Eeh, we've got nothing for *you*,' Eileen said.

'You've got Christmas dinner for me, haven't you? I'd be sitting in me room but for you.'

Eileen's mother took Becky's coat. 'You two have a natter and I'll peel the spuds.' She shuffled into a tiny pantry.

Eileen sank into one of the fireside chairs and indicated the other to Becky. 'Your dress looks nice.'

'Thank you. Aren't you even going to take off your apron today?' Eileen wore a sacking apron over her work frock.

'Ha! That's a joke. Christmas day's a working day for me.'

Now that the room was empty of children, Becky saw that it contained only a scrubbed table and chairs and the usual two stuffed fireside chairs. Against the outside wall, rising damp spread dark stains over the clean whitewash.

She sat opposite Eileen. 'You won't believe I actually went out last night, to the pub with Janine, and a lad took a fancy to me.'

'Eey, that's grand! Are you seeing him again?'

Becky wrinkled her nose. 'Nah, I liked him, but he's all pink and freckly. There *was* one who made me knees knock though, but that fish got away.'

'At least you got out of that garret for a change.'

'Aye, but getting home was awful.' Becky explained about Mildred.

Eileen's face turned the colour of the whitewashed walls. It was some time before she spoke. 'Poor lass! She was right lucky you found her. She'd have died. I nearly did.'

'I, I'm sorry. I didn't know.'

'How could you? Only me ma and me know, not even me husband. I don't usually blab about me private affairs, especially at work. I've got seven bairns, Beck, but I had three miscarriages an' all, and a fourth just last year, after one of Fred's social calls.' She pushed a stray lock of hair from her strained face.

Becky felt a surge of sadness, mixed with surprise. 'I'm so sorry. I had no idea. I thought you were free of him.'

'Hinny, once you marry a man, you're his for life, unless you can afford a fancy divorce.'

'It's not fair! People with money can get divorced and they can afford those *things*, you know . . .' Becky felt too embarrassed to go on.

'Aye, he *could* buy those at the chemist, but it would mean one less pint of beer, wouldn't it? Anyway, he's usually too far gone to use them.'

Becky's voice grew heated as her anger increased. 'You wouldn't be in this state if you'd had any control over your *own* body.'

'Hey, luv, calm yourself. I'm sorry I've upset you.'

'You haven't upset me,' Becky said. 'You've just made me all the more determined not to fall into the trap of letting a man own me.'

'Good for you, then.' Eileen rose. 'I'd better help Ma with those spuds or we'll be having Christmas dinner for tea.'

Becky still felt angry as she sat in the waiting room at the General Hospital. Eileen's story flapped around in her head like a bat after its prey.

'You can go in now,' said a starched white nurse from the gynaecological ward. Everyone rose.

Becky meandered down the aisle, between the two rows of narrow beds covered with grey blankets. Some women were raised, others lying, staring at the ceiling or groaning with pain. A sickening smell of illness and antiseptic suffused the ward.

In an end bed Mildred lay staring at the ceiling, her face almost transparent. A tube dripped blood into her arm from a bottle attached to a stand. Becky had read in a newspaper article that during the war they had refrigerated blood to make it more available for transfusion. So, just a few years ago, the hospital might not have had enough blood and Mildred would have died.

'Hello, how are you feeling?' She stood awkwardly at the bedside.

'Oh, Becky!' Mildred burst into tears, then sniffed them back. 'I . . . I'm so ashamed. Thank you for what you did, and thank you for coming.'

'It was nothing you wouldn't do for me. And it was Janine who told me what to do. She's coming to see you tomorrow.'

'I suppose Mrs Dunn's packed my belongings?'

Becky managed a smile. 'Mrs Dunn was zonked out on sedatives and didn't know a thing till this morning. You've got appendicitis *and only family visitors are allowed.*'

'Oh, wonderful! I bet that was Janine's idea.'

'Good guess. And your room's all clean and ready when you are.'

Mildred's lower lip quivered. 'I can't believe how kind you both are to me.'

'Rubbish!'

'Would you . . .' Mildred plucked at the sheet. 'Would you make a telephone call for me?'

'Of course.'

'The number's in the book. It's St Peter's Church Vicarage, Reverend Pringle. Just say I have flu. He'd better get Mrs Joyce to clean the house.' Obviously trying not to cry, she sounded as if she had hiccups.

'I'll telephone on the way home. What about work?'

'I'm not due back until Monday.'

'Is there anyone else?' Becky knew there was some problem with her family.

Mildred shook her head. 'No, just Reverend Pringle, and . . . tell him I'm sorry.' Tears squeezed through her eyelids and disappeared into her hair.

Becky clasped the hand without the drip. 'Sshh, Mildred, it's over.'

'It'll never be over. I'm a mess. I can never have children.' She wept openly now.

'What's wrong here?' One of the starched white uniforms approached the bed.

'She's just a bit upset,' Becky said.

'Aye, she has a right to be.' She turned to Mildred. 'You still won't tell us anything?'

Mildred stopped crying, sealed her face and shook her head.

The nurse shrugged. 'Have it your own way.' She marched back down the ward, calling, 'Time, visitors, time.'

Becky stood and put a hand on Mildred's shoulder. 'It'll get over. Everything does.'

Mildred gave an unconvincing nod. 'Could you let me know what Reverend Pringle says?'

'Of course. Now you rest.' Becky left, puzzled. Mildred was concerned only about this vicar. Why should she want to know what he says to a simple message that she's got flu? And why should she say she's sorry? Could it be? She spent most of her free time at church. Oh well, that was Mildred's business.

When she reached home, she was overflowing with an emotion she didn't understand. Anger? Yes! But not aimed at any one person. It was the same frustrated, helpless anger she'd always felt about her own life and the unfair power Dora and Ma had over her. Yet it was different. This was a general sort of anger at the way things were for women. She could not accept that the law allowed men to act like pollinators and flutter away as free as butterflies after they'd had their fun.

Eighteen

One day in March Becky returned to work early from her midday break, her head huddled into her overcoat collar and her hands in her pockets. She'd read the headlines at the newspaper stand and was confused and worried. She needed to sit down and it would be warm in the canteen. Eileen would have finished her sandwich by now. Becky still pretended she ate with a friend.

Eileen gave her a close look as she dumped herself into an empty chair beside her. 'You all right?'

'I was before I read the headlines. Now I'm worried. The government's just raised the price of domestic and export coal *again*. Can you believe it? It's barely two weeks since they fobbed off the miners with a puny wage increase. Will got two shillings extra a shift because he's eighteen and the younger ones even less. What good will that do now that the bosses have whacked up coal prices? Coal affects the cost of *everything*. We'll all suffer, not just the miners.'

'Aye, pet, just when you think things can't get any worse, they do. We'll have to tighten our belts a bit more.'

Becky snorted with anger. 'If we tighten them any more, we'll split in two.'

On returning from work the following month, Becky grabbed the familiar letter from the hall table. Upstairs she tore it open. Liz had given birth to a healthy baby girl, Mary Rebecca. Tears ran down Becky's face – Liz had named the baby after her. A shower of joy and relief flowed over her. They were both all right.

Reading on, her spirits plunged. The owners were pressing for further pay cuts. There'd be a strike.

Janine banged on the door, invaded the room and flung herself on the bed. 'Old pie face told me not to bother to come in tomorrow.'

Becky's jaw dropped. 'You've got the sack?'

'Nah, but that'll be next. Women can't spend money at the hairdressers like they did.'

'Oh, Jan, I'll help you. I can cut out every treat – no pictures, no cups of tea, no biscuits or anything. I could manage a couple of bob a week.'

Janine expelled a puff of air, as if about to laugh, then her face turned serious. 'Thank you, luv, but don't deny yourself yet. We're going to the pictures tonight to obliterate me misery. And I'm spending tomorrow and every day off Madame gives me after that looking for another job.'

Mildred tapped on the door and opened it. They'd become friends since the barriers between them had been broken, though she'd never satisfied their unspoken curiosity about her lover. 'Mind if I join you?'

Janine made room on the bed. 'Come in. It's not altogether a happy party though.'

'The good news is that Liz has had a baby girl, Mary Rebecca,' Becky said.

'Splendid! And the bad news?'

Janine pulled a face. 'I'm on the verge of joining the unemployed masses.'

Mildred's brown eyes opened wide like a deer's. 'Oh, no, Jan! I'm sorry.' She fingered her blouse collar and held out the gold-and-sapphire pin she wore every day. It had been her grandmother's and was the only piece of jewellery she possessed. 'Here, you can pawn this to tide you over till you find something.'

'Don't be daft,' Janine said.

'I mean it. Don't argue.' Mildred's usually gentle voice sounded like an auctioneer's. 'Ask fifteen pounds and you'll get twelve from the pawn shop in Pink Lane.'

Janine's eyes suddenly looked moist. 'You're barmy,' she said. 'It's worth a fortune more than twelve pounds. It'd take me a lifetime to pay you back. But it's wonderful of you to offer.'

'I got twelve pounds for it last time.'

They stared at her in surprise.

'I needed money for . . .' A crimson flush crawled up Mildred's face. 'But my friend redeemed it when he found out. The stones aren't very clear. It isn't worth a lot. Please, Janine, you and Becky helped me, probably saved my life. I'd like to do something for you.'

'It would be nice to have some money to fall back on in an emergency, Jan,' Becky said.

Janine's confused expression cleared and her eyes brightened. 'Aye, that's right. I'm not sacked yet, but if it happens and I'm desperate, I promise I'll take you up on it, Mildred.' Then tears filmed her eyes. 'You're both too bloody kind to me. Beck's offered to give up breathing to help me out. But I've always got me ever-loving Victor to protect me, haven't I?'

Becky wondered. She'd met Victor only once. He was charming, but didn't seem responsible enough to look after any woman.

When Janine and Mildred had left, Becky picked up the letter again. She reread the end, which she'd skimmed earlier:

> Will's really down, though I know he's happy about the baby. He looks like a man with a load on his back. There's still talk about cutbacks and short time.
>
> Dora's been unusually nice to me, though she hasn't lifted a finger to help. She actually said I was lucky to have such a grand husband. Though she's not thrilled about the baby. Sometimes she looks at her as if she's a piece of snot. She pretended to gag yesterday while I was feeding her. Then she gave me one of her triumphant smiles. You know the kind, when she's won a battle. As if she's cleverer than me because

she's not lumbered with a bairn and I'm stupid for falling pregnant.

Anyway, Ma coos over little Mary and seems to love her, and Will's mother adores her, though she hasn't the energy to help much.

Why was Dora being nice to Liz? That triumphant smile that Becky knew so well worried her. It *could* be simply that she's glad she's not the one with the baby. Or it could be something else. Surely she hadn't got her clutches into Will?

She'd read in the *Women's Weekly* problem page that men were vulnerable to other women when their wives were pregnant. If Will was depressed about work and Dora took him into her arms with words of comfort, he might be swayed by her.

Becky banished the thought. Tomorrow she would start looking for another job. As an experienced worker, she could do better than Jacob & Sons. It was time she started saving seriously. Liz or Janine might need her help, and if they didn't, her savings would go towards her future business.

A month later Becky received another letter from Liz:

Dearest Beck,

I didn't want to tell you but I need to because I can't keep it in and I can't tell anyone else. Will and I had a terrible row, but it's all right now. He's been in a bad way since the baby came, hardly talking to me, hardly looking at me, and he never touched me. Not even a goodnight kiss.

The other night I couldn't take it any longer. I leaned over in bed to kiss him goodnight and he turned away. I burst into tears, and *he* did, just like a baby. We held each other until we'd cried ourselves out and then he told me. He'd had to stay away from me because he'd felt too dirty and too ashamed to touch me.

When he came home from wetting the baby's head the night Mary was born, Dora was waiting downstairs, starkers under her dressing gown. The bitch knew he'd be drunk after celebrating with the lads and it would be easy to cop him.

Anyhow, he fell for her bait. But he's cursed himself ever since. Oh, if you knew how tortured he was, you'd forgive him, just as I have. When we stopped crying we made love, the first time since the baby. It was heaven to be together again.

I'm so glad it's over, and I can't hold a grudge against Will, just as I hope you won't. He's his wonderful loving self again, and we're as happy as before.

Now I know why Dora was so nice to me just after the baby – gloating over her victory. I'm such a daft bugger, I should have guessed. Will told her he'd confessed and that I'd forgiven him because I knew he wouldn't have gone near her sober. I wish I could have seen her face when he said that. She'd tried more than once, but he only gave in the time he was drunk, so that tells her plenty. Now she knows she could never cause a rift between Will and me. She doesn't speak to me except about her meals and washing and things, but that suits me. Me life with me lovely baby and husband is wonderful, even though Ma's as grumpy as ever.

I'm bringing Mary to see her auntie next month. I'll come when Will's got a day off and we can escape to visit his *friends*. Ma and Dora's never found out we go our different ways at the bus station.

Will sends his love. Please forgive him as I have.

Your loving sis,

Liz

Boiling lava bubbled in Becky's head as she folded the letter. She'd like to put her hands round Dora's neck and— What was the point? She'd always known it was a matter of time before Dora made a play for Will. Thank heavens it was over.

Nineteen

In July Becky started a new job with Harold Walker & Sons, Gentlemen's Tailors, at 12 Bigg Market. She couldn't believe her luck. While buying bruised pears for tuppence a bag at the market at closing time, she saw a man placing a notice in a tailor's window. 'Seamstress required.' She hammered on the locked door and a startled elderly man opened it.

'I'd like the job, sir.'

He gave her a quizzical look. 'Wouldn't you like to know something about it first?'

'It can only be better than what I'm doing now, sir.'

His face relaxed into a smile and he opened the door. 'Come in, Miss . . . ?'

'Becky Ryan, sir.'

He led her down a passage to a large workshop. Three sewing machines stood in a row between two large cutting tables; several dummies stood around like silent overseers, and at least a hundred bales of material covered the shelved walls. The man entered a small office partitioned off in one corner and sat at a littered desk. He nodded towards the leather-covered chair opposite. Becky sat and placed the soggy paper bag of bruised pears on her lap.

'Well, well!' A suggestion of a smile glinted in his blue eyes. 'You waste no time, Miss Ryan.'

A cool feeling spread over Becky's lap as pear juice oozed through the paper to her thighs. She spread her hands under the bag to trap the sticky mess and smiled nervously.

He rested his elbows on a mountain of papers on the desk and laced his fingers. 'I need someone experienced in men's

147

tailoring. I've lost two seamstresses, one forced to retire with arthritis and the other about to marry a man from Sunderland. I'm replacing them with only one for the moment, as business isn't up to par.' He smiled. 'What is, these days?'

'I have experience, sir. I can cope with all the work you want.' Becky poured out her history with only slight embellishment.

He rose to indicate the interview was over. 'I shall telephone your employer regarding your references. Call in for confirmation at this time tomorrow and, all being well, you can hand in your notice and start next week.'

'Thank you, sir.' Becky prayed as she grasped the soggy bottom of the bag before she stood, but God didn't hear her. Mushy brown pears plopped to the floor with moist thuds and oozed over the grey linoleum. Her stomach felt as if it had also fallen to the floor. 'Oh, I'm so sorry, sir.' She bent to wipe up the mess with what was left of the paper bag, but he gave her a newspaper from his desk.

When she'd finished he handed her sixpence from his pocket. 'Buy some fresh pears on the way home.'

'That's kind of you, sir, but it's all right.' Tension plaited every muscle in her body into tight cords.

He smiled encouragement. 'That fruit seller's a rogue. He bags the rotten fruit at the end of the day, and places a couple of only slightly bruised ones on top. It would give me pleasure to replace them.'

'Then thank you, sir. You're very kind.'

She accepted the sixpence and walked home, oblivious to the motors and trams honking at her. A kind boss! And nineteen and six a week! Her references should be good. Even Miss Pratt had praised her work.

The months ran as fast as a ladder in a stocking. By October 1920 Becky felt as if she'd always worked at Harold Walker & Sons, and that she'd known her workmate, Norma, all her life.

Occasionally Mr Walker joined them for tea during the

midday break. Becky was surprised one day to find herself confiding her secret desire to become a dress designer.

He raised his eyebrows. 'That's quite an ambition!'

She felt herself blush. 'It's nothing, sir. I've done it since I was little.'

'And how do you intend to make it a career?'

Becky warmed to his question. 'I've already started, in a small way, sir. I design and make clothes at home for my friends, and I get other recommendations that way. It keeps me busy.'

'Aye, she hardly sleeps,' Norma said. 'Work, work, work! She goes to Paddy's Market on Sundays to buy second-hand clothes to cut up, and even *reads* to better herself. She never goes out to have a good time.'

Becky blushed. 'I only buy the best quality ladies' gowns, sir, and take them apart for the material. The new styles are so much shorter and skimpier, there's often enough left over to make matching handbags and hats.' She glowered at Norma for mentioning her reading. 'And I *have* to read, sir, to learn proper English, and I listen to me friend, who talks nicely. If I want rich clients, I have to sound as good as they are.'

Mr Walker put his cup on the paraffin stove. He'd bought a stove for each room, as coal prices had risen again. He gave Becky a look of mixed admiration and sadness. 'So, you do the same thing in your spare time as you do all day?'

'Not quite the same, sir. I sew by hand. It's slower, of course, but one day I'm going to buy a second-hand machine.'

Mr Walker leaned back in his chair until it creaked danger-ously. He fingered his chin. 'My third machine is lying idle, Becky. If you wish, you may borrow it until business looks up – and the chair.'

Had he taken her remarks as a hint? In her embarrassment, Becky kneaded her overall as if making pastry. 'Oh, I . . . I couldn't, sir—'

'Why not? I'll have it delivered for you. You work hard and deserve a rise, but business won't allow it just now. Think of the loan as a bonus.'

Her mind raced like a greyhound round a track. Now that Janine had moved in with Victor and she, Becky, had the larger room, she could squeeze in the machine. But what about Dunners? Already she complained about the doorknocker going constantly. But Becky's old room remained empty after nine months. Many people were so broke they slept in the streets. Dunners couldn't afford to lose another tenant. Becky raised her eyes to Mr Walker, who was looking expectantly at her.

'You don't wish to accept it?'

'Oh, yes, sir. I can't thank you enough.' She wanted to fling her arms round him and kiss him, but instead gave him a grateful smile.

'Splendid! Let me know when to order a cart.' He pulled out his pocket watch. 'Back to work,' he said, smiling, then paused. 'If there are any offcuts and scraps suitable for handbags and hats, please take them.'

'Thank you, sir.' Mr Walker used only the best flannels, tweeds and gaberdines, and the suit linings were quality silks and satins. Becky almost danced back to her machine.

While the driver and his mate were loading the sewing machine on to the cart, Becky saw a tall young man picking up a bag of bruised pears from the stall she'd learned to avoid. He seemed familiar. The student with the books! 'That fruit's always rotten at the bottom,' she said. 'Try the next stall.'

'Oh, er, thanks.' He stared at her and she grew bold.

'We've met before. I sent your library books flying.'

He peered more closely through his glasses. 'Oh, yes. A long time ago. My name's Paul.'

'I never forget faces. Mine's Becky. Just remember, that man's a rogue.'

'Thanks for the tip.'

The men were ready and waiting for her. She didn't want the young man to see her riding on a cart. 'I must rush now,' she said and dodged into the crowd, her heart pounding. How ridiculous to have a schoolgirl crush on a stranger!

She clattered her way home beside the driver, his mate clutching the rope that tied down the sewing machine and chair. At the door they helped her down, unloaded the machine and manoeuvred it up the narrow flight.

Mrs Dunn policed the operation from the hallway, arms folded, face grim. 'And don't you damage the paintwork or you'll pay for it to be redone.' Her face turned purple as they laid the machine on its side to squeeze it around the first landing. 'Watch out now!'

Around the corner and out of hearing, one of the men said, 'I know what I'd do if that was *my* missus.'

'I'd bloody well put her over me knee and let her have it,' the other said.

Becky giggled at the vision.

As she'd hoped, the machine fitted into the corner, leaving enough floor space to cut out the garments. The men tipped their caps and made for the door. 'Oh, please . . .' Becky opened her handbag.

'Nah, hinny,' the older one said. 'Your boss tipped us.'

Becky's eyes filled. If only she could repay Mr Walker for his kindness!

The tailor's dummy stood beside the machine. She'd bought it at the Quayside for sixpence, restuffed it and covered it in flesh-coloured cotton. It looked almost new.

She sat on the bed and gazed at the work area she'd created – the row of hooks on the wall to hang garments, the fruit crates she'd bought for a penny each from the errand boy at the market. She'd covered them inside and out with brown paper and stacked them to form shelves for work in progress. Now, with the sewing machine, it looked almost like a professional workshop.

As all her business was by recommendation, people didn't seem to mind climbing the stairs to the shabby little room. Janine and Norma always explained to prospective clients that Becky kept her overheads low to keep her prices affordable. And they didn't mention that her quality materials came from second-hand gowns. These she washed and ironed before taking them apart and cutting them into dress lengths. The clients chose from small swatches she cut and stuck in her sample book. Garments waiting to be unpicked she stored in boxes under her bed. It wasn't exactly deceit, she told herself. The customers never enquired where the materials came from.

After a meal of ham-and-pea soup, with the usual sliver of bread, Becky wrote a quick note to Liz and began her sewing. She was transforming an old wedding gown into an evening dress. From the now daringly low neckline held up only by two thin straps, layers of gossamer georgette floated to the knee over a satin sheath, a matching satin bow attached to the lower back. She was sure she would get requests for copies of this one. Humming with pleasure, she threaded the machine. She could finish the dress this evening and start on the black silk jersey waiting to be cut out.

A light tap, and the door jerked opened. Becky turned.

Janine stood in the doorway, staring at the sewing machine. 'Hey, have you won on the horses?'

'Mr Walker's lent it to me until business gets better.'

Janine hung her coat behind the door and sank on to the bed. She wore a blue wool day dress Becky had made for her, her hair a black satin halo round her face. Despite her glum expression, she looked stunning.

Becky sat beside her. 'What's wrong?'

'Nothing I can prove, but I swear that bugger's been at it again.'

Becky took Janine's hand. 'Oh, no!' When she'd lost her job and spent the money the pawnshop paid for Mildred's pin, Janine had been ecstatic when Victor let her move in with him.

But Becky's first fear that he wouldn't want to be responsible for a clinging vine had been right. He used Janine as a free housekeeper and a model for hire. Her earnings more than paid for her keep. Becky sighed. 'What's he done now, luv?'

'I was sitting for Henry last night. The bugger mauls me all the time, but he pays Victor well. Anyway, Victor didn't come home till five this morning, drunk as a louse, and stinking of cheap scent. He said he'd popped into the pub and they'd dragged him to a party. If I find out he's doing it with other women while he's using me as his standby mistress and skivvy, I'll—' She burst into tears.

Becky put her arms about her. 'All right, his friends persuaded him to go to a party, but that doesn't mean he slept with another woman. You know you love him too much to leave him, and what choice do you have?'

Janine sniffed and ran her fingers under her eyes to catch the mascara running with her tears. 'Aw, I know there are no jobs out there. With Victor at least I've got a roof over me head and food in me belly. That's an achievement during a depression, I suppose.' She twisted her face into a warped smile. 'But sometimes I think I'm no different from a prostitute. Little though it is, I'm getting money for giving myself to Victor.'

'But you love him. It's different. And you're not *only* his lover, you run after him hand and foot. You earn every penny you get, and more.'

Janine wiped her eyes again and nodded. 'Thanks, luv. I needed a pep talk. But I'm keeping you from your work. I'll make us a cup of tea and then unpick something for you.' She foraged under the bed for the tea things.

'Thanks, there's loads to do.'

Janine returned with the hot-water bottle glugging and dribbling on the stairs, Mildred in tow. 'Mildred's going to help an' all.'

Persuaded by Becky and Janine, Mildred had abandoned her brown skirts and cardigans. She wore a modified version of Janine's day dress, in a sober grey, non-clinging gaberdine, and Janine had coaxed her into letting her cut her hair to just below the ears. Out of its restricting knot it fell into natural curls. They would never have guessed that Mildred could look so chic and pretty.

'Thanks, Mildred,' Becky said. 'Work's more fun with two assistants to talk to.' She made a sweeping gesture with her arm towards the sewing machine, as if Mildred couldn't see for herself. 'Say hello to my latest assistant.'

'I know. Janine told me. I'm so happy for you, Becky. You're bound to be a success one day.'

Twenty

Two weeks later, on 5 October, a disturbance outside drew Becky and Norma to the window. People were shouting and waving placards saying, FIGHT FOR MINERS' RIGHTS. The miners' request for a fair wage increase had been denied and the men had come out on strike.

Numb with despair, Becky returned to her machine. 'Come on,' she said. 'We'd better get on with our work.'

Becky sewed mechanically, her mind looping painfully in all directions. Liz was four months pregnant again. She wiped her eyes on her sleeves as tears fell and made black dots on the grey silk lining she was sewing. Her worst fears were happening – Will out of work and a baby every year. And when the miners did go back, she doubted the owners would take Will. He was a strong union member – what the owners called a troublemaker.

By 4 November the strike was over, though not a total victory. The government had succumbed to the miners' wage demands, but had guaranteed the increase only until 31 December.

Still, it was a reprieve. Becky's business was thriving with the aid of the sewing machine and Liz refused to accept money while Will was working. Whatever money Becky didn't spend on necessities, she placed in a Post Office account. Though intended for the future to expand the business to new premises, it was also a reserve in case of more problems at the pit.

'Hey, look what the wind blew in. You haven't been in for

155

ages.' Annie advanced on Becky as she entered the café. 'My God, lass, you look like a ghost.'

'I'm just tired.'

'Aye,' Janine's voice hailed from behind Becky. 'She never gets more than four hours' sleep a night. She's making more money but not putting it in her belly. I had to force her to come out for a decent meal and get away from that damned sewing machine. I never see her unless I go and unpick frocks or tack seams. She bloody well owes me a good dinner.'

'I've got just the thing – mince and dumplings. Back in a minute.' Annie returned with two laden plates.

'Thanks, Annie.' Becky realized she *was* hungry.

Annie joined them. 'How's your Liz?'

'In the club again. Due in February,' Becky said miserably.

'I hear they're opening a new women's clinic,' Janine said, cutting into her dumpling. 'They're giving free advice on how not to get in the pudding club *and* giving away *free you-know-whats* for women. It's all hush-hush, word of mouth only. Why not drag Liz to a couple of meetings?'

Becky's ears pricked up like a dog's at the sound of his master's whistle. 'A women's clinic? Here?'

'Aye, I wouldn't mind getting a job there, even part-time,' Janine said.

Annie chuckled. 'Don't be daft, lass. They only employ respectable married women, and it's *voluntary work*.'

Playing with her dinner, Becky decided she would volunteer one night a week, if they would accept her. If necessary, she'd wear a ring. It wouldn't hurt to learn about birth control. She smiled, excited about her secret. She'd have less time for her business but it wouldn't take long to learn what she needed to know.

Becky followed the daily negotiations between miners and the government and was dismayed by the lack of progress, though work helped to keep her mind occupied. On 31 March 1921, unusual activity in the streets and glaring newspaper placards confirmed her worst fears. The government had given back price control to the coal owners, who had locked out one million miners that morning. Dear Lord! And Liz not even fully recovered after Billy.

She bought a *Daily Herald* and scanned it as she pushed through the noisy crowds on her way to work. Mr Walker arrived at the same time, also carrying a newspaper.

'Good morning, Becky. Would you like to make a cup of tea and we'll have a break before we start?' he said.

'Yes, sir. Morning, sir.' Becky lit the stove and filled the kettle.

Mr Walker sat by the stove. 'Have you read the news?'

'Some of it, sir, on me way here. That's why I'm late, I'm sorry.'

'No need, but Norma's late too often these days. I must talk to her.'

As soon as his words were out, a breathless Norma barged in. On seeing Mr Walker in the workshop, her face turned poppy-coloured. 'Oh, sir, I'm that sorry I'm late. The trams were held up with everybody jamming the roads. It would've been quicker to get out and walk.'

Mr Walker raised a hand to silence her. 'It's all right today, but in future be on time. We're having an early cup of tea. Please join us.'

'Yes, sir.' After donning her overall, Norma helped Becky to wash yesterday's mugs.

'Is it another strike?' she whispered to her.

'No, a lock-out. The coal owners posted notices terminating the men's contracts, including the safety men.'

Mr Walker looked up from his newspaper. 'It says here the drastic cuts in wages proposed by the owners are the most savage in the history of the coal industry. A man with a wife and two children would earn less than is paid by some boards of guardians as relief to such a family.'

'Dear God!' Becky forgot Mr Walker's presence. 'They'd be better off on relief than working.'

'Indeed, but the miners can't get relief while they're locked out,' Mr Walker said, then obviously regretted his words. 'I'm sorry, Becky, I know this affects your family. Come and have your tea. I bought some ginger snaps on the way.'

Becky accepted a ginger snap and cradled her stiff hands round her hot mug. 'They'll starve to death,' she said, deciding to draw out her savings and go to see Liz on Sunday. She knew Liz lied to shield her, but this was more serious than last time. 'What else do they say, sir?'

'The government are moving in troops to keep order. It seems they're worried the railway union and the Transport Workers' Federation will support the miners by striking.'

'But the whole country would come to a stop,' Becky said, pleased about the amazing support for the miners but wondering how she could get to Ashington if there were no buses.

The transport federation and railway union threatened to strike on 12 April, which gave Becky time to visit Liz before the buses stopped. On Sunday she was relieved to be on her way, though she felt sick in her stomach at the thought of seeing Ma and Dora. They had, of course, guessed she'd gone to Newcastle, but had no idea Liz visited her.

Leaving the bus station she thought she would gag. The familiar sulphurous fumes of coke and coal dust blending with the stench of the ash middens floated heavily on the air, as always. It would take a century to clean up this dump, she thought.

She walked towards Long Row, eager to see Liz and little Mary and the new baby, and of course Will. But she was afraid of the inevitable scene with Ma and Dora.

In the fields beyond town, pit ponies grazed. Thank goodness the men had brought them to the surface. As usual, when she saw the ponies, Becky wanted to cry. They were so small and defenceless, and most were blind from being constantly underground. The poor creatures led such terrible lives it must be heaven to simply move freely, breathe in fresh air, such as it was, and eat fresh grass instead of a nosebag of hay. She wondered what would happen to the animals who'd grown too large or too old to get out of the pit, but knew that the miners loved their ponies. Some would go in to feed them.

Outside the house, she took a deep breath. As arranged with Liz and Will, she knocked, and they managed to show as much amazement at her appearance as did Ma and Dora.

'Hell's bells!' Dora's eyes bulged and her mouth fell open. She looked like a gargoyle on a doorknocker.

Ma clasped her heart, and squeaked, 'Becky!'

'Oh, Beck, how lovely to see you,' Liz said, as if she hadn't seen her for years.

Will followed with, 'Aye, it's been a while.'

Dora leaned back in her chair as if preening herself on her throne. 'I suppose you're broke and hungry and homeless, eh? Well, you can bugger off. We don't owe you nowt, you little tart. And where did you get the fancy haircut?'

'Me friend cuts it.' Becky took a deep breath.

'Are you all right?' Ma strained forward to peer at her. 'You look thin. Are you starving? We haven't got much but we can give you something.'

'I'm not starving, Ma. I've lost weight because I'm working hard, but I'm fine. I just came to see how you all are.' Her eyes fixed on Liz, seated with the baby in her arms, and she bent to take the tiny wrinkled hand. 'He's lovely, Liz. He's the image of his Da, no mistaking he's a little lad.'

'Aye, he is that. How long can you stay?' Liz looked exhausted and sounded strained.

'I have to catch the eight o'clock bus to be at work in the morning. But I'd like to talk to Will. I can get the truth from him. You can't believe the newspapers.'

Although it was only ten o'clock, Dora poured herself a gin. 'Eey, by!' She raised the glass to Becky. 'Since when did you start reading newspapers and keeping up with politics?'

'Since it's been important to know what's going on in the world.'

'So, you're educating yourself at last.' She sipped her gin and drove mocking eyes into Becky's like two corkscrews.

Little Mary climbed down the stairs, whimpering. Dear God!

159

Becky hadn't thought about Mary giving away the fact that she knew her from Liz's visits.

Liz saved the day. 'Mary, this is your Auntie Becky. Why not give her a big cuddle?'

'Auntie Becky,' Mary cried with delight and bumped down the remaining stairs on her bottom.

Becky scooped her up. 'Well, aren't you a lovely little girl, and you've got a lovely little brother.' She must keep talking to keep Mary quiet.

'Billy!' Mary pointed a grubby finger at the baby. 'Like Dada.'

Will took over and threw Mary over his shoulders. 'You need cleaning up before we eat. We've got rabbit stew and your Auntie Becky's going to have some.' He paused and said to Becky, as if in apology. 'I planted early but there's nowt up in the garden yet. We've had bad frost. I do a bit of poaching.'

For the first time, Liz looked directly at Becky. 'Everybody's doing it. It's not a crime for a man to feed his family.' She gave a wan smile. 'Since Will's been off work he's been doing the cooking and cleaning. It's me first day up. This one –' she nodded to the infant in her lap – 'took eighteen hours to decide to come out into the world.' She chucked the baby's chin. 'But he was worth every minute!'

'Two already! You've been busy, Liz.' Becky remembered to keep up the act too. She turned to her mother, who still sat with her mouth open and a glazed expression in her eyes. 'Are you all right, Ma?'

The expression hardened. 'Still alive, no thanks to you. Not even a penny from me runaway daughter to help her old mother in sickness and hard times. And you've got a job.'

Becky lowered her gaze. Since leaving home, she'd lost the habit of lying. 'Aye, Ma, but it only pays me rent and food. It's got prospects though.'

Dora knocked back her gin and sneered. 'What the hell sort of job could *you* get? And prospects, my foot! Keeping some dirty old man happy till he kicks the bucket and you inherit his money, is that it?'

Becky forced a deep breath.

'Hey!' Ma pointed to Dora's glass, seeming only to have noticed the gin since she'd come out of her stupor at Becky's arrival. 'One for me an' all, our Dora.'

'It's too early for you.'

Becky glanced at Liz, who returned a knowing look. So now that money was tighter Dora wasn't so free with her gin. A warped blessing.

Will returned with Mary and pulled out a chair from the table for Becky. Mary, wiped clean, climbed on to Becky's lap. 'Auntie Becky, hair like Mamma's,' she grabbed at Becky's short crop and bounced with glee.

'Yes, my hair's the same colour as your mamma's.' She bounced Mary on her lap to keep her quiet. 'How long do you think it'll last, Will?'

He shrugged. 'The owners can string it out as long as they want. They've always got grub on their tables. If we accept their wage offer we starve, so, lock-out or not, either way we starve.'

On the journey home Becky slumped into her seat in a black cloud of depression. What would happen to Liz and Will and the children now? She'd sneaked four pounds into Liz's hand, but there was no knowing how long the lock-out would last. She would send more each week.

Twenty-One

One evening in May, Becky was working on a backlog of orders when a thump on the door made her start.

'Come in,' she shouted, continuing treadling. Only Janine knocked like that.

Janine leaned on the sewing machine and drummed her fingers. 'I've come to take you to a fabulous party, where, a little bird told me, Andrew is the guest of honour.' She paused for effect. 'Remember, *Andrew*?'

Becky swivelled round on her chair. 'How do you know?' She didn't need to be reminded who Andrew was.

'Victor met him in town today,' Janine said. 'Just back from London. A friend in Gosforth's giving him a welcome party.' She removed her purple wool coat and matching cloche hat and sat on the bed. Though Becky preferred to design her own work, she'd helped Janine to copy a Coco Chanel original. Janine gave an exaggerated sigh. 'I'm nuts to expose you to Andrew, but anything to get you out of here.'

Becky managed to swallow. 'But I'm not invited.'

'Don't be an idiot, darling.' Janine paused to light a gold-tipped cigarette and placed it into a foot-long black holder. 'The whole world's invited, as always, especially gatecrashers.'

Janine was right. Nobody seemed to care who invaded their homes, drank their booze, or even who slept with whom. It seemed the aftermath of the war and the depression had made those who could afford it live only for whatever pleasure they could gain for the moment.

162

Becky didn't even deliberate. She couldn't miss the chance to see Andrew again. She stood. 'What time does it start?'

Janine flicked cigarette ash on the floor. 'After the pub, as usual. I'll wait while you change into something more fetching. Victor's coming later.' She shrugged, having accepted that she played only a walk-on part in Victor's life. But she still loved him.

Becky's mind raced. What to wear? On impulse, she took from the row of finished work a red satin creation with a matching bandeau beaded with pearls. 'Would this do?' She held it up.

Janine's eyebrows disappeared under her fringe. 'Good God! Since when did you make anything like that for yourself?'

'I didn't, but my client isn't collecting it till the weekend, so what the hell!' She flung it at Janine. 'It needs hemming. Do it while I sneak a wash and do my hair.'

'Go on, sweetie. It should only take a couple of hours to make you look respectable.' Janine grinned as she rose to get a needle and thread from the table.

It was Friday and the Barley Inn was packed. As Becky followed Janine through the crowd, her stomach fluttered but she kept her expression calm.

She threw her black coat carelessly over her arm and raised her head, the sparkling red bandeau over her cropped curls. The satin, cut on the bias, shimmered and clung to her fashionably slim body. She might even stand a chance with Andrew.

'Hello, Janine.' Andrew disengaged himself from the crowd as they approached. 'And who have we here?' He appraised Becky.

'Don't be daft. You've met my friend, Becky.'

Embarrassed, yet also pleased that he didn't recognize her from the way she used to look, Becky said, 'Oh, that was centuries ago. My hair's different.'

He took her hand as if to kiss it and gave her a mock

bow. 'Delighted to meet you again, Becky. What would you like?'

Janine spoke up. 'Two pink ladies, please.'

'What the devil's that?' Becky hissed at her.

'Gin with grenadine, and brandy and egg white.'

'Ugh!' Becky felt ignorant and out of her depth, but was confident that her speech had improved and came more naturally since she'd been friendly with Mildred.

'Hey, thanks, I will,' Janine said, as Dot, one of the artists' models, whispered something in her ear and disappeared into the crowd.

'Will what?' Becky tore her eyes from Andrew.

'That clinic I told you about's just opened. Dot got fitted out. It's dead easy. Just a sponge contraption and a bottle of oil, even olive oil will do. I'm going tomorrow, before the police find out and close the place down.'

'The clinic! Wonderful!' She would offer her services and could perhaps get some advice and a sponge for Liz.

'Here you are, ladies.' Andrew handed them each a glass of pink-tinted liquid.

They thanked him, and Becky forced herself to look into his blue eyes as if it cost her no effort. 'So you've been living in London?'

He returned her gaze coolly. 'Not *living* exactly. I never *live* anywhere, just stay here and there with friends. Don't like to be pegged down, you know.'

'You must have lots of friends to stay with.' Becky wanted to kick herself for this stupid remark.

'Enough.' He smiled at Janine, who, like Becky, had removed her coat to show off her Chanel design. 'I must say, you ladies are enough to gladden any man's eye,' he said.

'Becky's a dress designer.' Janine sipped her drink while Becky nudged her to shut up, to no avail. Janine continued, 'She works from home at night but soon she's starting her own business during the day.'

Andrew raised his eyebrows. 'Fascinating. It must be a lucrative as well as a glamorous occupation.'

Becky met his bright-blue eyes again. 'Reasonably, considering the depression.'

'Andrew, glad to see you back.'

Becky groaned inside. It was Jake, thoroughly nice, pink-saveloy-sausage Jake. She prayed he'd lost interest in her, but his eyes lighted on her. 'Becky! I hardly recognized you. You look grand. Are you going to the party?'

'Yes, are you?'

'I am now.' He grinned.

Becky's spirits sank. She'd get nowhere with Andrew if Jake glued himself to her side again. She must be firm with him. 'Good, see you later, then. Excuse me.' She pushed her way to the ladies and powdered her nose, before making for Andrew, cutting through the dense undergrowth of bodies like a scout forging a path. Being so tall and striking, he was easy to spot.

'Ah, the talented and beautiful Becky,' he said to Ronny, whom Becky remembered for his dark-red hair, pleasant manner and generosity with drinks.

'How do you do, Becky.' She was pleased that he didn't recognize her.

The pub grew busier and noisier and, at closing time, Becky found herself squashed into a large motor that someone said was a Sunbeam Coupé. The interior was packed with bodies, women splayed across men's knees. Andrew had left earlier and Becky wondered with envy who had sat on his knee, but she was glad she was on Ronny's. He clasped his arms round her to steady her but his hands didn't rove.

The motor stopped and the driver got out to open two heavy wooden gates. Although on the main North Road, a high brick wall, shrubs, and a long curved drive concealed the house in Gosforth from prying eyes. It was a huge, three-storied square structure with every window lit. Inside, from the wide hallway, Becky gaped into the drawing room at the extravagant modern furniture. White and black lacquered cocktail tables and white brocade sofas and chairs, all heavily fringed, stood on dark red oriental rugs. She blinked to adjust her eyes to the colourful theme.

Gerry, Andrew's host, also large and sumptuous, greeted the newcomers in the hallway. 'Come in, my dears, one and all.' He was perhaps forty but had the look of a man who overindulged. Soggy flesh hung from his face as he bent to kiss the women's hands. His body was spongy, and the pearl buttons on his black satin waistcoat strained over the bulge of his belly.

Two servants, dressed in tight black jackets and trousers with red cummerbunds, took their coats. Becky's throat constricted as Andrew appeared and inclined his head in greeting. Already the gesture was familiar.

'I hope you weren't too squashed in the car,' he said, leading her to the black satin-quilted bar. Here two men dressed like the other servants, except with white jackets and gloves, were shaking cocktails in silver shakers. Andrew turned to her. 'Another pink lady?'

Becky confessed. 'Actually, I'd love a lemonade, but in one of those tall glasses with a straw and a cherry please.'

He laughed. 'So, the lady doesn't care for cocktails but wishes to keep it a secret.'

'I'd feel silly,' she said, feeling silly anyway.

She stayed close to him and accepted the lemonade with a smile. He held a Martini in his left hand and ran his right forefinger round her jaw and down her profile. 'You have fine bones. A wonderful face. I need look no further. Without that head gear and make-up, you could pass for a beautiful choirboy. I want to paint you.'

'A choirboy?' She looked puzzled and he laughed.

'My latest commission. It is to be a present to my host's uncle. He's a choirmaster.'

'I see,' Becky said, not seeing at all.

He held her shoulders and leaned her against the white grand piano, studying her.

Becky felt thrilled yet thrown at the same time. 'Am I

supposed to accept it as a compliment that you think I look like a boy?'

'Absolutely! There is such purity in the faces of beautiful boys, as in their voices. It's rarely found in girls of similar age.' He lifted her hand and touched his lips to her fingers.

A warm shiver ran through her. 'Then I should be glad to sit for you.' She ignored the voice in her head asking how she would find time for modelling, work at the clinic, *and* her business.

Andrew sipped his drink. 'Shall we say Wednesday at seven. Gerry has kindly provided me with a magnificent studio in the attic.'

'That would be fine.'

'Splendid! I look forward to it.'

'Andrew,' Gerry called, and Andrew waved acknowledgement. He gave a mock bow to Becky. 'Excuse me, I must attend to my other guests.'

Janine appeared from nowhere and leaned on the piano. 'If my eyes don't deceive me, you've made a hit with dream boy.'

'I can hardly believe it. He's asked me to model for him – as a choirboy.'

Janine spluttered and the pink lady she held spilled on to the carpet. She placed it on the piano, forming a sticky ring on the white lacquer. 'A choirboy! My foot! That's a new line if ever I heard one.'

Becky felt defensive. 'He said I have the pure face of a choirboy.'

'Is he going to make you sing an' all?' Janine spluttered again and supported herself against the piano.

'You're drunk. I thought you'd be happy for me. He wants me to come here on Wednesday.'

Janine's tone suddenly sobered. 'How much is he paying you?'

'We didn't discuss money. It's not a business arrangement.'

'I see,' she said, furrowing her brow. 'Andrew seems to

get a lot free, doesn't he? He's always staying with friends. Rent-free and all that.'

Becky glowered at her. 'What are you driving at?'

'Sorry, but I'm a bit worried, luv. I wish now I hadn't got you into this. We don't know much about our Andrew, do we?'

'He's a perfect gentleman.'

Janine relented. 'Aye, you're probably right, and the only way you'll find out is to get to know him. God knows you've had a pash on him long enough.'

Becky worked furiously in order to make time go faster and get ahead with her work. At seven on Wednesday she stood outside the wooden gates. Panic seized her. She wiggled her toes in the tight high heels she'd bought for the occasion, then crunched slowly up the gravel drive.

A servant answered the doorbell. His cummerbund was now black. 'I'm Becky Ryan,' she said. 'Mr, er, Andrew is expecting me.'

'Ah, oui, please come in. I will fetch him. Please be seated.' He helped her out of the grey wool coat and hat she'd made for Mildred and borrowed for the occasion, and indicated one of two tasselled sofas in the hallway.

Again, she felt overwhelmed by the grandeur, but took a deep breath. She'd watched her elocution carefully when she'd been with Andrew. Surely he wouldn't have taken an interest in her had he suspected she was a lowly pitman's daughter. She thanked Mildred silently for her influence, but she must still be careful not to slip up.

'This way, mademoiselle.' The man returned and led her up the red-carpeted stairway. After climbing three flights they reached an attic cluttered with articles – old chairs, vases, a white marble mantelpiece removed from its mooring, statues and other oddments.

Andrew appeared from behind a curtain, wearing a white overall covered in paint. He wiped his hands on a paint-spattered rag as he approached. 'Good evening, Becky. Please, sit down.' He indicated a dilapidated horsehair sofa of dubious vintage.

As she sat, his eyes explored her face. 'So pure! I'm impatient to start.'

From behind a mahogany dressing screen he produced a black cassock and white lace surplice. 'Please stand.' He dropped the cassock over her head and she sought the wide armholes. Then, almost with reverence, he placed the surplice round her neck and buttoned it down the back. A small quiver ran through her as he smoothed her curls back from her face and secured them with metal hair clips he took from his overall pocket.

'And please, in future, no make-up, except a little childlike glow to the cheeks perhaps, and absolutely no lipstick – just Vaseline for a little shine.' He wiped off her lipstick with his paint rag. 'I need the natural line of the lips. No cupid's bow.'

Becky felt herself blush. She'd painstakingly painted the fashionable points above her lip line. But he was right. She must look the part.

Surveying her with narrowed eyes, he nodded. 'Now you look the perfect choirboy. Please come.' He took her by the shoulders and placed her behind a piece of old banister, propped upright by bricks at either end. Then he handed her an open black-bound hymn book. 'Please hold it but don't look at it. Keep your chin and eyes up as if you were singing directly to the Lord himself.'

Becky hoped she wouldn't have to stand like this for long. Her toes throbbed in the tight shoes. The cassock covered her feet. Perhaps she could sneak off the shoes. She forced each foot out of its prison and almost sighed aloud. He didn't seem to notice that she'd shrunk a couple of inches.

'Now, please open your mouth in a long *O* shape, as if you were emitting the purest of notes.'

Becky swallowed. She had to stand like this *and* hold her mouth open! 'Do I have to keep my mouth open *all* the time?'

'Don't worry, I'll sketch your head first, then you can relax your mouth.'

He raised her chin, lowered her shoulders, and stepped back to study her. Frowning with concentration, with his thumb and forefinger he pressed the corners of her mouth closer to open it further. His touch on her lips made her feel faint.

'That's perfect. Hold it.' He disappeared behind his easel and chuckled. 'Think pure thoughts.'

Becky stood rigid. Her muscles shrivelled. Her throat dried up.

After a while he said, 'I suppose the other artists at the pub have painted you.'

She wanted to say, No, *oh no, you're the first and will be the only*, but all she managed was a sound like Ah, ha.

'So, this is your first time?'

At least he'd understood her. She remained motionless and learned to swallow when necessary by closing her throat with only the slightest movement of her lips.

After an eternity he stood back, surveyed his work, studied her again, added one or two strokes, then placed his brush in a jar of water on the table. 'Time for a break.'

The words sounded like angels singing. Becky grunted agreement as she closed her mouth with difficulty and indulged in a genuine swallow. Then came the trial of forcing her body back into action and her feet back into her shoes.

'Let me give you a hand.' He held out his arm and she took it, walking like an old woman leaning heavily on a walking stick. He stared at her in surprise. 'Oh, my dear girl, I'm so sorry. I kept you too long. You should have said so. I do get carried away.'

'I'm fine,' she said, resolving to take his advice and say so in future. She sank into the lumpy sofa with as much pleasure as if it were a feather bed.

He hovered over her. 'I'll make you tea.'

Becky watched him fill a tin kettle at the paint-splattered sink and set it on a Bunsen burner on the bench. He struck a match and she enjoyed watching his slender fingers at work

170

and his elegant movements. Everything about him showed
refinement and breeding. By comparison, Will moved like a
carthorse with corns on its hooves.

Feeling her blood beginning to circulate again, she asked,
'May I see the painting?'

'Ah, never! Never, that is, until it is finished.'

Becky felt as if she'd been scolded and smiled to cover
her embarrassment. 'I told you, this is my first time.'

He rinsed two dirty mugs under the tap, rather too briefly,
but still she was glad when he set them on the floor beside
her and filled them with steaming dark tea. Only now she
realized she was shivering.

He handed her a mug and raised his. 'To the most patient
model I've ever found.'

Becky would have stood there all night if he'd asked her to,
but he went on, 'You've had enough, and so have I, at least for
tonight. Could you manage tomorrow at the same time?'

She cast all thoughts of work from her mind. 'Of course.'

'I'll get Gerry's chauffeur to drive you home. It's too dark
and cold to take the tram.'

'Thank you.' She wanted to add, *And I'm too exhausted
to make it to the tram stop*. Instead she smiled. 'You're
very thoughtful.'

He wove through the various objects in the room and paused
at the door. 'Shan't be long.'

She changed into her own clothes and stood by the paraffin
heater, still shivering.

At last he returned with the servant who had shown her
up. 'George will see you to the car. Thank you, Becky. Till
tomorrow.'

George escorted her downstairs, wrapped her in her outer
clothes and helped her into the waiting motor.

She leaned back, grateful to be driven home, though she
couldn't help wishing that Andrew had escorted her himself.
But, she reasoned, why have servants if you don't use them?
She gave the chauffeur directions only to the corner of Pink
Lane, in order to avoid Mrs Dunn's hawk eyes.

171

She was seeing Andrew again! Tomorrow! And he was a gentleman. He'd had every opportunity to take advantage of her tonight and hadn't, though he seemed to think her attractive.

Twenty-Two

B ecky continued to sit for Andrew twice a week. Some nights she sewed until morning to keep up with her work. With the lock-out still on, she couldn't afford to lose clients, but neither could she afford to lose Andrew. Becky was blissfully, crazily in love.

Though he had never invited her out, after her Friday evening sittings he would say, 'See you tomorrow.' So she became a regular at the Barley Inn on Saturday evenings. One such evening when she and Andrew stood discussing his work, Rosemary, a chic redhead with a talent for tittle-tattle and an obvious interest in Andrew, squirmed her way through the crowd. 'I see you come here every week now, Becky – since Andrew rejoined our ranks.' She bathed Andrew in a honeyed smile. 'Watch out, my man. Before you know it you'll be snared into respectability.'

Becky's blood rushed to her face, but Andrew gave Rosemary a disarming grin. 'And *you* also come every week, my dear, though I can't imagine your ever becoming respectable.' He was adept at making witty, but frequently caustic, remarks, which often made Becky feel uncomfortable.

Rosemary's lingering smile froze. 'My, my! It's a rare joy to meet a *man* with a sense of humour.'

There had been no open declaration of feelings between them, but Becky knew Andrew liked her. Why else would he spend his time chatting to her at the pub when there were dozens of women craving his attention? He never mentioned his family nor asked about Becky's. For this she was grateful. She locked within herself her sadness about that other part of her life.

*   *   *

At last, on 1 July, starved into submission, the miners gave up their fight for the national principle. They accepted the government's offer, though the drastic wage cuts proposed by the owners were the most savage in the coal industry's history.

Becky couldn't concentrate on her sewing. For the second time that morning she withdrew the letter she'd received from Liz the previous night and read it:

> Dearest Beck,
>
> I'm so glad it's finally over. You know what reductions of three-and-six a day mean to most families. The unemployment queues are a mile long. They had to accept the cut in manpower as well as wages to return to work at all. I'm sorry for those who didn't get their jobs back and thank God Will was one of the lucky ones. I thought the owners might consider him a risk, but they know he can hew several more loads a day than most men.
>
> Thanks to you, my dearest sister, we survived. The bairns are fine. Ma's faring a bit better but she's a terrible grouch. Dora's still allowing her just one gin a day.
>
> The garden's thriving with all Will's hard work and we can manage now. Please don't send more money, luv. I want you to save up and start that business, *please*.
>
> I'll close now. I'm a bit tired.
>
> All my love, and Will's, and kisses from the bairns.
> Liz

Becky replaced the letter in her skirt pocket. A swarm of wasps attacked her conscience. She kept her own expenses to a minimum, but at the pub, every time she drank an expensive cocktail – she'd learned to like them now – or at the frequent parties, she cringed at the extravagance.

'What you gawping at?' Norma broke into Becky's thoughts. 'You've been staring into space for the last ten minutes.'

'Then, if you were watching me, you can't have been working.' Becky resumed stitching a Harris tweed waistcoat. 'I've decided to go to see Liz this Sunday.'

'What?' Norma's jaw dropped. 'I thought you were never going back.'

'Liz sounded so weary in her letter.'

'Then go, luv, if it'll ease your mind. But you shouldn't feel guilty that you've got a better life than hers. It was her choice. And your Andrew sounds like a real catch. If I wasn't so in love with Larry, I'd be dead jealous.' She examined the narrow gold ring with the imitation diamond on her left hand and sighed as if admiring the crown jewels. 'Eey, I can't believe he chose me.'

Becky smiled. 'I can. You'll make a wonderful wife.'

Mr Walker emerged from his office, his face grey and strained. 'May I see you for a few minutes, Becky?'

'Yes, sir.'

He smiled at Norma. 'The blooming bride can take off early if she wishes.'

'Oh, thank you, sir.' Norma was on her feet and out of her overall and cap before Becky had removed her work from the machine.

Mr Walker sat at his desk, as usual littered with samples of materials and invoices. He nodded for Becky to take the chair opposite and cleared his throat.

Becky clenched her teeth. Business was slow. Was this the end? She felt the blood drain from her face.

'Don't look so stricken, my dear, I'm not closing down, but I need to cut back. I can't afford to replace Norma.'

Relief drenched Becky like warm rain. He was keeping her on.

He placed his elbows on the desk and pressed his fingertips together. 'I will have to scale down and concentrate on the wealthier clients.'

Becky had known for some time that Mr Walker had a

shifting price scale, depending on the customers' ability to pay. Though all garments were of equal quality, the so-called less expensive lines were often sold at minimal profit. 'I'm not surprised, sir, but I'm sorry you have to do it.'

He pinched the two vertical worry lines above his nose. 'I expect to retain my wealthier clients, and as you will be carrying the load alone, I shall raise your wages, say five shillings until we see how profits go.'

'Thank you, sir.'

He looked into Becky's face and she noticed that his eyes over his half-spectacles were sunk deeper into their sockets, the lines in his face more heavily etched, like furrows in ploughed soil. Was he simply getting older, or was he ill? Her concern and liking for this man who had been so kind to her overcame her inhibitions. 'You're feeling well, sir?'

He smiled. 'Just old, and tired.'

Again Becky dared to be personal. 'Couldn't one of your sons help you out with the business, sir?'

He raised his white eyebrows. 'My sons?'

'Well, the firm's name, sir – Walker & Sons.'

He shook his head. 'I have no sons. When I started the business I certainly hoped to have sons and I got a bit ahead of myself naming the firm. My wife died in childbirth shortly afterwards, but I couldn't make myself change the name.'

Becky's eyes welled with tears. 'I'm so sorry, sir.'

'It was a long time ago, Becky.' He raised himself slowly, his hands pressed against the desk as if for support. 'It's past closing time. You be off. I'll lock up.'

'Goodnight, sir,' she said with a catch in her voice. How sad and lonely he must be!

Passing the vegetable stalls a voice hailed her. 'Hello, again!' It was the student, carrying a bag of apples under one arm, a pile of books under the other.

'Oh! Hello.'

He fell into step. 'You were right. The fruit's better at the stall you recommended.' His eyes were still on her. 'I hardly recognized you. You look different.'

'Perhaps it's my hair.' Becky felt embarrassed but pleased. She *had* changed, she knew. Her face looked as if it glowed from the inside. 'I go this way,' she said as they reached Grainger Street. 'Nice to see you again.'

She waved and crossed the road. She still thought him attractive but, now that she was in love with Andrew, other men were just people.

Becky walked from the bus station to Long Row. The pit ponies were back underground. She sighed. The company had probably killed off the less productive and older ones just as they'd laid off the men. The groups of unemployed on street corners playing marbles were larger, their faces more haggard, their clothes looser on their bodies.

Liz showed her surprise with the others. 'Becky! How lovely to see you.'

Mary ran to her with a squeal of delight. Becky hugged her but couldn't take her eyes off Liz. Her face was the colour of fog. Her belly was flat but Becky knew instinctively she was in the club again, and Billy not five months old.

'Good God! The big city sister returns!'

Becky ignored the sneer in Dora's voice. Ma, in her chair opposite Dora, looked thinner, but better for it. Her ankles were less swollen. 'Our Becky! Why didn't you come earlier and help us out, or at least send us some money?' she whined.

'Send us money! Don't be daft,' Dora broke in. 'She's probably come for some, now that Will's working again.' She aimed cigarette smoke towards Becky as if spitting at her.

Becky ignored her and put her arms about Liz, who had straightened from laying Billy in his cot. Fear hissed in Becky's throat like a steaming kettle. Liz had that look about her. She *was* in the club again. 'How far on are you?' she managed to whisper.

Liz looked astonished and gave Becky one of their schoolgirl kicks that meant *shut up*. 'Take your coat off and sit down, Beck. I'll make some tea.'

Becky groaned inside. She was right! And Liz was afraid to

177

tell Ma and Dora. But they'd have to know eventually. Becky hung up her coat, pulled out a chair from the table and slumped into it. Mary climbed on to her lap and Becky held her. 'All right, Mary, but only if you sit still. Auntie Becky's tired.'

'How you doing, then? Making big money in the town now, I suppose?' Ma still sounded peevish.

'No, Ma, but enough to survive.' Becky wore her old serge dress and no make-up. Only her stylish hair showed.

'Your friend couldn't cut your hair *that* fancy! You go to a hairdresser,' Dora said.

'My friend *is* a hairdresser.' Becky strove to keep her patience.

Dora opened her mouth to retort, but Ma cut in. 'Stop bickering and let's hear how Becky's faring.'

'The same, Ma. I'm sewing.'

'Sewing what?'

'Overalls, at a factory.' That would make it difficult for Dora to find her.

'Sounds awful.' Dora turned up her nose.

'It *is*, but some of us have to work for our living and pay the taxes for those who don't.'

Seeming not to notice the jibe, Dora pulled on her cigarette.

Becky took the mug of tea Liz handed her. What had happened to all those dreams they used to share? But, now that she was madly in love, she understood why Liz couldn't give up Will. She sipped her tea and smiled at her sister. 'Nobody makes a cuppa like you, Liz.'

Dora let out a bored yawn. 'Hell, if you two's going to sit gawping at each other, I'm off to see Ted.'

Ma waved away the mug of tea Liz handed her and clawed at Dora's arm as she tried to rise. 'Oh, luv! Bring me back some gin from Mr Brown's, please?'

'Got any money?'

'You know I haven't.' Ma's face twisted and she began to cry.

'No money, no gin. Mr Brown can't afford to give it

away. I only get me free nips because I'm Ted's lass, you know that.'

'Please *try*, Dora.' Ma grabbed Dora's hand but she shook her off and left.

'So, Dora's going out with Ted Brown,' Becky said. 'She'll do whatever it takes to survive, I suppose. She wouldn't look at him if his da didn't have the distillery. Or has the frog turned into a handsome prince?'

Liz smiled. 'Nah, he's still skinny, chinless, and his glasses get thicker every year, *plus*, he's losing his hair. The poor lad thinks he's been blessed by the Lord that Dora fancies him.'

'Stop talking about your sister like that,' Ma said. 'He's a nice lad and he's good to her. I pray to God she brings some gin back.'

The day wore on and Will came home but Dora didn't. Becky was pleased to see Will, despite her initial despair at Liz's condition. It wasn't simply carelessness, but also ignorance. She would volunteer at the clinic the next day. It was too late for Liz this time but she would get her a sponge before she fell again. She found herself smiling. Perhaps she may need one herself soon.

Twenty-Three

'It's a girl!' Becky said to Janine as she read Liz's letter. 'Nancy Elizabeth! As soon as Liz's on her feet, I'm taking her to that clinic. And I'm going myself.'

Janine, sewing sequins on an evening bag, looked up in surprise. 'Don't be daft, why would they give their precious free sponges to a virgin?'

Becky jutted her chin. 'I'll borrow Norma's ring and say I'm engaged. If anything happens with Andrew, I want to be prepared.'

At this, Janine exhaled a theatrical sigh. 'Beck, you've known him for nine months. Do you really think anything's ever going to happen?'

'He's a gentleman and he respects me. He says I'm precious and different.'

Another sigh, then Janine giggled. 'Aye, it wouldn't hurt to be prepared. Somebody else might get in there before him.'

'Stop your cheap talk,' Becky said angrily.

Janine looked penitent. 'I'm sorry, luv. They might be especially nice to you if you offer to volunteer. Marie Stopes is giving public lectures in favour of clinics, but we can't afford any bad publicity before the idea's officially accepted.'

In April, after an ugly spell of riots by the unemployed had come to an uneasy halt, Liz ventured to Newcastle with the new baby. Will, working short time, stayed with Mary and Billy.

'Oh, she's lovely, Liz.' Becky felt an unaccustomed twinge of longing as she looked into the crumpled face.

'Aye, she's like Mary.'

'Move along, let people off the bus.' The driver flicked them away with his hands as if they were bothersome insects.

Becky frowned. Liz's face was thin and pale. 'Are you all right?'

'Just a bit tired.'

'The clinic's only open two hours on Saturdays. We'll go straight there. You can rest after that.' Becky took the baby and again felt that strange longing. No, she mustn't start feeling mushy about babies!

'I've got some news,' Liz said as they walked.

Becky's stomach tightened. 'What?'

'Our Dora's getting married, to Ted Brown and his gin machine. The father's furious, but guess what else.'

'Thank God! A miracle! But don't tease. What else?'

'She's preggers, so Ted has to do the right thing.'

'Our Dora! With a bairn? I can't imagine it in a million years.'

'I'm sure it was deliberate. She's avoided it all this time, and suddenly when her only source of gin and money is Ted, she gets in the club.'

'Cooking and cleaning and looking after a bairn? Dora?' Becky laughed aloud at the idea.

'You know better than that, Beck. The father's done the housework and cooking, besides his business, since the ma died last year. If he thinks Dora's going to take over, he's got another think coming.'

'Thank God you'll be rid of her. That's the best news I've heard for years.'

Following Janine's directions, they turned on Grainger Street and made their way to the Cloth Market. Hey's Court was a narrow, dirty street, the clinic a converted stable with no name on the door.

Becky paused outside. 'How come you're not shocked that I'm getting one as well?'

Liz shrugged. 'Times have changed, Beck, and I know you love this Andrew fellah. I wish I could meet him.'

'Maybe soon.'

Cautiously, Liz opened the door. Inside, the stone floors were scrubbed and the walls whitewashed. They joined the women lined shoulder to shoulder on the hard benches along the waiting-room walls, some with babies or squirming toddlers on their laps.

Becky shivered. All the women had the same hopeless expression of total acceptance of adversity and poverty. She'd become too embroiled in material ambitions. It was important to make money, yes, but making pretty dresses seemed frivolous compared to the magnitude of these women's need.

A woman in a white overall came in. 'Next, please.'

Becky watched the women ahead of her file in and out of the office. Each clasped a brown paper bag and, before leaving, stuffed it furtively into her skirt pocket.

At their turn, Becky, still holding the sleeping baby, nudged Liz to go. When she returned, her face whiter than ever, she took the baby.

On jelly legs, Becky followed the woman into a sparse room containing a small desk, a high leather bench, a chest of drawers and a sink. Another, greying-haired woman in white was washing her hands.

'I'm Nurse Morgan and that's Dr Simons.'

The other woman nodded. 'Please, remove your knickers, then raise your skirt and climb on to the table.'

Becky stood rigid. 'I've, er, come about two things. I want to work here, and I'm getting married and would like to be prepared.'

Dr Simons studied her. 'Volunteer, eh? We'll discuss that later. Let's fix you up first.'

As Nurse Morgan had instructed, Becky arranged herself on the table and opened her legs with bent knees. They trembled violently.

She bit her lip as Dr Simons approached, drying her hands on a white towel. 'No need to be nervous. The more you relax the less you'll feel. First, a quick examination for size and shape and possible problems.' She opened Becky's legs wider.

Becky screamed. It felt as if the woman's clenched fist was poking up her insides.

'Oh, we've got a virgin here. Sorry, pet, but you'll be glad on your wedding night. Take a deep breath and relax.'

The hand poked around inside her and Becky ground her teeth. Was this what sex was like? She wanted to cry.

Eventually, it was over and, with her knickers back on, she felt like a human being again.

Dr Simons leaned against the bench and folded her arms. 'So, you want to work for us? Had any medical training?'

'No, but I'm good at clerical work. I run my own business and make out invoices and receipts and orders and things.'

The doctor looked thoughtful. 'We could use somebody a couple of hours a week to order supplies and keep the ledger. But we can't pay.'

'I know, but what you're doing is important and I want to help.'

'Splendid! Could you manage a couple of hours on Thursday evenings?'

Becky nodded. 'Yes.'

'Then we'll see you at seven.'

Nurse Morgan handed Becky her brown paper bag. 'Good luck, pet.'

By September Becky's sponge still sat in its bag, hidden among the box of scrap materials under the bed.

Tonight she was sitting for Andrew. She dressed in a soft pink wool that flared from her thighs and ended above the knee. Her breasts hadn't grown much, but her legs were her best feature, and the dress showed them off.

She patted her hair into place, smeared Vaseline on her lips, and dabbed 4711 behind her ears. One of her clients had given her the scent as partial payment. Next she put on the tweed coat made from off-cuts Mr Walker had given her and, as always, retrieved the brown paper bag from its hiding place and tucked it into her handbag. It could be tonight.

She would follow Janine's advice and *come on* to him. She'd listened to many lectures on sex at the clinic and was probably the most sexually informed virgin in Newcastle. But the clinic didn't teach you how to *come on* to a man. She giggled aloud. How to look alluring in that oversized white angel gown? She was posing as three angels ascending to heaven.

Andrew had moved out of Gerry's house after some silly argument. He was now staying with Roger, an artist with a small flat and studio in Colliery Lane above a fish-and-chip shop. Quite a comedown from Andrew's last lodgings, but he and Roger got on well. Roger was visiting his ailing mother tonight. Her heart somersaulted. She and Andrew would be alone.

The smell of fish and chips and boiling lard met her half-way up Colliery Lane. It permeated the flat and sickened Andrew, but Becky didn't mind it. Andrew opened the door at her knock. He seemed a little drunk.

'Hello, my angel.' He giggled. 'Or, I should say, my three angels.' He flourished his arm towards the dim interior. 'Enter my palace and we shall finish the bottle together.'

'What bottle?'

'The bottle my dearest Roger left me to keep me company while he's away.' The sitting room was lit with a bare bulb hanging from the ceiling, and a half-empty whisky bottle stood on the oilcloth-covered table. He waved the bottle before her.

'Andrew, you can't paint drunk!' She tried to scold him, but his shock of black hair, in need of cutting, flopped over his face. His shirt collar drooped open, his tie hung loose, and his red braces were twisted. She had to smile. He looked like a lost little boy. She longed to take him in her arms, smooth his hair and kiss him.

'Not drunk! One little drink together, then I'll paint.'

While he filled two glasses, she threw her coat on the tattered armchair. A bunk bed against the wall scattered with a few cushions served as a sofa during the day and as Andrew's bed at night. 'Half water for me, please.' Shamelessly, she decided that tonight was a good time. Tiddled and alone with her, he might forget he was a gentleman.

She sat on the bunk and, following Janine's instructions, raised her skirt, crossed her legs and made little circles with the toe of her raised foot.

He handed her a glass and flopped beside her with his own, spilling whisky on her pink skirt. 'Oops a daisy! Sorry.' Unsteadily, he wove his way to the corner that served as a kitchen. This comprised a sink, a wooden draining board, a kitchen dresser, and a paint-spattered rag that doubled as a dish-cloth, which he ran under the tap. 'Now, this'll be cold. But you can't go home smelling like a brewery.' He wiped the stain vigorously.

Becky was acutely aware of the pressure of his hand on her thigh. She felt that tingle between her legs.

'That should do it.' He dropped the rag, flopped again beside her and emptied his glass.

Becky grew anxious. 'Haven't you had enough?'

'Must drink it. Present from my best friend. Anyway, I'm drowning my sorrows.'

'What sorrows?'

'Got no money, got no commissions, got no talent. Nobody wants my lovely paintings.' He put his hand to his forehead and squinted at her, then his head fell back against the cushions, his eyes closed.

Dear Lord! He'd passed out. When Becky looked at this dishevelled, vulnerable man, always so sophisticated and self-assured in company, her heart swelled with love. His confidence needed bolstering. His work was good. He would be a success one day. She told him so constantly. But why should he believe her? What did she know about art?

After undoing his shoes she was stumped. How to pull out the blankets from under his dead weight? Roger wouldn't need his blankets tonight. She ventured into his bedroom and looked around, surprised. The only furniture was a double feather bed in total disarray and a huge mahogany-framed mirror on the facing wall. A pile of dirty laundry in the corner caught her eye. Andrew's pink shirt on top! They must do, or rather *not* do their laundry together. Next time she would arrive early for a sitting and do the washing.

She took the blankets off the bed and covered Andrew. Asleep, he looked so innocent. She smoothed his hair and kissed his cheek. He didn't stir. On an impulse, she pressed her lips gently to his, *soft and warm*. Then she jumped back, ashamed. He respected her. He had standards. She must let him take his own time. Before leaving, she took one last, longing look at his sleeping face.

The next day a letter from Liz awaited Becky on her return from work. She flopped on to the bed and tore it open:

Dearest Beck,

Just thought I'd tell you that the bride of only three weeks made the sad announcement today that she's lost the baby. Baby, my foot! Dora never *was* pregnant.

I'm dead sorry for Ted, but I confess it's a relief not having her here. Ma's been crochetier than ever but I think she's just missing Dora, *and* the gin.

The bairns are treasures, and Will is working four shifts a week. Better than nothing, but we couldn't manage without your help. Bless you for that.

Your loving sis,
Liz

Twenty-Four

O n a raw morning in March 1923, Becky unlocked the door to Harold Walker & Sons, lit the stove and filled the kettle. She and Mr Walker always had a quick cup of tea before starting work.

Singing, she took the biscuits from the cupboard. The kettle gurgled. She made tea and set the metal pot on the stove to keep hot. Mr Walker was unusually late. Just then, the office telephone screeched for attention. She ran, and said, 'Walker and Sons,' into the receiver.

'This is Mrs Foster, Mr Walker's housekeeper. I have to tell you, luv, the poor man died in his sleep last night. I found him this morning when I came.'

Becky's head floated above her body. She gripped the receiver as if to anchor herself. She'd grown very fond of Mr Walker. 'What did he die of?' Her voice came from someone else's throat.

'A heart attack. Sudden like, hinny. He can't have suffered long.'

'But he died alone,' Becky wailed, and hot tears scalded her cheeks. 'He didn't have anyone at the end.'

'Aye, but there's folk as'll miss him. Me and you, especially. He sometimes talked about you. Anyway, hen, his solicitor said to close the shop and go home.'

'But Mr Walker would want me to finish the orders in hand, I *know* he would. He'd never let his customers down.'

'Well, if that's what you want, hinny, but I don't know as you'll get paid. The solicitor told me to stay on till the funeral. That's all. And me looking after Mr Walker

187

for thirty years.' The voice broke and the woman took a racked breath.

'When is the funeral?'

'I'll let you know, pet. It'll be a few days.'

'Thank you.' Becky replaced the receiver. Suddenly everything seemed loud – the tick of the clock on the wall, the market vendors' shouts outside, the hiss from the paraffin stove. Steam gushed from the now stewed tea she'd forgotten. Automatically she rescued the pot, then sat by the stove, staring at Mr Walker's empty chair. Her thoughts dwelled on him for a long time before they turned to her own dilemma. How to find another job with hundreds of applicants for every job available? She couldn't live on the income from her clients *and* send money to Liz. And Mrs Dunn wouldn't tolerate her working full-time from home.

With the back of her hand, Becky wiped her tears and returned to her sewing machine. She would work overtime to finish the current orders this week. Next week she would look for a job.

The following day Mrs Foster telephoned again. The funeral would be at eleven o'clock on Friday, at St Michael's Church near Mr Walker's home. The solicitor had asked that Mrs Foster and Becky stay after the funeral to discuss certain matters.

By Friday Becky was still behind with the outstanding orders. No doubt the solicitor would want the keys. She took them but would ask to stay on a few more days. She also took the books, which she'd kept up to date, and the cash and cheques she'd received.

After the funeral, Becky helped Mrs Foster, a hollow-cheeked, scrawny woman in her sixties, to serve refreshments at the house. They were clearing away the dishes after the last guests when the solicitor, Mr Corwin-Smith, summoned them to the study.

They followed the stout, balding man as he waddled into Mr Walker's study, a quiet, green room, with shining cherry-wood furniture Mrs Foster must have spent hours polishing over the years.

Mr Corwin-Smith sat behind the desk and laced his hands over his belly. 'Please be seated.' He nodded towards the chairs opposite, then cleared his throat. 'Ladies, I have now gone over Mr Walker's affairs, and must inform you that the good man remembered you in his will.'

His jowels wobbled as he spoke and Becky failed to detect any note of pleasure in his educated voice. How kind of Mr Walker to think of his workers, she thought.

'To you, Mrs Foster,' the man went on, 'Mr Walker bequeaths out of the proceeds of the sale of the house whatever sum necessary to buy a comfortable flat. In this endeavour I am to help you.' He squinted through the glasses perched on his red nose to read the wording of the will. 'Er . . . as a thankyou for your thirty years of devotion to his well-being.'

A squeak escaped from Mrs Foster's lips before she burst into tears. 'My oh my!' She covered her face with her scrawny hands and continued to weep.

'There's more.' Mr Corwin-Smith ignored her outburst. 'Mr Walker also arranged a pension in the sum of two pounds a week until your death.'

'Eey, by!' Mrs Foster exploded again and dabbed at her face with her handkerchief. 'He knew I had nobody. Such a kind man, he was. And here I was thinking I had to find another job at *my* age.'

Over his spectacles, Mr Corwin-Smith looked at Becky, then again at the will. 'To you, Miss Ryan, he bequeaths his business premises and contents. There are seventy years left on his hundred-year lease. The annual ground rent and rates of twenty pounds will be paid from his remaining funds until your death, or until such time as you wish to vacate the premises for any reason.'

Bewildered, Becky clutched the keys she'd been about to return until they cut into her hand.

Mr Corwin-Smith squinted again at the print. 'He wishes you to close his business and start your own. Aware that you have already a small clientele and will be successful, he offers the sum of thirty pounds to help you to start. Afterwards, you will receive a weekly stipend of two pounds for five years, or until your business affords you a good life and you no longer need assistance. He thanks you for your devoted service and hard work, without which his business would have failed.'

Becky swallowed hard. She could say nothing.

Mrs Foster addressed Mr Corwin-Smith, her voice quavering. 'We're very grateful, sir, but begging your pardon, I know Mr Walker had relatives, and his house and business are worth a lot of money.'

'Indeed they are.' He continued, throwing out his words like a handful of coppers to street urchins: 'Mr Walker discloses in his will that his two cousins' wealth far exceeds his own. Though he bequeaths to them family furniture, paintings and trinkets, he prefers the money to go where it is needed.'

'Eey, my!' Mrs Foster wiped her eyes again. 'Do I stay on then, sir?'

'You may stay until you find a suitable flat. Miss Ryan, kindly call at my office at two o'clock tomorrow to sign the transfer deeds.' He handed her a gold-embossed card.

'Thank you.' Holding out a trembling hand for the card, Becky realized that she was still clutching the keys.

She found herself back at Walker & Sons and opened the door.

Dizzy with disbelief and delight, she toured the premises, seeing them with new eyes. She would paint the woodwork a deep pink, drape the walls of the window display with white muslin, and buy two mannequins to show her models. What to call it? Becky's Boutique? No, 'Becky' wasn't elegant enough. Rebecca! Simply that! In large pink letters on white, and underneath, *Couturier* in smaller letters. Her present clients wouldn't know that the word meant ladies' tailor, but the wealthier clients she hoped to attract would.

Her excitement mounted as she studied the kitchen area adjacent to the office. It had a window and was larger than her present room. She could partition it off and live on the premises until she could afford her own flat.

Happiness went to her head like a strong cocktail. She couldn't work today. It was four o'clock. She returned to Mr Walker's office and stroked the desk. Tears plopped on to the leather surface. Dear Mr Walker. He'd thought enough of her to give her such happiness. Yet how she would miss him! In a silent prayer of thanks to him she vowed she would justify his confidence in her. Dabbing her eyes with the black-rimmed mourning handkerchief she'd bought for the funeral, she walked home. First she would write to Liz, then, after tea, pay Andrew a surprise visit. She'd never visited without an appointment, but this was a special occasion. He would be pleased that her career was taking off, even though his own wasn't.

Outside the door she heard Andrew and Roger, voices raised in anger. She hesitated. It was a bad time. She would wait until tomorrow. But Andrew's words rooted her to the spot.

'You bloody traitor! If that's what you want, you can play around as much as you like in future, but not under my nose. I'm leaving.'

'Oh, yes? And who've you got lined up for free bed and board this time?' A loud sneer came from Roger.

Feet stamped across the floor and the door flew open. Andrew was carrying his coat.

Becky found her voice. 'Oh, Andrew, I was just about to knock. I . . . I'm sorry.'

'What the hell are you doing here? You don't have a sitting.'

Boiling blood crept up her neck to her face. 'No, I just have some good news I wanted to tell you.'

He gripped her arm tightly. 'Come on then, you can celebrate and I can drown my sorrows.'

He marched her downstairs and up the street to the Black

Crow, a seamy pub with dark oak-panelled walls, uncomfortable wooden chairs and tables that looked as if they hadn't
been wiped for months. Becky sat at a corner table, away
from the throng at the bar.

Andrew stood over her, his face like stone. 'What would
you like?'

'A pink lady, please.' Becky realized this was the first
time he'd bought her a drink since the night he'd asked her
to model.

He returned with a pink lady and a large whisky for himself.
'All right, what news?'

His bad mood clouded Becky's joy at telling him, but she
perserved. 'Mr Walker's left the premises to me to start my
own business, plus a lump sum to get started, and two pounds
a week until I'm independent.'

His cool blue eyes looked up from his glass. 'How much
lump sum?'

'Thirty pounds.'

'Congratulations! I suppose you won't want to sit for a
down-and-out artist any more.'

'Of course I do! You know I enjoy it . . . *and* our friendship.'
Her voice trailed off. They'd never discussed their personal
relationship.

He took her hand across the table. 'Thank you, Beck. You're
the best friend a man could wish for.' He knocked back his
whisky. 'I need another.'

'Please, let me pay. It's my celebration.' Becky delved into
her purse and produced a florin.

'Absolutely not.' Andrew folded his arms in a school-boyish
gesture, his lips pouting. 'I've never yet let a lady buy me a
drink and I'm not starting now.'

Becky laughed. 'I'm not a *lady*, Andrew, I'm your *friend*.
Or so you keep saying.'

His face cheered. 'You're right, and my soon-to-be-rich
friend at that.' He took the florin and returned to the bar.

Two drinks later, he rose. 'I have to go. Have a model
coming at nine.'

Becky felt like a child who'd had a treat whisked away. She forced a smile. 'Who's the model? Do I know her?'

'No, and it's a *he*.'

Relief, like a team of carthorses, crashed into the fragile stable of her love. Then she remembered the row. 'But can you go back? I couldn't help overhearing you and Roger.' She cast her eyes down.

'Oh, that!' He buttoned his overcoat. 'We snarl at each other several times a week. Just our artists' temperaments. We get on pretty well really.'

Twenty-Five

'This bloody machine! Me thread's snapped again.' Janine slumped in her chair like a rag doll.

'You've set the tension too tight.' Becky, at the neighbouring machine, went to her aid. 'Remember – turn knob *right* for big stitches, *left* for small. You'll get the hang of it.'

'Never!'

'I thought you liked sewing.'

'It beats posing starkers for six-handed groping artists.' Janine threaded the needle again. 'And, talking about groping! Has Saint Andrew's halo slipped yet? I can't believe he still hasn't—'

'*No, he hasn't,*' Becky's voice always rose when protecting Andrew, but now softened. 'He *is* beginning to show affection, though. He held my hand in the pictures last night.' She could still feel his long fingers wrapped round hers.

'The pictures?' Janine dropped her jaw in exaggerated surprise. 'He actually took you out?'

'I wish you weren't so hard on him, Jan.'

'*You* paid, I suppose.'

'What if I did?' Becky changed the subject. 'Got a letter from Liz today.'

'How's your Dora? Preggers again yet?' Janine giggled.

'I'm glad Dora lied to make Ted marry her. It's made Liz's life easier.'

The doorbell clanged. Becky stood and straightened the fluted skirt of her grey jersey dress. She had to look fashionable for business.

As she opened the door, excitement boiled inside her like

lard in a chip pan. Andrew was leaning against the doorpost. Then she smelled whisky on his breath and noticed his blood-shot eyes.

'Had another little tiff with Roger. Thought I'd visit my sweet angel for tea and sympathy.' He began to slide down the post.

'Come in, for goodness sake.' Becky grabbed his arm and supported him through the workshop.

'I'm just leaving.' Janine gave Becky a warning shake of her head and stalked out.

In her room, Andrew fell on to the divan bed that doubled as a sofa. She propped up his head with cushions.

'Ooh! Nice! You're so good to me, Beck.'

'Back in a moment,' she said, running to lock the front door and turn the sign in the window to *Closed*. When she returned, she wet a flannel and laid it on Andrew's forehead.

'Ouch! Cold.' He always reverted to his childish voice when drunk or unhappy.

Becky felt like a mother tending him. 'Lie still and I'll make tea.'

'Coffee.'

'All right, coffee. What did you argue about this time?'

Andrew pouted. 'Roger was a pig. It wasn't my fault.'

From experience, Becky knew that was all he would tell her. She made coffee, pouring boiling water into the pot and, as he'd taught her, letting it stand until the grounds settled. He disliked floating grains. 'Sit up. Here's your coffee,' she said. 'You look terrible.'

His hands shook as he took the mug. 'Ooooh, you're so good to me.'

'Someone needs to look after you. You obviously can't do it yourself.' Becky felt overwhelmed by tenderness at his dishevelled, helpless appearance.

He sipped the coffee and handed it back. 'No more. Just sleep.' As he spoke, his head fell back on the pillows and his eyes closed.

Becky smiled. Andrew wasn't a habitual drunk like some

at the pub. He only drank excessively when he rowed with his flatmates. While he slept, she sautéed potatoes, mixed an omelette and opened the drop-leaf dining table for two. She loved her little room – the two bentwood dining chairs, the coffee table – an old butler's table she'd stripped and restained herself – and in the window corner a wicker armchair with brocade cushions. She'd hung matching curtains and whitewashed the backyard wall to reflect the light.

Dreamily, she took two plates from the cupboard. How wonderful to be married and set the table for two – or more – for ever!

She was sitting in the wicker chair sketching designs when Andrew groaned. He blinked and peered about until his gaze lighted on Becky. 'What the blazes—?'

'It's all right. You've slept for three hours.'

He jerked up and rubbed his hands over his face as if washing it. 'Oh, Lord, why do I make such a mess of my life?'

She knelt beside him. 'Don't be silly, your life's just starting. You're going to be a success. Splash your face and comb your hair. Supper's almost ready.'

He stumbled to the sink and removed his jacket. Becky smiled. Only the front and cuffs of his shirt had been ironed. Washed, groomed, and wearing his jacket, he sat at the table and ate in silence.

'I know you and Roger disagree a lot, but he'll be sorry and ask you back as usual.' Becky decided to draw him out.

He looked up at her. 'Nope.'

'Why not?'

'He's found another flatmate.'

'Already! What will you do?'

'I thought you might be kind enough to let me doss down on your floor until I get sorted out.'

Becky's world shifted. Giddily she confronted the prospect! The people they knew didn't care about such matters any more.

'Of course you can stay.' Did she sound too eager?

'Thanks, Beck. You're the sort of girl a man can count on.'

'Where are your things?'

'At the left-luggage office. I'll get them.' He scraped back his chair.

Becky felt as if she had a fever or were entering the final phase of some serious illness. Surely he'd suggested sleeping on the floor out of good manners. They couldn't go from friends to lovers overnight. But, just in case, she would insert her sponge.

While he was out, she arranged bales of heavy tweed from Mr Walker's old stock under the window wall. She covered the makeshift mattress with a sheet and added one of her own blankets and pillows.

Her heart hammered in her chest when the doorbell rang. He followed her in and dumped a battered but expensive pigskin suitcase on the improvised bed. 'I had to leave my painting things at Roger's. You're a gem, Beck. Where does a man wash around here?'

Becky smiled to cover her embarrassment. 'At the kitchen sink, and the lavatory's down the corridor.'

While he was in the lavatory, she undressed, washed quickly at the sink and threw on her nightgown. She switched off the light and opened the curtains, allowing the full moon to shed a pale light into the room. Slipping into bed, she pulled the blanket up to her chin and waited. When the door squeaked, her voice croaked, 'The light switch is on the right.'

'I can manage.'

'I'm sorry it's not more comfortable.'

'Please stop saying sorry. It's fine. Goodnight.'

She had no idea how long she'd lain there waiting, listening to him tossing and turning, when the floorboards creaked and soft footsteps padded towards her. He raised the blanket and slipped in beside her. Her heart leaped like a salmon in a stream.

'Angel,' he whispered, as if the dark had ears. 'Can't sleep, angel.'

She turned to face him and his lips brushed hers, then travelled down the side of her neck. His stubble prickled her skin but even that excited her. He was still kissing the curve between her neck and shoulder but she wanted his mouth on hers again. As she tried to seek his lips, he rolled her on to her stomach and raised her nightgown. She gasped with surprise as he gripped her buttocks and entered her, but stopped herself from crying out.

'Angel, my little angel, you're so good to me,' he moaned.

Gritting her teeth as he gripped her tighter and his movements became more urgent, she told herself it was all right. She'd learned at the clinic there were many ways a man and a woman could please each other. She tried to relax and to feel his pleasure as her own.

When he groaned and fell over her she fought back tears. She'd wanted him to caress her naked body, to explore his, to kiss while they were joined. But, she told herself, it was the first time. In his eagerness he'd got carried away.

'Sorry, angel, am I heavy?' He rolled off her and pulled down her nightgown, then adjusted his pyjamas. He hadn't undone them. Again she reminded herself, after tonight they would take more time. He turned his back to her and she nestled into him.

'If you want, you can stay,' she said. 'Soon I'll be able to afford a proper flat. You could use the window corner for painting. Most of the time I'm in the shop or the office anyway.'

'It's a kind thought, sweet pie. Thanks. Nighty night.'

One Sunday, after buying second-hand clothes at Paddy's Market, Becky returned home. Though it was ten o'clock, Andrew was still asleep. She smiled at his face in repose, his lock of black hair covering one eye. She removed her shoes so as not to wake him, lit the stove and put the kettle on. Then she fried sausages, tomatoes and cut thick chunks of bread. Her grocery bills had more than doubled recently, but her happiness had increased beyond measure. She'd adapted

198

to Andrew's preferences in love-making and wanted to please him. Wasn't that what love was all about?

While waiting for the sausages, she tidied the room, picking up props, costumes, sketches and crumpled paper, which Andrew tossed anywhere when frustrated.

When breakfast was ready, she set a tray on the butler's table by the divan and gently shook Andrew. 'Wakey, wakey, Breakfast!'

He turned over and muttered into the pillow.

'Andrew! I have customers coming. You'll be trapped in here till they go.'

He faced her and opened one eye. 'Do I smell coffee?'

'You do.'

'Well, that makes getting up more tolerable.' He sat up in his grey silk pyjamas and blinked. 'You bitch! It's Sunday. You have no bloody customers.' He reached out to grab her but she laughed and drew back.

He jumped up, threw on his dressing gown, glanced at the tray and pulled a face. 'Sausages and egg! Becky's version of a gourmet breakfast.'

'It's all I can afford. On my own I eat porridge.' She hated the hurt note that had crept into her voice.

'That's all right, my love. When I strike it rich, I'll make up for these threadbare days. A fancy house, fancy servants, fancy everything.' He sat on the divan and sliced into a steaming sausage.

Becky wondered if he were thinking in the singular or the plural. 'And perhaps a fancy little brood of artists and dress designers?' she ventured. Was she included in his dream?

'God, no! Too many of those already. Nice coffee. Hardly any floating grounds. You're improving.'

She accepted the compliment and began eating. Andrew couldn't be drawn out.

'Got a model coming later.'

Becky's heart tumbled to the floor. 'But it's the only day we spend together.'

'Only day he's free too,' he said, pricking his egg yolk with his fork.

'Do you have to pay him?' Andrew rarely paid for anything, but she knew he was broke.

'No, it's a chap I know, Bob Williams.'

Becky felt relieved but still disappointed. She would have to leave the room. Although she always used the time working, she would rather do that with Andrew nearby.

That evening Andrew was in a playful mood.

'More?' He waved the whisky bottle his friend, Bob, had given him over her glass and she nodded. It was her third, but why not relax. She'd worked all day.

They read the Sunday papers in companionable silence, until he yawned. 'Time for beddy-byes.'

'Mmm,' she agreed, longing to be close to him.

After their nightly ritual, criss-crossing to the lavatory, the sink, the dressing room and office, she stood between him and the bed as he approached. She undressed slowly and deliberately in front of him, the summer evening light slanting through the window. It was the first time she'd done this. When she was down to her satin shift she dropped it to the floor and stood naked before him.

'My, my! I suspect angel's feeling lovey-dovey tonight.'

Quivering with excitement and yearning, she shamelessly drew his hands to her breasts. She longed for him to caress her there but he never did.

'Nice flat little titties,' he said, slipping his hands down to her belly. 'And nice hard little belly.' Almost immediately he slid to her buttocks and gripped them. 'And *lovely* tight little arse. Angel *is* raring to go tonight. Get into bed before you get cold.'

Disappointed but hopeful, Becky decided she must let him know gently what *she* would like. At the clinic they said a woman should make her needs known, and so far she'd only tried to please Andrew.

She slipped under the covers and when he joined her she

clasped him to her. He embraced her and stroked her back. Dizzy with desire, she kissed his lips. After a moment he pulled away and patted her hair. Gently she again placed his hands over her breasts, shuddering with pleasure.

'Such hard little nipples for an angel,' he said, and stroked down to her belly.

Then he turned her over and made love passionately in his customary fashion. Afterwards, her body sagged and, as usual, he took that to mean she was satisfied.

At least she'd made a start. Next time she would go further and *show* him what she longed for. But gently. She couldn't insult his manhood by telling him his love-making left her unfulfilled.

Twenty-Six

S hivering, Becky slipped out of bed, threw on her dressing gown and lit the stove. She sat in the wicker chair to sift through the post, eagerly opening the familiar envelope.

24 January 1924

Dearest Beck

I didn't want to tell you that Ma's been bad, but Dr Maynard says she might not last the week. She's got bronchitis and her heart can't take the strain.

Please don't think you have to come, or that you owe her anything. Dora's here a lot, wailing and weeping and giving Ma gallons of gin. The doctor says it doesn't matter now, and it cheers her up. Of course, I'm sad about Ma, but Dora's wild with grief.

Otherwise, the family's well. Do what *you* feel is right, Beck. No guilty conscience.

The bairns send kisses.

Your loving sis, Liz

Becky clutched the letter. Her childish fears about God taking her ma had stopped when she'd turned to Liz for the love her ma denied her. Yet she felt sad that Ma was dying.

Today was Friday. Janine would look after the shop, and Norma would help.

As she looked at Andrew's sleeping face, she felt a swell of sadness at leaving him, even for a short time. But she must make her peace with Ma. She left a note for him and one for Janine and Norma, saying she would be back on Sunday evening.

*   *   *

At Ashington, grey clouds hung low over the belching pit chimneys. Becky set out for Long Row. She couldn't pretend this visit was purely social. Ma and Dora knew by now she kept in touch with Liz, though they didn't know it was through Miss Miles at the Co-op.

Liz must have heard her footsteps. The door opened and she threw her arms round her.

'How is she?' Becky asked when they'd untangled themselves.

'Bad. I'm glad you came. She'll be that thrilled to see you.'

Becky hung her coat on the door and set down her suitcase.

'You're staying?' Liz's tired eyes brightened.

'For the weekend.'

'You don't have to, but I'm glad. I'll bring some tea. Will's on shift and his folks have taken the bairns off me hands.'

'I'll go up now.'

'Dora's there.' Liz looked anxious. 'She's sat with her all night. She's taking it hard.'

'Don't worry. I promise – no rows.' Nervously Becky entered her mother's room and stood by the bed. 'It's me, Ma.'

'Eey, our Becky!' Florrie's voice was thick and wheezy. Propped up with pillows, she held out a wizened hand. 'Come to see your old Ma, have you?'

Becky tried not to show dismay at how thin and wasted her mother was. She took her hand. 'How're you feeling, Ma?'

'How do you bloody think she's feeling?' Dora, wrapped in a blanket, was sitting on the bedside chair. Her face was pale and drawn, devoid of makeup, her hair scraggy.

'Hello, Dora.' Becky sat on the bed, still holding Ma's hand. 'Liz told me you weren't well, Ma.'

'Aye, we know you keep in touch,' Dora said.

'But I'm that glad you've got each other.' Ma stifled a cough. 'And I'm glad our Dora's got a good man to look after her.'

Dora stood. 'I'll go home for a nap, Ma. I'll be back later.' She gave Florrie an almost reverent hug and left, ignoring Becky.

'Eey, it's grand to see you, Beck.' Tears filmed Florrie's rheumy eyes and zigzagged down her cracked cheeks. 'And you an' all, Liz,' she said as Liz brought in the tea. A violent coughing fit overtook her, and Becky handed her a square of old sheet from a pile on the bedside table. Then she spooned red medicine from a bottle beside the rags. Florrie sucked it in.

'There now, Ma, relax and have your tea.' Liz sounded as exhausted as Florrie.

'Nah, nothing. I just need to talk to you both.'

Liz gave Becky a mug and sat in the chair with her own. They looked at their mother expectantly.

Florrie drew a rasping breath. 'How's work, Beck?'

Becky told her about her growing success and her artist boyfriend. It would please Ma. She didn't care that Dora would find out.

'Eey, I'm that glad for you, luv. You've got guts. You've worked hard, and you even talk like a posh businesswoman. And Liz here, with a lovely husband and bairns! I'm glad you're both happy. I've lain here day after day thinking what a rotten mother I've been to the both of you. I want to tell you I'm sorry!'

'No, Ma!' Guilt clutched Becky like a giant fist. She should have visited Ma earlier.

Florrie opened and shut her mouth as if to say more but was seized by another coughing fit. It subsided after Liz had rubbed her back and she lay against the pillows, one wizened hand kneading the rag.

'It's all right, Ma,' Liz said. 'You don't need to apologize for anything.'

Becky rose and kissed her cheek. 'Rest now. We love you, Ma.'

They walked downstairs in silence. 'Poor Ma,' Liz said at last.

They sank into the chairs flanking the fireplace.

'She's so pathetic,' Becky said. 'I feel something like love for her again. I wish I hadn't had all those bad thoughts about her.'

'Oh, luv, don't feel guilty. You had a lifetime of good reasons for those bad thoughts.' Liz dried her eyes on her apron and stood. 'Eey, me head's still in a jumble. I've got the soup to make.'

'I'll help.' Becky felt nostalgic following Liz into the pantry. How many hours had they spent here chopping vegetables and soothing each other after trouble with Ma or Dora? She leaned against the draining board. 'I'll try to be civil to Dora from now on, but I think it's too late for me to try to love her.'

Liz dumped carrots into the sink. 'You don't have to, pet. She doesn't play a big part in your life any more. Though she'll know about your shop now. I was glad you told Ma, but Dora could be a nuisance.'

'She never goes to Newcastle, and she doesn't know the address. I'll send her the odd dress to keep her happy. It'll be a relief in a way. I can make more for you and the children.'

Liz gave her a fond look. 'The *children*! I still call them the bairns. You're getting such a posh accent from your Andrew and his friends.'

Becky plopped a peeled carrot into a bowl. Did Liz think she was getting snooty? 'It's not only Andrew, luv, I'm trying to sound right for the business as well.'

'I hope you're not ashamed of your old sis.'

'Never!' Becky's wet hands flapped as she flung her arms round Liz's neck. 'I've always been proud you're my sister and I always will be.'

They jumped as the back door opened. Liz squeaked in surprise. 'Dora!'

As she hung her coat on the door, Dora pulled a bottle of gin from the pocket. She glared at their stunned faces. 'What's the matter? Did I interrupt your tittle-tattle about me?'

'We were complaining about these rotten carrots.' Becky tried to adopt a new voice – light, pleasant, but not overdone.

Dora stared at her, seeming to notice the stylish dress for the first time. 'Got a fancy man to buy your clothes now, eh?'

'I made it myself. I'll make you one for your birthday if you like.'

Dora studied the dress, obviously tempted, then the red lights flashed in her eyes and she glowered at Becky. 'Dresses! Ma's up there breathing her last and all you can think of is dresses? You're still a vain selfish little bitch.'

Becky silently continued peeling carrots.

Dora stood in the pantry doorway, clutching the bottle. 'What's the matter? Pussy got your tongue?'

'No, I just don't feel like arguing when Ma's so poorly.' She'd struck the right chord. Dora didn't retaliate. Becky had turned her own words back on her. The red dots left Dora's eyes and she flounced off, grabbed two tumblers and turned at the stairs. Her eyes were wet and her voice trembled. 'If you'd ever had any feeling for her, you wouldn't have run away and left her.' The stairs groaned as she thumped up them.

Becky popped a puff of air through her lips. She looked into Liz's frightened face and smiled. 'Don't worry, I won't let her get to me, if only for your sake, and Ma's.'

When the soup was ready, Liz mixed the dumplings. She hesitated, then reached for the salt. 'Ma might as well enjoy some salt now.' A tear trailed down her cheek. Becky set two bowls on the table while Liz took up Ma's and Dora's.

'I have to tell you, Beck,' Liz said when she joined her, 'Will was going to write to ask you to stop sending money. Now that he's working part time we can manage. We don't have our Dora's face to feed any more.' Her face crumpled. 'And soon we won't have Ma.'

Becky handed her her handkerchief. 'She wants to go, luv. It's a blessing. I'm so stunned, I forgot to ask. How *is* Will?'

Liz sniffed and returned the handkerchief. 'Excited about Labour getting in. He's convinced they're going to do wonders for the workers, especially the miners.'

'Let's wait and see. At the moment you still need help.'

Liz put down her spoon and turned to Becky with a sigh. 'Please, Beck, it hurts his pride to take money from you.'

'But I can't have you scrimping when I'm running my own business.' She paused, a dumpling balanced on her spoon. 'I'll stop for now if you'll promise me one thing.'

'What?'

'That you'll tell me on the quiet if you're in trouble. Will needn't know I've sent anything.'

'I couldn't lie to him.'

'If it means your family eats or half starves, you could. For now, instead of money I'll send clothes for you all. Will can't object to clothes.'

'Sending her clothes, eh?' Dora stood at the foot of the stairs. 'Ma says you've got your own shop. By God! What silly bugger's paying for that?'

'It's just a tiny rented shop I live in.'

'Aye, probably in a posh flat over it. Who would have thought it? Our mangy little Becky—'

'If you like, I'll take your measurements before I leave,' she cut in.

'Aye, I thought you'd be off soon. We're honoured you showed your face at all.'

'I came to see Ma.'

Dora laughed and the smell of gin wafted across the table. 'I know you didn't come to see *me*. Ma and I know you and Liz send each other secret letters.'

'Not secret. Private. I like to keep in touch.' Becky was proud of her calm voice.

After five, Will returned, Nancy, still a toddler, and Billy, clinging to his pit-blackened hands. Mary, playing the little mother, held Nancy's other hand. 'Becky!' Will said, freeing his charges. 'What a nice surprise!'

Becky barely had time to return the greeting before a rush of miniature bodies threw themselves at her. 'My, such a lovely welcome!'

Liz wiped their hands with a wet rag. 'Auntie Becky's going

to play with you in the front room while your da has his bath. Then we're having sausages and mash for tea.'

Becky ushered the children next door. Sorrow rippled through her as she looked around her father's old room. But it was cheerful now. Two bunks and a cot were the only furniture. But toys littered the floor – peg dolls, some stuffed dolls she'd made from scraps, and brightly painted wooden lorries and trains. They were beautifully crafted. Will's handiwork, she guessed. He'd made toys for the children before, but this work looked professional. 'Let's play with your lovely new trains,' she said.

Twenty-Seven

B y Sunday morning Becky felt drained. She'd managed to ignore Dora's insults, but she'd had a bad headache the previous evening.

When Becky emerged from the front room, Liz was making tea and Will had taken the children to his parents.

Liz frowned. 'Oh, luv, you look terrible. *Please*, go home after breakfast. You've done your duty by Ma. You need a rest before work tomorrow.'

The thought of seeing Andrew quickened Becky's pulse. She sat at the table. 'You're right. I'll catch the next bus. It was wonderful seeing you and the bairns and Will, but I've had a bellyful of Dora for one weekend.'

Liz handed her tea and a sausage sandwich. 'You did well.'

'I'll be back soon,' Becky said, unable to add, *for Ma's funeral*. After finishing the tea and half the sandwich, she pushed back her chair. 'I'll get my things, then say goodbye to Ma.'

'Aye, she's probably awake now. Why don't you take her tea up.'

'Right, that'll perk her up.'

When she peeked round the bedroom door, Ma's eyes were closed but she clicked her gums and said, 'That you, our Liz?'

'No, it's Becky, Ma. I've brought your tea.'

Florrie's eyes opened. 'Eey, I could do with that. Me mouth feels full of gravel.'

Becky sat gently on the bed and gave her the mug. 'I'm catching the morning bus, Ma. I have things to do.'

Florrie's toothless mouth fell open, then she nodded. 'Aye, I knew you'd have to be off soon. Thank you for coming, lass. I'm that glad I managed to see you.'

'Me too, Ma, and I'll be back.'

Florrie's skinny hands shook as she gripped the mug, spilling tea on the coverlet. Becky took the mug and hugged her mother. For one so frail, Florrie's arms clasped Becky surprisingly tightly. Becky's eyes filled. Ma had never held her like this. They rocked with emotion.

She kissed her mother on the cheek. 'I love you, Ma,' she heard her voice saying. She couldn't remember saying that in her entire life.

Florrie wiped her eyes on the sheet. 'Eey, and I love you, lass. I don't deserve such good bairns.'

Tears filmed Becky's eyes as she slipped out. She'd never imagined she would feel anything like affection for Ma. How sad that they hadn't enjoyed a loving relationship earlier!

Alighting from the bus, Becky felt a rush of happiness. Newcastle was her home now. In just a few minutes she would be cosy in front of the stove with Andrew. Despite the gale-force wind that blew dust into her eyes, she marched on, head down, then stopped. She should pick up some groceries, but it was Sunday. Perhaps Andrew had shopped. She'd left thirty shillings in the grocery money jar. No, he hated shopping. But she had tins of soup, sardines and bread. They wouldn't starve.

Excitement hastened her steps as she reached home. With passing pleasure, she noticed her name in large letters above the shop and, trembling with excitement, unlocked the door. The wall clock said ten o'clock. Andrew would still be asleep.

She tiptoed to the living quarters and quietly opened the door, where she stopped. A surge of sensations clamoured in her head. Andrew was sleeping, and beside him lay a tousle-haired man with one hairy arm outside the blankets round Andrew's waist. The man's fingernails were black.

The noises in her head gave way to a pain in her temples.

Unable to move, she squeezed her head between her palms, while her fragile happiness crumbled as silently as coal ash. But she must have made a sound. Andrew sat up, naked as far as she could see. He said nothing.

His companion opened his eyes. Black, greasy hair hung over his forehead. He looked as dirty and wretched and dispirited as the husbands of the women at the clinic, or those unemployed men who hung around street corners. So this was what people would do for money! It had to be a business transaction.

'Jesus!' The man pulled the sheets up to his chin.

'Get out, Becky.' Andrew's voice was dangerously quiet.

Somehow, she found her way to the lavatory. There she vomited until, exhausted, she lay curled up on the cold linoleum, her hands gripping her head, trying to contain the searing pain shooting through it, then everything went dark.

When she opened her eyes, she had no idea how long she'd lain there. Awareness of the horror slithered back into her head like a slimy monster. What to do? Where to go? She couldn't go to her room, but she couldn't go anywhere else in this state. She must at least wash her face. Knowing Andrew, he'd probably gone out to avoid facing her.

She prised herself up, her head now a dull ache. On feet like lead weights she made her way to her room. It was empty. It was also like a pigsty. Earlier, consumed by the scene on the bed, she hadn't noticed the empty bottle of whisky and two glasses, together with a mess of dirty dishes.

She lifted the lid of the housekeeping money jar. Empty. Still wearing her coat, she sat in the wicker chair. She hugged herself and rocked but couldn't cry. All the moisture had been sapped out of her.

Andrew, oh, Andrew, she wailed inside. *How could you? And how could I not have known? I love you. I still love you.* She rocked harder. What a blind fool she'd been! Janine had tried to tell her. Probably everybody knew but her. In her wild consuming love she'd ignored the signs. She longed

211

to lie down and sleep for ever, but she couldn't go near that bed.

She forced herself up on wobbly legs, splashed her face and cleaned her teeth. Rubbing her cheeks hard with the towel, she tried to *feel* something, but she was numb. Again she curled up in the wicker chair and hugged herself, as if to hold herself together. She stared ahead at nothing.

An eternity later she looked about her. The room was dark. She couldn't stay here. Janine would be with Victor. Annie! She would go to Annie.

Needles of icy rain stung her face, yet she was glad she was still able to feel something.

At the café, the sign said, 'closed', but the light was on and Annie was sweeping the floor. Becky tapped on the glass. Annie opened the door. 'Becky! What's wrong? Come upstairs, luv. The fire's on.'

Becky followed her to the flat above, where she lived with her daughter, Vera. The small living room was furnished with two comfortable chairs beside an old-fashioned black stove, and a chenille-covered dining table with four chairs.

Annie indicated a fireside chair. 'Take off that wet coat and sit yourself down, pet.' She pushed the sooty kettle on the trivet over the flames. 'I'll mash us a nice pot of tea. Just tell me what's wrong when you're ready.'

It was like Annie not to probe. Becky absorbed the warmth. She knew if she said only that she wanted to sit there all night, Annie wouldn't question it.

'Would you like a scone or a biscuit? You look half starved.'

'No, thank you.' The mundane words seemed to bring back her voice. 'Annie, I . . .' But she didn't know how to begin.

'It's all right, pet, take your time. We've got all night.'

Night! The word sparked Becky off. 'Could I stay the night, Annie? I . . . I can't go home. It's Andrew.'

'Aye, I thought as much.' Annie handed her a mug of tea.

She struggled to find words to explain. 'I didn't tell you, but he's been living with me for six months. I was blind and stupid not to know what I'm sure the whole world knows.' Hot tears seared her cheeks like pellets of molten lead.

Annie sat opposite. 'Take your time, now.'

'I went to see my mother. She's dying.'

'Eey, I'm sorry, hen.'

Becky nodded and wiped her eyes with her knuckles. 'I came home early and . . . and found Andrew in bed . . . with . . .' Her voice fell apart and scattered like a broken string of beads.

'Another woman, eh?'

'I wish! It was a man.' She covered her face with her hands and wailed.

'Me poor bairn.' Annie leaned over her and took Becky in her arms.

Whimpering like a lost puppy, Becky dissolved into her.

At last she raised her head. 'I don't know what to do. My life's a blank wall. I can't go forward any more.'

'Beck, you've *got* to go forward, no matter how bad life gets. That shop has to be open tomorrow. Your customers rely on you.'

Becky shuddered. 'Even the shop seems contaminated by Andrew's presence. How could I love him so much one minute and *loathe* him the next?'

'You know you don't loathe him. You were in love.'

'That, and blind and stupid! I know Janine suspected. And I might have seen the signs if I hadn't worshipped him like a God.'

'You have to put him out of your life now, luv. Vera doesn't start work till nine. She'll go with you before work and help you to clear out his things and clean the place up.'

Becky felt as though she stood on the edge of a frozen river, forced to cross, not knowing how thick the ice was. The thought of going back to that place, that bed, packing Andrew's belongings, almost paralysed her. 'I think I could cope with Vera there. But he has a key. What if he's come back?'

'Just say you'll ring for the coppers if he doesn't give you the key and leave. He'll scarper. He won't want his secret made public.'

The thought of calling the police to take Andrew away made Becky feel giddy. And tomorrow, when she must confront him! She counted to ten and breathed deeply. 'Thank you Annie,' she said, 'I don't know what I'd do without you.'

Annie rose. 'You'd manage. You're stronger than you think. Look how you've got on since you came here without a penny.'

'But you don't know how scared I've always been of everything I've ever done, even trying to hold me own against our Dora. Everyone thinks I'm brave and clever and successful, when really I'm all jelly inside.'

'You have good reason to be proud of yourself. Never forget that. Now, give me a hand with the bunk, luv, and I'll show you where the lavatory is. Our Vera's out with her lad.'

After helping Annie to set up the folding bunk near the fire, Becky climbed in, wearing one of Vera's nightgowns. She closed her eyes but the alarm clock, set for five, ticked relentlessly. She heard the flat door open and Annie's stage whisper from the bedroom. 'Vera! Come in here. Becky's asleep in the bunk.'

She was relieved not to have to explain any more tonight.

The alarm clock clamoured and Becky jumped up. She would start the fire and the kettle. She hadn't closed her eyes all night. The rain had drummed over her head constantly, like a team of workmen driving nails into her coffin.

She pulled on her coat and crept around in her bare feet. The fire took easily and she filled the kettle from the pantry tap and set it over the growing flames. By the time she'd washed and dressed, the kettle was steaming.

'Eey, what a welcome sight!' Annie shuffled in, wrapped in an oversized dressing gown. 'One of these days our Vera'll get up first and make the tea.' She yelled into the bedroom, 'Vera! Get your lazy backside in here.'

Annie bustled to the pantry as Vera trailed into the kitchen wearing a newer version of her mother's dressing gown. She put her arms round Becky. 'Hello, luv, I'm that sorry about Andrew. Ma told me everything. Of course I'll help you to clean up.'

'Thank you. I couldn't face it alone.' Becky changed the subject. 'You look wonderful.' Vera had transformed her schoolgirl plaits into a shining black bob with a fringe almost down to her eyes.

'You two had better eat,' Annie said, setting a loaf on the table. 'There's not much up here but plenty of sausages and bacon and eggs in the kitchen downstairs.'

At the thought of food Becky felt her stomach rising. 'Just tea, please.'

'Me an' all, Ma.'

'You're both at least having some bread and marmalade. You can't go out in that on empty bellies.' Annie indicated the rain battering the windowpanes like pebbles hurled by the wind. Tutting at Becky, she cut two slices of bread. 'Our Vera's starving herself to look like you and Janine. In my day, women had a bit of flesh on them.'

Vera struggled to hold a broken umbrella over them as they hurried, heads down, to the Bigg Market. Still, they were soaked when they reached the shop.

Becky turned the key and stamped her feet along the corridor. No sound. She opened the workshop door and, Vera behind her, walked heavily towards her room. As she flung open the door, a rush of blood surged to her head, then drained, as if an overflowing sink had been unplugged. The room was empty.

Vera stripped the bed and put the soiled linen into a pillowcase. 'I'll take this home and do it with me ma's.'

Becky was grateful. She couldn't have touched those sheets. With a grimace, she pulled the battered pigskin suitcase from under the bed and stuffed Andrew's clothing, clean or dirty, into it. Let his next lover sort out his washing. Yesterday, in her shock and confusion, she'd felt a medley of emotions, but now anger alone shook her like a gale. She concentrated on the anger instead of self-pity, rubbing at it as if it were a brass mantel rail she could mist with a puff of breath then shine with a rag.

She closed the suitcase with a snap and dragged it to the front entrance, propping it against the inside of the door. Angry as she was, she couldn't leave his possessions outside in the rain.

When she returned, Vera was attacking the mountain of dirty paint jars and dishes on the draining board. 'I'll help,' Becky said. 'Perhaps scrubbing with carbolic will help to scrub him out of my mind as well.'

'Aye, pretend it's his face you're scrubbing.'

Becky winced. The remark cut through her anger like a knife on cake icing to the flesh of the futile love she still felt.

By eight o'clock they had finished. Andrew's painting supplies, portfolio and easel were stacked along the corridor. She looked round the spotless room. 'Thanks, Vera, I couldn't have done it without your help and moral support.'

'It was nowt. I'll be off now or I'll be late for work. And don't forget! Ring the police if he makes any trouble, and come back to us whenever you want.'

Becky's lips quivered. 'Thank you, and thank your ma for me, but this is my place and I'm going to stay. I'll be back to see you soon though.'

After attending to several customers, Becky went to the workshop to cut out a bridal gown, her first wedding order. Work didn't exactly keep Andrew out of her mind, but the enforced concentration pushed him further into the shadows.

She looked up as she heard the door open. Andrew stood there. The rain had plastered his hair to his scalp, his face was the colour of ashes, and his macintosh was soaked.

Her legs came undone like ribbons. She gripped the cutting table. 'Your things are in the passage.'

'I'm not blind.'

'Everything's there.'

'My trilby and my umbrella?'

Of course, he never went out without his trilby. He must have been in a state yesterday or still drunk. 'Where are they?'

'On top of the wardrobe.'

'I'll get them.' Becky pushed one leg in front of the other and reached her room. When she returned with the hat and umbrella he stood in the same spot. His belongings were gone. No doubt he had a friend outside with a motor.

'Thank you.' He pulled his trilby over his sodden hair, clasped his umbrella, and left.

She stared at the spot where he'd stood. *That was it*! After all they'd been to each other. He'd turned off their relationship like a tap, without a word of regret, apology. Not *any* word. She felt her grief, inside her skull, under her skin to the soles of her feet, but she couldn't cry.

Twenty-Eight

A t midday Janine poked her head round the door. 'Just popped in to say hello.'

Becky raised her ravaged face from her sewing machine.

Janine was beside her in a second. 'What's wrong?'

'Andrew,' was all Becky could get out.

'Oh, pet.' She put her arms round Becky's quivering shoulders. 'Another woman?'

'No, a man. I should have known there were always men before me, and even during me.'

Janine groaned. 'Aye, I'm not surprised. You poor lamb!'

Janine turned the window sign to *Closed*, locked the door, and shepherded Becky to the sitting room, where she seated her at the table. 'You need to eat.' She puttered about and asked no questions, but Becky found herself relating the tale of her visit to Ashington and her early return.

'The bastard!' Janine stirred a pan of soup vigorously. 'And you already in a state over your ma.'

'I never want another man in my life.'

'Oh, you'll get over that.'

'I won't. Now my life is my shop, and the clinic. I'll have more time to help those poor women.' She made a sound like a sneer. 'Now I'm better qualified – an expert on men and their needs. Yet I still don't know what my own needs are.'

'You will. Here, have the soup while it's hot.' She set the bowls and sandwiches on the table.

Becky ate mechanically. She needed the energy to work.

'I'm staying with you this afternoon,' Janine said.

'Thanks. Norma's coming tomorrow.'

Janine bit on her sandwich. 'Good. You need company as well as help.'

Becky's eyes filled. 'Oh, Jan. I don't need to be looked after like a baby.'

'But there's nothing like friends when you need them. Funny, I bumped into Mildred today and she's looking for a job in London. Has friends there. She says it's time she started a new life.'

'Oh, poor Mildred! I'll miss her. And she's even worse off than I am. At least my *body*'s still whole. She'll always have that to remind her.'

Janine attempted a cheerful note. 'Me ma always says, *Time heals all things.* It used to drive me potty but it's true.'

Becky sighed. 'Thanks for staying, Janine,' she said.

'My pleasure, luv. Look, if Mildred comes tonight and Norma's coming tomorrow, give yourself a break and start your spring designs. You enjoy that more than sewing. I'm free this week so I'll come an' all.'

'You're a good friend, Jan.' Becky was the only person Janine allowed to call her that.

Janine grinned. 'Aye, but I'll expect one of those newfangled spring creations when they're ready.'

By autumn Becky was inundated with orders and had started buying new materials for the more expensive outfits. She had adapted her own versions of Chanel's boyish look – Norfolk-jacketed walking or travelling suits, boyish caps only slightly softened with a ribbon or bright feathers, though evening dresses became more daring than ever. Despite the cold weather, no woman seemed to mind shedding her outer garments and emerging like a chrysalis, half-naked in skimpy short or full-length sheaths, sleeveless, or with caftan sleeves almost trailing the floor.

Becky employed Norma three days a week for a wage, and Janine, Mildred and Eileen helped when free. She wished she could employ Eileen full-time, especially after Mildred left for

London. The thought of Eileen still at that sweatshop upset her, but she couldn't yet afford full-time help.

Despite her success, Andrew still haunted her thoughts. Yet time passed, and fruitfully.

She worked at the clinic, often giving talks on birth control and hygiene. Helping those poor women improve their lives, however little, was therapeutic.

She also joined Mrs Pankhurst's Women's Social and Political Union, attending meetings, but joining only peaceful marches, as she refused to employ violence to achieve women's rights. Birth control alone was not enough to gain power over their lives. It was six years since the Representation of the People Act had given the vote to women householders and wives of householders over thirty, and university graduates, but every man over twenty-one could now vote. Why not women?

One evening, as Becky returned from the clinic, Janine was waiting outside the shop. She wore an outfit she'd made herself, from Becky's design – a straight knee-length satin skirt topped with a Chinese-style tunic and feathered cap.

'You look like a fashion model,' Becky said, an idea striking her as she spoke. 'Why don't you model for me? I could get another couple of girls from the pub or from an agency and give fashion shows on Saturday afternoons.' She opened the door and Janine skipped across the showroom after her.

'I'd love to show your swanky clients that I look better in your creations than they do.'

'We could serve tea and dainty sandwiches. I wish I'd thought of it earlier.' Becky stopped at her room door. 'But why are you here so late?'

'I'm taking you to a fabulous party.'

'You know I don't go to parties any more.'

'You'll like this one. It's at a posh house in Jesmond, given by one of Victor's new acquaintances, an old but very successful publisher.'

'I'm not interested in an old publisher.' Becky threw off her coat and shoes and flopped on to the divan.

'But this old publisher has two sons.'

'I'm not interested in his sons.'

Janine knelt by her and took her hands. 'Beck! You *know* Andrew won't be there. Nobody's seen him since January.'

'I'd rather have an early night.'

'Aw, come on. These are *new* people – only a few of the old crowd.' She clenched Becky's hands tighter. 'You're getting awfully boring – obsessed with work and women's rights. You need to enjoy yourself sometimes.'

'You know I don't feel sociable.'

'Oh, go on. Wear that cream satin thing with the fringes. You look fab in that. We're all meeting at Victor's and the men are clubbing together for a taxi. You can't miss it, Beck.'

Becky wavered. 'All right, I'll take my new business cards. I might find some rich clients. But that's the only reason I'm going. No more men!'

Janine clapped her hands in satisfaction. 'Thank God! Whatever your reason, it'll be fun to go out with you again. Victor will be occupied with business, as usual. Now get ready or we'll be late.'

In no time, Becky was made-up and dressed in the cream satin, an elegant black coat and matching cloche hat, and carrying a cream beaded evening bag.

Janine appraised her. 'You look divine. I definitely can't promise the men won't swarm.'

Becky gritted her teeth in the crowded taxi. Victor was in a jovial mood and shouted from the front seat, 'Nice to see you back among the living, Becky.'

'Yes, welcome back,' the others called.

She was glad Jake wasn't there. She couldn't take his cloying adoration.

The taxi stopped at a large detached house on Osborne Road. Inside it was exquisite, furnished in traditional style with oriental rugs and antique furniture.

A lace-capped, uniformed housekeeper led them to the cloakroom, then to an elegant drawing room furnished with green velvet chairs and sofas and low tables.

A bevy of bejewelled bosoms and bloated bellies under straining waistcoats filled the room. Apprehensive, Becky joined the crowd, sticking close to Janine and hoping to disappear. 'See,' Janine said, 'they're all turning to look at you.'

'And you!' Becky had long ago admitted proudly yet shyly that people did turn to look at her, though Andrew hadn't given her confidence in her femininity.

The host, flanked by two younger men, approached the new arrivals.

'Ah, Victor! Where have you been hiding your lovely ladies?'

'Janine and Becky, this is Howard Gray, and his sons Michael and Clive,' Victor said.

Becky noticed he didn't introduce Janine as his girlfriend. She murmured a greeting and took in the trio. No bulging waistcoats here. Howard Gray was tall and slim with a shock of white hair and cheerful hazel eyes. With chestnut hair, the sons looked like younger versions of their father. They were a handsome family.

Michael and Clive shepherded the girls to the bar. Victor, already inebriated, took Howard Gray aside and began earnest conversation. The man looked too respectable to be doing business with Victor, Becky thought.

The son on the right, whom she remembered was Michael, took Becky's arm, and Clive took Janine's. 'What would you like to drink?' Michael led them to a walnut buffet.

Becky resumed her old habit. 'A pink lady, please.'

'The same, please,' Janine said.

It was difficult to tell the brothers apart, except that Michael was about an inch taller than his brother and had a mole on his cheekbone. Janine appeared happy with her handsome new attendant, although, as always, she would seek Victor out before going home.

The men returned with two pink ladies and two Martinis.

'It's nice to see some new faces,' Michael said. Both men surveyed the girls openly.

'Victor's doing business with your father. We came with him and some friends,' Janine said. 'Are you in the business too?'

Michael smiled at her. 'Clive and I are medical students. The medical streak comes from my mother's side. How do you ladies occupy your time?'

Becky felt flattered yet indignant. Did they look like the idle rich women that filled the room? She supposed they did.

'Becky's a couturier,' Janine said with a hint of pride.

Clive's eyebrows rose. 'Sounds jolly impressive.'

'I enjoy it, but it's also hard work.' Becky felt her business cards burning a hole in her bag.

Janine added, 'Becky's a brilliant designer. She'll be famous one day.'

'Where *is* your business?' Michael asked Becky.

'In the Bigg Market,' she said, then laughed. 'A shop, not a stall.'

'It's Mother's birthday next week,' Michael went on. 'If I brought her along could you make her something as my birthday present?'

'Damn! Why didn't I think of that?' Clive said.

Becky thought rapidly. The window display and showroom were quite impressive, but she mustn't let it slip that she lived in a corner of the workshop. 'Is your mother here this evening?'

'No, she's in bed with a cold,' Michael said.

Clive took Janine's glass, which to Becky's surprise was already empty. Then he reached for Becky's. 'Another?'

She held up her full glass. 'Not yet, thank you.'

When Clive returned, Michael said, 'We're being remiss, we must introduce you.'

They shepherded them around the room. Though Becky felt dizzy with all the introductions, she professionally summed up the women's clothes. She could do as well and better. But she kept her business cards in her bag, realizing that this exclusive party was not the place to ply for business. She'd gained the mother as a client. Perhaps it would spread from there.

At the end of the evening, Michael and Clive still clung to the girls' sides, and Becky found their natural, well-bred charm had put her at ease. Victor and the pub crowd lingered and Mr Gray insisted on sending them off in his chauffeur-driven Daimler-Benz.

Michael took Becky's hand as she left. 'What's the name of your shop?'

'Rebecca.' She felt justified in handing him a card.

He slipped it into his top pocket. 'I've enjoyed meeting you, Becky.'

'Thank you. It was a wonderful evening.'

As she climbed into the car she noticed Janine, laced around Victor, while Clive stood by looking puzzled. *Oh, Janine, you silly bitch*, Becky thought. Clive was obviously taken by her, and was charming and eligible. Yet *she* was no better than Janine. Michael was extremely personable but she had no interest in him other than acquiring his mother and her friends as clients.

On Monday morning Becky was rushing an order for a client expected at eleven. She'd awoken, crying out, after a nightmare that Andrew was making passionate love to a man and forcing her to watch. A bad start to the day.

The showroom bell rang. Groaning at the interruption, she removed her apron and smoothed her green pleated dress. Michael and his mother stood waiting. *Oh, no*! *Not today*! Becky switched on her professional smile. 'Good morning.'

Michael smiled back. He wore his Kings College scarf. 'Good morning, Becky. Mother, this is Becky, alias Rebecca. Becky, my mother.'

They shook hands. 'Michael tells me you're a talented designer.'

'That's kind of him,' she said, leading them to the showroom and indicating the two pink velvet chairs. 'Please sit down.' She stood before them, forcing a smile as if posing for a snapshot. Like her family, Mrs Gray was tall and slim, and wearing a mink-trimmed coat and matching cloche. 'Please, let me take your coat.' Becky wished she'd remembered to light the showroom stove earlier. Luckily, Mrs Gray's dress was a sturdy tweed. Returning from hanging the coat, Becky said, 'Perhaps you would like to see my present stock first, Mrs Gray. Then we can go through my designs.'

'Splendid.'

Becky smiled at Michael. 'There are magazines.' She indicated the glass coffee table, then flushed. Of course, she had only women's fashion magazines.

He grinned and pulled from his Burberry inside pocket a small hardback book. 'I came prepared. Mother has trouble making decisions.'

Mrs Gray clucked appreciation at Becky's selection. 'My dear, you have so many delightful things, how am I supposed to choose?'

'Perhaps you'd like to try on a few.'

In the dressing room Becky helped Mrs Gray out of her dress. It had fashionable straight lines, but was plain and boring. She looked like a schoolmistress, yet she was a beautiful woman. Her shining blonde hair was plaited and coiled round her head. It looked perfect on her. This was one time Becky wouldn't advocate a fashionable bob. She held out a black crêpe de Chine with chiffon sleeves and a matching stole that floated in two panels down the back. 'This is one of my favourite cocktail dresses, or, if you prefer, I could make a full-length formal version.'

'It's lovely.' She slipped it on, and twisted and turned to examine her reflection, the chiffon floating elegantly with her movements. 'I've never worn anything quite so . . . so glamorous.' She gave Becky a mischievous smile. 'I'll wear it on my birthday. I know Howard's cooking up a surprise. Now I shall surprise him.'

Becky too was surprised. 'You'll take it off the rack?'

'My goodness me, why not? It could have been made for me, and I shan't have to go through boring fittings.'

'It's one of a kind. You won't find anyone else wearing anything similar.'

Becky helped her out of the dress. No price had been mentioned but, as it was a present, she should discuss that with Michael. She helped Mrs Gray to dress and noticed the goose pimples on her arms. Yet she hadn't complained.

She packed the dress in tissue paper inside one of her pink paper bags with her name written in white.

When they returned to the showroom Michael closed his book and rose. 'I'll make out the invoice in the office,' she said, to gain time to decide on a price. She couldn't make it too cheap, but didn't want to overcharge.

'Please bill me.' He tucked the bag under one arm, handed her a card from his wallet and grinned.

'Michael, dear . . .' Mrs Gray joined them, buttoning her coat. 'While you're doing business would you please have Miss . . . ?'

'Becky,' Michael said.

She smiled. 'Would you please have Becky open an account for me.'

'It's the same as my card, except that my mother's name is Elsa.' He grinned, then took his mother's arm, shaking the bag. 'Am I allowed to know what I've bought you?'

Mrs Gray shook her head. 'Not until my birthday.'

Becky was relieved when the showroom bell clanged and Mrs Winston, a dumpling of a woman in her thirties who felt that Becky's creations took pounds off her, shouted, 'Yoo hoo!' But, remembering the woman's unfinished dress in the sewing machine, Becky's relief dissipated.

'Well, my dear, we won't keep you. Thank you so much.' Mrs Gray pulled on her kid gloves.

'Thank *you*.' Becky added silently, *for your money*, and clamped her lips into a smile. She said her goodbyes and turned, clearing her throat. 'Sorry to keep you, Mrs Winston.'

On Thursday, Becky and Janine were in the workshop when the telephone rang. Becky went to the office.

'Becky?' a male voice said as she picked up the receiver.
'Yes.'

'This is Michael. I wanted to tell you that we've never seen our mother look so glamorous. Everyone at her birthday dinner was quite bowled over by her.'

'Thank you. It was kind of you to let me know.'

'I rang for two reasons.'

'Oh, yes?'

For the first time, he sounded unsure of himself. He cleared his throat. 'I'd like to see you again.' Becky's legs felt as flimsy as the chiffon drapes of his mother's dress. He was nice. It wasn't his fault she didn't want to see him. It was Andrew's.

'That's kind of you, but I'm afraid I'm much too busy for social life at the moment.'

'Perhaps if I try later?'

'Perhaps.' Her eye caught Janine in the doorway, gesticulating and making grotesque faces. 'Goodbye, Michael, and thank you. I'm so glad about the dress.' She put down the receiver.

'You bloody idiot! You bloody, bloody, idiot!'

Becky brushed past her. 'Please don't listen in to my private telephone conversations.'

Undaunted, Janine followed her. 'Michael's wonderful! You can't carry a torch for Andrew for ever.'

'*You* dumped Clive the minute Victor decided to reappear the other night.'

'That's different! Victor is my life, the bastard! Otherwise, I'd have jumped at Clive. Andrew is out of your life for good.'

Becky's eyes filmed. 'I know it's crazy, but when I see someone who resembles him my heart jumps into my throat, then falls to my boots when it's not him. He still has that power over me. It wouldn't be fair to go out with Michael when I'm still in love with Andrew.'

Janine groaned. 'Beck, your whole life is before you. You need a man's love – and perhaps a family.'

'Do me a favour, Jan. Get back to work.'

Twenty-Nine

A t the end of November the expected telegram came. Though she'd prayed to die, Florrie had lingered. Becky had visited Ashington regularly and avoided a major row with Dora, but each time she returned with a headache.

Tears of sadness and relief glistened in her eyes as she folded the telegram. Ma was out of her misery.

'Your ma?' Norma asked.

Becky nodded.

Janine ushered her to the sitting room. 'Soup's ready, luv. Something hot will do you good.'

Becky ate the vegetable soup and glanced up. 'I could make the one o'clock bus. Would you mind? Liz will need help. Dora's going to be a handful.'

Janine carried the dishes to the sink. 'Hurry up then. But before you go, is there anything I should know? What's the money situation?'

'The books are up to date, but I'm still waiting for Mrs Wainright to cough up. If she comes in, no more credit till she pays.'

'Don't worry, I'll be firm. And I promise I'll put on me best voice to your clients.'

Liz, wearing her coat, started in surprise when Becky opened the kitchen door. 'Oh, Beck!' They clung together and wept, until Liz pulled away. 'I'll take you straight up. Leave your coat on.'

The kitchen was gloomy and the bedroom dark except for a candle burning on the bedside table. Dora, wrapped in a blanket in her chair, was wailing and clutching a bottle of gin.

'Hello, Dora,' Becky said. Dora stared at her blankly and continued to wail.

Gazing at her mother's lifeless face on the pillow, profound and confused feelings whirled inside Becky's head like a wire whisk beating an omelette. Love, hate, guilt, sorrow and grief were blended inseparably. Yet when she kissed the cold cheek, love surfaced. Her mother's face looked more peaceful than she'd ever seen it.

Dora stopped howling long enough to speak. 'All right, now you've gauped at her, get out! Stop pretending to play the loving daughter now she's dead.'

They left silently. In the kitchen Liz let out an explosion of air as if trying to deflate herself.'

'How long has Dora been like that?' Becky asked.

'Since the minute Ma went. She won't let me near Ma either. She even washed her herself.'

'It's probably guilt as well, for all the times she treated her badly.' Becky shivered and stared at the empty grate. 'Why no fire? It's freezing in here. Don't tell me you have no coal.'

Liz raised her eyes. 'Dora's orders. Ma must have a traditional funeral. The men are setting up the special bed this afternoon. She's sent Ted to order the flowers – roses! At this time of year! And would you believe it? She asked him to order for us an' all. She'll probably regret it when she sobers up. I asked for a wreath of yellow roses from you, and pink from Will and me. Dora wanted red – red for love, she said.'

'It's amazing she's getting the flowers. But of all the crazy ideas – an old-fashioned funeral.' They sat by the empty stove, Becky huddling deeper into her coat. 'As if you don't have enough problems organizing a funeral, you've got to do it in the dark and without heat. And what about the children?'

'They're at Will's folks, then Lettie, Will's mate's wife, is having them on the day. I don't want them to see this misery.'

'How will you do the cooking?' Becky asked.

'At Will's folks'. But we only need stuff for sandwiches. Dora's ordered fancy cakes from the bakery.'

Becky jumped up. 'Then let's go shopping now. At least it'll get you out of this house. And I'm paying.'

'I don't know what I'd do without you, Beck.' Liz rose stiffly and unhooked two canvas shopping bags from the wall. 'We'd better go now. Dora'll be furious if we leave her to deal with the funeral men herself.'

Becky snorted. 'Poor Dora! She'll have to get her arse off that chair and put down her bottle for a while.'

She thanked God that Liz had a good man and, for the first time in her married life, would have only her husband and family to look after. She tucked her arm in her's and they walked down Long Row as they'd done for so many years.

'How's Will?' Becky asked

'Poor lamb, with Labour losing the election, he's worried sick about work. They've cut him back to half time again.'

Becky stopped dead. 'Liz! You promised you would tell me if things got worse.'

'I know. I just couldn't. You make our clothes and that's enough. You could be making money from clients instead. Come on, don't stand there like a statue.'

Becky walked on, her face rigid with anger. 'Liz! You broke your promise! I'm sending you something every week again, whether you tell Will or not.'

'All right, luv. Thanks. Just till Will's on back-shift. We'd better get home before him. I don't want him in the house alone with Dora, and I can't let him get his own bath today, especially with no fire on. I have to boil the water next door.'

'Bloody hell! He comes home from a miserable day's work to a freezing house, cold water, and that madwoman up there.'

Liz sighed heavily. 'Aye, and the manager's got it in for him at work. He's deliberately giving him old or useless marras because Will had the nerve to tell him one of the ponies was too old and lame to work.'

'So they're giving him rotten mates to work with to punish him for trying to save a pony.'

'It's more than that. It's really because he's such an activist. They only keep him on because he's a good worker.'

'And he can't complain?'

'Phweew! One more word from him to the bosses and he'd be sacked. It costs him a lot to keep his trap shut, but he does it for me and the bairns.'

'Be patient, luv. It's got to get better.'

'Ha! That's what they all say.' It was strange for Liz to be pessimistic.

When Becky returned with the last of the shopping, Will was washed, wearing a clean shirt, and Ma lay in state in the sitting room. Dora had rented a black and brass bed and had it placed in the corner.

According to tradition, the wall and bed were draped in white sheets with black ribbons tied round the bed ends. The curtains were closed and a single candle illuminated Ma's face. From the brass rails above Ma's head hung a gigantic wreath of red roses. Becky drew in a breath. At the foot of the bed lay two scrawny bunches of yellow chrysanthemums held together with elastic bands.

'The witch!' Becky screamed, then clapped her hand over her mouth. *Not in front of Ma.*

'I couldn't believe it either,' Liz said. 'But *please* don't say anything. At least we can write what we like on the cards. Promise you'll ignore it when she comes back. That'll really goad her. Pretend you haven't noticed, or don't care.'

Becky sniffed. 'You're right! I'd die before I'd give her the satisfaction of knowing how much she's upset me.'

The house was warm again. Traditional funeral or not, Dora wanted an extravagant wake to give Ma a better send-off than Da had had. She'd ordered a selection of drinks, and bought fancy cakes from the baker's.

The more gin Dora drank the more she howled and put on

her mourning performance. She was too far gone to notice the guests' quiet departures and passed out before the last had left.

'Help me to get her upstairs and come back for her later,' Will said to Ted, whose eyes behind his thick glasses were half closed. He was almost as drunk as Dora, Becky thought. They made a fine pair.

'So much for a happy wake for Ma,' Liz said as they cleared away the left-over food. 'I'll hide some of these cakes under the bed for the bairns. Dora'll be back for them tomorrow.'

'She was too far gone to remember what was left,' Becky said.

While Liz packed cakes into a large tin, Becky picked up an armful of bottles. 'Some of these are full. I'll stash them under the bed for Will.'

The men came downstairs. 'She'll be out for the night. I'll bring her home in the morning,' Will said.

'Aye, thanks.' Ted staggered out.

Will sat by the fire with a sigh. 'Heaven! Dora's passed out and we've got the fire back on.'

'And when Dora leaves, we've actually got our own house, all to ourselves,' Liz said. 'Our real family life starts tomorrow, Will.'

'Aye, I'm that grateful I'd do a jig if I wasn't so tired.'

Becky felt happy for them. A home of their own at last!

Always, after visiting Ashington, Becky remembered that fateful homecoming to Andrew. Would he ever stop haunting her?

Norma looked up from her machine. 'Hello, luv. Was it awful?'

Becky pulled a face. 'Worse than I'd thought possible. How have things been here?'

'Busy.' Janine grinned. 'Michael's mother bought two more outfits – that chiffon dress you were working on, and the red and black two-piece. And her friend loved the black gown Michael bought for her birthday and would like something similar.'

The horrors of the past days evaporated like a murky puddle in warm sunshine. '*Two* rich customers! Or, should I call them clients?' Becky said, delighted.

Norma giggled. 'Tell her the other bit.'

'Oh, I forgot. Michael telephoned. I told him you were away for a few days and he said he'd try later.'

'Damn! I am *not* going out with him – and that's that. I don't owe Michael my company because his mother buys my clothes.'

Thirty

B ecky was about to insert the key in the lock when the door opened. 'Oh, you startled me! I was just locking up.'

Michael Gray stood on the doorstep wearing a tweed overcoat and trilby, looking not at all like a student. 'As you won't talk to me on the telephone, I'm trying the direct approach.'

In her surprise, Becky stammered, 'Well, eh, won't you come in. It's cold.' Not wanting him to know she lived on the premises, she went to her desk and indicated the chair opposite.

He'd removed his hat and his hair was tousled, his face fresh from the cold air. He did look attractive.

'You look as though you're about to do business with me.' He broke the awkward silence. 'I came to invite you out. Just *one* evening. I'd enjoy a companionable meal and friendly conversation, but if you'd prefer, we could go to the cinema.'

Becky's hollow stomach reminded her it was after six, and she'd only had a sardine sandwich since breakfast. She smiled. 'You caught me at the right moment. I'm ravenous. If you don't mind waiting until I tidy myself.'

She felt his eyes on her as she left. In her room, she renewed her makeup and put on her black coat with astrakhan trim and matching hat. He would probably take her somewhere nice, and he *was* good company. It wouldn't hurt for once.

To her surprise, he opened the passenger door of a black Ford motor car parked outside and helped her inside. He cranked the handle until the engine ticked over, then jumped in. 'Hold on to your hat. I've only had it a week.'

'A birthday present?' The Grays must be richer than she'd thought – a student owning a car!

'My twenty-first.'

'Happy birthday. When was it?'

'Next week, but my parents gave it to me early. I'm having a big bash. You're invited.'

They turned on to Grainger Street, missing a tramcar by inches, and took the next corner almost on two wheels. Becky gripped the leather seat.

'Sorry, I'll get better at it, and we're not going far tonight.'

'Where *are* we going?'

'My favourite restaurant. Small, cosy, and superb food. Only the initiated know it.'

'I suppose your parents initiated you.' She sensed his embarrassment and regretted her words.

'Yes, I'm lucky, but I'm *not* a spoilt brat. Clive and I always had to do chores for pocket money. Though I do appreciate my good fortune, especially during such a hard time.'

The car stoppd abruptly outside what at one time must have been a shop, the large windows now heavily draped with red velvet.

Inside, the carpets and chairs were red plush and the table-cloths crisp white damask. There were barely a dozen tables, and only a few occupied. It was still early.

The head waiter, in a black evening suit, greeted Michael. 'Good evening, sir. Nice to see you again.'

'Evening, George.'

He seated them at a rear table and handed them two menus.

Becky looked aghast at the list. It was in French – except for the name, Barron's, printed in gold letters.

Michael grinned and turned it over for her. 'This side's in English.'

She was relieved to see that he also read the English side – or was it to make her feel more comfortable? They decided on the same items, prawn cocktails, followed by veal cutlet with chocolate mousse for dessert. Michael consulted with the wine waiter and asked if she'd like a Sauvignon Blanc.

'That'll be fine.' She wondered how long she could keep up the pretence that she was used to such dining. The pub crowd drank only cocktails and beer.

He seemed to read her mind. 'Perhaps a pink lady to start?'

'No, thank you. The wine will be wonderful. I'm surprised, you remember what I drank at your party.'

'I remember much more than that.'

Becky felt her cheeks burn.

When the wine was served, he held his glass to hers. 'Here's to my success at finally managing to drag you out with me. What did I do right this time?'

She couldn't help giggling. 'I was hungry.'

'I love your honesty.'

She lowered her eyes. 'I'm sorry if I've seemed rude, but there's a reason I don't want to go out with anyone.'

'Another chap?'

The painful scene of the man in bed with Andrew flashed through her mind. 'There *was* one. I'm just not ready to start again.'

'I'm sorry.'

She sipped her wine without even tasting it. 'I'm well rid of him.'

The prawn cocktails arrived and she attacked hers with enthusiasm. When she looked up, he was smiling. 'You *were* hungry. I'm delighted I came at the right moment. Will there be another right moment?'

She looked at his handsome face, his hopeful expression. Andrew had never looked at her like that. It did feel nice to be wanted as a woman. And he was pleasant company. She hesitated. 'Just friends?'

'For as long as you like.'

'Thank you. Most men would have given up long ago.'

'I'm tenacious. Now you *must* come to my twenty-first on Saturday.'

'I haven't been to a party since your last one. Thank you.'

'Splendid!' He looked as if he'd just picked the winner at the Grand National. 'Any chance your girlfriend could come too? Clive found her fascinating.'

'She's sort of Victor's girlfriend,' Becky admitted reluctantly.

'But last time Victor ignored her all evening.'

'He usually does. But they're a couple.'

The waiter arrived and saved Becky further embarrassment.

After the main course, Michael summoned the wine waiter again. 'Any preference for a dessert wine?'

He obviously thought she was used to such fancy dining. She felt like a fraud. She must let him know the truth. 'If you'll let me treat you to my own version of coffee.' She realized this sounded rather forward, but the motto these days was *anything goes*.

'Invitation accepted.'

'Where to?'

'The shop.'

They returned as they had left, in a series of hair-raising bumps and jerks and hooting horns. Michael stopped outside the shop, grinning. 'I *promise* to practise more.'

Becky led him to her room. 'This is it. I expect you thought I had a fancy flat.' She smiled to lessen her embarrassment.

'I didn't think anything. And this is charming.' He appraised the tiny room.

'It's all I can afford until the business grows. Please sit down.'

He sat on the divan. 'You're very enterprising.'

She lit the stove to boil the kettle. 'I had to be. I come from a mining family in Ashington. They couldn't help me. In fact, I help my sister and her family.'

'Then you're even more exceptional than I thought. I'm impressed.'

So, he didn't mind! Why did she feel relieved? 'I suppose you've only known girls with rich mummies and daddies.'

He grinned. 'It's the girls I take out, not their mummies and daddies.'

They chatted easily. Becky told him about Liz, her husband and children, and their hard life. She mentioned that she also had an older sister, who was difficult, but left it at that.

He talked about his ambition to own a family practice. Clive wanted to be a surgeon, but Michael preferred the more personal approach to the clinical hospital atmosphere.

With obvious reluctance he looked at his wristwatch. Becky noticed it was gold. 'I'm keeping you up. How inconsiderate!' He stood and she retrieved his coat and hat from the wardrobe.

'I admit I'm tired, but I enjoyed the evening. Thank you.'

'No! Thank *you*.'

At the door, he said, 'I'll pick you up at seven on Saturday.'

'*Please*, you should be at home to greet your guests.'

'They aren't coming until eight.' He grinned and she found herself laughing.

'All right, I'll get an early start on the pink ladies.'

He gave a mock bow. 'And I promise you a smoother ride than tonight.'

It seemed every window was lit. After taking her coat, Michael led her to a large room upstairs. 'This *was* the playroom, but Mother had it converted into a party room for dancing.'

Becky gazed at the shining dance floor as if it were a bed of stinging nettles. She wished she'd taken more notice when Janine had tried to teach her the new dances. Stupidly, she'd thought this would be drinks and conversation, like the last party.

He led her to the bar in the corner. 'A pink lady?'

She smiled. 'I suppose.'

The band tuned up, sounding like cats meowing. Becky

began to feel festive. Clive approached her and, again, she was struck by the brothers' similarity.

'So, the lucky sod managed to ensnare you.'

'It took a while,' Michael said, handing Becky her drink.

Clive leaned on the bar sipping a Martini, and Becky suspected it wasn't his first of the evening. 'How's your friend?' he asked.

'Her mother has flu. She's looking after her.' Becky ignored the question of Victor, still hoping Janine would leave him.

The guests began to arrive and Becky became lost in a flurry of introductions until the band struck up and everyone started hopping around to the tune of 'Margie, I'm always dreaming of you Margie'.

'Dance with me?' Michael said.

'I . . . I can't.' Becky's face went hot.

He looked surprised. 'Then I'll teach you. It's the jogtrot. I promise, it's easy.'

He led her to the dance floor, and Becky was grateful that the crowd was large enough to hide in.

Afterwards they returned to the bar. 'You lied to me,' Michael said. 'You did splendidly.'

'Janine's tried to teach me, but this is my first time on a dance floor.'

'And not the last. They're playing the twinkle.' He led her back to the floor protesting.

'I like that one,' Becky said afterwards, sipping her drink.

The band was playing. 'It's three o'clock in the morning, and we've danced the whole night through'. Becky giggled. 'We have!' Though tired, she was enjoying herself.

'It's time I took you home.'

Becky looked at the thinning dance floor. 'Half the guests have left anyway.'

'Some have. Others are upstairs playing musical bedrooms.'

In the car Becky's head felt funny. She was tipsy! Mustn't let it show. 'I had a lovely time, thank you,' she enunciated slowly.

'No, thank *you* for making it the best twenty-first I shall ever have.'

The car jerked to a stop outside her door. 'Oooh, that was fast.'

He unlocked the door for her, then kissed her cheek lightly. 'That was my happy-birthday kiss. You forgot earlier.'

'So I did! I'm sorry.' She held up her face and, with puckered lips, kissed him playfully on the mouth. 'Happy Birthday, birthday boy, and thank you for bringing me home.'

She floated to her room, still feeling the touch of Michael's lips against hers. But she reminded herself she was tipsy.

Thirty-One

Becky and Janine carried the suitcases to Paddy's Market. 'How were things at home?' Becky asked.

'Bloody awful. I felt like you – a prisoner in the house.'

'I went out . . . with Michael Gray.' Becky slid her eyes to Janine's face and enjoyed her friend's stupefied expression. 'Close your mouth, Janine. People might think you're an idiot. We went out twice, actually – first to a wonderful restaurant and, on Saturday, I was his partner at his twenty-first birthday party.'

Janine raised her eyes to the murky sky. 'Praise the Lord! Did you *do* anything?'

'*Just friends*!'

Janine moaned. 'You daft thing! That rich hunk!'

'And the same to you. Clive was disappointed you weren't there.'

'Really?' Janine sounded pleased. 'But you know I couldn't two-time Victor.'

'Michael's parents bought him a motor.'

'Then why not ask him to give you a lift instead of lugging these bloody suitcases?'

'I told him about my background and he's not a snob. I don't think he'd be shocked that I use second-hand clothes.' She giggled. 'But I'd have to assure him his mother's outfits are made from new materials.'

'Don't let him go, Beck. He's a catch.' Janine's tone was serious.

They had to weave their way through the crowds as they approached the market. Once there, they selected the best

241

offerings and lumbered back to the shop. As Becky turned the key in the lock, the telephone was ringing. She ran to the office. It could only be Michael. Breathless, she lifted the receiver.

'Morning, Becky! Father's taking me out today to refine my driving. Would you like to risk a spin this evening, then perhaps dinner. You can't work *all* day.'

'I'm afraid I must, *and* this evening, but thank you anyway. Another time. Bye, Michael.' She replaced the receiver.

'Flaming idiot!' Janine stood in the doorway shaking her head. 'Why didn't you accept?'

'Because I have two evening gowns to finish for tomorrow and I haven't even cut them out yet.'

'Then I'll help you, and telephone him right back and say you can see him at ten for a late supper.'

Becky fluttered her eyelashes in weary exasperation. 'Jan, I have a business to run. Thanks for the offer to help, I accept. But I can't see Michael. I need to sleep as well as work.'

'What you need is a good—'

'That's enough, Jan.'

Janine's face unfolded like a flower as she burst into laughter. 'I was going to say *a good time again*, you dirty-minded sod.

'What you also need is extra permanent help, Beck.' Janine set the sugar on the table. 'I'll volunteer my services three days a week, for the meagre sum of – ten bob. Night work for my own clothes only. Then you'll have more time to see Michael. And I'd rather help you than pose for naughty pictures. Anyway, Victor's increased my allowance.'

'All right, I accept your offer, but you deserve more than ten bob.'

'Then you'll go out with Michael?'

'I give in.' Becky threw up her hands in surrender.

The following evening Michael drove only slightly more competently. Becky gripped the door strap.

He flashed her a good-natured grin. 'Sorry. Father says I'm too impatient – and, incidentally, Mother asked me to invite you to Christmas dinner.'

'That's kind of her, but I always spend Christmas with Janine. Victor's Jewish and goes home, to avoid the Christmas celebrations.'

'Then invite Janine too. Clive would be delighted.'

Becky calculated quickly. She'd planned to take Janine to Ashington for Christmas, but an opportunity to get her alone with Clive was tempting. Instead, she would spend New Year at Ashington. 'Your mother won't mind?' she asked.

'Of course not. She loves young people.' He squeezed between a lorry and a horse and cart to take the corner on to Northumberland Street. 'Made it!' he said, triumphant. 'Let's go to the refectory for a drink.'

Becky held her breath. 'What's the refectory?' she said, releasing her breath.

'The university bar. It can be fun, especially tonight. Finals are over.'

The noise was ear-splitting and the refectory grubby. The rough wooden floor was crammed with trestle tables full of students waving pint mugs, singing bawdy songs, or simply swilling beer.

Becky slid on to a bench and he patted the space beside her. 'Keep this for me. What would you like?'

Becky grinned, falling into the spirit of the holiday. 'I'll try a beer.'

While she waited, a large student slopping a pint of beer squeezed into Michael's space. 'I can't believe I've found you when you're not running off somewhere.'

'Paul! What a surprise! Merry Christmas.' Even in his shabby overcoat he looked strangely attractive.

'*That* it is! I'm finally out of here for good and I meet you again.'

Becky smiled. 'Congratulations! Have you found a job?'

'Sort of. I've been working for solicitors part-time and now

I'm joining them full-time. Now that I've finally caught you, let me buy you a drink.'

'My friend's getting me a beer, thank you.' Becky felt herself flushing under his gaze.

'Oh! Male friend?'

'Yes.' Why did she feel embarrassed?

Michael returned with two glasses. He stood blinking at them.

'Michael, this is Paul. He's just become a fully-fledged lawyer.' Becky took her glass and Michael shook Paul's hand.

'Congratulations!' he said, without enthusiasm.

Becky tried to lighten the atmosphere. 'Michael will be a fully-fledged doctor one day.'

'Not in the near future.' Michael's tone was now positively grim.

Paul seemed to get his message. He offered Michael his space on the bench. 'I'm afraid I've taken your seat.'

'It's all right. I'll get in on this side.' Michael thrust one leg over the bench between Becky and her neighbour.

After an uncomfortable silence, she cleared her throat. 'A century ago I bumped into Paul and knocked his library books flying.'

'We've been bumping into each about once a year ever since,' Paul said.

Becky felt Michael's body relax.

Paul emptied his glass and stood. 'I'd better be off. Nice to see you again, Becky, and nice to meet you, Michael.'

'And you.' As Michael spoke, he nudged Becky along the bench to take up Paul's space. 'Nice chap,' he said, but Becky doubted he meant it.

Christmas dinner was superb. Mr and Mrs Gray were gracious hosts and the conversation was as abundant as the food. Janine used her showroom voice and Clive was obviously enchanted. He rarely took his eyes off her.

'When are you going to start your fashion shows, my dear?' Mrs Gray asked.

'As soon as I have enough spring outfits ready. It's been such a busy winter, we're still working on winter clothes.'

'Don't push yourself too hard, Becky,' Michael said. 'You have so many commitments already, I rarely see you.'

'Thank you, Michael,' Janine said. 'I'm tired of telling her that.'

'I get bored if I slow down,' Becky said. Michael was becoming more demanding of her time, and his earlier, chaste goodnight kisses more urgent. Was she being fair?

After dinner they played the gramophone and chatted. Mr and Mrs Gray retired at ten o'clock.

In great spirits, Clive put on the jog trot and bowed to Janine. 'Please dance with me.'

A slightly tipsy Janine said, 'Delighted.'

Tired though Becky was, a plan formed in her mind. She nudged Michael. 'Take me home and give your brother a chance.'

He nodded and shouted above the music. 'We're off now. Have fun.'

Becky sat beside Michael on the divan and kissed him on the cheek. 'I'm sorry if I spoiled the party.'

'Actually, leaving was a splendid idea. And a real cup of coffee would be another splendid idea.'

She laughed and filled the shiny metal coffee percolator he'd given her for Christmas. 'I'm not sure how to do this, but I'll try.'

'That was a joke. This is real.' He placed a small box on the table.

'Oh, Michael, another present!' She opened the fancy box, feeling guiltier than ever that she was so distant with him. 'Oh, 4711! My favourite scent. You spoil me.' She dabbed a little behind each ear and sat beside him, taking his hand. 'I promise I'll have more free time when the holidays are over.' She kissed him lightly on the lips and he pulled her to him, increasing the pressure. A long-forgotten feeling awakened in her.

Just then the percolator made alarming noises.

'Damn that thing!' he said as she jumped up to rescue it.

She poured two mugs of dark liquid and handed him one.

He sipped and gagged. 'Next time try half as much coffee. I promise to drink it quickly like a good boy, then I'll be off and let you sleep.'

'Thank you for being so understanding.'

Sleep wouldn't come. Becky found herself thinking of that kiss. For the first time in so long she'd felt a response awakening in her. Perhaps she'd been wrong to think she couldn't make love to any man after Andrew.

Thirty-Two

'Michael, didn't you hear me?' Becky shouted into the receiver. 'I'm inviting you to dinner.'

There was a pause, broken by Michael's delighted laugh. 'I *thought* so, but couldn't believe it. Only a couple of days since we saw each other and you're inviting me to a cosy evening for two?'

'Six o'clock?'

'I'll be there.'

'Oh, and, casual dress. Remember, it's not Barron's Restaurant.'

Michael arrived looking splendid in a Harris Tweed jacket and cavalry-twill trousers. He held out a bottle of wine and kissed her cheek. She grabbed his hand.

'Come on, it's freezing out here.'

She'd put the workshop stove in her room as a second hotplate. On one stove stood a steaming pot of lamb stew, on the other a pan of rice – more sophisticated than potatoes, she'd decided.

'Smells delicious.' Michael looked at the candlelit table, set for two, a bottle of red wine open and partially used. 'I'm impressed.' He handed her the bottle he'd brought. 'We'll save this for later.'

He poured the wine and she sat on the divan. He gazed at her as he handed her a glass. Wearing her green skirt and white satin blouse, tied at the hips with a sash, she knew she looked nice. Round her neck hung a cascade of glass beads she'd picked up at the quayside, together with a second-hand

247

cookery book and white serving dishes to match her crockery. She hadn't used the white table cloth she'd embroidered herself since . . . She must put Andrew out of her mind.

'You look stunning.' Michael sat beside her and touched glasses. 'To the grand chef.'

'Taste my cooking first.'

'I'm sure it's delicious.' He sipped his wine. 'And this is perfect.'

'It was half-price at the off-licence,' she admitted. 'I have to learn about wines.' Funny, she thought, there was a slight tension between them, almost a shyness. She put her glass on the coffee table. 'I'd better check dinner.'

'I didn't know you were multi-talented.'

'I learned basic cookery at school. But I'm trying more exotic dishes now. I even put wine and herbs in the stew – sort of half followed a recipe with an unpronounceable French name.' She transferred the food to the serving dishes and set them on the table. It was much nicer than serving directly from the pans as they did at home. Strange, she'd cooked only simple meals for Andrew. She thrust him out of her mind.

Michael ate with gusto. The dinner was excellent. They'd opened the second bottle of wine and Becky felt mellow and pleased with her first effort at entertaining.

'You won't believe the coffee. I've finally conquered the percolator,' she said, rising and setting it on the stove.

He sank on to the divan with a sigh of contentment.

'I'll be with you in a moment.' She cleared the dishes with the minimum of fuss. The washing up could wait.

'A man could get used to this,' he said when she joined him on the divan. His fingers explored her hand and she felt a frisson of pleasure throughout her body. Must slow down, she thought. Though she'd inserted her sponge earlier, knowing that tonight they would make love, she didn't want to rush it.

'Janine said she saw Clive last night.'

'Mmmm, but that blasted boyfriend came back today. Clive's all morose.' Michael's middle finger travelled up the inside of her arm to her elbow, then, in a caressing movement, stroked down to her hand again. He lifted it to his lips in an almost worshipful gesture.

She laid her head on his shoulder and savoured this new feeling of being wanted and revered.

Leaning towards her, he kissed her on the lips, lightly at first, then searching. His hands cupped her face, and again she had the strange feeling of being cherished. Her arms went round his neck and she returned his kiss, each searching and exploring the other. It seemed to go on for ever until, at last, breathless, they broke away.

His breathing was heavy but his voice gentle. 'I've loved you since I first saw you.' He kissed her, all over her face, tender butterfly kisses on her eyelids, her nose, her cheeks.

Tears squeezed through her closed eyes. It was wonderful to be loved like this, yet she couldn't say the words back to him. She knew only that she felt a strange warmth for him and wanted him in a way she'd never experienced before. It wasn't a wild passion, but a deep longing.

He stopped kissing her and looked at her, alarmed. 'You're crying. Have I upset you?'

'No, no, it's just that you're so gentle and tender . . . I didn't expect . . .' She ran out of words and held his face, kissing him as he'd kissed her, until their passion grew. His mouth still on hers, he laid her down and stroked her shoulders, her neck, her breasts. She moaned and shuddered with delight.

Michael undid her blouse and camisole. His hands cupped her bare breasts, and stroked and fondled them. She thought she would die with the pleasure of it, then, incredibly, his mouth was on her breasts, her nipples, transporting her to another world where only sensation existed. She clung to him and one sensation overtook another. Hardly realizing how it had happened, she found herself naked with Michael's long body beside hers.

They explored each other, slowly and thoroughly. She kissed the hills and dales of his body, inhaling the warm clean scent of his skin. His lips, his hands, covered every inch of her, but when he stroked her buttocks she stiffened.

'What's wrong?' He sounded alarmed.

'I just don't enjoy being stroked there. One of my quirks.' She kissed him before he could say more.

His lips traced her breasts and down her belly to the insides of her thighs. That forbidden area that Andrew had never touched. She gasped with surprise and delight and felt no embarrassment. The room reeled about her, then Michael's mouth was back on hers. 'Don't worry, I'll be careful,' he whispered.

'No need, I'm ready for you.' Every nerve in her body trembled with delight. She heard her own voice make some sound, as if from far away, as she arched her back and clasped him tightly. She followed his movements, slow and delicious, then increasing in intensity, until she thought she could stand no more pleasure. Yet it went on, and on, until at last a myriad of sensations burst within her and she heard something like a scream in her head. Had it come from her? He called out her name over and over and she felt his joy mingled with her own.

Eventually he stroked the hair from her damp forehead and said, 'That was the most incredible thing that has ever happened to me. I'm crazily in love with you, Becky.'

She was silent for a moment, trying to sort out her confused feelings. 'I feel something – a deep, delightful longing and caring – but I'm not quite sure what love is any more. I'm afraid to call it that.'

He kissed her gently. 'Don't worry if you can't say the words. You couldn't make love like that if you didn't feel something special for me.' He stroked her cheek. 'Somebody must have hurt you terribly. I've felt it since we first met.'

The depth of his perception surprised her. She owed him *some* explanation, though she couldn't tell him everything. 'It was the first time I've made love like that,' was all she could say.

'I'm honoured.' He pressed her face into the curve of his neck.

Her head swam with confused thoughts. She'd never felt for Michael the heady infatuation she had for Andrew. But had that been love? Or was this warm deep caring she felt for Michael what people called love? She tried to remember what Eileen had said that Christmas about the different kinds of love. Whatever this was, she wanted more of it.

She opened her eyes and felt Michael's warm body next to hers under the covers. They'd made love most of the night, each time as wonderful as the next. She wanted to hold him and make love again, but both stoves had burned out. Stealthily she slipped out of bed, grabbed her dressing gown and slippers, and lit the stoves. After filling the kettle for a warm wash, she prepared the coffee.

When she dropped her dressing gown and slid back into bed. Michael opened his eyes. She watched with delight as he blinked in astonishment. 'I'm in heaven,' he said, and took her in his arms.

'You won't be for much longer,' she said. 'I have clients coming at nine.'

He looked at his wristwatch. 'Half past seven. Plenty of time.' He kissed her and she responded as before.

Afterwards, though she longed to stay with him, she flung off the covers. 'Back to reality. You must get out of here.' She was amazed at how unself-consciously he got out of bed, naked. 'Wash before the water gets cold,' she said, filling the bowl.

'No, you first. You look frozen. I'll brave the elements and wait.' He put on his sports jacket and turned to her with a grin. 'How do I look?'

She giggled at the sight of him dressed only in his shoes and jacket. 'Not quite fit for a night on the town.'

'But adequate for a visit to the lavatory?'

'You'll do.' The kitchen was littered with last night's dishes. She plunked them on the draining board and put the bowl

251

in the sink. Singing, she washed herself. With Andrew, the ablution rituals had always been conducted as if they were doing something else. Rarely a word had passed between them, and never laughter.

When Michael returned, she refilled the bowl, laughing again at the sight of him. He took off his jacket to wash and faced her. 'That better?'

'Only slightly. You still look ridiculous in those shoes.'

'Then I shall bring a pair of elegant slippers and dressing gown. I refuse to be a laughing stock around here.'

'Who said you were coming back?' Becky sat on the bed pulling on her silk stockings.

'*You* did, all night long, and again this morning.'

She dropped her dress over her head. 'Was I that obvious?'

'Magnificently obvious.' He strode over to her and kissed her.

Thirty-Three

'You *must* love him, you silly bat,' Janine said. 'For five months you've never stopped talking about him.'

Becky laid down the trousers she was making for Billy. 'Aw, Jan, I definitely feel something, though I don't know what. Sometimes I wonder if *being loved* is what I feel. It's heaven to be in Michael's arms and know he loves and wants me. I feel almost part of him, but my knees don't knock when he walks into the room, not like Andrew.'

Janine stopped treadling and rolled her eyes to the ceiling. 'And you can thank the Lord for that. It was a stupid schoolgirl crush you had on that lout.'

'Do *your* knees knock when Victor walks into the room?'

Janine stopped work again and moaned. 'You know the main feeling I have for Victor is sex. I can't do without him. When he turns on the charm, I melt.'

'Why not give Clive a try and see what he does for you? He still asks after you.'

'I *live* with Victor, you nit, and Clive lives with his parents. Do you want us to have it off up a back lane?'

Becky laughed. 'You have such a ladylike way of putting things. Let's change the subject. It's already July and I *have* to start the Saturday fashion shows. I need full-time help. Norma can't do more while she's looking after her mother-in-law. Now that you're a talented seamstress, would you like to work full-time? I need your help in the showroom as much as in here. To start, I could manage – say, twenty-five shillings.'

Janine's eyes looked like marbles. 'Twenty-five bob, plus Victor's piddling pocket money! I could even save some.'

'Then it's settled.'

Glancing through the paper as she sipped her coffee, Becky groaned. Baldwin had refused a government subsidy to the coal owners, who in turn insisted upon longer hours, lower wages and more profits.

Janine arrived, her smile freezing as she studied Becky's face. 'Why so glum?'

'The coal owners are going to cut miners' wages by forty-eight percent.'

Janine sighed. 'You'll have to send more to Liz. Can you manage?'

'I've been saving for the worst.'

'You can pay me less.'

'No, you twit, I can do it. But we'd better get our bottoms on those chairs and work.'

Janine and Norma looked up when Becky waltzed across the workroom. 'The end of July and I had enough money to buy for the winter season.'

'Is that why you look so chirpy?' Norma asked.

'Only partly! I'm seeing Michael later, and there's been nothing but good news in the papers for days. The Trades Union Council is supporting the miners and keeping an eye on negotiations on their behalf. *And* the General Workers Union and Amalgamated Society of Locomotive Enginemen and Firemen are supporting them.'

Norma pulled a face. 'I don't know about all those fancy names, but if *you're* happy with the news, I am.'

'Me too,' Janine said.

At six o'clock Michael poked a cheerful face round the sitting-room door, though his voice was serious. 'Have you seen the paper?'

She reached up to kiss him. 'Haven't had time yet. Been snowed under.'

'They're calling today Red Friday. The transport and rail

unions have agreed not to handle coal. Trade union solidarity wins over capitalism. A humiliating defeat for the government.'

She raised her eyebrows. 'Sounds wonderful. Why so serious? You're on the workers' side.'

'But if there's a total strike, you know the whole country will come to a stop.'

'No! The unions are in control. There won't be a strike. Let's go out and celebrate.'

He cupped her face in his hands and kissed her nose. 'I love your optimism. What would you like to do? One, go to the cinema. Two, see if the Theatre Royal has tickets left for *The Barber of Seville*. Or, three, have dinner.'

'Or we could kiss.' She found his mouth again and he drew her close. He kissed her until her lips felt like bruised fruit and her body called out to him.

'That's settled,' he said. 'We're going nowhere.' He pulled her dress down to expose one shoulder. When he pressed his lips to her skin she shivered.

'Are you cold?'

'No.'

He undressed her, kissing each area of skin he unveiled. As her silk underwear fell to the floor, he ran his hands down her back and over her buttocks and she tensed. The flickers of recollection were becoming fainter. Still, for a moment she saw Andrew, but then the image swam away.

Michael never asked about this one anxiety in their lovemaking and she'd been unable to bring herself to tell him. Perhaps if she did, it would go away. 'You must think I'm wierd,' she began.

He pressed his forefinger against her lips. 'My darling, I don't need to know what happened before, but I do need *you* to know that I love every inch of your body and would never do anything to hurt you. In time, I'll make you forget.'

He carried her to the bed, where she lay propped on one elbow. 'I'm forgetting already.' She smiled as he threw his expensive jacket to the floor. And while he bent to remove his shoes she grabbed his tie and pulled him down, kissing him playfully and undoing his shirt.

Within moments she felt his familiar nakedness against hers with a pure shiver of joy. His skin smelled so light and fresh. In a room filled with a thousand naked bodies she would go unerringly to his. It seemed as if they'd been together all their lives, and as if each time they made love he left a small part of himself with her and she with him. Eventually, even when apart, they would be one person.

He kissed her throat, her breasts and she thought she would explode with pleasure. Her hands searched his body – the smooth hollow between his shoulder blades, the muscles that rippled like a horse's flanks when she stroked his back. His mouth moved down her body to her thighs, where he kissed her until she could bear it no longer. She lay over him and gave herself to him with an urgency that made him gasp.

They soared together to the highest points their senses could endure. She'd read Dr Stopes's theories, the wholesome handbooks at the clinic, but only since she'd met Michael had everything she'd learned become more than mere words on paper.

'Jesus,' Michael moaned. 'I didn't dream it could get any better. You're incredible, Becky Ryan. Please telephone me whenever you feel like that again and I'll be straight over.'

She let out an exhausted sigh. 'If you give me a few minutes, perhaps I can tell you to your face. Who needs technology?'

A few days later Becky put her shopping bag on the ground while she fumbled with her key. A voice from behind surprised her.

'Let me help you.'

She turned. Paul stood grinning at her, wearing a badly cut suit and white shirt.

'Oh, thanks.' She gave him the key and he opened the door, picked up the bag, then followed her to her room. 'Thank you,' she said again.

'Feels like a load of rocks in here.'

'Potatoes, and groceries for the week.'

After putting the bag on the bench, he looked around the room and through to the workshop. 'You live here?'

'Live and work.'

'Nice. You must have a good boss.'

'I do.' Becky put the food in the cupboards, careful to keep the wine in the bag. She didn't want to flaunt her good fortune.

'That's a lot of food for one little girl.'

'I . . . Would you like a cup of coffee?'

'Yes, please.' He watched as she filled the percolator. 'Wow! The real thing. I thought it would be that bottled rubbish.'

Again Becky felt embarrassed. 'The percolator was a Christmas present from Michael.'

'Oh, yes, Michael.'

She set the coffee on one of the electric hotplates Michael had bought for her birthday.

'Why don't you sit down?' She pulled out a chair from the table and he folded himself into it. He was even taller than Michael, and broader, but less graceful. Though she'd intended to give him a quick cup of coffee and work all evening, something needy in him held her back. 'Are you hungry?' she asked.

He grinned and showed his exceptionally fine teeth. 'Always. Food is secondary to my rent and my parents. I finally found them a cottage at Hexham.'

He seemed the type to look after his parents. 'How does a large lamb chop, new potatoes and fresh peas with mint sauce sound to you?'

'Like heaven.' He feigned a swoon.

The chops had been for Michael tomorrow but she would get something else.

The coffee gurgled. 'Would you like coffee now or after dinner?'

'Now, please.'

She found herself smiling. It was a pleasure to give to

257

someone so eager. 'Milk or sugar?' she asked as she set the coffee in front of him.

'Both, please.'

She burst out laughing. 'Do you realize that since I mentioned food you've hardly said more than a two-word sentence.'

'I'm sorry.'

They laughed together. Then he ran his hand through his hair. 'Fact is, I'm overwhelmed. A beautiful girl, serving me fabulous goodies in her delightful flat. It doesn't happen every day.' He added milk and three spoons of sugar to his coffee.

Becky made an effort not to smile again. Michael took his coffee black.

'Can I help?'

'You could shell the peas.' She set the bowl of peas on the table and a pan of water, and began peeling potatoes at the sink.

'I gather you're some sort of dressmaker. I've never noticed this shop, yet I come to the market often. Isn't Becky short for Rebecca?'

Becky's face grew hot. But why should she be embarrassed about her success? 'It's *my* business.' Nevertheless, she added to downplay her accomplishment, 'I had a stroke of luck and some help to get started.'

'Still, that's quite a feat!'

'One day you'll see headlines in the paper: Lowly Seamstress from Ashington Rises to Top Couturier in Newcastle.' She put the potatoes and chops on the burners.

'You don't seem like a girl from Ashington.'

'You should have met me when I first came.'

'I'm from Stockton.'

'You don't sound like it either.'

'My parents saved to send me to the right schools. I'm trying to pay them back. My father was a stoker. He's over seventy and didn't retire till I qualified. My mother's in her sixties. I arrived on the scene late. As soon as I reached school age she worked as a cleaner to help with school fees.'

'You're lucky to have such wonderful parents.'

'I wish I could do more for them.'

She felt drawn to him. 'Thanks for the peas.'

Opening the cutlery and linen drawer, she hesitated. Should she use her white cloth or would he think she was showing off? What the hell! Why should she treat him differently from Michael because he was poor? She would also open the wine.

She set the table then handed him the wine and a corkscrew.

'I can't believe you're going to all this trouble and expense for *me.*'

'Surely you deserve a treat now and then. It's a treat for me too.'

'It was meant for *him*, wasn't it? Michael, I mean.'

She continued setting the table. 'Sometimes I make a special dinner to show my appreciation. He buys me expensive meals. It saves a lot on food bills, so I can afford an odd splurge.'

Over Paul's face spread a film of embarrassment. He took off his glasses and wiped them on his handkerchief, as if the action deflected his discomfort. 'Look, it's very kind of you but I feel . . .'

'*Hungry!* That's what you feel. And so do I.' She nodded towards the wine. 'Please open it. It's supposed to breathe. I've just learned that. I've learned a lot since I left Ashington. I come from a mining family. We couldn't afford wine with dinner. In fact, sometimes we couldn't afford dinner.'

He opened the wine and a grin relaxed his face. 'I feel like Goldilocks eating Daddy Bear's porridge.'

Unlike Michael, who could spend the entire evening over a leisurely meal, Paul was eager, though well-mannered. She found herself keeping pace with him.

The bowls were empty and his plate clean when he sat back with a sigh. 'That was delicious, thank you.'

Becky rose to collect the dishes and realized she felt tipsy. She'd also consumed the wine faster than usual. She made an effort to keep her head together. 'I have no oven to make desserts but I do have home-made chocolate cake from my friend who runs a café,' she said. 'You must go there. She'll feed you well for a sensible price. She'd love to mother you.'

'Is that what you're doing? Mothering me?'

Embarrassed, she lowered her eyes and placed the cake on the table. 'Nonsense! I'm simply being friendly.'

'I'd like to be your friend, Becky.' The wistful way he looked at her made her glance away. The wine seemed to have loosened his reserve.

She felt flustered. 'I kept the coffee warm. Would you like some with dessert?'

'Yes, please.'

Though wobbly on her feet, she was glad of the diversion. How could she be attracted to another man? Her confused thoughts swarmed like bees buzzing in her head. She concentrated on serving the cake.

After dessert, she rose. 'I have to work this evening.' She couldn't possibly work now but she must stop this madness.

Obviously reluctant, he stood. 'Can't I help with the dishes?'

'I let them soak till morning.' She led him to the door. 'That café is Johnson's, on Pink Lane. Tell Annie you're a friend of mine.'

'I'd like to see you again, Becky. And I don't mean for a meal.' He'd turned in the doorway, his face barely an inch from hers.

'I . . .You know, it's Michael.'

'Of course.' He leaned forward and kissed her lightly on the mouth. She felt her head reel as if he'd just given her a passionate embrace.

'If you change your mind . . .'

She closed the door. Was she going mad? That one kiss had made her want to drag Paul back to her room and into her bed. She shuddered. Was one man not enough for her?

No! There was simply something extremely attractive about Paul, and she'd had too much wine.

*   *   *

Becky's breath steamed in the lamplight. Though May, the evening was chilly. She hurried to Johnson's Café to deliver the dress she'd made for Vera's birthday.

The miners, threatened with further wage cuts, had asked the Trades Union Congress for help. They had called out transport workers, printers, builders, and heavy industry workers. The Baldwin government had recruited special constables, volunteers to run essential services, and troops to maintain food supplies. Nevertheless, life was slowing to a halt.

'Hello, hen, it's been ages.' Annie hugged Becky. 'Paul's over there. I'm that glad you recommended him.'

From a corner table, Paul waved.

'I'll join him.' Becky hadn't seen the young lawyer for months, but was conscious that there was a tension between them. Half reluctantly, Becky followed Annie.

Paul rose. 'Hello, Becky. Nice to see you.'

'Nice to see you too.' She handed Annie the white paper bag with pink lettering. 'I brought Vera's dress.'

Annie beamed as she took it. 'Eey, hen, our Vera'll be that pleased. She's out with her lad, but she'll pop round to thank you tomorrow. You're too generous to her.'

Becky smiled at Paul. 'Hark at Annie complaining about *my* generosity.'

He gave Annie an affectionate look. 'She feeds me like a mother.'

'Aye, he needed fattening up.' She picked up his empty plate. 'We were lucky to get any deliveries today. The boss had to motor to North Shields to pick up the fish. In fact, he has to pick up almost everything himself. He moans, but he's bloody lucky he's got a motor to do it or he'd have to close the business. It's baked halibut, mashed potatoes and peas. All right, Becky?'

'Lovely, thank you.'

'And keep your coat on. I have to save the paraffin for cooking.'

Paul pulled out a chair. 'Messy business, the strike. I'm sorry about your family.'

Becky sighed. 'My sister's husband is convinced that the people are for the miners, not the government.'

'But the tension's running higher every day.' Pulling a newspaper from his pocket, he glanced at it. 'It says that in London eighty buses were damaged yesterday and the drivers have to wear steel helmets and carry truncheons.' He threw the paper aside. 'But the *British Worker* tells people *why* the miners are so angry. It says a Welsh pit labourer earns one pound, eleven shillings and seven pence a week. And the government pays its Special Constables two pounds six shillings and three pence a week to deal with the crisis, plus accommodation and two-and-six a day food allowance.'

Annie brought Becky's meal. 'Here you are, luv.' She slid a plate of apple tart and custard towards Paul.

He grinned. 'Thanks, Annie. I love you.'

'Aye, belly love. A cup of tea?'

'I have real coffee at home. I'll give him a cup and send him packing.' Becky felt her stomach knot. She was inviting trouble.

Paul sat on the divan. 'I thought you went to Annie's a lot. I've hardly seen you.'

'I've been busy.' Becky filled the percolator. Her hands trembled. Why was she testing herself like this? Until the coffee was ready, she dried the already dry dishes on the draining board.

'You look nice in that dress.'

It was the latest military look, double-breasted with brass buttons. 'Thank you. How's work?'

'All right.'

She set his mug on the coffee table and sat beside him, holding her own.

'You seem different tonight.'

'The strike's getting everyone down.' She shivered as she felt his closeness and tried to inch away. But a magnet held her still.

'You cold?' He took off his jacket and draped it round her shoulders.

She tried to banish the image of Michael, who had made ecstatic love to her on this same divan only last night. She snuggled into the jacket. 'Thank you. I've been trying not to light the stove. Paraffin's impossible to find.'

'Drink your coffee. It'll warm you up.'

Obediently she drank, then he took the mug and placed it on the table. She knew he was going to kiss her and felt helpless to stop him.

The kiss came, soft at first, and when she responded he increased the pressure and searched her mouth with his. His lips were insistent. She needed desperately to experience this man. He kissed her neck while he undid her dress. Her hands groped to remove his shirt, to feel his skin, to inhale his scent.

They were naked, oblivious to the cold, exploring each other with wild impatience. There was no time for the loving, tender kisses Michael bestowed on her before their passion mounted. Paul murmured her name, and they joined, his movements urgent.

She felt as if her insides were on fire and grasped him fiercely, winding her legs about him, greedy to feel more. She had no idea how long it lasted but she heard herself crying like a hurt animal, and then Paul's cries joined hers, like two wild creatures in the woods.

Despite the cold, their bodies were bathed in perspiration. They lay, clasped together, breathless and exhausted. After a few moments he pulled the divan cover over them and spoke for the first time. 'I never imagined anything like this.'

Becky regained her breath, though her thoughts were confused. 'I don't understand it. I don't want to want you.'

He stroked her hair with his big hands. 'It's Michael, isn't it?'

'I love him. We've just got engaged. How could I want you too? I feel terrible.'

'No, *I* feel terrible. I wish I'd found you first. But I'm pleased you feel bad about us. I don't like playing musical bedrooms either, though it seems to be the latest party game.'

'It's not a game, Paul. I've wanted you and felt guilty about it ever since that night you came here. I've avoided going to Annie's in case this happened. Is it possible to be in love with two people at once, especially with someone you hardly know?'

'It's possible to be in lust with any number of people and, as you love Michael, it must be only lust you feel for me. Flattering as it should be, I wish you felt more than that. I'm in love with you, Becky.'

She put her hand over his mouth. 'Don't say it.'

'I must see you again.'

'I can't.' Dear God! She had to tell him. 'The wedding's in a couple of weeks.'

Paul winced as if she'd whipped him with her words. 'A couple of weeks!' He gave her an uncomprehending stare.

'Forgive me. I don't understand it myself.'

'I like Michael, though I could cheerfully put a bullet through his skull. He has everything. But I only envy him you.'

Becky's mind was spinning. 'You'd better go. I'm sorry. But you're wrong. I feel more than lust for you, yet I can't explain. If I didn't love Michael, things would be different.'

He clasped her to him. 'I'm not going now, not on the one and only night you're giving me.' When he kissed her she felt her head reeling. She wanted him again as much as before.

The next morning Becky woke in Paul's arms and jumped out of bed in dismay. She glanced at the gold watch Michael had given her on her birthday and gasped. She shook Paul roughly. 'Wake up! You have to go. My helpers will be here in twenty minutes.'

In seconds she was in her dressing gown.

Paul said nothing as he quickly pulled on his clothes. Becky looked at him in despair. He took her in his arms and kissed her lightly. 'I shall never forget last night. Thank you for that memory.'

Tears filled her eyes. 'Please don't say that. Just go.'

Janine pranced into the room. 'Morning, luv. I put the *Open* sign on the door.'

'Thanks.'

Janine stared at her. 'You look ravaged. Are you all right? Had a night of it, eh? How's Michael?'

'It wasn't Michael.' The confession came out. She had to tell someone.

Janine's eyebrows disappeared under her hat. 'What! You sit down and I'll make the tea.' She led Becky to the table and pushed her into a chair. 'Not Andrew, for God's sake?'

'No, Paul, that lawyer.'

'Oh, that's better, but not much. Are you in love with him?'

'No! I love Michael. As Paul says, I'm probably simply in lust with him.'

The kettle steamed and Janine made the tea. 'Here, you need this.'

Becky picked up her cup. 'I don't know what to do. Should I confess to Michael? If I don't, I'll have it on my conscience for ever. And—'

'And if you *do*,' Janine interrupted, 'you'll crush him, perhaps even ruin your relationship.'

Becky nodded in misery.

'Take my advice, Beck. Don't hurt Michael. He's a sensitive soul. I think he loves you too much to let it change his mind about marrying you, but it'll haunt him. Why spoil everything you've got? Honesty isn't necessarily what it's cracked up to be. It doesn't always consider other people's feelings. Better that *you* suffer than Michael.'

Becky looked relieved. 'Funny, isn't it? Paul said that musical bedrooms are the latest party game, and here I am, an emancipated independent woman, yet I'm still old-fashioned about some things.'

'Aye, me an' all. I don't *think* I could be unfaithful to Victor, even though I'm almost sure he is to me. But I might give in. I do feel curious about other men sometimes. It's normal, especially when you've only slept with one.'

Becky put her hand over Janine's on the table. 'Thanks for the pep talk. I won't tell Michael, and I certainly won't repeat last night.' She thumped her forehead with her fist in horror. 'Good Lord! I was out of my mind. I forgot my sponge.'

Janine plunked her tea on to the table, spilling it. 'What?'

Becky counted on her fingers. 'By sheer good luck it was my safe time.'

'And you know what they say at the clinic about relying on that. You *must* have been carried away. Was it better than with Michael?' Janine sounded worried.

'Not better – different – and the difference excited me. I suppose you're right. I just needed to know what other men are like.'

'And now you know. You've no need to experiment again.'

'Paul said he loved me.'

'Aye, they all say that in the heat of the moment. Don't worry. A handsome lad like him can get any girl he wants.'

Becky was puzzled. 'I didn't know you knew him.'

'Annie introduced us. He's always hanging around there. Waiting for you, I suppose.'

Thirty-Four

W hen Michael arrived that evening to take her to dinner at his parents', she clung to him and strove to keep back the tears of guilt. She felt as though she'd stabbed him in the back.

'Here! What's this? Anyone would think you hadn't seen me for a month.' He gripped her tightly, then searched her face. 'What's wrong, darling? You look pale.'

'Oh, it's just the strike and everything. I haven't seen Liz and the family since it started. And I don't know if the money I send is getting through.'

'I'll take you on Sunday and you can find out for yourself.'

'Oh, you *are* an angel. Do you have enough petrol?'

'I'll make sure I do, if I have to siphon some out of Clive's motor.'

Becky found herself smiling. 'He'd kill you if you went near his new toy.'

The drive was pleasant, but Becky was tense. The trade unions had been forced to end the strike because the government had been better prepared than they. But the miners felt betrayed by the unions and stayed on strike, causing bitterness on all sides.

'Will's going to be in a state,' Becky said.

'Your family won't suffer. I shall add something each week to whatever you send.'

Her heart swelled with love and, once again, she was struck by guilt that she had betrayed Michael. 'You're so wonderful to me and my family.'

'Soon they'll be my family too. That reminds me, Mother says there's a gorgeous Georgian house for sale in Gosforth. A doctor owned it, so there's a surgery built on, and five bedrooms to fill with children – after I've qualified. Father suggested we make an offer and he'll arrange for my marriage settlement to be released.'

Becky put her hand over his on the steering wheel. 'Buy a house before we're married! I thought we were going to rent first.'

'Why, if we can afford to buy? Father says it's ridiculously cheap because of the depression.'

'It sounds like a dream. Can we furnish it before we're married?'

'Enough rooms to live in and some guest rooms for your family – and our friends.'

Becky felt ecstatic, but as they approached Ashington, she saw the ponies out to grass again, and her spirits slumped. She and Liz lived in different worlds.

'At least those poor beasts are having a holiday.' Michael had a knack for reading her thoughts.

Tears of pity for the creatures ran down Becky's cheeks. 'Some are blind from spending their lives underground, but at least they can feel the sun on their backs and eat fresh grass.' The men too could enjoy the sunshine, but filling their bellies was not so easy, she thought.

They bumped along the cobbles of Long Row and, when Michael pulled up, the three children crawled like beetles over the motor car. This was not his first visit and they knew he would take them for a ride.

Liz ran out, drying her hands on her apron, Will behind her.

'What a lovely surprise!' Liz hugged Becky and they all greeted one another warmly.

The children, now in the back seat waiting for a ride, shouted in impatience.

Michael wagged his finger at them. 'If you sit quietly like that while I have a cup of tea, I promise to take you for the longest ride ever.'

Liz was already in the kitchen making tea. 'I wish I'd known you were coming. I've only got scones.'

'Wait until you taste Liz's scones,' Becky said to Michael to put Liz at ease. 'Anyway, we brought you some presents.'

'Oops! I forgot.' Michael retrieved several boxes from the car boot, followed by the children, whose curiosity had overcome their impatience for a ride.

Liz opened the first box and three little blond heads exclaimed in delight. It was packed with biscuits, crackers, cheeses, sausages and fresh fruit. And on top sat a box of Cadbury's chocolates. 'Oh, thank you, but you shouldn't.' Liz seemed overwhelmed.

'Aye, it's kind of you, but we're managing.' Will rumpled his hair in embarrassment.

The second box contained an assortment of tinned goods.

'Tinned pears,' Mary said in awe.

'And peaches,' Billy stood on tiptoe to see what else was in the box.

Mary found her voice. 'Thank you for all the lovely things you brought, and for the lovely wedding invitation.' She pointed to the mantel, where the silver and white card Becky had sent was propped against the clock. 'Da's going to make a frame with wood and glass so we can keep it for always,' she said.

Billy nodded. 'It's called a keepsake.'

'Can we have the chocolates now, Ma?' Mary asked.

'We brought some special ones for you.' Becky rummaged in the box and came up with three cellophane bags of chocolate drops. 'If you go next door and eat these quietly, I'll bring you some milk. Then you can go back to the car and wait for Uncle Michael.'

She took a bottle of milk from the box and half-filled three tumblers. Liz looked at her anxiously. 'It's all right,' Becky said. 'We brought two bottles and some tins of evaporated.'

In the front room, Becky gazed at the three eager faces. They sat in a row on one of the bunks, the floor strewn with the soft toys she made for them and the brightly painted wooden toys

Will carved. She picked up a locomotive. It was beautifully tooled, with precise detail. Will had become a superb craftsman in the free time the strikes and lock-outs had afforded him.

'You've turned into a professional toy maker, Will,' she said, returning with the locomotive.

'Aye, when I've finished with the garden it keeps me hands busy. Tom at Brock's Hardware gives me damaged tins of paint and old stuff they can't sell. In return I give him toys for his bairns.'

Michael examined the toy and whistled. 'This would cost a fortune to buy.'

'Aye, and who could afford to buy them around here? Though sometimes I trade them for favours or extra food. I got a pound of cooking apples from the farm for one like that.'

Michael shook his head. 'They would sell in the big shops at Newcastle for much more than a pound of apples.'

Becky suddenly became eager. 'Would you make some for me to put in the showroom and to decorate the window? They'll catch people's eye, and I'm sure I could sell them.'

Will shifted in his chair. 'You think so?'

'It's worth a try,' Liz said.

'Well, as I've nowt else to do, I'll have a go.'

Liz put the scones and biscuits on the table and poured the tea. 'This should keep the pangs away till dinner. It's rabbit stew.'

Will looked embarrassed. 'I do a bit of poaching like the rest. It saves on butcher's bills.' He glanced at Becky's anxious face. 'It's all right, Beck. What you send is plenty to keep us going, but I economize in case there's an even rainier day.'

Michael helped himself to a scone. 'What's the real situation, Will? There are so many different stories.'

'Bloody awful! I can't see a quick end to it, and the union's relief funds won't last much longer. The Distress Committee's doing the soup kitchen again and the Co-op's giving credit. Some of the clubs are even running competitions to make money. But sooner or later we'll have to fall back on the Poor Law and the Board of Guardians. Problem is, they give out relief money to claimants who aren't miners, but they only loan it to us.'

Becky could see Michael's face turning white with anger. He glanced from Liz to Will. 'I know from my father what it was like to be poor. Let me help. I'd like to add a bit to what Becky sends. I'll be part of the family soon anyway.'

Will turned the colour of a peony. 'It's right kind of you, but we're still managing. I promise, though, if it ever comes to me wife and bairns starving, I won't be too ashamed to ask for help.'

Becky saw Liz's eyes filling and bit her lip to check her own tears. She felt such love for Michael. She groped for his hand under the table and squeezed it. 'I was worried that I hadn't heard from you,' she said to Liz.

'Oh, Beck. I'm sorry you were worried. I've written twice since the strike.'

'Aye, the postal service is up the creek like everything else.' Will's voice was bitter.

The children arrived, smothered in chocolate. 'Can we have the ride now, Uncle Michael?'

'Not until I've cleaned you up,' Liz said.

Michael swallowed the last of his tea. 'I can't ward them off any longer. Liz, your scones make Cadbury's biscuits taste like compressed sawdust.' He turned to Will. 'Want to drive?'

'Aye, I'll give the old girl a spin.'

'I'm so glad you found Michael,' Liz said when they'd left.

'I love him as much as you love Will,' Becky said, though her conscience gnawed her. She'd never kept a secret from Liz – except not telling everything about Andrew until the end. Should she tell her about Paul? No! Liz would worry. Janine was right. Only *she* deserved to bear the burden of her secret. The memory of that night was like a sensitive tooth that hurt only when touched. 'How's Dora?' she said.

'Getting more like Ma every day. She looks ill and old.'

Becky sighed. 'I feel guilty about not asking her to my wedding. It's breaking my promise to Ma, but I just couldn't

271

have her making a drunken scene. I'm still afraid she may just turn up.'

'It's *your* day, Beck. And anyway, when I told Dora you were getting married, she said she'd have to be bound, gagged and carried there by force, and that she has no desire to meet the idiot who wants to marry you. Better to keep it from her that you're marrying into money. If she finds out, she'll pester you to death. She doesn't come *here* because we have nowt.' Liz sighed. 'Life's so peaceful since she's been keeping away. She's better off financially than most people here. I'm sure she's afraid we're going to beg for money.'

'You deserve some peace, and I must stop this guilt about not asking her to my wedding. Michael and his family know all about her. I just don't want anything to spoil that day.'

'Nothing will, Beck. It's going to be the most wonderful day of your life.'

'I'm working on the dresses, but don't ask.' She wagged a finger at Liz who had opened her mouth to speak. 'I want them to be a surprise. You'll all look gorgeous. I hope I still have a figure like yours after three pregnancies.'

Liz grimaced. 'The answer's easy. Hard work. Of course, I wish the strike would stop, but I'm dead happy with me man and bairns.'

Becky felt humbled by Liz's simple attitude. Happiness had fallen into her lap in this ugly little town. She hugged her. 'I love you, sis. I'm always there for you, and so is Michael.'

Liz hugged her back. 'Thanks, luv. I know you'll be as happy as we are. If I had to choose between having money or me happy family, I'd choose me family, but I'm that glad you're going to have both.'

'Well, well!' a familiar voice hailed from the doorway. 'If it isn't the two ugly sisters.'

They turned in dismay. 'Dora!'

'Aye, it's me. I saw Will driving a fancy motor and I gathered it could only be our Beck's idiot fiancé's. I've come to make his acquaintance.'

Becky's stomach boiled over with anger and horror, but she remembered to count to ten and kept calm. 'How are you, Dora?'

'So-so.' She staggered in and surveyed the expensive biscuits on the table.

'Would you like a cup of tea?' Liz stood wringing her hands.

'Nah, I've got me own refreshment, but I'll have one of them biscuits.' She crammed a chocolate biscuit into her mouth, pulled a bottle of gin from her oversized handbag and took a long draught. Tottering towards her old chair, she noticed the wedding invitation and grabbed it. 'My! Fancy! Why didn't you send me one, then?'

'Because you told Liz you didn't want to come.' That was partly the truth.

Dora skimmed the card and read aloud, 'Fancy shop address, Becky . . . Eldest son of . . . oooh . . . reception to be held at *The Grange*. La-di-da! Is that where the rich idiot lives then?'

Becky's fingernails bit into her palms.

Dropping the wedding invitation into her handbag, Dora gave one of her sly smiles. 'I'll hang on to this for a keepsake.'

The motor stopped outside. Becky dreaded the pending confrontation.

Michael removed his trilby and Will his cap.

'Hello, Dora,' Will said.

Liz shooed the children out. 'You lot go and play outside.'

'What's brought *you* here?' Will approached Dora's chair and stood by, as if ready for trouble.

Dora patted her hair and smiled at Michael. 'Well, I saw you riding around the block. I thought, Now that must be our Beck's fiancé and I ought to meet him.'

Michael bowed slightly and took the hand she languidly held up to him. 'How do you do?' he said.

'Fancy car! How do you make your money?'

'Forgive Dora's rudeness, darling. She's had too much to drink,' Becky said.

Dora rose and stood over her. 'Too much! Not enough to put up with your insolence. You come here with your fancy man in his fancy car and think your family's not good enough!'

Will had come up behind Dora and twisted her arm, immobilizing her.

She wriggled to free herself but Will's grip was firm. 'I'm walking you home quietly, Dora. You're welcome here when you're sober, but not in this state.'

'Me bag!'

Liz gave her the bag.

'You rotten sod.' She kicked Will's shins. 'I'll get you all back for this.'

Michael stood beside Becky and she took his hand. 'I'm sorry, sweetheart.'

'She needs help and treatment.' Michael sounded troubled.

'Don't we know that,' Liz said. 'She's been drinking since she was twelve or thirteen. It's already killing her. Half the time she can't get out of bed. Our mother went the same way.'

'Thank goodness she's not coming to the wedding,' Becky said, relieved yet sad.

Liz stood beside them with clenched fists. 'Beck, I don't want to frighten you, but she just might go now to get back at you. She took the invitation.'

Becky put her hand to her head. 'Oh Lord! Let's hope she's too drunk to remember.'

On the return journey, Becky gripped Michael's knee. 'Thank you for being so understanding about Dora, and so wonderful to my family.'

'I like your family and I'm sorry for Dora.'

In the hazy reflection of the headlights, she saw him flash her a caring look. Guilt smote her once more. How could she have been unfaithful to this dear man she loved so much? 'I promise I'll be the best wife any man ever had – and mother, when the time comes,' she said. 'You need never, never worry that I'll let you down in any way.'

'You sound so serious. How could you ever let me down?'

Thirty-Five

B ecky peered through the window as fingers of sunlight poked through fluffy white clouds, spreading them apart. It was going to be a nice day. For the last time, she jumped out of the divan bed, feeling a tiny pang of regret at leaving the world she'd created. Janine would take charge while she was away, and Eileen, who'd left the coat factory to join them full-time. Becky felt relieved, though a little piqued, that the business would survive her absence.

After a honeymoon in London, they would move into their home, now mostly furnished. Liz and family had come yesterday for a practice ceremoney and were staying at the house. They would be here any minute to change into their wedding clothes.

When the doorbell rang, she barely had time to open it before the children bounded down the passage, Liz behind, raising her eyebrows in despair, and Will carrying a bag of comics.

'Everyone into the workshop, please,' Becky shouted, then to Will. 'You look almost as handsome as the bridegroom.' He was wearing the grey suit she'd made him for the occasion. She giggled and pointed to the formal dress of top hat and tails hanging on the rail. 'Pity you have to change.'

He grimaced. 'I wouldn't do this for anybody but you.'

'And I wouldn't want anybody but you to give me away. I sold three more toys last week. Let me give you the money.'

'No, keep it towards our debt.'

She had no time to argue, as Mary tugged at her hand. 'When can we wear our dresses?'

'Now, if you sit still like statues afterwards.'

Liz gazed at the dresses on the rack. 'They're absolutely gorgeous! Just look what Auntie Becky's made for us.'

'They're fairy dresses.' Nancy touched one of the pink and white creations.

Footsteps sounded in the corridor. Becky froze and stared aghast at Liz. Had she left the door open? Surely no customer would come in with the *Closed* sign up.

'I finally made it,' Janine said as she reached the work-room.

'For a horrible moment I thought you were Dora,' Becky squeaked.

'Oh, hen, calm down. I locked the door.'

Janine took Mary's hand. 'Come on my beauty, let's trans-form you into a fairy princess.' As she buttoned Mary's dress, she gave Becky a sideways glance. 'Guess what? Victor's invited me to meet his parents next weekend. Jewish boy takes gentile girl home to meet Momma and Poppa. If I pass that test, perhaps the next one will be my conversion to the faith . . . followed by?'

'Matrimony?'

'What else? I'm sure his parents are nagging him to wed a nice Jewish girl and have sons. The next best thing's a converted Jewish girl. And I look the part. Perhaps you and Michael getting wed gave him a push.'

Becky pulled Nancy's dress over her blonde curls. 'Con-gratulations!' she said, then froze as the doorbell rang again.

Dora's drunken voice penetrated the door. 'If you don't open this bloody door, I'll throw a bloody brick through the window.'

Will hurried out, yelling, 'You do that and you'll spend the night at the police station.'

The door opened and Will and Dora came down the hall. 'Bloody hell! Fancy place! And you've been hiding this from me all these years.'

She must have spent the entire bus journey swigging from her bottle. It dangled, three-quarters empty, from her hand.

'There now, Dora. You can watch everybody getting ready.' Will spoke as if soothing a child.

'Aye, Beck. What are *you*? The queen of tarts?'

Becky stood rigid.

Will picked up the bag of comics and took the children to Becky's room, returning with the wicker chair and a tumbler. He set the chair before Dora. 'There now. You can watch them finishing off in comfort. You look tired.'

She fanned her forehead, over which hung a grotesque bunch of feathers, attached to a black hat. She was dressed entirely in black, even black stockings. 'Aye, tired and hot.' She sank into the chair.

Will took from his inside jacket pocket a flat bottle of Gordon's gin. 'You need another drink, Dora. It'll cool you off and perk you up.' He filled the tumbler.

'Well I never!' Dora snatched it and swallowed half before stopping for breath. 'How come you're suddenly so thoughtful, Will?'

'I know that's how your Ted makes you feel better.' He pulled another flat bottle from his pocket.

Dora raised her glass to the array of white faces staring at the scene. 'Here's to the bride and groom.' She hiccupped. 'Whey now, I decided to have a peek at the shop first, then I can go to the church in the wedding cars. I *am* family.' She drained her glass and hiccupped again.

Then Becky saw a familiar and welcome sight. Dora fluttered her eyelids as she did when trying to stay awake.

'There's time for a little nap, Dora,' Will said, before he turned and whispered to Becky. 'Telephone for a taxi.'

'Aye, a nap.' Dora's eyes closed and she was out in seconds.

'It's all right, Becky,' Liz said. 'Ted says it's the only way he can manage her. She'll wake up with a hangover but she'll be in Ashington by then and in no state to come back.'

Will lifted her and half dragged, half carried her across the room. 'Don't worry, the bus driver'll put her off at Ashington and somebody'll help her home. It won't be the first time.'

Sorrow engulfed Becky's joy and the tears she'd tried to hold back broke loose. 'You didn't tell me she was so much worse.'

Liz put an arm round her. 'You know she grew worse after she got married, with free gin on tap day and night. But, after Ma died, she went really downhill. Don't let it ruin your big day, luv,' Liz begged. 'It's nothing new for Dora to wake up with a hangover.'

'You and Will had it planned,' Becky said with gratitude. 'Thanks for looking after me once again. I dread to think what would have happened.'

'Don't think!' Liz said. 'Relax. It's going to be the most wonderful day of your life.'

Janine had suggested pink and white to repeat the shop theme. Becky was swathed in a sheath of white satin, a train attached with pink rosebuds. Pink rosebuds also anchored the lace veil her mother and Liz had worn. Liz, as maid of honour, and Janine and the girls as bridesmaids, wore identical creations of white lace floating over pink satin, tied at the hips with pink satin sashes. The girls were delighted, but Billy looked unhappy in his white sailor suit.

'Eey, you look gorgeous, Beck.' Liz sniffed back tears.

Becky turned to Liz with a smile, 'Norma was miffed that she couldn't be a bridesmaid. But she looks ten months gone. Let's pray she doesn't go pop in the church.'

The wedding cars were soon filled with pink and white satin and lace. Seated next to Will in the bride's car, Becky realized it was finally happening. After all the planning and work, and the shock of Dora's surprise visit, she felt suddenly dreamy with happiness.

Michael stood at the altar, Clive next to him as best man. Still in a dream state, Becky walked up the aisle followed by her retinue of trainbearers.

The words of the service sounded like babble yet she managed to say *I do* at the right time and felt the gold circle

Michael slipped on to her finger with cold hands. He's nervous, poor lamb, she thought, a surge of love flowing over her.

As she walked down the aisle, her arm in his, she smiled at familiar faces in the pews. Suddenly she froze. Paul's face was smiling at her. He mouthed, *Congratulations*, then nodded as if in approval. He was telling her he understood their brief affair was over. She returned his nod with gratitude and, outside the church, smiled again as the confetti rained on them and the photographer pounced.

After the reception at the Grays' house, Liz and Janine helped Becky into her going-away costume, a blue tunic over a knee-length skirt. At the car, she deliberately threw her bouquet to the front of the crowd, where Janine caught it.

Becky reclined against the soft leather of the car and let out a long sigh. 'All day I haven't even felt my feet on the ground. I think I've dreamed the whole thing.'

He leaned over and kissed her lightly on the mouth. 'Could you feel that?'

She smiled and gripped his hand. 'Definitely.'

'Then you're waking up, Mrs Gray.'

They spent the night at a small hotel in Durham, from where they would motor to London for two weeks. The petrol was a wedding present from Victor.

'Do you think I overdid it wearing white?' Becky asked, as they returned to their room after dinner.

'Rubbish! I doubt there's such a thing as a virgin bride these days, and spare me from marrying one. I like to try on my clothes before I buy them.'

Becky feigned anger. 'You talk as if I were a piece of merchandise.'

He kissed her ear. 'So you are – the best business deal I've made since buying the house.'

'You took longer to look me over than you did the house.'

'That's because I can always sell the house, but I'm stuck with you for ever.'

He took her in his arms and kissed her and Becky responded as if it were their first kiss. Then he carried her to the bed.

'But I'm supposed to disappear and reappear in a white negligée,' she protested.

'Takes too long.' He removed her costume jacket.

She pulled him down and they tumbled on the bed, laughing as they undressed each other and flung their clothes to the floor.

When their passion rose and they were joined, Becky felt as if her head floated above her body and she was looking down, watching Michael making love to her. It was a sweet sensation, but then her own urgency overcame her and tongues of flame licked at her insides and up into her head until Michael's body, so attuned to hers, shuddered and they cried out as if in one voice.

'So this is what married life is like,' she said later as they lay together.

He nuzzled her neck. 'No, this is what *heaven* is like.'

The grey stone house had simple lines, except for the surgery addition on one side and, on the other, a conservatory. The lawn and flower beds flanking the drive were neatly tended. 'Mother has obviously sent the gardener round,' Michael said.

Hand in hand, they climbed the four steps to the door. He unlocked it and whisked Becky into his arms and over the threshold, kissing her. 'Welcome home, Mrs Gray.'

'And you, sweetheart. Let's dump the luggage in the hall and have a look around. I want to gloat over my first real home.'

'Then I'll have to dump you first.' He let her down and she took his hand. Michael picked up a pile of letters from the hall table. 'Mother's been looking after the post for us.'

Becky felt the dreamlike quality of her wedding day that had lasted throughout her honeymoon begin to float away. Though she wanted to know how Liz and the family were, she was reluctant to face reality so soon. 'Later,' she said.

She led him to the drawing room, facing the manicured lawn. They'd chosen traditional furnishings. A green and beige patterned carpet blended with the beige velvet chairs and sofas, which were accented with gold satin cushions to match the curtains. The walnut occasional tables and gramophone stand completed the earth-tone effect.

They wandered around and Becky assumed her showroom voice. 'As you will see, the dining room is a study in blue—'

Michael put a hand over her mouth. 'How about feeding me?'

'We have no food.'

Michael dragged her to the kitchen. 'You don't know my mother.' The larder was crammed with bread, home-made pies, cold meats, fruits and vegetables and a selection of cheeses.

Becky gasped. 'Your mother's an angel.'

'Nope! Just a mother. Mothers do things like that.'

'Not mine.' Becky felt saddened for a moment.

'I'm sorry, my love. I didn't think.'

'We'd better look at the post first,' she said.

Michael skimmed through the letters and handed her an envelope with an Ashington postmark.

Almost reluctantly, Becky opened it, then sighed with relief. 'Liz sounds cheerful, but then she wouldn't tell me if anything was wrong. She says Will's more and more impatient about work, but he's made a mountain of toys, and a mate who runs a delivery service is bringing them in a couple of days. I'll try Bainbridge's, Binns, and Fenwick's. They stock up early for Christmas.'

Michael chomped on an apple as he glanced through the rest of the post.

Becky felt guilty. 'I'll make dinner now.'

'And about time.'

Thirty-Six

'I insist!' Michael thumped his fist on the breakfast table, then rubbed the offending hand.

'Darling, being a few days late doesn't mean I'm pregnant. It's not unusual after all the hustle and bustle of the wedding. I'd feel guilty having a maid do my housework. All I'd do for you is cook.'

'And keep me happy in bed.' He looked at the clock and pushed back his chair. 'Come on, I'd better get you to work.'

'I know we don't have much time to relax together,' she said, rising.

'When you're not cleaning or cooking, you're falling asleep. A bride should be blooming, not wasting away. And if you *are* pregnant, you'll *need* help.'

They reached the car and he helped her in. Becky closed her eyes and prayed. *Please God, not now. Not when it could be Paul's or Michael's.* 'Let's discuss it if and when we know for sure,' she said.

'In any case, it's ridiculous to feel guilty. You earn much more at the shop than we would pay for part-time help.'

He cranked the car and jumped in. 'I'm not having my wife working herself to death.'

Becky raised her hands in surrender. 'I give in. I'll advertise today, but I don't want anyone living in.'

'All right, we'll compromise.' Backing out of the drive, he almost collided with another motorist and slammed on the brakes. 'Sorry, darling.'

Becky said nothing. She tried not to nag about his impatience behind the wheel. 'With a maid, I could start those fashion shows I've been promising myself forever.'

'That's right, as soon as you get some free time, create more work for yourself.'

He stopped outside the shop and leaned over to kiss her. 'I'll pick you up at six and we'll have a relaxing evening playing records.'

'Sounds wonderful.'

Michael's family doctor wiped his glasses on his handkerchief. 'I'd say you're about three months. Congratulations! And to Michael.'

'Thank you, Dr Stone.' Her head spun as he showed her to the door. Before returning to Michael in the waiting room she tried to collect herself.

He put down the magazine he was reading.

She nodded and he jumped up and took her in his arms, disregarding the waiting patients. She hurried him out.

'How far on?'

'About three months.' Somehow her feet carried her to the car.

'Wow! We might have hit the jackpot before we were married. We got respectable just in time.' Michael laughed and put his arm round her. 'Now you *must* take life easier.'

'I can't give up the shop.'

'Janine can take more responsibility.'

'And I can use my sitting room as a day nursery. I *can* do both, darling.' She *would* be a good mother, she thought, and would try to stop these thoughts about Paul. The chances of it being Michael's child were much greater. They pulled up outside the house and she kissed his hand. 'You're a nice man, Michael Gray. You'll make a wonderful father.'

That evening Michael sorted the post and handed Becky the familiar envelope.

Dearest Becky and Michael,

Will's had an accident at the pit. He's in hospital. On his first day back a runaway pony took off at a trot with a full load. Will tried to grab it to slow it down but the harness broke and Will fell and his leg got caught between the wheels. It's bad. The doctors don't think they can save it. It's fractured in two places below the knee, and the wheels tore some flesh off his calf. They've given him something to keep him out during the operation but he'll be in a bad way when he wakes up. My poor Will.

Now, don't think you've got to come running to help us. Will's folks and I are taking turns at the hospital and looking after the bairns. I'll keep you informed.

All my love,

Liz

'Dear God!' Becky gripped the table for support.

Michael ran from the kitchen. 'What's wrong?'

'Will's had a bad accident.' She broke into quiet little sobs.

He led her to the sofa and read the letter. 'Oh, no! And on his first day.'

'That's probably why it happened. The ponies feel so well after being in fresh air and grazing, some are skittish when they're forced to work underground again. They call them tickly-backs.' She wiped her eyes on her handkerchief. 'I must help Liz and be with her.'

'I'm going with you. I'll pack a few things for both of us, and fruit to eat in the car.' He kissed her before he rose. 'Bear up, darling. Just telephone Janine to take over.'

Liz flung open the kitchen door and put her hand to her heart. 'Oh, Beck, Michael!'

Becky hugged her tightly. 'Any more word about Will?'

'They couldn't save his leg.'

'Oh, Liz!' They held each other and sobbed as they'd done so many times.

Michael guided them to the fireside and produced a flask of brandy from his pocket. He poured a tot into three mugs. 'Here, it's medicinal.' He knocked back his own and they obediently sipped.

'Does Will know?' Becky asked.

Liz nodded. 'Dear God! If they'd only let me be with him when they told him. When they did let me in he sobbed. Can you imagine my Will sobbing like a bairn? He says he's no good any more. He's not a whole man.

'The bosses are trying to get out of paying compensation by saying it was Will's carelessness. They say, if it hadn't been for the strike, the pony wouldn't have turned into a tickly-back, and that, in any case, Will should have known better than to use it on its first day down.'

'But it's impossible to know which ones might turn skittish when they go back,' Becky said.

Liz sighed. 'Not only that, it was somebody else's cart. If Will had harnessed the pony, he would have known it was too excitable, but he would never tell on a mate.' She sniffed and dried her eyes on her apron. 'But his mates are fighting for him. They're taking it to the unions and even clubbing together for legal help. They say he fought hard for them and now they'll fight for him.'

'How are the children taking it?' Becky sipped her brandy again but it burned her throat.

'They don't know yet. Will's ma and da have them.' Liz burst into tears and Michael lifted the brandy to her lips.

'Can we see him?' Becky's voice was hesitant. She didn't know if she could stand seeing Will in such a pitiable state.

'If you tell them you've motored from Newcastle, they might let you see him.'

Will lay on a bunk in the middle of a crowded ward, a cage visible under the blankets where his right leg should have been. Becky felt faint with horror and the smell of disinfectant and disease. She leaned heavily on Michael's arm as they approached Will.

He looked from one to the other.

'How are you feeling?' Becky knew the question sounded ridiculous but didn't know what else to say.

'Bloody awful, but thanks for coming.' He closed his eyes and tears squeezed out. 'My poor Liz. As if I haven't put her through enough! Now she's married to a cripple for the rest of her life.'

'Don't say that, Will.' Michael's voice was sharp. 'You'll soon be able to get around. They've made great improvements in artificial limbs since the war.'

'Aye, so the war did *some* good.'

'Don't worry about the future. Your mates are helping, and I'll drum up my father's solicitor.'

'Thanks. I'll be the best one-legged miner down the pit. I'm not trained to do anything else, man.'

'But you *can* do something else, Will.' Becky's voice became animated. 'You can make wonderful toys with wood. Perhaps you could branch out and make other things too – clock cases, cigar boxes, even furniture. Either get a job with a carpenter, or just do it on your own.'

'Oh, aye, from home? What home?'

Becky swallowed hard. Of course! They would be evicted.

'Move in with us,' Michael said.

She wanted to sink to her knees to thank him.

Closing his eyes in a vain attempt to hide his tears, Will said, 'Thanks, but I can't accept any more help from you. I'm such a feeble bugger, always in trouble.'

'People have accidents, and bad luck, Will,' Becky said. 'You've had more than your share, that's all. We'd love to have you until you get on your feet.' Too late, she realized her choice of words.

Will grunted. 'Aye, one of them anyway.'

The nurse bustled up to them. 'I'm afraid you'll have to go now.'

Becky bent to kiss Will's cheek. 'We'll be back.'

'How is he?' Liz was at the door when they arrived.

Becky held her. 'The same old Will, feeling guilty about not being able to take care of his family.'

'I wish he'd stop worrying about us or he'll never get better.'

'You're coming to live with us until you can afford your own place. He can start off using the garden shed as a workshop, then if he moves on to furniture, there's an entire basement.' Becky paused for breath.

'Furniture? What are you talking about?' Liz put her hand to her head.

'You're babbling, Beck,' Michael said. 'Slow down and start again. And *sit* down, both of you.'

They obeyed and Becky retold her story.

Liz burst into tears. 'You're both that good to us. But I don't want to land a whole family on you. You're just newly-weds.'

'Newly-weds with too much house and too much to do and now a baby on the way. I posted a letter to you today.'

'A baby! Oh, that's wonderful. When?'

'About six months.'

Michael leaned against the mantelpiece. 'Mrs Jackson, our new part-time help, does the heavy work, but you could help Becky with the baby and cooking and light housework, or you could have separate quarters.'

'Both,' Liz said. 'Separate quarters'll keep the bairns out of your hair, except when you want them, but I bags the kitchen and the baby and the housework.'

Michael looked puzzled. 'Bags?'

Becky couldn't help smiling. 'It's a childhood expression. It means she claims it and I lose all rights.'

Liz folded her arms. 'I wouldn't come otherwise. It'll be a joy to help you.'

'Don't think you're coming as a maid,' Becky said. 'It's your home for as long as you need it. Will's so talented, you'll have your own house one day.'

'Aye, he's been whittling since he was a bairn. He can do magic things with wood. But it'll take him a while to make enough to live on.'

'Not necessarily, and he'll get his compensation, no matter how long we have to fight for it,' Michael said.

Becky sighed. 'Thank God! You'll never have to worry about that damn siren going again.'

'Aye, that'll be a relief.' Liz pushed the kettle over the flames and stood. 'You must be starving. I made you some sandwiches.'

Becky looked across at Michael and felt her love overflow. He must have noticed the change in Liz's voice. She sounded almost like her old self again. 'You're a miracle worker, darling,' she whispered.

He blew her a kiss.

With the tea tray on the floor beside them Michael said, 'After I've demolished a few sandwiches, would you give me the name and address of the chap who's leading the crusade for Will? I'll pop out and tell him I'm joining the ranks.'

'But you can't do much from Newcastle.'

'I can do plenty, and I can come when necessary. Think about it. They're denying Will compensation on the basis that it was his own fault for trying to restrain a pony who'd grown healthy by being allowed above ground. Some adverse publicity might change their minds.'

A tear rolled down Liz's cheek. 'Aye, and if he hadn't stopped it, it could have been a major disaster for the pit and cost them a fortune. Eey, it's that kind of you. The one to see is Dick Travers. He's at number twelve Third Row.'

When Michael had finished the last sandwich and his second cup of tea, he rose. 'See you ladies later.'

As the door closed behind him, Liz said in a voice quivering with emotion, 'Eey, you married a wonderful man, Beck. And I'm that thrilled about the bairn.'

'So are we.' As she said the words, Becky realized she *was* thrilled. 'Sooner or later, I bet Will carns enough to buy or rent one of those nice little semi-detached houses they're building up the road from us. I've been saving those boxes of toys till nearer Christmas. When I get back I'll try out the big shops.'

'There's a new pile in our bedroom Will was going to send to you. You can take them back.' Liz leaned forward and took Becky's hand. 'Thanks for your help, Beck. I never thought you'd turn out to be such a businesswoman. And I still can't believe that Will could earn enough to live on from his whittling.'

'I started small, remember?'

A smile lifted the corners of Liz's mouth. 'Aye, nobody could get much smaller than that.'

Thirty-Seven

C atherine Elizabeth Gray was born on 15 February 1927. Becky stroked the baby's blonde hair and searched the puckered face for signs of Michael, but wide blue eyes stared back at her.

'She's your image, darling,' Michael said. 'She's a beauty.'

'Your mother has the same colouring.' Becky prayed the baby would resemble the Gray side of the family more as she grew older. She tried not to think of Paul's blue eyes.

Michael opened the tiny clenched fist and the baby grasped his index finger. 'I'll get Liz to see her now. We'll wait till you're rested before Will and the gang come.'

'Thank you, sweetheart – for Catherine, and everything.' Becky felt grateful and happy. She couldn't ask for more.

At six months, everyone agreed that Catherine was like her mother. Becky had just got her off to sleep in the cot in her old sitting room at work – now the nursery – when the telephone rang and Catherine whimpered.

'I'll see to her. You answer the telephone.' Janine picked up Catherine. 'Sshh now. Back to sleep.' Becky ran to the office.

'That was Bainbridge's. Only August, and they've doubled last year's Christmas toy orders. I've collared the three largest markets in town.'

'I want to see Will's face when you tell him,' Liz said. 'I wish I had your knack as a saleslady.'

'Come with me next week to the small shops and I'll train you.'

'I'd rather look after Catherine.'

'Everyone wants to look after Catherine, including her mother. Will would be proud to have you as his partner.'

Liz gave a resigned shrug. 'You've got me there. I'll try.'

Peeking into the sitting room, where Janine was rocking Catherine on her lap and making cooing noises, Becky attempted a stern voice: 'Have you nothing better to do?'

Janine grinned. 'Not better than this.' Then, sniffing the air like a bulldog, she handed a puce-faced Catherine to Becky. 'Pooh! I've just changed me mind. I'd rather make the tea.'

Will was at his workbench in the basement. He could now manage the stairs on his artificial leg. He looked up when they all arrived and stood beaming at him.

'What's up?'

'Nothing much,' Becky said. 'Except that the three biggest shops in the town have almost doubled last year's Christmas toy orders.'

Will looked stunned. 'I can't believe people'll spend good money for my whittlings.'

'Congratulations!' Michael said. 'Perhaps next year would be a good time to branch out into ornaments and furniture – cigar boxes, clock cases, rocking chairs, or whatever.'

Will scratched his head. 'Furniture would be hard to deliver.'

'Rent a van and driver at first,' Becky broke in. 'Once your work is known, you can send out brochures.'

Will wiped his hands on his sawdust-and-paint-covered overalls. 'If sales keep up, and with me weekly compensation, we can rent a house soon and get out of your way.'

'You're not in our way,' Michael said.

'We owe you both so much . . .' Will was visibly over-come.

'Nonsense!' Becky also felt emotional. 'We'll hate it when you go. But you can't go too far. You'll still need the basement to work in.'

Catherine whimpered and Liz rocked her. 'And I'll still need the kitchen and Catherine. I'm not giving up neither.'

As Becky and Michael climbed the stairs, she said, 'I wish Will weren't so reluctant to accept our help. I'm encouraging Liz to do the sales side so he can feel more independent.'

'Splendid idea. They'd make a good team.'

'How about relaxing with a drink,' Becky said. 'I admit I'm tired today, but I didn't think it was possible to be so happy.'

On Christmas Eve Michael dropped Becky and Catherine off at the shop. The van behind tooted its horn and Michael tooted back angrily. 'Sorry I can't help you out, darling. That bastard behind's in a hurry.'

She was juggling the baby and her handbag to find her keys when a voice hailed her: 'Hello, there! Let me help.'

'Paul!' Her heart thumped. She hadn't seen him since the wedding. 'Thank you,' she said. 'You always appear in the nick of time.'

He took her bag and looked at Catherine. 'My! She's a beauty. How old is she?'

'Almost ten months.' Too late, Becky wished she'd lied. He might wonder.

'It's nice to see you again.' He followed her to the sitting room and set down her bag. 'So, your room's now a nursery. But I spy the coffee percolator. Any chance of a cup? I still eat at Annie's but I can't stand her coffee.'

Becky tucked Catherine into her cot. Janine and Eileen would be here soon but she couldn't refuse. 'Of course,' she said. 'Please sit down and I'll light the stove.'

He bent over Catherine's cot. 'May I pick her up?'

'She loves being spoiled.' Her fingers shaking, Becky struck a match. Was he wondering if he were holding his own child? No, he would naturally assume the baby was Michael's. Still, it was unnerving to see him gazing at her.

The stoves lit, she filled the percolator. 'How's your job?'

He sat on the divan, Catherine's fist wrapped round his big forefinger. 'It's hard work and underpaid but I love it. I work with a partner in Byker – only one crummy room but it's our own practice. We mostly represent poor clients. Sometimes the parish pays. Otherwise, we charge cut rates and get paid on tick. If it's a workman's compensation case and we win, we take a percentage – if we lose, we get nothing. I'm still in the same digs.'

'So, you'll never be a rich lawyer.'

He flashed his familiar grin. 'Oh, I don't intend to stay poor for ever. When we get enough capital together we'll expand the firm.' Suddenly, his grin faded and his voice softened. 'You look wonderful. Obviously, marriage and motherhood suit you.'

A lump rose in Becky's throat. 'If you're still in the same digs, I take it you're not married.'

He bounced Catherine on his lap. 'Haven't found a likely candidate. How come I never see you at Annie's?'

'We must just miss each other.' She felt flustered. She deliberately visited Annie between meal times to avoid meeting Paul.

Janine appeared in the doorway. 'Paul! Why aren't you having breakfast at Annie's?'

Setting the percolator on the stove, Becky realized Janine must see Paul quite often at Annie's, yet she never mentioned him. Clearly, she didn't want to remind her of her lapse.

'Morning, Becky,' Eileen shouted from the workroom. 'Something smells nice.'

'Coffee. Would you like a cup?' Becky was glad of the diversion.

'Aye, I'd love one.' She joined them in the sitting room and started with surprise on seeing Paul.

'This is Paul, an old friend,' Becky said, then to Paul, 'Eileen and I have known each other since my first job.'

Becky looked at her with affection. 'I'd never have survived the first day without her. We wouldn't be here now.'

'Oh, yes you would. Everything you do turns out right in the end,' Eileen said.

Becky looked at Catherine on Paul's lap and wondered.

Thirty-Eight

Wednesday 28 July 1928. Becky circled the date on the calendar and wrote, *Moving Day!* 'Your own house in one more week, Liz.'

Liz continued peeling apples. 'Aye, it's not quite next door, as you always wanted, but I never thought we'd find a semi-detached in this area at a rent we could afford.'

'Let's go shopping for furniture tomorrow. We can leave Catherine at the shop, though I must go in on Saturday to organize the fashion show. Trust Janine to get in the club when I finally need her to model.'

'Besides the agency models, you could always use Annie's Vera. She's glamorous enough and carries herself well.'

'Of course! Vera! She'd love to.'

'All gone!' Catherine announced from her high chair.

Becky wiped the chocolate cake from Catherine's face with her bib. 'Now drink your milk, sweetheart.' The telephone rang and Becky's shoulders slumped as she left to answer it. She returned, sighing. 'Sometimes I'd like to pull that telephone out of the wall. We're going to his parents' – *if* Michael finishes his evening surgery in time, then a mile-long list of house calls.'

Becky looked at her watch. 'Only five past six and the surgery's almost full. Michael's going to be late as usual,' she said to Liz.

'He's probably got caught in the traffic,' Will said, stretching out in a deckchair between the women in the back garden.

'Don't throw the sand, Catherine,' Liz said, and called to

296

Mary. 'Make sand pies with Catherine, Mary. She's throwing sand all over the place.'

The telephone clanged and Becky groaned. 'If that's another patient—'

'I'll get it.' Liz ran through the open French windows.

'Dr Gray's residence,' she said into the receiver. She listened, then her voice rose, 'What? Oh, no! Where is he?'

In a second, Becky was out of her chair and by the telephone. 'Michael? Is he all right?' She grabbed the receiver from Liz, who stood like a statue.

'Mrs Gray here.' She heard the voice at the other end and felt Liz's arms go round her waist. 'No! No! Dear God!' She replaced the receiver and stared at Liz. 'Michael's dead.'

'I know, luv.' Liz's arm tightened round Becky's middle. 'Will,' she called. 'Come, quickly.'

He was there in seconds. 'What's wrong?'

'Michael's been killed in an accident.'

Becky leaned against Liz, muttering to herself, 'They've made a mistake. It's not him. Please God! It's *not* him.'

The next thing she knew, Will's strong arms were helping her into a taxi, and then she was in a white room, with a white sheet over a bed, and a man in white standing beside it.

'I want to see Michael. Let me see him.' The man pulled back the sheet and she saw Michael's face. It was swollen and covered in red gashes and bruises. 'It's not him!' She heard her voice, loud, then Will said something to the man and he covered the bed again.

Becky's hands went to her temples and pressed hard, nausea overcame her before everything went black.

She opened her eyes and looked at the alarm clock by the bed. Liz and Will were sitting beside her. Drawing her hand across Michael's side of the bed, she realized it was empty. 'Oh God! It's not true . . . is it?' she begged.

Liz reached for Becky's hand and held it. 'He couldn't have felt much, luv. He was gone before they got him to the hospital.'

'He was in the car?'

'Aye, he must have been hurrying home,' Will said.

'Dear God! He was rushing for surgery and I'd begged him not to be late for dinner at his parents'.' Moaning, she buried her head in the pillow, then turned a tortured face to Liz. 'Heaven forgive me.' The first tears came and her agony wracked her body.

'You can't blame yourself. He was always rushing for surgery, luv. Anyway, have a good cry. It's time,' Liz said.

'What happened?'

Becky squeezed her wet eyes shut. She wasn't sure she wanted to know. But she heard Will's voice: 'He couldn't have done anything, Beck. A lorry came out of a side street without warning. He had no time to stop, and an old Ford doesn't stand a chance against a lorry.'

Dear God! She'd wanted him to get a better car, but he was emotionally attached to the old Ford because it was his parents' twenty-first birthday present. She ran a hand over her forehead. 'Oh, heavens! His parents!'

'We telephoned them,' Liz said. 'They'll be over tomorrow, if Mrs Gray's up to it.'

'Where's Catherine? My poor baby!'

'She's with the bairns, playing at the neighbours. Now *you* have a good cry.'

Becky exhaled deeply and it seemed the breath released the tide of grief she'd been afraid to let go until now. She sobbed as freely as she used to when a child, and Liz sat on the bed and rocked her, just as she'd done then.

Becky awoke with a start. Liz lay beside her on the bed, still dressed from the night before. 'Are you all right, Beck?'

Becky blinked and remembered. 'Oh, God! Michael! I don't want to wake up.' She wailed and thrust her face into the pillow.

Liz stroked her back.

'How could he leave us?' Becky cried.

'Sshh, you don't want Catherine to see you like this.'

298

'Where is she? What time is it?'

'In the kitchen with Mrs Jackson. The bairns are at school.'

Becky took a painful breath. 'I have to tell her. She'll be asking for her daddy. First I'll wash my face. I mustn't let her see me upset.'

Liz rose. 'I'll help you. I got out clean underwear and a dress for you.'

Becky saw the pile of silk on the bedside chair and a black dress draped beside it. She shuddered. Of course, black.

Washed and dressed, with a dusting of powder attempting to conceal her ravaged face, Becky took Liz's hand. But when she reached the kitchen door and heard Catherine's laughter, she recoiled. 'I can't do it.'

'You *can.*' Liz pushed her forward.

'Mummy, Mummy.' Catherine peered behind her at the empty doorway. 'Daddy?'

Becky picked her up and held her tightly. 'Daddy can't come, darling. He had to go on a long journey to heaven last night. He's with the angels now and smiling down on both of us.'

Catherine's face contorted. 'Daddy coming?'

Becky reached the nearest chair and cradled Catherine on her lap. 'He can't come now that he's with the angels in heaven. But Mummy's here. Mummy will always be here.'

'Daddy! Daddy!' Catherine yelled, and looked behind Becky to where Liz stood.

'Yes, baby. That's Auntie Liz. She's here, and Uncle Will's downstairs.'

Catherine opened her mouth and wailed, the tears glittering like pearls on her lashes. Becky kissed them away, but more came and silvered the pink cheeks. 'Sshh, baby, sshh. Mummy's got you.' She locked in her own tears. She must be strong for Catherine. 'Let's sit in the garden. Uncle Will's made it very pretty for us.' She felt her arms would break under Catherine's weight but eased her over her shoulder.

Mrs Jackson opened the French windows for them. 'I'll bring you a cup of tea.'

'No, but thank you.' Becky sat on the stone bench, and lowered Catherine to her lap. She wondered if the child somehow understood that her daddy would never come back, or was simply upset by his immediate absence. As she tilted the face, so like her own, and wiped the wet cheeks, Liz ushered Mr and Mrs Gray towards her.

Becky put on a bright voice. 'Look who's here, Catherine. It's Grandma and Grandpa.'

Howard Gray lifted Catherine and held her out to his wife. 'Give Grandma a kiss, then it's my turn. And now I have a kiss for your mummy.' As he bent to kiss Becky's cheek, he whispered something she couldn't hear, but she saw his dark-grey suit and black armband.

'My dear!' Elsa Gray sat by Becky and took her hand. Behind the black veil of her hat, Elsa's face looked white-washed, her eyes red and swollen.

Liz brought a tray with coffee and biscuits and set it on the wrought-iron table in front of the bench. 'Mrs Jackson said Becky didn't want tea, so she's made coffee.'

Mr Gray nodded. 'Thank you. You ladies have yours now. I'll take Catherine for a walk round the garden.' His voice was cracked and Becky guessed he felt too emotional to talk.

When he'd gone with Catherine, Mrs Gray broke down. 'Oh, God! He was so young!' She put her arms round Becky and they wept together.

Becky could feel the woman's pain. It must be as terrible to lose a son as to lose a husband. 'Would you help with the arrangements?' she said.

'Of course, my dear. Clive's at the hospital now.' She shaded her eyes to watch Catherine clasping her grandpa's hand and smelling the roses he held out to her. 'How's Catherine?'

'She was more upset than usual that her daddy wasn't here this morning. I think she might have sensed something from me.'

'She'll absorb it gradually. We'll help you with her all we can.'

'Thank you. I'm so glad she has you and Grandpa, and loving aunts and uncles.' Becky lifted her coffee cup to her lips with a trembling hand. The hot liquid burned her throat and brought back happy memories that had turned painful overnight. That first Christmas when Michael had given her a percolator; their nights of love on the little divan, and later in their own bedroom; his voice encouraging her when he'd helped Dr Stone to bring Catherine into the world. Suddenly, reality clenched her in its jaws anew and she cried out in anguish. She would never hear Michael's voice again.

Thirty-Nine

M ourning lay like dust over the house. The coffin, sealed because of Michael's disfigurement, stood in the centre of the sitting room covered in wreaths. The curtains were closed.

Mrs Jackson had taken the children for the day and for Becky it was a relief to let her misery out. Keeping up an act in front of the little ones had been a strain for everyone.

Becky lingered by the coffin as the motors arrived. The pallbearers would be coming to carry Michael to the hearse. Through the flowers, she touched the wood where his heart would be, and whispered, 'Goodbye, my darling.' This would be her last moment alone with him.

Clive, his father and Will, together with some of Michael's friends, acted as pallbearers, and Becky sat between Mrs Gray and Liz in the first car behind the hearse. Dust motes danced in the July sun pouring through the windows. After the dark coolness of the house, Becky couldn't take the sunlight. She reached over to pull the blinds. As she did so a small girl in the crowd of children on the pavement watching the scene put her hand to her dress collar and hopped up and down, chanting. Becky saw herself as a child and knew the girl was saying, *Touch collar, never follow to my door.* She'd said those same words so many times, but they hadn't protected her. She pulled the blind.

As the driver opened the door to help them out, Becky saw the open grave. She gave an involuntary gasp, then gritted her teeth and squinted against the sun. So far, she'd managed to stay calm and avoid a major headache, and she'd done her crying only in private. But that cold black pit . . . Breathing deeply, she took Mrs Gray's arm. The other mourners arrived and the white-surpliced vicar said words over the grave after the coffin had been lowered, but Becky couldn't make them out. Everything and everyone seemed distant and blurred. Only her grief was sharp, slicing like a razor through her heart.

At length she felt Liz ease her forward and heard her words, 'Just a handful, luv.'

She bent and took a handful of earth. It was dark and damp, freshly dug. Her knees didn't want to let her rise, but she leaned on Liz. She crumbled the earth as she let it fall into the black hole. God wasn't fair. Why had he taken Michael from them?

At the house, Mrs Jackson served sherry and refreshments. In a stupor Becky acknowledged the guests as they offered condolences, hardly realizing who they were, except for Janine. Janine engulfed her in a tight embrace, the mound of her large belly pressing into Becky and her wet cheek against hers. 'Keep it up, luv. You're doing fine,' she said.

Becky nodded. Janine was just embarking on family life with her husband. She was glad for her.

Liz placed a glass of sherry in her hand. 'Drink it and I'll get you another.' Becky sipped and gripped her glass. When the last guests had murmured their sympathies, she longed to sit. 'Thank goodness the procession's over,' she said, joining Mrs Gray on the sofa.

'You did well, my dear.' Mrs Gray's face, her black veil turned back over her hat, looked frail and old, her blue eyes darkly shadowed. But she kept her head up and her shoulders back. She'd retained her regal bearing.

Becky held her hand. 'I should take a lesson from you.'

'It's almost finished,' she said.

Looking about her, Becky realized that now the condolences were over, the guests were chatting as at any cocktail party. Strange, she thought, this custom of forced normality after a funeral. She sipped her sherry and Liz sat next to her with two triangular ham sandwiches on a plate.

'One for each of you or no more sherry.'

Mrs Gray took a sandwich and looked at Liz with affection. 'She's bossy today,' she said to Becky.

Becky gave in and took the other sandwich. 'I don't know how I managed to live without her all those years.' Suddenly she realized Liz and Will were to move into their house in a few days. In the light of her own tragedy she'd forgotten everything else.

'Liz! Your new house. It's moving day soon and you have no furniture.'

'Oh, that! Will and I cancelled that days ago. You're not getting rid of us yet.'

'But you were so looking forward to having your own home.' Becky heard a mixture of distress and relief in her voice. 'You're staying because of me? Oh, you know I would manage, you'd both be here every day anyway. You need a life of your own.'

'We've got our own life here, pet. So we decided to impose ourselves on you a bit longer, until you throw us out.'

Becky drew Liz close and, for the first time, she couldn't stop her tears. 'Oh, thank you both. I'm so glad you're staying.' She sniffed and foraged in her costume pocket for her handkerchief. 'Forgive me. Since Michael . . . I've been so wrapped up in . . .'

'I know, pet. But you can start your life again now. It's time you went back to work. I'll look after things at home.'

Becky felt warmed. Not everything had changed. Liz was still here for her.

Forty

W ill drove Becky to the shop in the new Ford she'd bought after Michael's death. Becky had had the car adapted to accommodate Will's wooden leg and he loved driving.

As they approached town, people jostled around a newspaper stand.

'Stop,' Becky said. 'Something's happened. I'll get a paper.'

She fought her way to the stand, thrust a penny into the owner's coin-blackened hand and grabbed a paper. 'Wall Street crash!' he shouted. 'Investors jump to death from skyscrapers.'

Becky returned to the car. 'How terrible!' Together they read.

He let out a low whistle. 'I'm sorry for them, but they knew the risks.'

Becky bit her lip. 'Do you think it will affect us over here? America's a long way off.'

'Aye, it could affect international trade, but it might just be a big scare.'

Will pulled up amid the pandemonium of the stall-holders setting up for the day, and Becky climbed out. 'Thanks, Will. You spoil me.'

The shop door was open. Janine or Eileen must have arrived early.

'That you, Beck?' Janine called from the sitting room.

'Yes, relax.'

'Oh, glad it's not a customer. I'm changing David's nappy.'

Becky walked over and tickled one-year-old David's bare belly. 'Tea or coffee, Jan?'

'Either, and biscuits. I was so busy feeding him I didn't have time to eat. Victor brought me early.' She cooed at David and made a kissing noise. 'Daddy had to take the car to the garage for petrol, didn't he, sweet boy?'

Becky smiled. She'd known Janine almost ten years and could never have imagined her as a doting mother. Yet here she was, her slim, dark good looks unchanged with motherhood, her scarlet-tipped fingers wielding a nappy pin. 'How's the doting daddy doing?' She filled the kettle.

'Fine. Still doing well on the horses during the day and managing the Rex part-time. It's amazing where people find the money these days to bet on horses and go to the pictures.'

Victor had turned to bookmaking when his artistic endeavours had failed. He'd proved successful, though only his close friends knew of his occupation. The cinema his father owned was his official source of income.

'Have you heard the news from America?' Becky set the biscuits and mugs on the table.

'Bloody awful! Poor sods. But that's where greed gets you.'

'Will thinks it might affect us.'

'Now, don't worry about that until and if the time comes.'

As usual, her words warmed Becky. 'Your optimism keeps me going, Jan.'

'Aye, well, if you expect the worst, that's most likely what you'll get.' She tucked the blankets over David's kicking legs. 'I have to finish that dress for Vera today and drop it off. She needs it for her boyfriend's twenty-first tonight.'

'Give Annie my love. Tell her I'll pop in soon.'

At six, Eileen poked her head round the office door. She'd filled out and looked years younger than when Becky had first met her. 'See you tomorrow, Beck.'

Becky glanced at her watch. 'Oh! Bye, Eileen.' She hadn't realized it was so late. The bills could wait. She went to turn off the sitting-room light before getting her coat. On the table sat the pink and white bag containing Vera's dress. Becky cursed Janine for forgetting it. She'd have to go herself, and she always avoided visiting Annie at meal times in case Paul was there. Though she knew from Annie that he was still a regular customer, she didn't want to see him. At times the memory of that one night tapped at the window of her mind, but she shooed it away. She'd behaved like a silly flapper.

She telephoned Liz from the office. 'I have to drop off something at Annie's. I'll be a little late. How's Catherine?'

'She's full of beans, had a good afternoon nap, ate a huge tea, and now she's playing with the bairns.'

'Thanks, Liz.' Becky put down the receiver and pulled on her grey wool coat and a cheerful red hat. Those endless days of mourning were over. She turned off the stoves and lights and braved the cold evening air.

Annie laboured her way around the tightly packed tables carrying a tray above her head. She greeted Becky and pointed with her free hand to a corner table. 'There's a seat next to Paul. Grand to see you. Won't be a minute.'

Paul was already standing, inclining his head in greeting.

'Hello, Paul.' She admonished her heart for skipping a beat as she reached his table.

He pulled out the vacant chair and Becky was glad to take the weight off her wobbly knees. He still had that physical power over her.

'I can't stay,' she said. 'I'm just delivering a dress for Vera.'

He looked disappointed. 'Won't you even have a cup of tea with me?'

Becky opened her mouth to decline, but Annie's voice boomed, 'Two teas coming up.'

Becky gave in and nodded.

'I was sorry to hear about your husband.'

'Thank you. How's life treating you?' She found she really wanted to know.

'My partner and I have a share in an office in town now and clients who pay real money.'

She noticed his grey wool suit was quality and his white shirt professionally starched, though his curls were as unruly as ever. Why was she surprised that she still found him attractive?

Annie came with the tea. 'Here you are. Where you been hiding, hinny?'

'Just busy, Annie. I came to drop this off for Vera. Janine says she needs it tonight.' Becky handed her the pink and white bag.

'Aye, thanks for bringing it, hen. You still spoil her like a bairn.' Annie took the bag and trudged off to the kitchen.

'Look,' Paul said when she'd gone. 'I know you're going to refuse but I intend to try. Please have dinner with me, somewhere quiet. I've been hoping you would come here one of these days.'

So, he still thought about her. A bird fluttered in her stomach. 'I really can't . . .' she began, not quite knowing why.

'Just a drink then?'

'All right.' She sipped her tea for something to do.

'Damn the tea!' He rose, placed half a crown on the table, and waved to Annie as he ushered Becky out. Annie waved back, looking not at all surprised.

At the touch of his hand on her arm, Becky felt a thrill of excitement she hadn't experienced for a long time. She let out her breath slowly and allowed herself to feel his touch. There was no reason why she shouldn't.

He guided her along Grainger Street among the crowd of shop and office workers on their way home. News vendors bellowed the latest news of the American disaster: 'More Investors Jump to Their Deaths.'

'How awful!' Becky was glad to talk about something impersonal.

'Yes, it's a bad day for America.'

'My brother-in-law thinks it could affect us over here.'

'It could, and other countries they trade with. But let's not worry about that tonight. We're going out to enjoy ourselves.'

Becky's thoughts raced as they walked. She wondered about the wisdom of getting involved with him again. After a year and two months of widowhood, her life was now her daughter and her business, plus her old job at the clinic and at the local chapter of the women's movement. Emmeline Pankhurst had died the previous year, but she'd won the vote for women. Now they sought equality in education and jobs. Though reluctant to give up the stability and freedom she'd struggled to regain, she couldn't deny the pleasure she felt as Paul's long legs moved next to hers. His voice brought her back.

'A shilling for your thoughts.'

'Oh, just that so much has happened since . . .' She stopped, unable to go on.

He piloted her across the busy road. 'How's Catherine?'

He remembered her baby's name! 'A constant delight,' she said. 'I usually take her to the shop with me. I miss her when I don't.'

He guided her through the entrance of the Douglas Hotel. She'd been here with Michael and felt a sudden emptiness inside, like an explosion. She gazed around the splendid Victorian building, its ceiling embellished with hand-painted canvas and covered with glass, its stained-glass windows and fine paintings on the walls. 'I love this place,' she said to Paul.

'So do I.' He took their coats and seated her at a table. She saw his eyes taking in her simple wool sheath dress and felt a long-lost flutter of pleasure at the admiration in his glance.

He sat opposite. 'What would you like?'

'A gin and orange, please.' She hadn't touched a pink lady since Michael's death. Damn! She must stop this self-torture. She was a free woman. Paul returned from the bar with her drink and a half-pint of beer.

He sat and raised his glass to hers. 'To your health.'

'And yours.' They touched glasses.

'You haven't changed a day.' He put his hand over hers as it rested on the table.

An electric charge ran through her. Embarrassed, she lowered her eyes. 'You've changed. At least, you've changed your tailor.' She found herself smiling.

He chuckled. 'Ah, yes, my threadbare years are over, I hope.'

She left her hand under his, savouring the heat of his touch.

'I might never have met you again that second time had I not been buying fruit outside your door.' He paused and in the dim light she *felt* rather than saw his eyes searching her face. 'I walk past often,' he went on. 'A hundred times I've wanted to go in.'

'Why didn't you?' Obviously, she'd been more than a one-night fling in his mind.

'I didn't want to push myself on you while you were in mourning. And, of course, I knew you were avoiding me by not going to Annie's. I was waiting for a suitable opening.'

'You certainly jumped in on the first one,' she said with a smile.

'Couldn't afford to miss the chance.' The hand over hers stroked her fingers.

'Why did you come to my wedding?' she asked suddenly.

He gave a wry smile. 'I wanted to sort of say goodbye to you officially.' He stopped stroking her hand and grasped it, knitting their fingers together. 'I can't deny my pleasure at sitting here with you now. Let me cook dinner for you.'

She felt torn. She hadn't seen Catherine all day. But she'd be asleep now anyway. There was no harm in spending more time with Paul. In fact, she felt a glow of pleasure at the thought. 'I can't stay long,' she said, 'and I'd like to telephone home first to say I'll be later than I expected.'

'Of course.' He rose and helped her into her coat. While she used a nearby public telephone, he hailed a taxi. On Westgate Road he stopped the driver at an off-licence. 'What would you like to go with an omelette? Afraid I need to catch up on my wine education.'

Becky drew on the knowledge of wines she'd gained from Michael. 'A Sauvignon Blanc would be nice.'

Paul's flat was small but pleasantly furnished in a man's fashion. A green sofa, two high-backed chairs and occasional tables were arranged around the fitted gas fire in the sitting room, and crammed bookcases lined the walls. An alcove off the kitchen served as a dining area, and the entire flat was immaculate.

'I'm impressed,' Becky said, while Paul opened the wine.

He filled a glass each, then raised his to hers. 'To us.'

'To us,' she repeated and it sounded strange. For the second time in her life this man had undone all her resolutions. But it felt as natural being here with Paul now as it had done being with Michael.

They stood in the kitchen sipping their wine. Paul took her hand. 'Why so serious?'

'I was thinking how life plays unexpected tricks on us. When I left home this morning I never dreamed I'd be having dinner with you this evening.'

'Dinner? I'd forgotten.' He grinned and put down his glass.

As if in a dream, Becky leaned against the wall and watched as his large frame navigated the small kitchen. He set the table with a white cloth and cutlery and in no time produced a fluffy cheese omelette with tinned peas and crusty bread and butter, while the coffee bubbled in the percolator.

He put two plates on the table. 'Dinner is served.'

'This looks and smells wonderful,' she said as he seated her. 'Why do you eat at Annie's?'

He grinned and adjusted his glasses on his nose. 'Because I can only eat so many omelettes and tinned peas in a week, and because I knew that one day you'd walk into Annie's.'

Becky looked down at her plate. 'I'd been warding off meeting you again.'

'I know. I know everything about you. I read the births, marriages and deaths, and then of course there's Annie. I

311

ask polite questions about you and she answers, pretending she believes my interest is purely friendly.'

'She never told me.'

'Of course not. She knew you'd need time.'

'So you've been keeping track of me.' Becky let out a breath. 'Even when I was married?'

'I still wanted to know how you were. I know that your sister and her husband live with you and help with the house and Catherine. I know that you've returned to your old interests in women's affairs. I know that the business is doing well. And I know that the coffee is boiling over.' He jumped up and turned it off, then returned and took her hand. 'Coffee can wait.' He pulled her up and kissed her on the mouth.

Becky felt as though she'd been thrust back in time. How could they have spent only one night together? The taste of him, the smell of him, so familiar. She was dizzy with desire. Eventually she eased him away to take a breath. 'I was wondering when you'd get round to that,' she whispered.

'It's been the only thing on my mind all evening, but I promised to feed you. I couldn't get you here under false pretences.' He grazed his lips over hers again. 'You taste exactly as I remember.'

'I was thinking the same. It's strange, how sometimes we're given more than one chance at life.'

He held her to him almost roughly. 'And this is your *last* chance. This time I'm not letting you go.'